SORCEROUS
RIVALRY

Book One of the Mage-Born Chronicles

Kayleigh Nicol

Printed in the United States of America

First Printing: April 2018
Blue Feather Publishing

ISBN-13 978-1-7321317-1-2

To Eamon,
My first fan
And to Andy
My forever fan

1

Everything about him was perfect. From his wind-tossed hair to his mud-splattered boots, from his broad shoulders to his low-slung sword belt, he was pure perfection. He must have been a soldier once, judging by his steady, solid gait and the way his eyes swept the room, as if evaluating it as a potential battlefield. His face held no expression at all, even as he approached the bar and gestured to the innkeeper. He looked perfectly balanced, perfectly aware and perfectly prepared for anything.

He was my favorite kind of mark.

"What can I get for you, handsome?"

I watched from the shadows of the unlit common room as Wix bounced up to the possible patron. "Bounce" was the perfect word for Wix. As she approached the counter, her bosom rose and fell with each step. Her eyes sparkled and her curly hair, tied in pigtails, bobbed about her shoulders. Her smile was out-and-out devilish, tucked beneath a pert nose and a dusting of freckles on rosy cheeks.

"The innkeeper up the road suggested this inn might have a room at half the normal cost." The stranger's voice was soft, but it carried. He met Wix's eyes evenly. "Do you have such a room?"

"Matter of fact, I do." Wix smiled, perfect teeth glowing against scarlet lips. "How many nights will you need it for, honeysuckle?"

"Three nights, perhaps more. May I ask why the room is half price?"

"Ah, well." Wix set her elbows on the bar and propped her chin in her hands. She took a deep breath, bosom heaving with the effort. "A storm blew through about a while back and took the shutters clean off the window. I haven't had the carpenters around to fix it yet. Don't feel right charging full price for it, since the window won't close, you see? I figure I can at least make something out of it if I charge half. Fair's fair, right, sky-eyes?"

He kept his eyes on hers for a long moment. Any normal person would have been put off, but Wix just kept right on smiling. Finally, he nodded. "I'll take the room. Is your stable around back?"

"Yep, just take 'im around and set 'im up yourself. Don't have any of those stablehands or nothing, it's just me here." Wix bounced back from the bar. "Supper starts around sunset, if'n you're feeling hungry. I'm making lamb with sweetberry sauce and vegetables from the garden tonight."

"Thank you." The stranger nodded before stepping away from the bar. His eyes swept the room again and found me for the first time. Not many noticed me when I didn't want to be noticed; a little thrill danced along my spine when his piercing blue eyes met mine. A lazy smile spread across my face and I offered him a sloppy toast from my dented ale mug. His eyes snapped away and he strode out of the tavern.

"Seems I got you one, eh, Reshi?" Wix asked, flouncing up to my table.

"Yeah, great job, Wix." I smiled up at the tavern keeper. "He's perfect."

Wix pouted prettily. "Seems a bit off, don't you think? A little...peculiar?"

"You only think that because he didn't look down your dress." Using my ale cup, I nudged her breasts to make them bounce. "Not all us guys are into that, you know."

"Hm." Wix put her hands on her hips and looked down into her cleavage. "You don't think I need a lower-cut top, or maybe a corset? Really show 'em off?"

I laughed. "If you showed them off any more, Denson would have to cite you for unseemly behavior. Maybe he was just being respectful."

"A respectful guy would have given them an appreciative glance," Wix huffed, crossing her arms across her chest. She had a point; they were truly magnificent specimens. "But you can use him, right, starflower?"

I grinned, looking towards the door. "Yep. He's . . . perfect."

I watched him through the broken window, the night sky behind me keeping my cover. He had not left the room for dinner after returning from the stable. He had asked

Wix for a tub of bathwater and paid her a handful of coins, good for at least three nights in a half-price room at the Broken Wing. Afterwards, he had kept to himself. I'd had to wait until full dark to clamber up on the roof to peek through his window, which meant I had unfortunately missed seeing him bathe. The wooden tub still sat in the middle of his room, the water murky from soap and filth. He sat in the room's only chair, rubbing down his sword with a cloth. He seemed to be deep in thought as he cleaned his blade. Finally, his hand stilled, resting on the blade near the hilt, his bright blue eyes distant and downcast.

With a slight shake of his head, he set the blade down on the clothes chest, which had been moved so it sat near the bed. He didn't bother sheathing the blade but left it gleaming in the candlelight. He ran a hand through his hair, then drew his arm across his chest in a stretch, tilting his neck to the opposite side. I would have smiled if I could; people were so interesting to watch when they thought they were alone. He walked around the small room once, marking the distance from the bed to the window and again from the bed to the door. When he sat on the edge of the bed, the sword was within arm's reach. He was cautious. Too bad it wouldn't help.

One final stretch and then the shirt was cast off. For a brief moment I was treated to the sight of lightly tanned skin and perfectly toned muscles before he extinguished the candle. A rustle of cloth told me he'd settled into the bed. When my eyes adjusted to the dim light from torches along the street, his form was still.

I slipped through the open window with the ease of a shadow. On velvet feet, I circled the room, touching his few personal items—a travel sack that smelled of overripe fruit, recently cleaned boots that smelled of soap, a naked blade which smelled of steel. The sword had seen hard use, judging by the worn leather grip and notched cross guards. The blade was in excellent condition, however. Typical of a soldier. Although . . . I wandered back over to the boots and tipped one over to its side. The bottom of the boot was so worn it couldn't possibly provide any protection from mud and water. A soldier would have replaced these boots long ago. Come to think of it, since when did a soldier need a half-price room in the first place?

I looked towards the bed. He had been still for a long time, but his breathing had only just begun to even out. He wasn't quite asleep yet.

A shame, really. I didn't even know his name and I was about to crawl into bed with him.

Once his breath became deep and even, I slipped lightly onto the bed. Sudden moves could kill me here, I knew that. That sword was too close, and he had the look of a trained killer. But it had been weeks since Wix had set me up with a traveler like this and I couldn't waste the opportunity, not even for prey as dangerous as this.

Or as good looking as this.

With slow, cautious steps, I moved until I was poised above him, watching his face as he slept. He was beautiful. For a moment, I was captivated. His hair was a rich chestnut, and despite its recent wash, it still looked wind-tossed. Long lashes brushed his tanned cheek, his eyelids twitching in a dream that most likely had some sort of violence. Breath moved steadily through his partially open mouth, but no sound escaped—how nice that he didn't snore.

I found myself helpless to baser instincts in that moment, staring down at him. For someone who could look so deadly while awake, I couldn't help but want to see him startled, maybe hear him cry out. It wasn't necessary for what I needed, no, but . . . I had to see it just the same.

I crouched low, leaned in over his face and, gently, licked his lower lip.

He didn't startle the way I wanted him to; he didn't jump, and he certainly didn't shout in alarm. His eyes snapped open and caught mine like a snare. I froze under that stare, even my breath stopped. Who knew eyes could be that perfectly blue?

"Hello," he said. "Did you sneak in from outside or are you a mouser here?"

I responded with a deep, throaty purr. The strange traveler shifted beneath the blanket, turning so I slipped from his chest onto the bed beside him. One hand appeared over the blankets to rub my ears. His touch was unexpectedly gentle.

"I suppose you can stay the night. I can't exactly keep you out." He glanced over his shoulder at the open window. "But I have nothing to feed you."

I sat beside him and licked a paw to wash my face. I heard a soft chuckle and looked up. For the second time that night, the breath stopped in my chest. It was the first expression I had seen on his face and it was beautiful: a shy smile and soft eyes. I completely forgot what I was doing, my paw hovering halfway between my tongue and my ears. All I could do was stare.

Another ear rub broke the spell. I arched my neck into his fingers and reveled in the thrill of them running down my spine. I turned a circle and rolled on my side, tail twitching as I batted playfully at his hand. Another chuckle, then he withdrew his hand and tucked it back under the covers.

"You're a friendly beast. Stars help you if you brought fleas in with you."

I flicked an ear at him in irritation; I did not have fleas. He rolled beneath the blankets, turning his back to me. I moved until I was pressed right up against him, sharing his warmth. I purred loudly, using the sound and the vibration of my body to lull him back to sleep.

I felt it when he dropped off into the depths of sleep, not just in the relaxation of his body nor by the rhythm of his ribs rising and falling, but as a current of energy, like the flow of a river. His life force pooled invisibly around him, creating an aura I could feel as tangibly as his body heat, allowing me to draw magical energy from him as if drawing water from a well. It had been so long since the Broken Wing's last poor traveler that I wanted to draw deeper and deeper, but I forced myself to sip at it as if through a reed. He had paid for several nights here; I could afford to drink slowly and refill my wellspring of magic without alerting him. Tomorrow, he would awake feeling as if he lost a few hours of sleep but those were the only lasting effects of my theft. Once he left town and slept deeply, he would return to full vitality, as all my other victims did. Even so, I could tell I was drawing from dangerous prey tonight. If my well had been close to full, I would have let this opportunity slip by untried.

Or would I?

I opened one eye. All I could see was the back of his head, his dark hair splayed across the pillow haphazardly. His shoulders were strong and broad, I could tell that from the pull of the blanket. His fingers had been calloused and warm when they'd touched me. And his eyes . . . the sky should be jealous of that blueness.

I might have tried him on anyway, I told myself, shutting my eyes again. I drew on him for another few hours, gently, enjoying the meal by stretching it out. By the time midnight passed, I was slinking out the window again.

"G'morning, golden eyes!" Wix sang as she burst into my room the following morning. She dropped onto my bed, leaning across my chest to smile into my face. "Did you feast? How did he taste?"

"Ugh." I tried to roll over, but the blankets twined around my wrists, pinning me in place. I opened one eye to glare darkly at her. "Too early for your sunshine and babble."

"Oh? Not too early for your handsome friend." Wix wiggled atop me. "Did you even get any off him? He looks fresh as a bright-blossom this morning, already out and about."

"Isn't that nice for him?" I tried to twist my hands free of the blanket, but it just dug tighter. "Wix, could you let go, please? Don't you have to make breakfast or something?"

"Hm, if you'd fed, you could free yourself." Wix leaned back and the blankets slid free of my arms. "And breakfast has been finished for an hour, that's why I thought I'd check on you, nightbird."

I sat up and rubbed my eyes. True to what Wix said, bright morning light streamed through my window's shutters. I wanted to hiss at it and chase it away. Instead, I arched my back in a luxurious stretch and began the process of waking up.

"So?" Wix asked, still half-lying across my bed, her head propped in one hand.

"So what?" I asked. My hair had come undone while I'd slept; I searched beneath the pillow and covers for the tie.

"Why didn't you feed?"

"Oh, I did." I found the tie and smoothed my hair back into a horsetail. "He's here a few nights, right? I thought I'd just draw a little at a time to keep him from suspecting."

"That's not so fun." Wix pouted. "I like it when they stumble and curse and buy lots of wake-tea."

I smiled. Wix was easy to please. "I'll draw more on his last night, okay, Wix? Maybe he'll buy extra provisions from you the morning after."

"Well, I hope so. Otherwise, what am I getting out of this relationship?" Wix stood, adjusted her low-cut dress to show a little more bosom, then flounced out of my room.

"What indeed?" I muttered to myself. My clothes lay puddled about the tiny room and I began the laborious task of figuring out which were too soiled to wear, and which could stand another day out in the light. I almost wished I had drawn more deeply; at least then I could have motivated myself to wash my clothes. Once dressed, I stumbled out into the common room where Wix sat at a table, polishing silver candle holders.

"Wake-tea?" I asked.

Wix nodded, and where there had been nothing before, a steaming mug appeared.

I hesitated before reaching for it. "Is this under our agreement, or is this going to cost me?"

Wix giggled without looking up from her work. "Always so cautious. I'll catch you one day, Reshi."

"Maybe." I waited a moment before pointing out, "That wasn't an answer."

Wix sighed. "You're no fun." The mug disappeared, a final puff of steam curled once before fading from existence. "You can make your own tea."

"And have you catch me for the leaves, right?" I rolled my eyes. "I'm starting to see why the glen kicked you out. You're too predictable."

"Am I?" Wix's eyes flashed with mischief. "We'll see. I'll tell you one thing for free, though."

"How free is 'free'?" I checked my reflection in a polished silver plate over the mantle and smoothed my hair again. Wix watched me, her chin propped on the back of her hand. A coy smile turned the corners of her mouth up.

"Kestral."

"Hm? What's that?"

"It's his name." Wix's reflection grinned wolfishly from the plate. "But if you want to know where he went, it'll cost you."

Kestral. It had a hunter's ring to it. The hair on the back of my neck stood on end but I forced myself to shrug casually. "It's a small town. I could find him if I cared to."

Wix replied with her own shrug. "I'd be willing to barter food for a fun price. You interested?"

I tried to look like I didn't care one way or another but staying out of Wix's debt was always a tricky matter. And eating was always high on my list of priorities. "I'm interested, if the price is right."

Wix kicked one bare foot free of her dress and traced a whorl in the wood of the floor with her toes. "The oak thought it heard laughter last night, soft but warm, like early spring sunlight. If you can make him laugh for me, I'll consider it as payment for a day's food."

Had he laughed last night? No, it had been little more than a sharp breath, just short of a true chuckle. It had looked unfamiliar to his face, as if laughter were a language he had trouble speaking. I shook my head. "If I can make him laugh, you'll owe me three days of meals. Full meals, with drinks and butter and everything."

Wix tilted her head as she considered the bargain. "I suppose that will be a fair price. But only for true laughter. No chortles or wheezes, Reshi. You understand me?"

"Yeah, yeah." I set one hand on my hip and rubbed the back of my head with the other. "Out of curiosity, what would it cost to know where he went?"

"Oh? You're interested now?" Wix asked with a predatory smile.

"Well, yeah." I sighed. "I gotta go make friends with him before I can make him laugh."

In the end, Wix's "fair price" for information was too steep. But it was a small village out in the middle of nowhere, so there were only a few places he could be. I wandered out into the town, earning more than a few disapproving glares from housewives and tradesmen. A reputation as the town layabout didn't earn one many friends, but that was part of the reason I was here. In fact, if not for Wix, I wouldn't be here at all.

The first place I thought a travel-worn ex-soldier might go was to the tanner's. A leather shop was easy to find in any village, and by the state of Kestral's boots, I thought he might have been getting them repaired. But as I stopped in to say hello to the shop owner, it was clear my quarry hadn't been there.

Perhaps the smith, then. I followed the sounds of ringing steel to see if the traveler had stopped for a new edge on his sword, or some horseshoes or nails. After a moment of flirting with a young apprentice, I learned that he hadn't come here either. With a wink and a wave, I left the open-air shop.

Where else, then? He hadn't taken any meals at the Broken Wing and that was the cheapest inn in town. It seemed he was hard-up for funds, as he had taken Wix's broken window room, so it was unlikely he would eat anywhere else. Was he hunting for his own food? The town was surrounded by forests full of game birds and hoofed-beasts, so catching a free meal was certainly an option. Did he have a bow? I hadn't seen one in his room, but he could have left supplies in the stable with his mount.

In any case, if he was a hunter he would need arrows. With little hope of finding him, I meandered over to the only fletcher in town. With luck, it was the tradesman's daughter who tended the shop, and for the price of a smile she admitted that the mysterious Kestral had stopped by early that morning. He had paid a copper sliver for unfletched shafts, nothing more. I left before her father could chase me out of the shop; I had learned by accident that he kept a bevy of loaded crossbows below the sales counter and had frightfully good aim. That wasn't quite enough to keep me from watching the girl bent over her work, gluing feathers to shafts, but it was enough to keep me from pinching her behind. Barely.

If Kestral was out hunting, there was no way I would find him. The forest was vast, and I wasn't an outdoorsman by any stretch. He would come back to the inn and with any luck he would have a fresh kill to gut and clean, which maybe meant some scraps for me if I was careful. Rather than continue my fruitless search, I returned to Wix's inn to wait. Not wanting to admit that I hadn't found Kestral, I circled around back to the stable. Maybe I could get an idea of what might make him laugh by checking out the gear he had stored with his mount.

A snorting, stamping, snapping mutt of a horse challenged me as I entered the stable. I tried letting him smell my hand, but he pinned his ears and lunged at me over the door of his stall, so I stepped back out of his reach. That was strange; animals generally found me likeable enough. I couldn't make out which breed he was, but he looked strong and sturdy, just like his rider. He had roan coloring with a white blaze and a black mane and tail.

Must be a trained warhorse, I decided. That would be why he didn't like me. He was probably trained to only accept his rider.

A heavy leather saddle was set just outside the horse's stall, along with a few other personal items—nothing worth stealing, of course. The saddle itself looked ready to fall apart and had been inexpertly patched in many places. Parts of the horse's bridle had also been tied together haphazardly, but the bit was shiny and clean, so at least he cared for the beast's health and comfort. The long haft of a spear was braced against the saddle. The wood was smooth but slightly thinner in the middle, perhaps from a lifetime of being carried, handled and thrown. A tied leather cloth covered the spearhead, but I imagined it was shiny and sharp as the sword had been.

Who is this guy? I wondered, leaning back against the far stable wall. The ill-tempered horse continued to eye me warily, pacing back and forth in his stall, daring me to come closer, but I wasn't that stupid. Instead, I pondered the enigma that was Kestral, the maybe-former-soldier. He took pains to keep his weapons in top condition and he cared for his mount better than he cared for himself, judging by the amount of quality hay scattered around the stall door. But his leathers were falling apart, and his clothing was patched. He'd paid half-price for a room in a no-name town and hunted for his own food rather than pay for it. Was he an army deserter? A disgraced knight? A bandit trying to turn his life around?

Well, whatever the story, he would be gone in three days, so I might as well not worry about it. I arched away from the wall, brushed the hay dust off my hands onto my pants and turned to leave.

And found myself face to face with the man I had been searching for all day.

His blue eyes were muted by the sunlight behind him, but I found them no less piercing. His hair was a mess, not just wind-tossed, but also decorated with leaves and small twigs. His shirt was unlaced near his throat, baring tanned skin that looked warm to the touch. Against his shoulder he carried an unstrung longbow, and in his other hand he held a pair of waterbirds. Clearly his hunt had been successful.

"Uh, hi," I said after a long pause.

A long moment passed before he spoke. "You were in the inn yesterday."

"I . . . uh—" He didn't mean last night, right? There was no way he could recognize—no, take a breath. He saw me in the bar when he reserved his room. "Yeah, I'm here most days."

His face betrayed no emotion at all; it made me more than a little uncomfortable. "Do you work for Miss Chesawick?"

Who? Oh, Wix. "Sometimes. Kind of. When I have to." I shrugged, offering an embarrassed smile. "I'm the town drunk when I can afford it. I do chores for Wi—Miss Chesawick when I can't."

He continued to stare me down. Finally, he nodded. He stepped past me to lay his bow against his saddle, but even as he shuffled through his personal affects, I got the feeling he was still watching me closely.

"I wasn't stealing anything," I said, folding my arms over my chest.

"You couldn't if you tried." He stood and held out his hand to his horse. "Shan would have kicked your teeth out."

The beastly horse lipped his master's hand with obvious affection.

"He tried that anyway," I muttered darkly.

"Sorry about that." He didn't sound sorry. In fact, his voice held no emotion. He turned back to face me and suddenly held out a hand. "I'm Kestral."

"Reshi." I reached out to grasp his hand but had to whip my hand away as Shan snapped at it. "Any chance we could finish introductions away from the carnivorous horse?"

A hint of a smile played on his lips as he turned his head, giving me only a glimpse of it. He gave Shan a final pat, then followed me outside.

"Can I clean these out here?" Kestral asked, indicating the waterbirds.

"Sure, the innkeeper won't mind. Use the fire pit."

Kestral sat on a stump, pulled a knife from his belt and began cleaning his kills. I sat opposite him and watched as he expertly feathered and gutted the birds, quickly reducing them down to mouthwatering cuts of flesh.

"Town drunk, hm?" Kestral asked, not looking up from his work.

"Oh, yeah, officially anyway." My stomach rolled as I watched him. I was hungry, sure, but his knife work was so good it was intimidating.

"And unofficially?" Kestral asked, dropping innards into a pile beside his boot.

"Hm?" I smiled across the fire pit at him. "I don't understand the question."

He glanced up, meeting my gaze for the first time since we sat down. "You have unusually colored eyes. Mage blood?"

I looked away hurriedly. Dust it, what had I gotten into? "Possibly. I grew up in an orphanage in Giltner until they kicked me out. Ended up here after a time." I shrugged. "Are you a mage hunter? Should I be running?"

Kestral turned his attention back to his waterbird. "Of a kind. There haven't been any reports of magic use in these parts, so maybe you're not. I don't recommend you run, though."

"Why is that?"

Those blue eyes pierced me again. "Because then I'll have to chase you."

My stomach dropped as if I had fallen from a height, my breath leaving my chest in a rush. I placed my hands against the stump I sat on just to have something to hold on to. My mouth went dry and a weird, fluttery sensation seized my gut. What kind of magic was this?

Kestral opened a belt pouch, took out his flint then frowned. "Is there a cooking tripod?"

"Yeah, Wix keeps it inside." I stood up. "I can get it."

"Wix?"

I flinched. "Miss Chesawick. Sorry, I usually only call her that when I've been drinking."

Kestral nodded slowly. He began setting fire to the logs as I trotted to the inn's back door for the cooking utensils. If I was lucky, maybe he'd share some meat with me. I caught my reflection in a silver bowl and silently cursed my golden eyes. Why hadn't I guessed that he could be a mage hunter? I should have started running yesterday, before he got a good look at me. Now all I could do was bluff and wait him out. I gathered Wix's cooking rods and carried them back outside with me.

"Copper?" Kestral asked as I set up the tripod.

"Yep. That's why she keeps them inside. Not as practical as iron, but prettier." I smiled. "The miss likes pretty things."

"Are you and she—"

"Wait, don't!" Kestral had just thrown the waterbird feathers and innards into the fire. I hadn't meant to cry out, but I had been hoping to make a meal of them after nightfall.

"What?" Kestral froze at my cry, but the damage was done. "You wanted the scraps for something?"

"No, no, just . . ." Something plausible, think of anything plausible! "Aren't you supposed to leave some for the fairies?" It was a poor excuse and I knew it. Worse, I would have to apologize to Wix for it later.

Kestral cocked an eyebrow, making the third facial expression I had seen from him so far. "I think that's milk and honey. Not bird guts."

"Well, sure, for most fairies." I shrugged. "What with your bloodthirsty horse, I thought maybe we should consider appeasing any carnivorous fairies he might summon."

It started as a chuckle, which he quickly tried to hide by covering his mouth with a hand. But then his shoulders shook, his sides trembled, and he tossed his head back and laughed. Loud and hard, his eyes shut, throat bared as peal after peal of laughter freed itself from his chest. It was such a beautiful sight that I almost forgot my bet with Wix. Almost.

Dust it all, why couldn't I be this witty inside the inn? I glanced around, looking for the nearest piece of living wood to confirm the laughter, but the barn was too far away, and the stumps were made of pine. Wix would never take the word of a pine.

Oh well, I thought, sighing out my frustration. At least now I knew he could laugh.

Wiping his eyes with the back of one hand, Kestral leaned forward, regaining his composure. He shook his head, but his smile lit his face for a few moments more. To distract himself, he rotated the waterbirds over the fire. Another head shake and the smile faded.

"Thanks."

"What for?"

"I haven't laughed like that in a long time."

"Oh." I leaned back, placing my hands behind me. "Why not?"

That was exactly the wrong question to ask. His face became so shadowed that I briefly wondered if I had imagined his laughter. Rather than answer, he reached out to the closest waterbird and snapped a wing free.

"Here." He threw it to me.

I was so surprised I bobbled it before catching it. "What's this for?"

"You aren't here to eat?"

"No, well . . . thank you." I had been drooling over the birds. The thicker pieces of meat still had a while to cook, but the wings had crisped up nicely.

Kestral snapped the second wing off for himself. He stared broodingly into the fire as he ate, stripping the bone in seconds, then cracked it open to suck out the marrow.

I wanted to ask him more about his past, to know if he had been a soldier, or if he really was a mage hunter. I wanted to know if he had participated in the Great Mage Hunt, though he seemed a little young for that. Come to that, how old was he? That wasn't too personal a question, right? As I opened my mouth to ask, the back door to the inn flew open.

"Here you boys are! Fast friends already, my doves?" Wix bounced through the back door bearing a strip of oilcloth. "I saw you cooking and I thought you might want to save one for later. Would you like me to wrap one and store it in the cold box?"

Wix leaned over to flourish the oilcloth in front of Kestral's face, displaying as much of her bosom as was possibly decent.

I leaned back on my stump, struggling to keep my mouth shut. I wanted to warn Kestral about Wix's exchanges but if I did she would certainly kick me out of her inn. My sense of self-preservation won out over the possibility of making a new friend.

Kestral met Wix's smile evenly as he wiped the grease from his fingers onto his pants. "No, thank you. I have my own oilcloth."

"Oh." Wix's face fell, but she recovered quickly. "I can still place it in my cold box until you want to eat it."

"I'll eat it tonight, so the cold box is unnecessary." Kestral shifted the tripod, dragging the waterbirds out from over the flames. He swiped his booted foot through the fire, scattering the logs into embers to burn out.

"If you're sure." Wix's mouth twisted. "Would you like any herbs for the meat? Or butter? How about some ale to wash it down?"

Kestral glanced across the fire pit to me. "Did you need some ale, town drunk?"

"Ah, well, if it's freely offered, I wouldn't say no." I smiled up at Wix.

Wix puffed up her cheeks and clenched her fists. She was far too easy to read sometimes. After a breath, she was able to force a smile. "I can't turn much of a profit, giving away free ale. If you flutterbugs get thirsty I'll serve you inside." With a wink and a flounce, Wix bounded back to the inn.

Kestral laid a finger against the copper cooking rod and seemed to decide it had cooled enough to free the cooked birds. He wrapped one in an oilcloth from his belt pouch, then cut pieces off the other one and split the meat into two piles.

"You don't have to share with me," I said.

He shot me a look with those piercing eyes.

"I mean, if that's what you were doing. It looks like—but, I'm saying I don't need any more. I just . . . I'm enjoying your company."

The expression on his face betrayed his skepticism as he went back to cutting up the waterbird. "Why not? Are you afraid of being in my debt?" He bundled half the meat in a pocket cloth and held it out to me. I hesitated before taking it. I would rather collect my bet from Wix, but then again, she probably wouldn't take the pine's word that I had managed to make Kestral laugh. And the waterbird did smell delicious, even if it was under-seasoned.

"Mmm." The skin was nice and crisp, and the meat was juicy. I noticed Kestral watching as I wiped my chin with a corner of the pocket cloth. "So now what? I guess I'm in your debt, right? Don't ask me to buy you anything, I'm flat broke."

Kestral chuckled. He took his time licking grease off his fingers before replying. "It's been several days of hard travel. I think Shan could use a good bath."

I shuddered. "That sounds like you're asking me to bleed for you. Isn't that a high price for a bit of bird?"

Those blue eyes studied me for a moment. "Is that a no?"

My brow furrowed as I studied him back. What game was this? "Do you really want me to wash that mean-tempered animal? You saw him try to take my hand off, didn't you?"

Kestral shrugged a dismissal. "If he wanted your hand, he'd have it."

"That doesn't make me feel any better about bathing him."

"All right. Then show me around town tomorrow."

"It's a pretty small town. Do you really need a guide?"

He shrugged again, dropping bird bones into the remains of the fire. "In my experience, small towns tend to take advantage of travelers. Having a local with me might keep more coin in my pocket."

"Ah." I leaned back on my stump, tucking my hands behind my head. "I don't know how much help I'd be with that. The town drunk isn't exactly the most respectable person in town."

"But I'll wager you're well known to everyone." Kestral pinned me with his eyes again. "It won't take long. An hour or two."

I rolled my shoulders, pretending to think it over. "Ah, fine. It's not like I had a lot planned for tomorrow, anyway." Actually, I had no plans at all, but he didn't need to know that.

"What exactly does the town drunk do, anyway?"

I smirked. "Hang around the bar tonight and find out." Having finished the waterbird, I wiped my fingers clean with the pocket cloth and stood to go inside. Kestral held his hand out to me and I looked at it in confusion.

"My cloth."

"I'll wash it and get it back to you."

"I'll have it now."

Was he worried I would steal it? "Okay." I handed it over and walked back to the inn. I felt his eyes on me the whole way.

"I swear, Wix, I made him laugh! Ask the wood around the fire pit, he really laughed!"

"Oh, ask the pine." Wix rolled her eyes. "I might as well ask a krupper for directions. Really, Reshi, I can't believe you would try to lie to me like this."

"I'm not lying." I leaned against the bar, my arms crossed over my chest. "He really laughed. It was beautiful."

"Just make him do it again." Wix stood atop the bar, refilling the oil in the ceiling sconces. "In front of respectable wood this time."

I sighed. "You know I don't really understand what you mean by that, right? What's so bad about pine?"

"If you don't know, I can't explain it to you." Wix sniffed. She hopped lithely from one end of the bar to the other, balancing on a single toe to reach the hanging sconce.

"Are there any other wagers you're willing to take in exchange for food?" I asked hopefully.

"As a matter of fact, yes." Wix set both feet down on the bar and placed her hands on her hips. "I will make you wake-tea tomorrow if you'll wash your clothes. The oak is beginning to complain."

"That's not much of a wager." I leaned my elbows on the bar and considered it. "Do I get the wake-tea first?"

"No, you'll get it after."

"Ugh, that's too hard." I dropped my chin to my chest, sulking. "You're probably going to charge me for using the well and the soap anyway."

Wix's mouth twisted in distaste; she hated getting caught double-dealing. "No milk or sugar in your tea and you can have the soap and water for free."

"Nope, not worth it." I flicked my fingers, dismissing the bet. It was my hope to get Wix up to a whole meal in exchange for me washing my own clothes. She had bent before; apparently, she liked keeping the oak floors happy. It just meant I would be wearing dirty clothes for a few days more.

Wix frowned, once again balancing precariously to reach a distant sconce. "You don't work, you don't wash your own clothes, you don't even make the guests stumbly and sleepy. Just what am I getting out of this—hello, sugar lump!"

Wix stepped off the bar, landing with a gentle, if bouncy, thump. Kestral stood just inside the door, one hand on the doorframe. Wix beamed brightly at him, holding her oilcan behind her back with both hands so that her chest was thrust forward. "Can I get you something from the bar?" Wix offered. "It's a little early for dinner, but I could fix something up right quick."

Kestral shook his head, frowning at the doorframe. "This is ash, isn't it?"

"It is." Wix positively beamed. "I had the carpenters work it special. Nothing is too good for my little Broken Wing."

"But your window frames." Kestral turned to the nearest window and ran his fingers over the sill. "These are hazel."

"Well, of course," Wix replied, tilting her chin. "What else would you use to keep out—"

I coughed, loudly. Both Wix and Kestral turned to stare at me. Slowly, Wix's face drained of color as understanding dawned on her. As she raised a hand to cover her mouth, Kestral's glare became more pointed.

He's too smart, I realized. He was smart, dangerous and had admitted to being a mage hunter. I should have started running before he ever got here.

"I was just setting up for the dinner crowd," Wix said, a little too loudly. She swung around behind the bar and began setting out mugs and plates. "Everyone in town knows I serve goose tonight, so we'll be busy. Will you join us for dinner tonight, bright eyes?"

"No." The pressure of his glare made me shift uncomfortably. "But maybe I'll come down later. For a drink."

"I hope you will. Timerie will be playing her lute tonight, so it should be fun!" Wix waved as Kestral made his way up the staircase. He ascended with excruciating slowness, staring darkly at the wooden railing as he went. Once he was out of sight, a heavy tankard of ale thunked down in front of me. I looked up at Wix, deliberately not setting a hand on the mug.

"In thanks for the warning." Wix gave the mug a little shove. "It's repayment, so don't worry about it."

"Well, in that case." I raised the mug to her. "Cheers." It was a nice, thick brown ale. Wix wasn't skimping at all; she must have been truly grateful.

"Ugh." Wix stretched her arms across to the far side of the bar and dropped her head in between them. "He's dangerous, isn't he?" Her voice echoed softly as she spoke into the wood.

"Yeah, I think so." I took another drink from my mug.

"What are you going to do about him?"

"Me?" I laughed quietly. "Nothing."

Wix turned her head to look up at me.

"I mean, I'll keep stealing his energy, of course." I stared down into my ale. "Maybe he'll feel so tired that he'll think he imagined . . . whatever it is he's thinking."

Wix bobbed her head. "I'll leave it to you, Reshi."

I toasted her again before drinking deeply, trying to hide my own trepidation.

As Wix predicted, it was a busy night for the bar. A few village families stopped by for an early dinner and the tradesmen and farmers came by later for drinks and a good time. As a seasoned bar mistress, Wix traded banter and dirty jokes while dodging overly-friendly hands. For myself, I went to work as the town's loveable drunk: flirting, story-telling and gambling. Most villagers were willing to at least buy me a drink, several even shared their meals with me, keeping me out of Wix's debt. A few even wanted a little more out of me, including a blacksmith apprentice who shyly wrapped his leg around mine during a game of dice, and the fletcher's daughter, who insisted I spin her about to the lutist's tune.

Kestral didn't come down to the bar for dinner, but after several drinks and sprightly dances, I noticed him sitting at the bar with a drink. I flashed him a grin and a wink before returning my affections to . . . wait, which tradesman's daughter was this, now? Whoever she was, she laughed and ordered me another drink, so we went back to dancing. But I couldn't shake that ice-blue stare as Kestral sat drinking at the bar.

As the dinner guests trickled out, I saw Kestral head upstairs to his room. I waited an appropriate amount of time—perhaps ten whole minutes—before ducking into my room to hide my transformation. In the form of a cat, I snuck outside and leapt onto a rain barrel, to the gutter, to Kestral's open window. He was already half-dressed, treating me to quite a view before he doused the candle and climbed into bed.

Once again, I circled his room in silence, sniffing his travel sack, boots and sword. I could smell the remains of his waterbird in the waste bucket but refrained from helping myself to them; once something hit the trash in Wix's inn, it became hers and I couldn't even afford the cost of garbage. At least I had eaten well that evening. Once Kestral's breathing evened out, I leapt into bed beside him and curled up. I didn't wake him this time—ever since he had admitted to being a mage hunter, I'd felt more than a little uncomfortable around him. But that didn't stop me from drawing from him to fill my wellspring as he slept.

"Reshi?" The voice had a tinny echo to it, as if the speaker was at the end of a long tunnel. "Reshi, can you hear me?"

It wasn't a dream. Not a real dream. My real dreams were a lot more interesting than this. Maybe if I ignored it, I'd find a better dream.

"Reshi, the hunters are closing in on us."

You have no idea, I thought. At the edge of my awareness, I could feel a warm body pressed against my back. I would have smirked if I could in the strange not-dream.

"We must join up, Reshi." The voice was pleading and edged with desperation. "It's the only way we'll survive. If we band together, we can be safe."

Or we'll all be one big target. I'd rather stay hidden. Besides, I've never met any of the others.

"Brother Velyn is on his way," the voice continued. "We can convince the others to come as well. We can be strong, Reshi. We don't have to be scared."

I'm not scared. I'm fine on my own.

"I can see the hunters, Reshi. They get closer every day."

Which one is Velyn? I never could keep them all straight.

"You're being stubborn, Reshi." The voice took on a stern quality.

From what I hear, that's the one trait we all share. I tried to sink deeper into sleep and drop beyond the voice's reach. It must have worked, because although the voice continued speaking, I could no longer make out the words. My shared bed was warm and the life force I sipped from its occupant made me feel stronger. Better to stay hidden in plain sight than to step out into the open with the others. I tucked my face beneath a paw and spiraled into a deep sleep.

Drawing from a person's life force should make them tired, and it should energize me, which normally meant the person I drew from slept much longer than I did. Imagine my surprise when I woke up to a rolling and stretching bed companion tossing blankets over my head. I twitched my tail and struggled to climb free.

"Sorry." Hands lifted the blanket, allowing me to step out with a little more dignity. "I didn't know you snuck in again last night. Did you smell my dinner and invite yourself in?"

I flicked an ear at him and glanced past him to the window. For stars' sake, it was still dark outside! What normal human wakes up so early? Pre-dawn light gave the room a soft illumination, giving the hunter just enough light to see by. Kestral moved around the room slowly, checking each of his belongings and sheathing the sword he had left within reach the night before. He shook fresh clothes out from his travel sack and laid them over a chair, then turned his boots over, frowning as he checked the worn soles.

That's right. We're running errands today, I remembered. I hope he gets those boots fixed. Wait, why do I care about his boots? He's a mage hunter. I began a vigorous cat bath to distract myself.

"Huh."

I looked up.

Kestral peered into the waste bucket. "You didn't steal any of the leftovers. You're either a very polite cat, or a very successful hunter."

I blinked slowly at him and went back to washing myself. I wondered idly if I could eat the scraps if he offered them to me, or if they were still considered Wix's property since they had been in the trash. Not that it should matter; I had eaten well the night before and felt full after filling my wellspring all night. But my animal instincts made it difficult to pass up any offered meal.

Wait, shouldn't he be at least a little sleepy? I glanced up from my bath to stare at him. I drew a lot more than I had meant to, but he looked completely refreshed. No stumbling or stretching or grumbling for wake-tea. In fact, he looked like he might—no!

He did. He started exercising.

Without a shirt on.

Kestral went through a series stretches that worked his arms, shoulders, chest and legs, flowing from one stretch into the next. I might have drooled a little; I had never seen a more perfect body move with that level of precision. It was an artform. Were all mage hunters like him? Or was this something from his past? His face looked completely blank as he worked up a thin sheen of sweat, as if his body didn't need his mind to take it through the motions.

He followed the stretching with sit-ups, then moved on to push-ups. I decided I could only be so good for so long, so while he counted out his repetitions, I hopped off the bed and walked beneath him, sliding my back along the muscles of his stomach and chest. He chuckled softly at first then scooted me out from beneath him. I walked in front of him, flicking my tail beneath his nose. He switched to one-handed push-ups and gently pushed me aside. My tail twitched. I wasn't sure what had me more irritated—the fact that I was being ignored or the fact that I couldn't do even a single one-handed push-up.

I walked around him and stepped carefully onto his back, riding the rise and fall as he continued to exercise.

"If you scratch me, I'll skin you," Kestral warned between counts.

I settled down into a crouch on his shoulder, adding weight to the side without support. He tucked his free hand behind his back for a while, then switched arms to work the other side. As I shifted my weight to the other shoulder, I thought I heard him chuckle softly.

"All right. Get down." Kestral rolled to one side, encouraging me to hop off his back. He stood, rolling his shoulders and cracking his knuckles. After wiping the sweat from his skin with a cloth, he dressed. I was surprised to see morning light streaming through the window; had he really worked out that long? Wix would be starting breakfast soon.

I sat beside the door, and before long, Kestral opened it. I trotted just ahead of him on the stairs down to the common room.

"Great morning, sun drop!" Wix called out cheerfully. I flicked an ear at her as I darted under the bar, heading for my room near the kitchen. She smiled at me knowingly.

"Does he work here?" Kestral asked, jerking his chin at me.

"Oh, well, I wouldn't really say that." Wix's grin was full of mischief. I stopped in my tracks and looked back at her over my shoulder. "But he is a welcome intruder."

"He comes in through the broken window," Kestral explained, sitting at the bar.

"I really do need to get that fixed." Wix sighed deeply, managing to look chagrined. "Let me get some breakfast started for you, morning lark."

I snuck away, trusting Wix to keep her mouth shut. She was a great friend, truly, but sometimes she could simply be forgetful. Once in my room, I nudged the door shut and shapeshifted. I sifted through my clothes, trying to find something remotely respectable for running errands in the village. At least I felt more awake this morning than I had in a long time. Did Kestral possess a depthless well of life force? Wix would probably chastise me again today, even though I had drawn quite a bit from him.

After smoothing my hair back into a tail, I made a show of yawning and stretching as I left my room and entered the common room.

"You two are so noisy," I complained, setting my elbows on the bar and dropping my head into my hands. "How's a guy supposed to get over a long night of drinking if he can't sleep in?"

"Try wake-tea," Kestral suggested, his voice even. He sounded a lot friendlier when he spoke to me as a cat.

"Mmm, wake-tea." I glanced across the bar at Wix. "Do I have enough credit for some of your most wonderful wake-tea, bar mistress?"

Wix smiled playfully. "You certainly do, tippy toes. But only enough for one cup."

"I'll take it."

Wix made a show of preparing the tea properly instead of blinking it into existence, as she did when we were alone. For as long as I live, I'll never understand how Wix calculates credits and debts, but I'd learned that often after a fun night of drinking and dancing, she almost always credited my account. I had asked about it once but Wix couldn't explain it well. It was a little like she paid me for entertainment. I could live with that.

"So where do you need to go today?" I asked Kestral, cupping the mug of hot tea between my hands. I inhaled deeply. The smell of fresh mint and warm honey were waking me up even before taking a sip.

"Blacksmith," Kestral replied. For the first time that morning I noticed he had his sword on his belt. How did I miss that? I had practically watched him dress. "General store. Any place that will sell oats for my horse."

"Not the tanner?" I raised the mug to my lips, letting the flavors tease my tongue before taking a tiny sip. Fresh tea was nothing short of pure starlight.

"Why the tanner?"

"Hm?" Oh, I had been thinking about his worn-out boots. I shouldn't know how worn his boots are. "For your saddle. Out in the barn. It looks a bit . . . broken in."

Kestral shook his head. "It will hold out a while yet."

"Where are you goin' at such a hard pace and on such little coin?" Wix asked, curious. "There's not much worth passing through these parts for."

"My journey is my own." Kestral stood as if to leave. He gave me a pointed look.

"Whu—it's still pretty early," I protested, hugging my tea to my chest. "Hardly anything is open just yet."

"In my experience, blacksmiths open early."

"Yeah, but they won't have the forges hot yet."

Kestral stared at me from the doorway. I heaved a sigh.

"Wix, I'm borrowing this mug," I said it just to be clear. "I'll return it later."

"Be sure that you do, Reshi, my starling." Wix winked at me before clearing away the breakfast dishes. I followed Kestral out into the street.

Kestral was right and the blacksmith's workyard was already occupied by a few sleepy apprentices. The forge fires had been lit but were still being worked to a high heat. After a brief introduction, Kestral told the head blacksmith that he needed to put a new edge on his sword as well as sharpen a few recovered arrowheads. The smith agreed to set his apprentices to the work quickly, the cost of which had Kestral grimacing. Rather than argue with the hard-headed blacksmith, I lifted myself onto a work table and called out to several of the young apprentices. I flirted with a few of them and joked about the village girls with the others, setting an alluring distraction from the early-morning work. The smith grumbled something to Kestral about letting him do the work himself for cheap, as his apprentices all seemed "too busy" for paid work. Kestral seemed relieved to hand over a few coppers for the use of the smith's tools before he shooed me off the table to begin his work.

"I thought you were here to help me," Kestral said as he gathered files, stones and cloths to begin his work.

"I did, didn't I?" I winked at him. "You're not paying full price for the work, are you?"

"No, but it could take me hours to do the work myself." Kestral eyed my critically. "Do you want to help?"

I laughed. "That wasn't part of the deal."

Kestral shrugged as he sat on the work bench, hunching over his blunted arrowheads.

It only took a few minutes for me to become extremely bored. There was nothing interesting in just sitting and watching someone else sharpen arrowheads. I sipped my tea and wandered around the shop aimlessly. I was considering attempting to juggle horseshoes when the young apprentice who had flirted with me the night before found me.

"I've never seen you out and about this early, Reshi." He smiled shyly at me. "Not enough fun for you last night?"

I laughed and leaned in towards him. "I didn't hear you offering to make my night any more fun."

The apprentice blushed. "Well, Alma seemed exceptionally keen on your affections last night."

Shoot, which one was Alma? "She couldn't keep up with me." I smirked playfully. "I prefer partners with a little more stamina."

The young blacksmith started to reply, then hesitated, looking over my shoulder.

I glanced back and found Kestral staring intensely at us.

The youth ran a hand through his hair nervously and dropped his gaze to the floor.

"Let's go outside," I offered. He nodded and led the way to the open-air work area.

"Who is he?" the cute apprentice asked.

Ugh, why could I not remember this kid's name? He had been flirting with me for several months now, you would think I could at least recall his name.

"His name is Kestral. He's staying at the Broken Wing for a few nights." I shrugged. "That's all I know about him."

"Master Nealan noticed him at the bar last night." The apprentice shifted from foot to foot. "He thinks the stranger must be an army deserter or something."

I rubbed the back of my neck. "Well, who knows. He should be leaving tomorrow, and he hasn't caused any trouble so . . ." I trailed off and the smith nodded his understanding. People in this village were pretty laidback. It was one of the big reasons I had stayed for so long. That, and Wix's protection.

My stomach rumbled and the young smith laughed. "Have you not eaten? We have some fresh bread if you'd like."

"I'd love some!"

The master smith's wife happened to be the village baker and her bread was like fluffy clouds baked inside a hearty crust. This morning's rolls had swirls of cinnamon baked into them, making them just a little sweet. I ate well more than my share, complete with honey and butter, before Kestral finished his work and asked me to take him to the general store.

We barely walked through the door before a cheerful blonde girl attached herself to my arm, asking what we were shopping for. Kestral recited a list, which was mostly rations for the road, as well as soap, oilcloth and a stretch of canvas tarp. The girl chatted constantly as she tugged me along to gather the supplies about the store. Just before she could wrap everything, I remembered to ask her about oats. She slung a sack of oats onto the counter and calculated a total. I pretended to swoon.

"How much? Sweetling, how will our little village continue to attract visitors at such prices?"

"Aw, Reshi, you know how it is." The girl pouted prettily. "But seeing as how it's you . . ." She hummed to herself for a moment before quoting a new price. A quick glance at Kestral showed me it was still too high. I leaned across the counter on my elbows, so I could look up at the shop girl.

"You know what I think?"

"What, Reshi?"

"I think you could go even lower." I reached out and tugged playfully on her apron, pulling her a step closer. "Can't you go lower?"

She giggled and blushed. "I don't want to get in any trouble."

"But getting in trouble is half the fun." I winked. "For me? Please?"

"Oh, Reshi . . . All right." The girl cut her second price nearly in half.

Kestral counted out a palmful of coins and gathered his groceries, shoving the sack of oats at me. I frowned at him as I hefted the bag—he hadn't said anything about me having to carry anything. I bid the girl farewell and caught up with Kestral on the street. Kestral shot me a look as I drew even with him.

"What?"

"You have an unusual method of bartering."

I grinned. "Can't argue with results, though."

"Hm." I waited for more but that seemed to be his entire response. We dropped most of Kestral's supplies in the barn near Shan's stall—the horse still hated me for some reason—and Kestral took a few minutes to care for the beast. I pulled myself up onto the stacked hay bales and watched him.

For the most part, Kestral ignored me. He checked Shan's hooves, teeth, and eyes before giving the monster a thorough brushing, even untangling his mane and tail. Afterwards, he tied Shan to a post and cleaned the stall before setting out fresh hay. Bored, I stretched out on top of the hay stack, rolling on my back and letting my head loll over the edge. After putting Shan back in his stall, Kestral stared up at me.

"What?"

"What is it that you actually do?" Kestral asked. He seemed puzzled, even though his expression and tone didn't change from their usual neutrality.

Shrugging while upside down was a difficult maneuver; as such, I nearly shrugged myself off the hay bale. "You're looking at it."

"You simply freeload off the villagers and Miss Chesawick?"

I rolled over to my stomach, grimacing as the blood rushed out of my head. "What's wrong with that? No one here seems to mind."

"Even when you're flirting with all the young people in the village?" He cocked an eyebrow at me.

"Especially not then." I smirked. "You may not have noticed, but I'm very pretty."

Kestral shook his head and looked away. Dust. I had been hoping to make him laugh with that comment.

"So, what do you do?" If it was fair for him to ask me, it must be okay for me to ask. "You were pretty mysterious this morning about your journey being your own. Where are you going? Where did you come from?"

"Beramin."

"Beramin?" I hadn't really expected an answer. It took me a moment to remember which direction that city was in. "You didn't just ride here from Beramin. That would have taken you—"

"It's been a long time since I was in Beramin." Kestral stared off into the distance, as if envisioning the journey. "I've been traveling the kingdom since I left."

Beramin was one of the military capitals of the kingdom. "Were you with the army there?"

He fingered the pommel of his sword unconsciously. "Yes."

Wow, such elaborate and telling answers! I couldn't be too upset, though; he didn't have to answer at all. "Are you traveling on army business now?"

"No."

"So where are you going?"

Those bright blue eyes snapped to mine so suddenly my breath caught. "Here."

"Wha—whoa!" I had tried to stand, lost my balance and tumbled backwards off the hay bale, pulling it on top of me in the process. Not my most graceful move ever. Kestral lifted the hay bale off me as I coughed and brushed hay from my clothes, trying to recover my dignity.

"I'm going hunting," Kestral said after restacking the hay bale. "Do you want to come?"

"No," I wheezed, still coughing up hay dust. "I just injured myself in a barn. What do you think I would do to myself around actual weapons?"

Kestral laughed. It wasn't the long, loud laugh he had yesterday, but it was an honest laugh. And the barn was made of what Wix considered "respectable wood", so I had just earned my next few days of food. Suddenly, my little tumble was worth it.

"All right. Instead of hunting, can you show me to the nearest stream? I may as well wash out my clothes before I head out again."

"Oh, that's actually a good idea."

Kestral raised an eyebrow at me.

"I have washing I've been putting off, too. I'll see if Wi—Chesawick will let us use her soap."

We walked back to the inn, Kestral heading upstairs to gather his clothes and me to the kitchen to find Wix. She made a face at me as I sauntered in, feeling more than a little cocky.

"Did you hear that I made him laugh?"

"Yes, you made him laugh." Wix pouted. "But you haven't made him sleepy. Isn't that the root of our agreement?"

"I drew pretty deeply last night. He should be falling over his own feet by now." I shrugged. "I found out he used to be a soldier. Maybe he just knows how to hide fatigue."

Wix puffed up her cheeks and balled her fists, clearly unsatisfied with my explanation. "You had better make him sleepy tomorrow."

I waved a hand dismissively. "Tomorrow, he'll feel like he hasn't slept in three nights. Believe me, he'll be tired. Oh, I need soap. For my clothes. I don't want to keep upsetting oak."

Wix tilted her head to the side. "Just for you?"

"I'm borrowing it for me and for Kestral."

"You're not borrowing it, you're using it," Wix clarified. "I suppose I could trade out one of the laughter-meals for soap."

"A whole meal for some soap?" I rolled my eyes. "Unfair, Wix. Soap should only be worth the cost of a buttered roll."

"For one person, maybe." Wix held up a finger to stop me from protesting. "If you're paying his cost too, then it's a half meal: meat and vegetables only."

I huffed at her. "With seasonings."

Wix nodded. "With seasonings." She handed me a small pouch of powdered soap. I took it with a shake of my head. Arguing with Wix was like reasoning with a chicken. After quickly gathering my clothes and stuffing them into a sack, I met up with Kestral in the bar.

"There's a stream I like to use not far from here," I told him, leading the way back outside. "There is a washer well in town, but I hate paying to use it."

Kestral nodded as he followed, his own sack of clothes slung over one shoulder. He still wore his sword at his belt and I now noticed a small crossbow hooked on the opposite hip. Perhaps he intended to catch another waterbird for lunch today.

"What made you leave the army?" I asked, trying to continue our earlier conversation.

He shrugged, eyes distant.

"How long have you been a mage hunter? Have you collected any notable bounties?"

He glanced sidelong at me. "There are only seven bounties in the whole kingdom right now. As far as I know, they're all still alive."

"Oh, so you weren't part of the Great Mage Hunt, then?"

"The Great Hunt was over by the time I enlisted. I did help take down a few small-time mages, though."

"So, you're about my age," I surmised. "Around twenty?"

"You don't seem too sure of that."

I gave him a one-shouldered shrug. "Orphanage, remember? They didn't exactly keep great records."

He nodded. We had taken a turn out of town and were following a well-worn path down to the creek I liked for washing and sometimes bathing. The grass grew high along the sides of the path, waving rhythmically in the breeze and hiding the stream from view, although I could hear it as we drew closer. The forest that secluded the tiny village from its neighbors and gave us our good hunting grounds rose on the far side of the stream. Not that I did anything as strenuous as hunting, of course. Sometimes I would go fishing upstream where the river widened. There was almost nothing I loved more than fresh fish.

I led Kestral off the beaten path towards my favorite washing spot along the stream, where a large shale shelf extended out over the water. The grass was tall enough that it reached my thighs, making it difficult to see where my footfalls landed. When Kestral stopped behind me, I looked back to see if he had tripped.

"Are you okay?" I asked as he peered into the depths of the tall grass.

Kestral stooped down and plucked something from the ground. He held up a bright orange flower. "We're walking over shura flowers."

"Oh, yeah, those are everywhere near the stream." I looked down and found a few of the sticky, orange petals stuck to my boots. Ugh, Wix was sure to make me take my boots off before she let me back in the inn. "They don't make you itch, do they? I should have asked earlier."

"No." Kestral frowned at the tiny flower, then at me. "I thought . . ."

"Hm?" I looked around. "They're not that uncommon here. Did Beramin not have shura flowers?"

Kestral shook his head, dropping the flower back into the depths of the grass. Then he did the most unexpected thing ever: he smiled at me. I grinned back, not quite certain what had just happened. I pointed out the shale overhang just ahead. We each sat down at one end of the shelf and dumped out our clothes sacks. I set the soap powder between us to share and we each set to work.

Silently.

I hated silence.

"What do mage hunters do now that almost all the kingdom's mages are dead?" I asked as I wrung out a shirt.

"Mages aren't the only magical forces in the kingdom," Kestral replied. "I mostly deal with magical beasts near villages and cities. Centaurs, griffons, elementals, fairies. Killed a slag once."

I shuddered. Meeting a slag was not something many people walked away from.

"We don't have many of those around here." I dunked a small handful of clothes in the water and swirled them around. "Occasionally, a krupper will waylay a hunter, but that's about it."

"Hm."

I felt him staring at me, but didn't meet his gaze. I ground some soap into my clothes and gave them another swish in the water.

"Usually when a small village isn't being bothered by supernatural forces, it's because something is keeping them away." He spoke softly, but the words sent a chill up my spine.

"Well, we have a lot of really good hunters here," I replied, trying to keep my tone light. "That's good enough to keep some monsters away, at least."

Kestral wrung out his last shirt, folded it and placed it back in his bag. He leaned back on one arm and turned to face me. "I came to this village because I thought it might have a mage protecting it."

I laughed, hoping it didn't sound too forced. I kept my golden eyes turned down as I finished up washing my clothes. "I'm pretty sure I would have heard about it if we had a mage in town."

Out of the corner of my eye, I saw Kestral smile. "Once I got here I realized I was wrong. I thought—"

A loud, snarling grunt pealed out from the forest across the stream. Kestral and I both froze, watching as the grass waved wildly before parting to reveal a beast on four legs, narrow in the chest and shoulders, wide in the gut, with pointed ears, a pig-like snout and long tusks.

Pigoblin.

And not just one. Behind the first was a herd of at least ten more of the beasts.

The first pigoblin stopped as it saw us watching it from across the stream. It rose up on its hind legs to a height just below my shoulders. Its tiny eyes darted over us, snout snuffling as it checked our scent. After a moment, it dropped back to all fours and continued along the stream away from us.

"Too bad I didn't bring my longbow," Kestral commented, watching them go. "I don't have time to salt the meat anyway, but—what's wrong? Are you shaking?"

I was rooted in place, hands trembling over the forgotten laundry. This was the biggest group of pigoblins I had ever seen, and they were already so close to the village. My sense of self-preservation went to war with my more sentimental side. I knew what the right choice was, but if I made it, everything would change.

"Hey."

I found myself staring into concerned blue eyes.

"They look scary, but pigoblins are cowards. They won't go into the village."

"They will," I rasped. My throat had gone dry. I swallowed and tried to find my voice.

Kestral shook his head. "Except for when they're defending their young, pigoblins never attack humans."

"No." I took a breath to steel myself. "But they kill fairies."

"But you're not—" Kestral's eyes widened. "The Broken Wing. Chesawick."

I nodded. "Her glen kicked her out. She's all on her own. She doesn't cause the villagers any trouble, you have to believe me."

Kestral swore quietly under his breath. He turned to look back at the trail of trampled grass behind the troop of pigoblins. They had crossed the stream a-ways up from us. From the waving of the grass, they were headed straight for Wix's inn. Kestral stood up, leaving his bag of wet clothes on the ground.

"I can turn the pigoblins back. After that, I'll deal with the fairy." He glanced back at me. "Try to beat them to the inn so she knows they're coming."

I nodded, climbing shakily to my feet. Before I could take a breath, Kestral exploded into motion, loosening his sword and racing after the pigoblins. I ran for the trail, hoping Kestral could slow the troop down before they reached the inn. My mind raced faster than my feet as I worried about what might happen to Wix. The pigoblins would eat her if they got to her, but what would Kestral do to her? Fairies could be terrible to humans, but Wix was a kind soul who enjoyed living among us. Would the villagers who had known her for years protect her, or would they turn on her when they learned the truth? I owed Wix so much more than she could ever know, but I wouldn't be able to protect her. Not if I wanted to keep my own skin intact.

Villagers stared at me as I pelted along the main avenue. I didn't bother trying to explain; it would have taken time and a horde of pigoblins wasn't normally a threat anyway. Distantly, I could hear the screaming snarls of the beasts. Hoping that Kestral had slowed them down, I leapt up the front steps of the Broken Wing and burst into the bar. Wix stood in the doorway of the kitchen, frozen in the act of drying her hands on a cloth.

"Reshi, what—"

"Seal it up, Wix!" I panted, leaning on a table to catch my breath. "Seal it all up. There's a huge group of pigoblins coming this way."

Wix cried out, dropping the cloth. She placed one hand against the doorframe causing the wood to instantly spring to life, sprouting leaves and growing thicker. All around me doors and shutters snapped closed, the wood growing together to form a seal.

"I had to tell Kestral." I put a hand on the front door, preventing it from shutting me inside. "I'm sorry. He knows you're a fairy. He says he's going to deal with you after."

"Reshi . . ." Wix trembled. She looked so tiny, so helpless, in that moment. I shook my head; fairies were most definitely not helpless, no matter how they appeared.

"Try to run after we kill the pigoblins," I told her. "I'll do my best to protect you."

Wix nodded, still shaking. I ducked out the door before it could seal itself shut. Kestral and the pigoblins had reached the street just in front of the inn. Most of the beasts were bleeding—a few lay injured or dead. The trouble with pigoblins was that they were faster than they looked and their skin was tough; an injury that would kill a human often just enraged a pigoblin.

Kestral moved through the pack of monsters like a scythe through wheat. His sword moved like liquid steel, carving a path of blood and flesh. No move was wasted, each step was sure and solid. He was a perfect warrior, beautiful and terrible all at once.

There was no way I could stand against this man.

Two pigoblins broke free of the massacre, heading straight for Wix's inn. I might be no match for Kestral, nor for such a large group of pigoblin all at once, but I'm not completely useless. I fell back into a familiar stance, one leg behind me for support, the other ahead for balance. I tucked my hands behind my back and as the pigoblins charged, I surged forward, drawing twin daggers from hidden sheaths. The blades bit deeply through the beasts' necks, spraying blood impossibly high on the inn's outer wall. A few quick steps brought me within reach of another pigoblin. I feinted with my right dagger, then plunged the left through its piggy eye. The beast screamed and whipped its head, trying to gore me with its tusks. I leaned back to avoid the swipe, kicked it down and sliced through its windpipe. Another came charging at me from the side and I had to kick off the thrashing body of the one in the dirt to leap out of the way. A sword whistled past me, striking the pigoblin from behind and biting deeply through its spine. I turned, putting my back to Kestral's, before reversing my blades with a flourish and taking a balanced stance.

"I didn't pick you for a fighter," Kestral said, his voice controlled if slightly breathless.

"I'm not, when I can avoid it." I tried counting the remaining pigoblins as they regrouped a short distance away. "How many are there?"

"There were almost twenty." I felt him shift to a new stance behind me. "Have you turned pigoblins away before?"

"At least once a month." The pigoblins were grunting to each other and spreading out. A new charge was coming. "Never a group this big before."

"They must have spread the word. It's not usual to find a single fairy without a glen to protect it." Kestral paused, then added, "I thought you were the fairy."

"What? But I—Oh." My eye color, the talk of 'debts,' his examination of the wood in the inn. "A lot of things just started making sense."

"I was only sure after the shura flowers. We're going to talk after this." I could hear the threat in his voice. I didn't expect I would enjoy the coming conversation.

"Well, we gotta live first."

A group of pigoblins charged at me on all fours. I tossed my right dagger to my left hand, shook my right wrist and flipped a long, thin throwing blade into my palm. Holding it at the tip of the blade, I threw it end-over-end into the center of the leading pigoblin's forehead. It went down with a crash, knocking another pigoblin off course. I spun neatly out of the way of the remaining pigoblin as I tossed my heavy dagger back to my right hand and slammed it into the base of its skull. I used my other dagger to deflect a tusk that would have ripped my stomach open. The pigoblin staggered a step before his head recoiled violently on his thick, piggy neck. I spun to the side, narrowly avoiding the ball of flying saliva pigoblins used to shoot fairies out of the air. It wasn't all that dangerous, but the impact could have knocked me off balance even if I didn't consider how gross it would be to be covered in pigoblin spit. Before the spitter could run, I darted towards him, driving a dagger deep between his ribs.

I couldn't keep track of Kestral's movements as I fought. His sword was little more than a red and silver blur as it cut down the pigoblins. I moved away, giving him the space he needed for those powerful swings. No way did I want to find myself between him and a pigoblin with that sword bearing down on me. At least this battle had come at a good time for me; my wellspring of power was full, giving me an edge against the hardy pigoblins.

I spun as a grunt and a clatter of steel on stone sounded behind me. Kestral had slipped in a gob of pigoblin spit and a lucky tusk ripped his sword from his grasp, tossing it several paces away. I couldn't tell if the blood on his clothes was from the pigoblins or from an injury. I didn't have long to look as a pigoblin reared up behind him, intent on crushing him.

Icy panic gripped my chest. This was my fault. Kestral was clearly a seasoned warrior; killing a few pigoblins should be nothing at all to him, but I had drained his energy the past two nights. He had to be feeling the effects of lost sleep now, at the worst possible moment. It was all my fault.

In that moment, the world seemed to spin a little slower. Everything came into sharp focus. Heat blossomed in my chest as my mind cooled. It wouldn't have happened if I hadn't been so full of magic, I'm sure of it. But I couldn't control what happened next, even if I had had the presence of mind to try.

Golden light flashed around me, giving me a thread to the consciousness of each pigoblin still fighting. Their minds were consumed with hunger and rage, but in a tiny corner of each of their minds, I found fear. The golden light seemed to hum as I nurtured that fear into terror, and from terror into a blind panic. The sounds of screams and the pounding of cloven feet surrounded me as the light faded. As the pigoblins fled, the world regained its normal speed and color.

Kestral stared up at me from one knee, one arm wrapped around his midsection. I held my breath as those blue eyes froze me in place.

"You're a son of Laurana." His voice held the promise of death. "Jereshin."

Could I talk my way out of this? Could he be convinced to let me live? As my mind struggled to find the right words to keep myself alive, I realized Kestral wasn't holding a wound—he was holding the small crossbow from his belt.

I can't honestly say what happened first. Did he fire first, or did I shapeshift first? I doubt even he could say. But quick as a shrug, I dropped into my cat form, a crossbow bolt zipping through the space where my head had been moments before. I leapt through the collar of my shirt as it dropped around me and ran toward Kestral, who was now on his feet, snapping a new bolt into place. I darted between his legs, racing for Wix's inn. A bolt shattered against the fence as I leapt through it, jumping to the rain barrel, to the gutter and in through the broken upstairs window. I didn't chance a look back, but I heard boots pounding the street below; I didn't have much time.

"Wix!" I shouted as soon as my shapeshifting was complete. "Wix? Where are—oof!"

She popped out of the wall, crashing into me, causing me stagger backwards. Her human veil was gone, revealing her true fairy form—short, curling hair and bright eyes, both the color of new growth in spring. Her ears were slightly pointed and the features of her face exaggerated. Her limbs appeared to be too long, too thin and she wore only a petal-pink sheath dress from her chest to her thighs. On her back, there were a pair of torn and broken wings, translucent like a dragonfly's. Her glen had broken them when they banished her.

"Reshi, what happened?" Wix's eyes were wide with fear and she gripped my arms tightly, her entire body trembling. "Did they hurt you? Is he coming for me?"

"He's coming for me." I pushed her away from me. My transformation had left me naked, as always, and I felt vulnerable in front of the magical being. She followed me as I ran for my room, where I hoped I had left some clothes. "Wix, you owe me a life debt. Can you get rid of him?"

Wix said nothing. She stood meekly in my doorway, shaking like a leaf.

"I don't have time for games and trades, Wix!" I flipped my mattress, revealing a tunic and a single sock. We both jumped as a fist pounded on the front door. It felt like the inn shook all around me. "Get rid of him! Turn him into a tree or pond scum or whatever fairies turn people into."

"Reshi, I can't." Tears streamed down Wix's face.

"You have to!" I pulled the shirt over my head, then gripped Wix's shoulders. "Wix, he's going to kill us both."

"I know, but . . . but . . ." Wix stared back at me, her mouth moving without sound.

"I'm calling in a life debt. I just saved—" I stopped, my mind finally catching up. "You owe him a life debt, too, don't you? We both saved you from the pigoblins."

Wix nodded.

Grind all fairies and their debts to dust! I dropped onto my tumbled mattress, putting my head into my hands. The pounding at the door grew louder. What now?

"Reshi?" Wix knelt in front of me. "Why is he after you? Is it the reason you've been hiding here for so long?"

I took a breath, trying to steady myself. I reached out and gripped Wix's hand, just for something to hold on to. "Wix, I'm . . . I'm one of the mistress mage's children."

She tilted her head to the side. "I don't know what that means. I always knew you were a mage, but you're not very strong."

How could I explain it in a way a fairy would understand? The pounding at the front door stopped suddenly, and I imagined Kestral circling the building, trying to find a way in.

"Wix, you remember the Great Mage Hunt, right? It should have happened before you lost your wings."

She shrugged. "Only a little. Humans killing humans aren't exactly something we take notice of. I remember the glens grew quite large, though, since there were so few magical humans to kill us."

"Right. A long time ago, the king decided the realm would be safer without mages and he ordered the army to find and kill everyone who could use magic. What he didn't know was that his long-time mistress, a woman named Laurana, was a very powerful sorceress. She had seven children with the king, all with minor magical abilities. When the king found out she was a sorceress, he locked her up and put bounties on all seven of his children by her." I took a shaky breath. "I'm the youngest. That's why I've been hiding. And that's why he's going to kill me."

"But why?" Wix asked. "You've never hurt anyone with your magic. You're not even very strong. Why even go to the trouble of killing all the magical humans in the first place?"

"I don't know, Wix. That all happened before I was born. I didn't even know I was one of Laurana's children until a few years ago when she was locked up." I looked up into Wix's eyes. "I need to escape, Wix. If you can't kill him, what can you do for me?"

Wix glanced away, her unnaturally thin shoulders rising and falling in a shrug. She met my eyes, then looked away again. "Does he know much about fairies?"

"I think so. He said he'd fought them before. Why?"

Wix hesitated, drawing her hand away from me. I took a deep breath and held it to keep from yelling at her. It wasn't her fault that she had to follow the rules of fairies.

"If he knows about fairies . . ." I turned my thoughts over, trying to follow the gnarled logic of the fae. "He might know he can call in a life debt. If he does, you would have to tell him where I am."

Wix nodded, fresh tears running down her cheeks.

"So, anything you do for me won't help me, will it?"

Wix shook her head. "I can buy time. I can give you any provisions you need. Food, clothes, anything you can take with you."

"No." I stood up, pulling my tunic off. "I won't be able to take anything with me."

"Reshi, I'm so sorry."

"Don't be." I tried to smile, but my chin trembled, betraying my fear. "Buy as much time as you can, please, Wix. I'll leave through the window upstairs."

"Where will you go?" Wix gripped my arm with both hands. She trailed along behind me as I walked back up the stairs. Somewhere outside I heard thumping. Was Kestral pounding on the back door?

"I can't tell you, but I'm sure you'll know when I get there." I peeled her fingers off my arm. "Stay safe, Wix. Thank you for hiding me all this time."

"I'm the one in your debt, Reshi." Wix hung her head. "If you—if you live, I will repay you. I swear it by silver."

"Thanks." I was able to force a small smile this time. "I'll do my best."

"Farewell, Reshi."

My throat closed up, so all I could do was nod. I looked to the open window and felt my body shift into a new form. I perched just inside the window frame, taking a careful look around. When Kestral didn't appear like a streaking star of justice, I leapt out the window.

Black wings caught the air and carried me aloft. I chanced only one look back. Sure enough, those piercing blue eyes followed me, but I was too far out of range for the tiny crossbow. I wheeled north, heading straight for my destination as the crow flies.

It was time to finally meet my family.

2

The journey pushed my abilities to the absolute limit. As a crow, I suffered from night-blindness, so I could only fly so long as the sun was up. When it set, I would catch an hour's worth of sleep on a high, hidden tree branch, then climb down as a cat. House cats don't move very quickly through what was mostly dense forest, but at least I could see. Most of my forms were useless at night. When the sun peeked over the horizon, I caught another quick nap, nestled between tree roots, before alighting to the skies as a crow once more. By the time I approached my destination, I was well and fully exhausted.

Each time I slept, my sister's voice called out to me, telling me where to go. She had been excited by my sudden decision to meet, less so about the hunter on my trail, but she welcomed me all the same. I tried to think positively about her, as well as my other siblings, but mostly I kept picturing Wix at Kestral's mercy. Would she be safe? Would he hurt her? I felt ten times the coward for running away, but Wix could take care of herself. I had been the one in real danger.

A thin plume of smoke marked the end of my journey. I angled my wings, swooping down cautiously in case I was flying into a trap. The tiny cottage was set at the edge of the forest, along the banks of a large, clear lake. It was picturesque, especially with the beautiful young woman sitting out front, looking out over the water as if in a trance. I landed on the roof of the cottage and studied her for a moment.

We looked nothing alike. Her hair, waist-length and straight, was the purest blonde I had ever seen, closer to white than blonde. She wore a simple dress of pale yellow, the sleeves only reaching to her elbows and the skirt dropping just below her knees. Brown boots laced up high beneath the dress. Her skin seemed to glow, pink and fair. With her back to me I couldn't see her eye color, but her body was slender and shapely for a young woman. How would I even know if this was my sister?

I ruffled my feathers, getting ready to take flight again if it became necessary, then cawed loudly. The girl stood gracefully and turned, a surprised smile on her lips. Her eyes were silver, like looking-glasses or twin full moons. When they met mine, I knew instantly that this woman was most certainly my sister.

"Reshi, is that you?" The woman stepped as close as she could, looking up at me on the roof. "I didn't think you would arrive before Velyn. You must have traveled so quickly!"

I responded with a flick of my wings.

"Oh, I understand." She smiled sweetly. "I have a robe inside that might fit you. I'm sorry I didn't think to have clothing prepared. Will you come inside?"

That was more than a little disconcerting. I had known about her far-speaking ability, but was she also a mind reader? I did need clothes, however, as well as food, and I thought I could smell something cooking inside. I fluttered down from the roof onto my sister's offered hand. She carried me inside and set me on a crudely-made table.

The cottage was even smaller inside, mostly due to the haphazardly arranged furniture. The front room looked to be a combination sitting room and bedroom. The back room was the kitchen, which contained a single table and chair surrounded by piles of clutter along the counters and pushed into the room's corners. A large pot bubbled on the stove and my stomach lurched. In that moment, I almost would have chosen nudity over hunger.

"Here it is." My sister stood after rummaging through a clothes chest. "I don't know how tall you are, but this robe should fit. After you shift, I'll see about finding you something else." She held it up to me and turned her face away, inviting me to shapeshift. The robe was longer than I was tall, with full sleeves and buttons up the front. It was a dark color, maybe once a deep green, but now it was mottled with stains and patches. After slipping back into my human form, I accepted the cloak from her, grateful that she kept her eyes averted until I had it wrapped snugly about my body.

"Thank you," I said, my voice rough. I coughed and swallowed. With my voice not having been used since I had fled Wix's inn, talking was even harder than shifting.

"Ah, now I can finally see you properly." Those silver eyes met mine. Small, long-fingered hands cupped my cheeks, a tiny smile curled on her lips. "Far-sight is a wonder, but it falls short of actually meeting family for the first time. You have such beautiful eyes, my brother."

I cleared my throat before speaking. "They're nothing compared to yours. Um, it's Cera, right?"

Her laughter was like starlight rippling on water. "I never did properly introduce myself, did I?" She released my face and stepped back. "Yes, Cera is fine. Mother named me Hacerathan, but none of us use our given names, do we, Jereshin?"

"Not since they posted our bounties," I replied dryly. I tried to hide a glance at the pot in the kitchen, but Cera smiled knowingly.

She led me to the small kitchen and pressed me into a rickety chair before ladling soup into a hand-carved bowl.

"So, you've spoken to all our brothers and sisters? Have you met any of them?"

Cera pressed the bowl into my hands before leaning back against the kitchen counter. It looked like a creamy potato soup full of herbs and tiny pieces of meat. It was a struggle to keep from wolfing it down in an instant.

"You are the first I have met in person," Cera admitted. "I have spoken to each of our siblings in the moments before they fall asleep, much as I have spoken to you in the past. I believe the only way for us to survive is to come together. Unfortunately, no one seems to feel the way I do. You can eat as much as you like, Reshi. I made plenty of soup and I have bread baking."

I tipped the rest of the soup down my throat at her invitation, wincing as the heat burned my mouth. I held the bowl out for a refill, trying to hide the temporary pain. Cera handed me back a full bowl as well as a cup of cool milk.

"Why is Velyn suddenly joining you?" I asked after sipping the milk to soothe my burned tongue. "Is he being hunted, too?"

"I don't think so. Not as closely as you, at least." Cera's eyes turned distant, and I wondered if she were far-seeing. "You and I and Velyn are the youngest. I think he saw the advantage in coming together. I feel that if we band together, the others will join us."

"Really?" I scooped up a spoonful and blew on it, watching curls of steam rise from it. "Even Kila?"

Cera sighed. "Oh, Kila. You must admire her strategy, though. I would never have thought to challenge the bounty so aggressively."

Through Cera's far-speaking ability, I knew most of us had gone into hiding after our bounties had been posted. But our sister Tekilashan had announced that anyone who wished to kill her could find her on the bloodiest battlefield of the kingdom. The last thing I had heard was that she had killed over forty mage hunters, all while participating in border skirmishes and house wars. There hadn't been much talk of any new challengers lately, so I suppose the strategy worked. Even after all those highly visible battles, no one was certain what type of magic she possessed.

Cera placed a still-steaming loaf of bread on the table and cut it into thick slices. "I'm not a very good cook, so I'm sorry this is all so plain." She handed me a slice of bread and pushed a carafe of butter towards me. "I'm known to a few local villages as a fortune teller, so I get by, but I try to keep mostly to myself."

"Did you get sent to the orphanage in Giltner, too?" I swiped out my soup bowl with the bread; no sense in wasting a single drop of it. "Were we ever there at the same time?"

"No." A shadow passed over Cera's face and her words became clipped. "I can't believe that woman sent you to Giltner. It was bitter and petty, and you were just a baby."

The venom in her voice made me pause, a handful of bread halfway to my mouth. "It wasn't so bad. I didn't think Laurana had any choice in where we were sent."

"No, not Mother." Cera folded her arms across her chest and glared darkly at the floor. "The queen chose our fates for us. She was upset that Mother was able to bear so many healthy children for the king when she only managed to have one herself. She was increasingly cruel with each child." She met my eyes, her expression melting to pity. "I'm so sorry."

I shrugged it off. My past wasn't something I was willing to discuss, not even with my older sister. "Where did the queen send you?"

"She gave me to a band of traveling performers." Cera smiled. "She intended that I be traded to fairies, but the performers kept me and raised me. I learned to read fortunes and I was able to travel widely. It wasn't as bad as some."

I avoided the look in her eyes this time. "What do you know about Velyn?" I asked, changing the subject.

"He is the fifth child of Laurana, Navelynstra. I think he grew up with fishermen in the far north." Cera shrugged. "We will learn more about him when he gets here."

"When will that be?"

"Any day now." Cera cleared the table. "Are you still hungry? I have some food set aside if you need it."

"No, I should stop eating before I burst." I pulled the robe around myself a little tighter. "Did you say you might have more clothes?"

"Yes, but I'm not sure if much will fit you." Cera placed the dishes I had used in a basin of soapy water. "Check the trunks in the front room for anything suitable."

I stood, trying not to sway on my feet. It had been far too long since I'd walked as a human. It didn't help that I had completely emptied my recently replenished well of magic. I could tell that one more transformation would wipe me out; I was lucky to have made it this far.

How long will it take for Kestral to find me? I wondered as I sifted through a trunk of old clothing. Wix must know where I was by now—the cottage was surrounded by elm and oak trees. Would my brother arrive before Kestral did? Could the three of us stand against him? I would have to find a way to refill my wellspring before that time came.

After a bit of digging through the trunks, I found pants that would fit if I cinched the waist with a belt, as well as a few shirts and tunics. There was a pair of boots that were a little too big, but I preferred that over too small anyway. By the time I finished dressing, Cera reappeared in the small front room.

"Why do you have all this?" I asked, gesturing to the trunks of clothes, the broken furniture, the hand-made trinkets and even a musical instrument or two.

Cera smiled, a blush rising in her cheeks. "I can't stand to see anything discarded. My family—the traveling performers—never threw anything away. Everything has a use, even if that use is no longer what the object was intended for. Old clothes could be costumes, broken chairs could be used as canvas anchors, old pots could be used to create sounds. When I pass through villages as a fortune teller, I collect anything that has been set aside. It may be silly, but I hate to think of anything being wasted."

I nodded as if I understood, even though I didn't. I had been forced to flee so many times that I had learned to leave everything behind—clothing, weapons, even dear friends. It wasn't worth getting attached to anything or anyone. But Cera seemed to have learned something completely different.

"You look half dead on your feet, Reshi. Let me set up a pallet for you." She moved some crates, clearing space on the floor. The sun was only just setting, but I was utterly exhausted and sure that I could sleep for a week. Maybe I would; maybe if Kestral arrived and killed me in my sleep, I wouldn't notice.

"Cera, can I ask you about your powers?"

She glanced up from fluffing a pillow. "Yes, but I may not answer."

"That's fair. You're a far-speaker, right? That's how you talk to me in my sleep?"

"I have the gifts of both far-speech and far-sight," Cera explained. "It isn't particularly strong magic, but it suits me just fine."

"Far-sight? Like, the future or mind-reading?"

Cera laughed. "No, not future-sight. Not normally, anyway. Far-sight is like scrying without crystal or glass; I can see people I have a connection with over great distances. Far-speech allows me to project thoughts and hear responses through dreams, but I cannot see inside someone's mind. I have been told that I am fairly intuitive, though, so I apologize for seeming off-putting."

"You don't have to apologize to me so much, sister." I offered her a sleepy smile as I helped her stretch a blanket over the pallet. "I truly appreciate you taking me in right now, especially with a hunter on my tail."

Cera smiled back. "Once Velyn is here, we will take care of the hunter. Sleep now, brother. Save your worries for the future."

The next day I awoke to a cool hand against my forehead. My first thought was of Wix, and strangely, my second was of Kestral. But the eyes greeting me were neither green nor blue, but that haunting silver color unique to my sister.

"Reshi, you've been sleeping all day," Cera told me, her voice soft. "It's nearly nightfall again and you've barely stirred. Are you well? Can I make you some dinner?"

My voice cracked as I tried to speak. Cera handed me a chipped clay mug. The water was cool, clearing sleep from my throat. "Perhaps a little dinner would help," I told her hoarsely.

Cera nodded and stood. I finished the water and set the mug aside, looking at all the broken junk filling Cera's small home.

"Has Velyn arrived yet?" I asked.

"He should arrive tomorrow," Cera replied. She reappeared from the kitchen bearing a bowl of soup and buttered bread.

I ate it on my pallet, still feeling a little too weak to stand.

"Reshi, may I ask about your magic?"

I coughed on my soup, surprised by the question. "I suppose so. I asked about yours."

"I know it's a bit personal and we don't know each other very well. But yours is a nature-based magic, isn't it? Can you do more than shapeshifting?"

I tore the bread into little chunks to dip into the soup, mulling over her question. No one had ever known enough about my magic to ask about it except Wix, and the only part she cared about was how I regained my magic. I didn't really know much about my magic; it had only manifested a few short years ago when Laurana had been revealed as a sorceress.

"Shapeshifting is almost all of it," I admitted. "And even that's fairly limited. I can only take the shapes of common mage familiars."

"And the shapes you take, are they all black like your hair?" Cera asked, reaching out to tuck a free strand behind my ear.

I pulled away from her reflexively.

She frowned but didn't reach for me again.

"Yes. The black cat, the crow . . . my eyes stay golden in all my forms, too." I shifted uncomfortably. "I never received any sort of mage-training, you know. I'm kind of still figuring this all out."

"Me too." Cera smiled. "It wasn't like any of us could approach a trainer once the bounties were placed on our heads. Even if we could, there are no more powerful mages left in the land. Except for Mother."

"I guess it's not possible for us to ask her for magic lessons." A thought came to me. "Can't you speak to her? With your magic?"

"I have, but it's . . . strange." Cera's mouth twisted and her eyes grew distant. "Speaking with her is like listening to someone speak underwater. I can only see her through dark mist. I think it has to do with the enchantments used to keep her locked away."

"Huh. Of course, it couldn't be that easy." I finished my meal and handed the bowl and mug back to Cera. "I'm sorry for being such a boring guest. I barely rested at all while traveling here, so it's all catching up to me now."

"That's understandable." Cera smiled at me. "Is there anything I can do for you to make you feel better?"

I shook my head. "I'll feel better with more sleep." Cera nodded and rose. On a whim, I caught her sleeve to keep her from leaving. "Maybe you could just sit with me while I sleep? For a little while?"

Cera beamed. "Of course, brother. I'll be right back."

I settled back into my pallet as Cera took care of the dishes. I felt like a rat for asking her to sit with me in the hopes that I could steal from her magical wellspring, but without it I would never get any better. I felt helpless without my magic, made worse by the knowledge that Kestral was most likely already on his way here. Besides, Cera must have to refill her well somehow, too, right? She probably even understood what I needed and would be happy to help.

So why not just tell her?

Cera came back and sat down beside my pallet. She set a broken lyre in her lap and toyed with it, as if to fix it. I turned so my back pressed against her and pulled the blankets up over my head to block out the light coming in through the windows. I could tell her, I supposed, but what if she refused? She was already doing so much for me, asking to pilfer from her wellspring just felt like asking too much of her. Better to take a little and not let her know it was done. Not that I could steal anything unless she fell asleep. I tried lying awake, hoping she might doze, but eventually sleep took me.

I woke to voices from outside the cottage. I was still tired and completely drained magically, but one of those voices held a masculine edge. Had Kestral arrived? Would he kill Cera? I tried to order my thoughts as I pulled my ill-fitting boots on hastily. Judging by the sunlight streaming through the windows, it was early afternoon. The voices spoke softly and calmly, nothing at all like Kestral's monotone. After quickly pulling my hair back into a tail, I crept through the kitchen and out the back door. Better to sneak up on possible attackers than be snuck up on.

Cera stood with someone at the edge of the lake. As I watched, she nodded seriously, eyes looking out over the placid water where a small boat had been anchored, its sails tightly furled. The stranger was of a height with her, making him shorter than me by an inch or two. His skin held a dark tan as if he spent most of his time in the sun. His hair was dark gray and curled around his head in a strange, nebulous fashion. As I watched, a phantom wind shifted his hair, and it seemed to flow and change shape. His clothes looked rough and weathered; the wide-legged pants didn't tuck into the thick boots. A faded blue vest covered a cut-sleeved undyed shirt, which he wore long and untucked.

"Come over and say hello."

I jumped. The voice was in my head, but it was clearly Cera's. She was still looking out over the lake, but somehow, she had noticed me lurking around the corner of the cottage. I should have known better than to try and sneak up on a far-seer. I made a show of slamming the cottage door to draw their attention before walking down towards the lake.

"I take it you are Reshi?" the newcomer asked, his smile friendly and his hand outstretched for a handshake. I gasped. His eyes were the same electric white-blue of a lightning bolt. He quickly looked away, hiding his eyes.

"Sorry." I took his hand and shook it. "You must get that a lot, with eyes like yours."

"I imagine you do, too." His eyes met mine again briefly. "I'm Velyn."

"Glad to meet you, Velyn." I felt a spark of power at his touch. I wanted to ask what his magic was, but it felt like a rude question after having just met someone.

"Oh, my brothers!" Cera leapt forward, wrapping an arm around each of our necks in a hug. "I have a shank of lamb I've been saving for just this occasion. Come inside, we'll have a nice family meal!" Without waiting for our response, she took us both by the hand and dragged us into the cottage. Velyn and I exchanged a bemused glance as we allowed her to tug us along.

Velyn stopped inside the doorway, surveying the amount of old broken furniture the same way I had when I arrived. Cera scampered into the kitchen, where a chorus of pots and pans clanged about as she prepared food. I sat back on my pallet, watching Velyn as he tried to make sense of the mess.

"Don't think about it too loudly or she'll hear you," I advised, tilting my head towards the kitchen.

Velyn snorted. "The trouble with far-speakers, right?" He glanced over at me. "Cera says you have a hunter after you."

I grimaced. "I do. It's selfish, but it's the only reason I agreed to meet up with you both."

Velyn moved a stack of unbound books from a chair and tested it before sitting down. As he moved, I noticed he wore a large, jagged tooth on a silver chain around his neck. Was it from some sort of sea beast? "Is he strong, this hunter?"

I shrugged. "I saw him slaughter a huge group of pigoblins all on his own with just a sword."

Velyn waved a hand dismissively. "Pigoblins aren't really a threat, though."

"They were in a frenzy over a fairy." I tried to find the right words to describe how dangerous Kestral really was. "He says he killed a slag once."

Velyn smirked. "And every fisherman I've ever met says he hooked a kraken once."

I let my head fall back against the wall with a thud. "If you knew him, you'd believe it. He's an ex-soldier from Beramin and he's . . . he's just intense."

"You think he'll find you here?" Velyn asked.

"That fairy he saved from pigoblins owes him a life debt, so yeah, I think he'll find me."

"Fairies." Velyn rolled his eyes. "Don't get me started."

I wanted to ask what he meant, but Cera came in balancing several bowls in her hands. "The lamb will take a while, but I found some cream and berries for us." She thrust one bowl at Velyn, then handed me another. She sat back against a wall with her own bowl. The berries were a little tart, but the sweetness of the cream was a perfect counterpoint in flavor. We fell quiet for a minute as we enjoyed the snack.

"Did Velyn tell you?" Cera asked, a smidge of cream adorning her upper lip, making her look like a little girl.

"Tell me what?" I replied, amused.

"He has weather magic." Cera beamed at our older brother. "It must be true that the elder siblings got the stronger magic."

Velyn shrugged modestly. "I don't know that you should call it 'weather magic.' Most of what I do is predict weather. Maybe change a wind here or there. It's nothing like far-sight or shapeshifting."

I flinched. So, Cera had told him about my powers. I guess it was all right. He was my brother after all. My powers had always been such a closely held secret that it felt strange to be discussing them out loud like this.

"What do you know of our other siblings' magic?" Velyn asked Cera. "You've spoken to all of them, right?"

"I have, but some of them aren't . . . well, they're not exactly friendly." Cera grimaced.

I caught Velyn's eye and could tell he was trying to hide the same laugh I was. From the small amount of information I knew about my so-called family, "friendly" was certainly not a word I would use to describe them.

"Most won't discuss their powers with me. The only one who actually answers me is our eldest brother, Eagan. He uses fire magic."

"Everyone knows that." Velyn shrugged. "It's part of his bounty information now."

"Is there new bounty information?" I asked. "I've been hiding out in the backwoods, so I haven't heard much."

"Every time a hunter gets away alive, they update our information. I passed through Kibernia on my way here and checked on the latest information."

I dropped my spoon with a clatter. Cera stared, her mouth hanging open.

"You passed through the capital city of the kingdom and no one recognized you?" I asked, incredulous.

Velyn shrugged. "The trick is not to let a hunter get away alive." He pointed at me with his spoon. "You'll be lucky if your hunter comes straight here without updating your information. You're the most mysterious of all of us."

I snorted. "If by mysterious you mean useless, then you're right."

Velyn laughed but Cera frowned at me. "I think shapeshifting is a powerful skill, Reshi. I doubt any of our other siblings can do it."

"They can't," Velyn confirmed. "At least, not according to their bounties."

"What do they know about us?" I asked. "Aside from our names and where we were sent."

"Next to nothing is known about Reina, the eldest, except for the name of her adoptive family and the schools she attended before she went into hiding. Eagan has been a bit more visible; he's beaten at least ten hunters so far, so they know about his fire magic. Then there are the twins."

"Kila and Laki," Cera put in. "Everyone knows about Kila. She's been killing hunters since the bounties came out, but they still don't know her power."

"Right, but they do know Laki's." Velyn rolled his eyes. "Supposedly he's a real softie, total opposite of Kila. He's never killed a hunter but he's strong enough to keep them away. His power is listed as 'life to the lifeless.'"

"What does that mean?" I asked.

Velyn shrugged. "No idea. I've never met him. Cera, they have a description of you, probably from the performers you traveled with. They have your powers listed as 'psychic.'"

Cera shook her head sadly. "I wish I was powerful enough to consider myself psychic. No hunters have come for me yet, though, so I suppose I'm well hidden here."

Velyn nodded. "It's a nice secluded spot. Doesn't your sight help protect you?"

"Sometimes I'll get a premonition." Cera shrugged. "It doesn't happen often, though."

"Maybe your magic only warns you when you need it," I suggested. Cera gave me a quick smile before staring into her empty bowl again. "What does it say about me?"

"Nothing." Velyn smirked at me. "Let's kill this hunter of yours so it stays that way."

"What about you?" Cera asked. "Do they know about your magic?"

"They describe it as 'wind magic.' A few people from my village remembered me enough to report it, but I haven't let any hunters get away with anything more specific." Velyn passed his bowl over to Cera. "That lamb isn't burning, right?"

Our sister cried out and ran to the kitchen.

Velyn chuckled softly.

"That's all of us, isn't it?" I said, more to myself than to Velyn. "I remember hearing their names the day the bounties were posted, but I'd forgotten them."

"Wasn't it strange, finding out you're half-royalty?" Velyn asked, a strange smile on his face. I felt my shoulders stiffen in surprise.

"I never even considered that." I shook my head. "Laurana was only a mistress; none of us have any claim to the throne. The heir is a true son of the king and queen."

"Right, but haven't you heard?" Those strange-colored eyes seemed to flash. "He's sickly, just like the queen. Imagine it, Reshi. The queen can have no more children and the heir might not be long for this world. Who stands to inherit?"

I couldn't help myself; I laughed. "I'm the youngest of seven bastards with a bounty on my head, which was placed by my own father. No, I don't think I stand to inherit one thin copper, Velyn. I'm a lot more concerned with keeping my skin intact than the succession of the throne."

Velyn shrugged easily. "It was just an idle thought, brother. I'm not about to go strutting into the throne room and demanding to be recognized as an heir. If they locked Mother away, I'm sure they would do the same to me. Or worse."

Cera came back into the room with plates of sliced mutton and fresh rolls slathered in jam. Once again, we lapsed into silence as we ate. I only got halfway through my meal before that nagging fatigue swept over me. Cera must not have fallen asleep against me last night, or else I would have restored at least a little of my magic. Maybe I would try sleeping against her tonight after she fell asleep. The thought filled me with shame, taking advantage of such a kind person, but at the same time I felt naked and vulnerable without my power.

"Cera, can you see the hunter coming for Reshi?" Velyn asked as he mopped up his plate with his roll.

"Not clearly," Cera replied. She shook her head back and stared up at the ceiling. After a moment, her eyes went blank. "I have no connection to the hunter, so I can't see his face. I can see he is drawing closer to us, but he is still far away. He wears a cloak of ice and purpose. He looks like freshly minted steel and moves like a predatory beast. He's . . . he's dangerous." Cera shook her head, surfacing from her trance. "But he's only human. We'll have a plan ready for him when he arrives."

"I'm sorry to drag you both into this." I set my plate aside and drew my knees up to rest my chin on them. "I couldn't face him alone, but that's no excuse to get you involved."

"Don't worry about it, Reshi." Cera placed a hand on my shoulder and smiled at me. "I'm grateful that it brought us together."

"And since we are together, killing him will be no problem at all." Velyn grinned darkly. "No one stands against the mistress's mage-born."

I felt a chill race along my spine. I had known, hadn't I? That the only thing that would keep Kestral from collecting my bounty was death? I should want him dead. With him dead, I could return to my village and to Wix. My secret would be safe, and I could continue living a normal-ish life. So why did the thought of killing him turn my stomach sour?

"Reshi? Are you still not well?" Cera placed her cool hand against my face. "Do you need to sleep more?"

"No." I grimaced. "Maybe. I feel terrible, just sleeping all the time."

"You should rest. You'll need your strength when the hunter comes." Cera gathered up the plates and stood. "Velyn, I'll set up a pallet for you after I clean up."

"No need." Velyn waved her off. "I have my own gear and I feel better sleeping outside anyway."

"Well, if it gets cold or if it starts to rain—" Cera cut herself off with a giggle. "I suppose a little rain is nothing to you. Let me know if I can get you anything."

"Thank you, sister." Velyn gave me a small wave then walked outside.

Cera clattered about in the kitchen as I lay down. I would have to wake myself up tonight and curl up next to one of them. The only way I would get my energy back was to steal it.

I managed to rouse myself later that night and found myself alone in Cera's cluttered room. If I had even a little magical energy stored up, I would have shifted to my cat form in order to see by the dim moonlight, but as weak as I was, I couldn't chance it. I kicked off the blankets and made a quick circuit around the room, just to make sure I was really all alone. I hissed as I bumped into several haphazardly placed items. How could Cera live in this mess?

When I couldn't find anyone, I opened the front door a crack and peeked out. Just enough light reflected off the lake to show me that a hammock had been strung from a tree just over the water. It swung low and heavy, giving the impression of a body inside it. I guessed that was Velyn, as I had never noticed the hammock before. After looking around a little more for Cera, I nearly jumped out of my skin when a voice called, "Up here, Reshi."

With my heart beating out of my chest, I glanced up to see Cera sitting on the roof of her house, smiling down at me. She waved at me and directed me to the chimney around back, which was an easy climb. I sat down beside her, already tired from my brief excursion out of bed.

"You're not regaining your magic, are you?" Cera asked bluntly.

"No," I replied with a sigh. I didn't really want to talk about it, but if she already knew, what was the harm? "How do you recover your magic, Cera?"

She looked up, a soft smile on her face. "Moonlight."

"Moonlight?" I looked up as well. The moon was a mere sliver, a day away from being black. "You just sit in the moonlight and your well refills?"

"That's right." Cera leaned back on her hands, staring up. "My power always waxes and wanes with the moon. When it's full, I can see further and hear more clearly. I've even seen glimpses of the future on nights of the full moon. I'm filling my wellspring now, in case your hunter shows up while the moon is dark."

I wrapped my arms around my knees, looking out over the lake. "That's lucky for you. You can soak up as much magical energy as you need most nights without even trying."

"How do you recover power, Reshi?"

I sighed. "I steal it. I have to draw it from a sleeping victim. It doesn't hurt the person, it usually just makes them sleep a little longer. But I have to be close enough to touch them to do it."

"Oh." Cera tilted her head to look at me, her hair falling behind her like a silvery curtain. "That makes sense."

I narrowed my eyes at her. "How does that make sense?"

"It just does, doesn't it?" Cera gave me a small smile. "It's like how some animals hibernate. They sleep to save their strength for the spring. It's like you're taking a small piece of that stored strength. Isn't it?"

"Huh." I leaned back on my hands, staring up at the sky. "When you put it like that, it does kind of make sense."

"The moon has always been a source of magical energy for seers," Cera explained, looking back up at the sliver of the moon. "Even weak ones, like me."

"What about him?" I asked, pointing to the hammock near the lake.

Cera shrugged. "Maybe the wind. He was telling me that he grew up on ships and boats in the seas up north. That's where he learned to control his magic."

I nodded. "Cera, can I ask you a favor?"

"Sure, Reshi."

I hesitated. "Could I sleep next to you tonight? I know it's asking a lot, but I really need to get my magic back."

Cera shook her head sadly. "I would if it could help you, but it won't. You can't siphon magic from a mage. Our bodies protect our magic until we decide to use it."

"Really?" How could there be this much that I didn't know about my own magic? "Well, I guess I'll have to visit a village or something."

"Reshi, that would be dangerous." Cera's silver eyes went wide. "What if your hunter visits the same village? What if he updated your bounty information and someone recognizes you?"

I laughed softly. "The best part about being a shapeshifter is that no one recognizes me. Don't worry, Cera. I'll be careful."

Cera bit her lip, turning to look out over the forest. "It's not just your hunter, Reshi. There are bandits in these woods. My sight keeps me safe from them, but anyone taking the roads in these woods has to bring trained guards along with them for safety."

I felt my eyebrows climb to the top of my head. "Is that so?"

It turns out that finding bandits isn't that difficult, especially using Cera's sight to cheat a little. It's just that sane people don't often go looking for bandit camps.

I never claimed to be a sane person.

Following Cera's directions, I found the bandit encampment only a few hours from her cottage. I traveled there as a human to save time, but once there I used the last vestiges of my magic to transform into my favorite all-purpose form: a rat. Not the most loveable of creatures but fitting for invading a bandit den. These bandits were fairly well set up, which meant they had robbed a lot of innocent travelers. There were three permanent buildings set up for housing and storage as well as tents or half-huts set up as shops, almost like a tiny village. I whisked around the settlement unnoticed, looking for anything worth stealing before sneaking into the main dormitory.

Even though I arrived at midday, a few of the bandits were fast asleep. Maybe these men had been guarding the camp overnight, or maybe they had been up late drinking, who could say? But it was the perfect opportunity to top off my wellspring. Hopefully, I could leave these louts too tired to attack any travelers for a day or two. I scrambled up a hanging blanket and tucked myself against the leg of a sleeping bandit, quickly drawing as much as I could. When he shifted about uncomfortably, I moved on to my next victim. As men drifted into and out of the barracks throughout the day, I continued filling my magic at a gluttonous pace. I had never drawn on so many so quickly before; the fear of discovery had made me cautious. Even if these men discovered a rat in their bedroom, I doubted they would associate their lethargy with me. It also helped that I felt a strong sense of justice, stealing from those who stole from helpless travelers.

An hour or so past midnight, my wellspring was full to bursting. Outside the barracks a few men were still awake in the camp, drinking around a blazing fire in the center of the settlement. I gave them a wide berth and snuck into the armory. The door was locked with three different-sized locks, but the gap beneath the door was just wide enough for a determined rat to squeeze through. While it was true that I felt vulnerable without my magic, I also felt naked without my daggers—like a cat without his claws. Luckily, there was no shortage of daggers here. It took me a while to find what I was looking for—a pair of heavy but thin daggers with sheaths designed to be tucked beneath a waistband. With a bit more work, I found a few leather bracers of throwing knives with flat sheaths that could be strapped to wrists or ankles. A sour taste filled my mouth as I noticed the crafting mark beneath the leather wrappings—these knives had come from a shop in my hometown.

After stockpiling the weapons, I investigated a few clothing chests that had been left inside the armory. Most held armor, either leather or studded, but one held the sleek black clothing sneak-thieves used to break into homes at night. After a bit of digging, I found a set of sneak-thief clothes in my size, much better than the ragged cast-offs I had been wearing. Even better, these clothes were designed to hide daggers. At the bottom of the chest I found a pair of boots that were a thief's dream—low ankle support for running, padded soles for sneaking and grips for climbing. They could even hide small knives or a lockpick set in hidden pockets.

So now the real question: how to get away with all this loot?

The heavy daggers would never fit under the door, and the thin knives risked reflecting fire light. The windows were boarded up tightly to prevent theft. Something about honor and thieves, I'm sure. I circled the room again, poking my nose behind chests and into corners, searching for a way out. My lucky star must have been at its zenith, for I found a floorboard that had all but rotted away unseen behind a chest of armor. With a little quick digging, I widened the gap between the floor and the back wall, creating just enough space to shove the daggers and rolled-up clothing through. Unfortunately, the hole was just a bit too small for the boots to fit. I started widening the hole with my little rat paws, peeking through occasionally to watch for the sunrise.

This is going to take forever, I realized. If only I had bigger paws, then I could . . . With an internal sigh, I shifted to my cat form, using my bigger paws to widen the hole quicker. Once deep enough, I seized one boot by the laces and dragged it outside, then returned to repeat the process for the other boot. Still in my cat form, I continued dragging the boot until I could conceal it the forest behind the shed. Piece by piece, I dragged my stolen treasure deep into the woods, not daring to shift back to my human form until I was too far from the bandit camp to smell their fire. By then the sun was fully up, and I suddenly realized how tired I was. My well was full, but my mind was fuzzy from lack of sleep and my body ached from all the digging and carrying.

A little nap, I promised myself, finding space between tree roots to hide my precious treasures. I'd get back to Cera before nightfall. With a yawn, I tucked my nose beneath a paw and fell asleep.

Hours later I awoke, more out of hunger than anything else. The nearby bandit camp was quiet, so either they had not yet discovered the robbery, or more likely, they were all still sleeping off the effects of my magical draining. As it would be impossible for me to drag all the clothing and weapons back to Cera's in an animal form, I shifted to my human self and dressed in my new favorite outfit. The sneak-thief's clothes were a near-perfect fit and had just the right drape to hide my daggers in the waistband, as well as the throwing knives on my wrists. I twirled the heavy daggers around, getting used to the feel of them. The hilts were shaped differently from my last set and they felt slightly off-balance. I would get used to them in time, but I missed my old daggers.

I began the long walk back to Cera's, wondering how long it would be before Kestral caught up to me. Did we have to wait for him to come to us? What if we left Cera's cottage and joined the next closest sibling? Kestral would eventually become outmatched and leave us alone, right?

No, more likely he would come back with an army. I sighed. I had been lucky to escape him once; the only way to be free of him would be to kill him. Even though he would have killed me without a second thought, I was having trouble wishing the same for him. But why? He had nearly killed me with a crossbow bolt; shouldn't I be angry and vengeful against him? So why didn't I feel that way?

It was a long walk back to Cera's cottage, so I took some time to consider the question. In the end, the only thought that kept popping up was that I had been expecting someone to come after me eventually, ever since the bounty had been posted. I had been able to enjoy a few quiet years so far, which was more than some of my siblings could say, so perhaps this attempt on my life was somehow justified. I couldn't really be upset with Kestral for doing his job, it just wasn't fair that I had to be his target.

With a mental shrug, I pushed back a branch and revealed Cera's cottage and the lake beyond it. Dark clouds had gathered over the lake, giving the setting a look of twilight, though it was only late afternoon. Despite the ominous look to the sky, I could see Velyn and Cera speaking near the edge of the lake. Velyn's boat rocked, pulling at its anchor. I couldn't feel a breeze but perhaps there was wind over the water. Velyn was facing away from me but Cera saw me, her silver eyes lighting up. She waved cheerfully, and I waved back with a smile. So, this was what it was like to come home to family.

Velyn moved as if to glance over his shoulder, then made a sudden, jerking movement towards Cera. Cera's smile dropped into an "oh" of surprise, her eyes widening frightfully. Her hands jumped to her chest and she stumbled backwards, Velyn following each step she took. I didn't understand what I was seeing until Cera collapsed to her knees, the front of her pale dress rapidly coloring red.

"Cera!" I broke into a sprint, mind trailing behind my feet. I shoved past Velyn, trying to catch Cera as she fell backwards, white-blonde hair swirling in the lapping waves of the lake. Her eyes were open and staring, her mouth gasping without sound. Her hands spasmed once, then fell limp. I felt her breath leave her body as I held her.

"Wh-what—?" I stammered, looking up at Velyn.

His hands were empty as he knelt opposite me, watching Cera as her chest stilled and her eyes glazed over.

"How did this . . . What—" A dim corner of my brain told me I was in shock; that I couldn't possibly process what had just happened. There was something important I needed to do immediately, but what that was simply wouldn't surface in my mind. I stared dumbly at Velyn as he placed his hand over the wound in Cera's chest.

As I watched, silvery mist drifted up from Cera's body, curling and twisting in the suddenly still air. It started as a trickle, then streamed up like a backwards waterfall. Velyn held his hand through the mist, a grim expression on his face. When the mist grew so thick that I could barely see past it, Velyn made a fist. The mist condensed, turning into an ice crystal enclosed in my brother's hand.

"What is—" my voice broke. My mind screamed at me to do something. *Do something! Do anything!*

I stayed still, holding Cera to my chest as Velyn's grim expression suddenly turned to relief.

"I was afraid it wouldn't work," he confessed, drawing the ice crystal close to his body. "It would have been a shame if it hadn't."

"What?" I couldn't raise my voice above a whisper. A corner of my mind was screaming, but I shoved it back, trying to understand.

Velyn held the ice crystal in both hands, staring intently into it. Suddenly, he crushed it between his hands, holding it close before him. He breathed in and silver light bloomed from between his fingers, seeping into his skin, flickering behind his eyes.

I had to get away.

That was the screaming thought.

I had to get away from him. I had to run away.

Now.

I lowered Cera as gently as possible. I want to say I was conflicted about leaving her, but the instinct to run had overcome all sentiment. Any care I took was to try and hide my actions from Velyn. If he was too focused to notice, maybe I could get away.

Eyes the color of lightning snapped to mine.

"Where are you going, brother?"

"How could you?" The strength in my voice surprised me. I eased back a step, getting my legs beneath me. "She was our sister. She fed us, took care of us. She loved us! How could you?"

Velyn glanced down at our sister's body, something like regret on his face. "I wanted to kill you first, you know. I thought I could do it while you were sleeping; I could sense you had no magical strength left. It would have been easy. But you ran off and the moon was dark, so it had to be her." Velyn looked back to me, stepping over Cera's body. "Do you know why they locked Mother up instead of just killing her?"

"What does that have to do with you murdering our sister?" A hysterical edge was creeping into my voice; I had to keep that under control. I eased back another step.

"Everything." Velyn's voice was low and calm. "The king couldn't have Mother killed because her bloodline would inherit all her magic, unleashing seven new powerful mages on the kingdom. But it doesn't just work that way, brother. For each of us who dies, the others gain the lost power."

"Is that—" I swallowed as bile rose in my throat. "That mist. Was that her power? You took it?"

Velyn nodded. "The powers of a far-seer are useful, but not very strong. But then again, neither are yours, are they, little brother?" His arm lashed out, a weapon glinting in his hand. I whipped out one of my new daggers, catching his weapon edge-to-edge. It was a dagger of ice. It shattered a moment after crashing against mine but reformed almost instantly, Velyn stepping in close to press the attack.

"I couldn't go after any of our older siblings," Velyn admitted, hair and clothing whipping in a sudden wind. "The eldest got the strongest magics. My power couldn't hope to beat any of theirs, so I had to go after the only two younger than me." His teeth flashed in a manic grin. "You can't believe how excited I was to hear that you were finally going to meet with Cera. Both my younger siblings together. It was like a gift."

My left boot splashed in the water as I was pressed back to the edge of the lake. I flicked a throwing knife free of my sleeve just as Velyn raised his free hand. His eyes flashed, and for a moment I thought he had blinded me before I realized that the light wasn't coming from him, but from the lightning bolt he'd called down. I leapt free of the water, simultaneously dropping my heavy dagger and whipping my knife at Velyn.

The lightning bolt found the steel of my dropped dagger before it could find me, turning the weapon into little more than a steel puddle. The throwing knife just missed burying itself in Velyn's eye, instead skipping across his cheekbone and nicking his ear. He raised a hand to his face in shock, as if surprised that I dared fight for my life. His other hand flew to the sky again, most likely to call down another bolt.

I lunged forward, catching my brother off guard. I'm the first to admit that I'm not a strong mage, nor am I a particularly skilled fighter, but when my back is against the wall, I can be as fierce as any beast. And my brother had revealed something he hadn't meant to. He was a poor fighter. His grip on the ice dagger was all wrong, he had no stance to speak of, and I would be willing to bet that the first person he had ever stabbed was our poor sister.

My second dagger appeared in my left hand as if summoned, and I spun, cutting a thin line across my brother's chest. He yanked his arm down as if to protect himself and tried to form another ice dagger, but I shattered it with my steel before it could take full shape.

"You should have killed me in my sleep," I hissed, settling into a low stance. "You should never have let me see you kill her."

"You got back sooner than I thought you would." Velyn held one arm across his chest, the other he held between us, as if to ward me off. "And I had to kill you both before the hunter got here. I can't have him chasing me. I have too much to do!" Velyn thrust both hands out at me and a strong wind shoved me backwards. The knife I had just thrown went wild, forcing me to duck out of the way of it coming back at me.

"Cera told me all about your shapeshifting," Velyn shouted over the wind. The water in the lake surged and the air filled with sand, leaves and twigs. I had to narrow my eyes to see through it. "Familiars are small, powerless creatures, useless for anything other than sneaking around. You can't fight me, so why even bother? It's either me or the hunter, Reshi!"

"I'd rather it be him," I muttered through clenched teeth. "And you don't know a stars-cursed thing about my magic!"

I shed my human form, alighting the winds as a crow. I was tossed about but I quickly learned to compensate, angling down towards my brother. The flash of his eyes was my only warning before another lightning bolt lit the sky. A rapid shift to cat helped me fall out of the bolt's path. I raced along the ground, skimming beneath the roaring wind and the objects it carried along with it. Claws and teeth bared, I launched myself at Velyn, biting and tearing at as much tender flesh as I could reach.

Another ice dagger formed in his right hand. I twisted out of its way at the last second, shifting once again, this time into the most powerful form I could take—a long, black, hooded snake. I wrapped myself around my brother, pinning one arm to his side and raising my head to look him in the eye. He cried out and struggled, revulsion clear on his face. My tongue flicked once before I hissed and struck, my fangs seeking his throat.

Velyn's body blurred, becoming mist. I fell, hissing as my heavy body struck the ground. Velyn reformed from mist only a few paces back from where he had been. He was panting, one hand pressed against his chest, blood dripping from my earlier slash. He stumbled back a step, his lips curled in disgust.

I undulated towards him, stopping short as his hand flew to the sky, preparing to call another lightning bolt. If I could get my fangs into him, it would be over. My venom was extremely deadly and it only required a scratch. But how to get close? I was quick as a snake, but not faster than lightning.

As the sky flashed, I shifted again. There was panic on Velyn's face as he searched for me. The wind picked up again, tossing forest detritus and lake water about wildly. I sprinted along the ground, my tiny form hidden by the very wind that sought to reveal me—a black rat against the tempest. A lightning bolt arced down at random, Velyn's eyes frantic as he tried to spot me. I managed to latch on to his boot before he noticed me and kicked out, sending me flying. I shifted to my cat form, twisting to land safely despite the violent launch.

If I shifted to crow, I could get above him and drop as a cobra. My thoughts halted as my vision blurred suddenly. I crouched, catching my breath, keeping a careful eye on Velyn. He staggered until he was leaning against a tree, watching me as I watched him.

We were both at our limit. He'd been using strong magic, trying to end the fight quickly. I'd been using my magic in rapid bursts, more than I ever had before in my life. I couldn't keep up like this.

I stole a furtive glance around for anything that might help me. My weapons were near the lake's edge, beyond where Velyn stood. Even if I could get to them, the throwing knives would go wide in the wind and lightning would catch anything steel. And if I shifted to human, I would be naked—not an appealing condition in a life-or-death battle.

Could I drown him in the lake? If I leapt at him as a cat, then turned human to hold him in the water—no good, he could just zap the lake and cook me. If I only had one shift left, it should be the cobra. One bite and this was all over.

"Give it up, Reshi," Velyn panted, still braced against a tree. "If it's any comfort, your magic will help me rise against our older siblings. If you—"

Velyn screamed, an arrow sprouting abruptly just beneath his collarbone. I flattened instinctively to the ground, eyes wide as a second arrow streaked towards the first. Once again Velyn turned to mist, the second arrow missing its mark and the first tumbling free of his flesh. He reappeared near the water's edge where his boat was anchored. Blood soaked the front of his shirt and ran down his left arm, but with his right he yanked the tether free and half-climbed, half-fell into the small vessel.

"Your hunter is here, brother!" Velyn shouted from the deck of his boat. One yank on a rope and his sails dropped. I felt the wind pick up as they bulged, hull scraping against sand as it struggled into deeper water. "It doesn't matter who kills you, your power will still disperse. You should have let me have it, Reshi!"

An arrow thunked into the side of Velyn's boat, humming as it vibrated against the wood. Velyn cursed and his sails billowed, the boat pulling free of the shore and heading out into open water. I raced for the water's edge, thinking vaguely that I could still catch him if I flew after him as a crow. Even as I thought it, I knew I'd never make it. I watched the boat shrink as worn leather boots stepped up beside me.

I won't look up at him, I told myself firmly. I had nothing left. He could go ahead and kill me. My tail twitched in irritation, but I held still, face turned away, waiting for the fatal blow to come.

Waiting was boring.

How long did it take to kill a cat, anyway?

I looked up. Kestral held his strung longbow in the hand closest to me, a quiver hooked through his belt. On his opposite hip, his sword was loosened, ready for a fight. He reeked of sweat, not just his own, but of horse-sweat, too. He had ridden hard to get here. I kept looking up until I met his eyes, orbs of ice glittering down at me. I held his gaze evenly, letting him know I wasn't going to run this time. Slowly his chin tipped, his eyes shifted. I followed his gaze to Cera's body, forgotten at the water's edge.

"I'm sorry."

My heart stuttered, leaping into my throat and choking me. The pain in my chest was suddenly too much to bear. My form trembled, blurred and dropped away, leaving me naked on my hands and knees, staring piteously at my poor sister's corpse.

It would have been kinder for him to kill me.

Instead, I heard a rustle of cloth before something dark dropped over my head. I reached up and found the edges of a short riding cloak. It wasn't much, but it helped me feel less exposed. I couldn't look at him again, couldn't bring myself to meet those eyes. If I did, the pain in my chest would rip free like a wounded, howling beast. I kept my eyes on Cera, biting my lip to keep the beast inside.

"Are you going to kill me?"

"Probably." His voice was the same as ever—cool, even, emotionless.

It took a moment before I was sure I could speak without my voice breaking. "Will you let me bury her first?"

Silence, followed shortly by one word, "Yes."

The boots beside me turned and he strode back into the forest. Was he leaving? Was he giving me the option to run?

No. No, I couldn't run. I would never forgive myself if I just left Cera like that. Holding the cloak closed at my throat, I stood on shaky legs and went to her side. She had already grown cold, lifeless eyes staring sightlessly, still wide with surprise. I moved her away from the water's edge, then stopped and changed back into my clothes. They were damp from the water, but I would be dead soon, so it didn't really matter.

After laying the borrowed riding cloak across the wound on Cera's chest, I lifted her. She was heavier than I expected, and I staggered under the weight before regaining my balance. When I had left the day before, I had made a circuit of the forest nearby and remembered a small clearing not too far from the cottage. I remembered it because it had been moonlit and beautiful, and made me think of Cera. After setting her down in the clearing, I picked up Kestral's cloak and turned back to the cottage. Hopefully, there was a shovel hidden away somewhere inside.

Kestral was tying his horse to a ground spike at the front of the cottage. I handed him back his cloak, trying not to make too much eye contact. Kestral jerked his chin at the door of the cottage, indicating a collection of digging tools in various states of disrepair.

"Do you want help?" he asked.

"No." I selected the sturdiest shovel from the pile, as well as a hoe. I started to walk back to the clearing, then stopped. "Did you hurt Wix?"

"No."

"Don't lie to me."

"I would have," Kestral admitted, voice soft, deadly. "But I called in the debt. She told me everything."

I nodded. I got the sense that he told the truth. The thought of Wix safe and warm back in her inn was a comforting one, and I carried it with me to Cera's final resting place.

It was full dark by the time I finished digging Cera's grave. Without a moon, the clearing seemed ghostly, sinister. At some point a small oil lantern was set nearby, though I never saw Kestral as I worked. I wondered vaguely if I shouldn't have dug two graves, but then, why make it easy for him? Kestral might not even bury me. He would need proof to collect my bounty.

After setting Cera in her grave as gently as possible, I stood back and tried to find something to say. I wasn't often lost for words, but even if I could find the right words, I couldn't speak past the knot in my throat. I brushed away hot tears, irritated that a far-speaker should meet her end in silence. An eternity passed before I knelt beside the grave and took one last look at her.

"Thank you, Cera." It was all I could manage. I looked away sharply, took a breath and began filling in the grave.

I don't know how long I sat beside the mound. I replayed every conversation I had ever had with her, both in person and in my dreams. I wished I hadn't shut her out so often. I could have known much more about her if I had cared to. It was all my fault; Cera had been the only one making an effort to bring our family together. Who was there now?

". . . shi . . ."

Was that a sound behind me? I couldn't bring myself to look. I half-hoped Kestral would sneak up and kill me, bringing a swift end to my mourning.

"Re . . . shi . . ."

It was the wind. How cruel of it to sound like Cera's voice.

"Reshi?"

Could a far-speaker be heard beyond the grave? I looked around. The clearing was awash in a soft light, not from the stars but from below, as if lanterns hid in the undergrowth.

"Reshi?"

"Cera?" Both my voice and my body trembled. Would I really be able to see her again?

Light flared from a nearby tree and a completely unexpected being leapt free of it. Long-limbed with softly glowing skin and a pair of broken wings. Wix.

"Reshi, I'm so glad I found you!" Wix stepped lightly, as if the ground had no real hold on her. She threw her arms around my neck and buried her face against my shoulder. "Do you hate me? He called in the debt. I didn't have a choice."

"No, I know. Wix." I tugged her shoulders, pushing her back. "I thought you couldn't leave the village. You said the terms of your banishment—"

"Don't apply when repaying a life debt." She unwound her unnaturally thin arms and bounced back a step. "I can't stay in your debt, Reshi. I made you something."

I shook my head, still sitting beside Cera's grave. "It won't make a difference if you repay me. Kestral is already here. I'll be dead in an hour."

Wix quirked her mouth. "If that were true, then why aren't you dead already?"

"I don't know." I glanced down at Cera's grave. "Human decency, I suppose."

"Well, then I especially have to pay you back before you die." Wix took my hands in hers. "It's terrible luck not to repay a life debt."

I sighed. "That was my strongest concern about dying: the run of luck you would have if you didn't pay me back first."

"Oh, Reshi." Wix shook her head. She held her hands out to me. One moment they were empty, the next they held a long, black cloak. "It's nothing too special, really. I've never been good with crafted items. But I think you'll really like it."

The cloak felt lighter than it looked. It was a perfect fit, though it was long enough to sweep the ground behind me. I tried to smile, but it was weak. "Thanks, Wix."

She held up a finger. "You know any gift from a fairy has magical qualities, right? Any guess what it does?"

"If it's all right with you, Wix, I'm not in the mood for guessing games."

"Hmph." Wix crossed her arms. "I guess I'll let it go this time. I made it for your transformations. As long as you're wearing the cloak, whenever you shapeshift your clothing will become part of your shadow. When you shift back, you'll still be fully clothed."

"Wow." I ran my fingers along the edges of the cloak. "That's really impressive magic. Thank you."

"The one thing it can't conceal is iron, of course. You'll lose your weapons during a shift." Wix now held a carved wooden box. "So you'll need these."

I set one hand on the box, then hesitated. I met Wix's eyes and asked: "Is this covered under the life debt?"

Wix shifted uncomfortably. "The cloak wasn't enough by itself, so I had to add something. You'll owe me a small price, but I promise you won't miss it."

I grimaced but curiosity got the better of me. The box opened to reveal the most beautiful daggers I had ever seen. Twin silver blades, delicately etched with fae runes, wickedly curved with points and curls, but small enough for easy concealment. I plucked one from the box to examine it. The hilt appeared to be made of a matte black metal and it fit my hand perfectly.

"What metal is this?" For a moment I forgot why I was in the middle of the woods at night. These blades could make murder an art. "Fairies can't work iron."

"It's black gold. That's why it's warm to the touch." Wix lifted the box, urging me to take the second dagger and the leather sheaths below them. "These are a fae treasure. I can't tell you their secrets, so you'll have to learn them as you use them. The cloak will hide them for you during transformations, though."

I had been about to slip the daggers into my waistband, then stopped. "I shouldn't take these. Once he kills me, he'll take them."

"They are only a gift to you, Reshi. When you die, they will return to me." Wix smiled; her hands were suddenly empty of the large box. "I'm not entirely sure he means to kill you anyway. Why else would you be out here all alone?"

She made a good point. I had been out here for hours. For all Kestral knew, I could have run away.

"And now." Wix stepped in close, driving me back half a step. "I need a price from you, Reshi."

"I don't—"

"Ssh, it's a small one." Wix wrapped her arms around my shoulders and tipped her face up to mine. She leaned in, rising on her toes. Or was she floating? I couldn't tell from the angle.

Was she about to kiss me? I held my hands stiffly out to my sides, unsure whether I could touch her or not. The last thing I wanted was to incur any more debt. Do fairies even kiss? I couldn't recall any lore about fairy kisses, but then, it was more than a little distracting having a half-clad female pressed against me.

Her lips brushed mine, petal soft. With great hesitance, I leaned down to meet her, then gasped as sharp, tiny fangs ripped at my lower lip. I shoved Wix away and stumbled back several steps, holding my hand to my mouth. Wix stepped back, her eyes glinting a feral red, matching the streaks of blood on her mouth. Light flickered around the clearing, seeming to emanate from her back.

"Mmm, king's blood." Wix wiped her mouth and licked her fingers. "I wish you had told me sooner, Reshi. The deals I could have made with you." She shook her head slowly, her eyes bleeding back to green.

"What did you do?" I asked, checking the bite with my tongue. She hadn't done too much damage, but it had been more than a little startling.

"I just took a taste, nothing more." Wix made a gesture with her hand, starlight tracing the motion. Supposedly that was a symbol of sincerity among fairies. "Be careful who you share your blood with, Reshi. King's blood mixed with mage blood is very valuable."

"I wouldn't have shared it with you, if you'd told me the price first!"

Wix shrugged, unapologetic. "That's why I didn't tell you. Don't worry, I can't do anything with these little droplets. But if you're ever willing to make a deal . . ."

"Right. I'll keep that in mind," I replied dryly.

Wix nodded, taking me at my word. "Good luck, Reshi. I hope not to see those daggers for a long, long while."

"We'll see." I still felt a little bitter about being bitten but I tried a wry smile for her. "I'm glad he didn't hurt you, Wix."

She smiled and nodded once before winking out of existence. The fairy lights that had lit the clearing winked out, leaving me in total darkness. I considered shifting to my cat form for the night vision, then decided against it. I didn't want Kestral to think I was trying to run. I glanced down at Cera's grave one last time, bidding her a farewell before picking up the lantern and turning towards the cottage.

Time to face the fates.

Light flickered through the windows of the cottage. Why not just run? With Wix's cloak, I could transform into a crow and fly for maybe an hour before exhausting myself. No, running wasn't my best option. Neither was walking right up to the headsman, but I really didn't have a lot of good options.

Shan snorted at me as I passed him to push open the cottage door. He pinned his ears and stamped his hooves, but he didn't lunge at me. Maybe Kestral had promised to feed me to him afterwards.

Kestral looked up from a plate of food as I entered the cottage. I felt a brief surge of annoyance that he had raided Cera's supplies, but then, it wasn't as if she could use them anymore. The blue eyes failed to pin me. I felt nothing but exhaustion as I leaned back against the cottage door.

Kestral's eyebrows knotted together, giving his eyes a shadowed look. Was that confusion on his face? Had he really expected me to run? Or did he think I'd come back to attack him? I kept my hands still and in plain sight, just in case.

"You came back," Kestral said finally, setting his plate of food aside and standing up. He loosened his sword from its sheath. My heart tried to climb up my throat to escape but I swallowed it back down.

"Wasn't that the deal?" I asked, voice soft. I felt that if I raised it, he would hear the fear in it. I spread my arms to the sides. "Go ahead and kill me."

Kestral hesitated, hand on his hilt. He drew, showing several inches of steel, then slammed the sword back into its sheath. Instead, he folded his arms across his chest and leaned back against the wall opposite me. "I want to ask you about some things."

I tried a casual shrug but I'm sure it looked jerky. "If it's about my other siblings, I don't really know anything."

"No." His voice was like leather-wrapped steel. "You were the cat."

I nodded.

"Why did you sneak into my room at the inn?"

I bit my lip, wincing as I tasted blood. "I need to draw life force to replenish my magic. It only works on sleeping people."

"Why me?"

I shrugged. "I worked it out with Wix. I only drew from travelers, no one living in the village. It doesn't hurt or cause any permanent damage or anything, but I was afraid someone would make the connection to me and . . ."

"Your bounty."

I nodded.

"Have you ever hurt anyone with your magic?"

I considered not answering the question. I mean, the worst he could do was kill me, right? "Not unless they were trying to hurt me first."

Kestral stared at me for a long time. It felt like hours, though it couldn't have been more than a minute or two. I locked my knees to keep them from trembling, but they were bound to give way any minute. Despite that, I kept my eyes on his. I didn't have the strength to run, nor did I have anywhere to go. A quick death now saved me from the borrowed time of a cat-and-mouse hunt.

"What are you going to do now?" Kestral asked.

A nervous laugh bubbled up from my chest. "I don't think that's up to me."

Kestral looked away, his eyes chasing thoughts I couldn't read. "If it were up to you, what would you do now?"

A dozen witty answers came to mind first, followed strongly by the urge to beg for my life. But before I could speak, I felt an icy hand grip my heart. There was really only one thing I wanted. If I could have that, I could die satisfied.

"Revenge." The ugly word fell from my lips like a drop of blood. "I want him to pay for killing Cera."

Another long stare, then, slowly, Kestral nodded. "I can help you with that."

"You would help me kill my brother?" My eyes narrowed. "For his bounty?"

Kestral nodded.

"Then what? Would you kill me for mine?"

Kestral shrugged. "I'd give you a head start."

Another nervous chuckle worked its way up my throat. "Why should I trust you? You've already tried to kill me once."

His face became shadowed, but only for an instant. What was that? Anger? Regret? Fear? "I saw your fight. You can't beat him on your own. Having you will give me an advantage, so there's no reason for me to harm you before. After . . ." He shrugged again. "If you run, I will kill you."

A shiver raced along my spine, making my knees quiver before I could lock them again. "So then, what are we? Allies? Am I your pet mage now?"

Kestral grunted. "You need someone to draw upon, don't you? I'll let you draw from me. Get too greedy and I will turn you into a cat-skinned belt pouch." He kicked off from the wall and jerked his chin at the plate of food. "Eat if you're hungry. We'll travel early tomorrow morning."

As he walked into the kitchen, my knees gave out. I slid down the door, sinking bonelessly to the floor. It was all I could do to simply breathe. I had seen death in his eyes as sure as anything, yet somehow my heart was still pounding. My insides were in knots, fear and grief keeping them tangled and unsettled. I knew sleep would help, but I wasn't sure I could, not after all of this.

Kestral stepped back into the room carrying two mugs, faintly steaming. He said nothing but held a mug down to me. Warm milk. He crossed back to the far wall and tipped his own mug back. I clutched mine to my chest; the warmth felt good.

"It will help," Kestral said, lifting his mug. "With sleep and with grief."

Maybe he poisoned it, I thought idly, taking a sip. No, I was sure if he were going to kill me, he would be upfront about it. He seemed like that kind of guy.

The warmth from the milk did help settle my stomach. I hadn't realized how exhausted I was from the battle with Velyn to digging Cera's grave, from grief to facing my own mortality. I was only halfway through the mug before my head drooped, mug slipping from my fingers.

Kestral was there to catch it. I blinked up at him, searching for the fear but mostly only feeling numb.

"Shift," he said, prodding me gently with a booted foot.

"Hm?"

"Change into a cat."

"Why?"

"So you can replenish your magic." He tilted his head towards my pallet, then went to the kitchen to clean our mugs.

Did he know I didn't have to be a cat to draw from him? I could do it just as easily as a human. Arguing the point would have taken more energy than simply shifting, and besides that, it was a fairly small pallet. By the time Kestral returned to the room, I was curled up on it with one paw over my face. I thought I felt a hand scratch my ears before I dropped into a deep, dreamless sleep.

3

I woke up in an empty pallet, dim morning light glowing through the cottage windows. I was allowed one delicious stretch before all of yesterday's traumatic events came flooding back to me: Velyn's betrayal, Cera's death, Kestral's . . . companionship? Alliance? What was this exactly? I had a vague memory of waking up enough to draw some energy from him, but after that I had slept like the dead.

My nose lifted to the air of its own accord. The scent of cooked eggs and freshly toasted bread danced in the morning light like dust motes. Had I really managed to sleep through Kestral cooking breakfast? My body shifted without me telling it to as I staggered into the kitchen, finding warm food on the stove. Cera's icebox still had half a bottle of cool milk in it, so I helped myself to that as well. Standing in her kitchen and eating her food gave me a pang in my chest, but beneath my grief was my sense of self-preservation that told me food should never be wasted.

After breakfast, I ducked out the back door and circled the cottage. I wasn't trying to sneak up on Kestral, I just wanted to see him before he saw me. It was still a lot to accept. Less than a week ago, he had nearly killed me. Now he was offering to help me avenge my sister. It made me feel just a bit skittish.

Kestral sat just outside the cottage, tying bags closed in preparation for the road. He wasn't wearing his travel leathers yet, only a long pair of pants and a barely laced shirt. His skin held a faint flush, as if he had just finished exercising. While Kestral prepared for the ride, Shan had been turned loose from his ground tie and grazed at the forest's edge.

I sidled around the side of the cottage, shuffling my boots in the dirt to draw attention to myself. The last thing I wanted to do was accidentally sneak up on him and earn a crossbow bolt for my efforts. Kestral glanced up, noted me, then went back to adjusting the ties on his satchel.

"Thanks for breakfast," I said, leaning back against the outer wall of the cottage. "And for letting me draw from you, I guess."

Kestral nodded.

"Oh, and uh, I think it slipped my mind yesterday, but thanks for saving me from my brother." I ran a hand through my hair, tugging my tie out to fix it. "And, you know, especially for . . . not killing me."

Kestral nodded again, still not speaking.

"So, was there not any wake-tea or are you just not a morning person?"

Kestral shot me a quick glare. "We don't know where our enemy is. Talking gives away our position."

"Enemy? Velyn?" My eyes were drawn eastward, roughly the direction Velyn had sailed yesterday. "He's not close. He still needs to recover from yesterday's fight."

Kestral stilled. "How do you know that?"

I blinked. "I don't. Not really, anyway. But I'm sure he's not close by."

Kestral narrowed his eyes at me skeptically. I shrugged and finished pulling my hair back into a tail.

"I don't have enough supplies for both of us, so we'll have to stop at the nearest village." Kestral stood, checking the weapons on his belt out of reflex. "Until we know if Velyn has updated your bounty information, you'll have to stay in an animal form. Preferably something small."

"Ugh, that's so boring." I thunked my head back against the cottage's side. "No one knows me out here, and even if he did update it, it'll take months for the new information to show up in all these little backwater villages."

"Regardless, you'll have to travel in animal form. Shan is not carrying both of us and I'm not walking." Kestral glared at me. "I recall seeing a bird form."

"Fine." I rolled my eyes. "But when we get to the village, I'll have to be human."

"Why." It wasn't a question.

"Because . . ." Because it was boring when I couldn't speak to other humans. Because it would already be a boring day, sticking to crow form while traveling. "Because I have to eat enough for my human shape and none of my animal forms can eat that much."

"I'll get a room at an inn and bring food up," Kestral replied. He put his fingers to his lips and gave a low whistle. Shan lifted his head from grazing, ears perked forward, then trotted towards us. "I saw your fight with Velyn yesterday. What was the small form you took? A frog?"

"Frog?" My feline sensitivities took offense at his guess. Had I a tail, it would be lashing in outrage. "Why would you say frog?"

Kestral shrugged before tossing the saddle over Shan's back. "It was small and fast. Most shape-shifters have limited forms, usually tied to one animal family. I guessed that yours all have to do with the animals mages use for their magic."

He really knew his stuff to have guessed all of that. "Well, mages don't use frogs. At least, not as familiars. Maybe as ingredients. Or to turn vexing humans into."

Kestral met my gaze evenly. A challenge.

I huffed and looked away.

"Then what was it?" Kestral persisted.

"A rat." I dug the toe of my boot into the dirt. I hated giving up any secrets of my magic, especially to someone who had tried to kill me.

"A rat," Kestral repeated, cinching the girth on his horse. "A cat, a crow and a snake. Any others?"

"Just one."

"Which is?"

"I'll show you." I kicked away from the cottage wall. It wasn't so much that I wanted to show Kestral my final form, as it was that I wanted to test out Wix's cloak. It had worked this morning, but I hadn't been awake enough to appreciate it. In fact, I was pretty sure my throwing knives were still inside where the cloak had dropped them the night before.

I had to close my eyes to begin the shift. I rarely ever took this form as it wasn't particularly useful, but it's always good to have a form no one knows about. After a breath, I was in my tiniest form—a large, black, hairy spider. When I opened my eyes to see Kestral's reaction, a large boot came down on me. In a panic, I coiled my legs beneath me and leapt, using some quickly spun silk to catch the wind and drift to Kestral's chest. He shuddered and a hand snapped up, shoving me away roughly. I managed to shift back to human, earning bruises as I hit the ground instead of broken limbs.

"What the dust, Kestral?" I shouted, wincing at the pain in my elbows and back. "You knew it was me!"

Kestral had backed up a pace, his eyes wide, his breath shallow. He held a hand up towards me as if warding me back.

"Never—" He stopped as a violent shudder wracked his body. "Never take that form again."

"You have got to be dusting kidding me." I stood up, brushing dirt from my clothes. At least I still wore clothes to dust off, which meant the cloak worked. "Sir I-killed-twenty-pigoblins-and-a-slag-with-my-bare-hands is afraid of a little spider? I'm not even a venomous spider! I mean, the hairs kinda sting, but I'm not actually dangerous—"

"Stop." Kestral held up a hand. "Stop talking." He unclipped a waterskin from his belt and drank deeply. Afterwards, he drew a deep breath, eyes closed.

"All this over a little—"

"Say it and I'll shoot you." He had his hand on his crossbow in the blink of an eye. It wasn't loaded, but the threat was real. I considered saying it anyway; his reaction was the funniest thing I had seen in days. Instead, I tucked my hands behind my head and waited for Kestral to recover from his vicious spider attack.

After another draught of water, Kestral straightened and turned back to preparing Shan for a long ride. "If you need to bring anything, go get it. It's a few hours to the closest village."

I pushed back the urge to continue teasing him and ducked inside the cottage. I gave in to a small laugh. I had never met anyone with a true phobia for one of my forms before. It was like having a minor weapon against the otherwise implacable mage hunter.

I gathered up my throwing knives from where they had fallen the night before. I checked the kitchen, but Kestral had already taken any food good for traveling. Nothing in the little house belonged to me, so I didn't feel right taking anything, but it was sad to think of all Cera's stuff being left as junk once more. I found myself pawing through a drawer of wooden carvings, trying to understand why she had felt the need to keep them. I stopped when a tiny, intricately carved lyre fell into my palm.

Hadn't Cera been trying to fix a full-size lyre? I looked around until I saw it, heaped in a corner along with other broken objects. I found myself wondering if she knew how to play or if she had been hoping to learn. I turned the carved lyre over in my hand, then tucked it in a pocket. At least I could keep one thing from being left by the wayside.

Kestral shot me a sharp look as I stepped back outside, as if checking that I wasn't a spider again. I hid my grin under a cough as I held out my bundle of knives to him.

"Can you carry my knives?" I asked. "I can't shift with them."

Kestral took the bundle and tucked it away in a satchel without breaking eye contact. His hand shot out suddenly, gripping the edge of my cloak and drawing me a step closer. I jerked backwards, preparing a spider-shift in my mind. Kestral ran his fingers over the cloak, staring at it intently.

"Fae made," he said finally, letting it go. "New?"

I took a few steps back and straightened the cloak. "Yeah. Wix stopped by last night. She needed to repay a debt."

Kestral nodded slowly. He had seen me shift before the cloak, so he probably already understood its function. He didn't say anything else but pulled himself up into the saddle. "We'll get to Bonham Village just after noon. I suggest you fly."

The hairs on the back of my neck stood on end and I felt like spitting. I hated being given orders. I could use my magic again now; maybe I could make my escape and go after Velyn on my own.

Just picturing those intense eyes as he promised to kill me if I ran brought that thought to a halt. Besides, Velyn had proven too much for me once already. I decided to have a strong talk with Kestral about ordering me around once we had a room at the village. Yes, that was sure to work.

I shifted to my crow form and took wing, getting just ahead of Kestral and Shan along the game trail that led from Cera's cottage. Shan moved slowly compared to me; it didn't take long for me to get bored of flying ahead and waiting for the pair of them to catch up. Kestral kept his eyes on me as I flitted back and forth overhead.

The thing about wearing an animal's shape was that it gave me that animal's instincts. I could ignore those instincts when I felt like it, but the road was long, and the horse was slow, making me give in to the crow's desire to collect shinies. Something glittered inside one of Kestral's overstuffed satchels and I wanted it. As the horse plodded past my perch, I dove for the satchel's buckle, thinking I might be able to unlatch it and free the shiny inside. Shan whipped his head around and nearly had me by the wing before I wheeled away with a warning caw. Kestral pulled his mount's head back around and shooed me away.

"Is there something that would keep you from being a pest?" Kestral called out to me.

I landed on a branch and ruffled up my feathers, conveying my irritation at the question. I waited until Shan got a bit ahead of me, then flew over to land on Kestral's shoulder. He shot me a sidelong glance but didn't say anything. Shan rolled one large eye back at me, daring me to come close enough to bite. I flicked my wingtips at him then settled in.

The trail eventually met a packed road and Shan picked up his pace. It was still slower than I could fly, however, so I stayed on Kestral's shoulder. He wore his riding cloak, so my nails didn't scratch him as I adjusted for the bumps in the road. Hours passed in slow silence. I think I napped. Once I tried preening Kestral's messy hair, but he waved me off. A little before noon, Kestral opened a bag on his belt and pulled out several strips of dried meat. He snapped one into small pieces and held each piece up to me to eat. I struggled internally as I ate; I wasn't fond of being fed like a pet, but I was hungry.

I was dozing off when Kestral suddenly shrugged. I tried to catch my grip, but a hand pushed me free. My wings caught me quick as thought, carrying me aloft as I got my bearings. The trees had dropped away suddenly, revealing a small village that looked almost like the one I had left behind. Kestral must have decided it would be strange to be seen riding with a crow on his shoulder, which was why he'd shrugged me off.

He could have just said something, I thought, flying above the village.

And risk being seen talking to a bird?

Well, that's a fair point. Wait, where did that thought come from? That didn't sound like me. I perched on a nearby rooftop and cocked my head, looking down at Kestral. He had dismounted and was leading Shan to an inn. He glanced up at me once before tying Shan to a post and disappearing inside the inn.

He's probably looking for a cheap room again, I realized, taking wing. It couldn't hurt to get a quick bird's eye view of the village. There were a few inns, several shops, a blacksmith yard and two tanners on separate ends of the street. Set back from the road were the villagers' homes with a few small gardens. The large building at the far end of town was the military outpost, where the local law enforcement was stationed along with mail-carrier services. It had a stable around back, but I noticed a pair of travel-worn horses hitched out front. I spiraled down, perching on a hitching post to get a look at them.

Just as I suspected, these horses looked similar to Shan—no distinct breed, sturdy and built for long journeys. One snorted at me, the other pinned its ears. Honestly, I was a friendly guy; horses and I usually got along great. I cocked my head, trying to get a better look at the saddlebags. No military insignia, but they were rolled and stowed with the same precision as Kestral's packs. Were these army outriders? I had to let Kestral—

Large teeth snapped in front of my beak. I leapt into the air, cawing loudly. Shan eyed me with pinned ears. When had the blood-thirsty animal gotten so close? Kestral tied the lead rope to the post I had been sitting on. He didn't look up at me but made a show of rooting through one of his saddlebags. I shot a dubious look at Shan's hooves before landing on the ground far behind Kestral, then pecked and scratched at the dirt.

Kestral turned slightly, talking softly over his shoulder. "I'm going to check for any updates on your bounty. I'm also going to update Velyn's information and report Cera's death. I'm not going to say anything about you, all right?"

I bird-shrugged. It was nice of him to check with me, but I couldn't exactly argue in this form. I cocked my head, fixing him with a beady-eyed stare. Did he intend to collect Cera's bounty? He hadn't killed her, but it wasn't as if Velyn could claim it.

"They won't pay on Cera's death without proof, if that's what you're wondering," Kestral said. "Keep out of sight. There are other mage hunters here."

I flapped my wings, sending road dust up at him as I took off, landing on the roof of the military building. Kestral swiped a hand over his leathers and kicked the dust from his boots before stepping inside. I gave it a ten-count before I swooped down into the shadow of the building and shifted. As a cat, I leapt through a ground-floor window and slunk inside.

The front room was mostly a receiving area with a long counter for the government officials to stand behind. Benches were set against the right wall; a small jail cell stood off to the left. Kestral was standing at the wall of posted bounties, luckily with his back to me. I crouched in the shadows beneath the counter and hoped he wouldn't notice me.

Raucous laughter bounced off the walls as a door behind the counter opened. Heavy boots strode across the floor and several voices spoke all at once.

"—won't be a problem for long. After that pigoblin raid in Hollager Village—"

"I still can't believe they reported that as a raid. Sure there were a lot of them, but all that means is that the village is eating good for—"

"Is that Kestral?" The boots stomped closer and a waist-high door in the counter swung open. Kestral turned, looking over the counter, one hand hooked casually over the hilt of his sword. "Captain Kestral of Duke Allaran's army? What are you doing way the dust out here?"

Two men dressed in army leathers held their hands out to Kestral. He shook each of their hands, grasping the inside of the wrist and pumping once: a formal military greeting. The taller one was blond with an easy smile and a nose that had been broken more than once. The shorter one was dark haired with a short, coarse beard. The newcomers smiled but Kestral's face remained stoic. Either he didn't recognize them or didn't like them.

"Didn't think I'd see you again without a mage-born's head on your spear," the tall one laughed. "To be honest, I'm still hoping to beat you for the first kill, though."

Kestral jerked a nod.

"Wow, as tight-lipped as ever, eh, Captain?" The other man threw a few soft punches at Kestral's arm. Kestral flexed and glared. The man backed away, holding his hands up in placating gesture.

"Aw, he opens up after a drink." The first man elbowed Kestral in the ribs. "Did you just get into town? Have a drink with us at The Coop tonight."

"Maybe." Kestral pushed past them, making his way to the counter. He stopped suddenly, eyes lighting on me. I had crept too far forward, interested by the men who had known Kestral before he became a mage hunter. He couldn't say anything to me, but there was cold fury in his eyes.

"Make sure you do, Captain." The blond smirked. "Unless The Coop isn't to your liking."

Kestral turned, his eyes flashing a warning as his hand tightened on his hilt. The second man drew back, surprise clear on his face, but the first just laughed.

"Kidding, Captain! We all know those charges were dust-ridden. But it'd help if you would tell your side of the story." He waved. "See you tonight, right?"

The ex-soldiers exited but Kestral stared after them, tension in every line of his body. My fur itched; I was torn between staying with Kestral or following the other men. Maybe I could get them to tell me why Kestral left the army.

"What can I do for you, sir?" A young male voice asked from beyond the counter.

I had forgotten that there must have been a clerk waiting to be of assistance.

"I'm looking for any updates on Laurana's children," Kestral replied, turning back to the counter. He glanced down at me briefly. "I may have updates as well."

I heard something heavy being set on the counter and pages being turned. After a moment, the youth said, "Nothing new has come in yet. The last information we have is almost a year old, about the daughter called Kila."

Kestral nodded. "Send out word that the siblings are fighting amongst each other. I witnessed Navelynstra kill Hacerathan."

There was silence, then a small squeak. "What?"

"The youngest daughter, Hacerathan, is dead," Kestral repeated slowly. "She lived not far from here, on the edge of the lake. She might even have come through here on occasion. Long, pale hair. Tall for a woman."

"Eyes like the moon?" the clerk gasped. Kestral shot a look at me. I bobbed my head in a nod. I doubted Kestral had gotten close enough to see her eyes. "She read fortunes. Everyone knew her. She was one of the mistress's seven?" The clerk's voice rose several octaves. "She's dead?"

A door was thrown open and heavy steps crossed the floor. "What's all this noise about?" a voice boomed. I was getting tired of not being able to see. I slunk along the shadow of the counter then darted between the bars of the jail cell. In the dark corner beneath the cell's bench, I was able to see the newcomer to the conversation—a military man, wearing a brown uniform with dark yellow trim. He would be the commander of this outpost. "Something about the mistress's seven?"

"Sir, this soldier—"

"Mage hunter," Kestral corrected.

"Mage hunter," the clerk amended, "says that the girl who used to pass through town telling fortunes was one of the mistress mage's daughters! But one of her brothers killed her."

"Is this all true?" the military man asked, sounding just as incredulous. "Do you have any proof of this?"

"I can tell you the location of her house," Kestral replied. "She's buried there, if you need such proof."

The uniformed man gave a low whistle. "I'll send some men to check it out. Which brother killed her? Did you get him?"

"Navelynstra. Calls himself Velyn. He got away." Kestral glanced down at where I had been hiding a moment ago. I noted a tiny flash of alarm cross his face when he didn't see me, but he played it off quickly. "I'd like to give an accounting of his powers. He is far stronger than previously believed."

"Come on back to my office, son. We should talk." The older man pushed the door in the counter open and Kestral walked through, but not before glancing around the room once more. He found me under the cell's bench, a look like relief passing over his face. I tried following him to the commander's room, but the door slammed shut before I could slip inside. I could hear their voices, so I sat down outside the door, trying to hear what they said.

"Oh, hi there."

I startled.

The clerk was talking to me. "I haven't seen you around before. Are you friendly?" He held his hand down to me.

I eyed it warily.

"Oh, wait right there!" The clerk—he couldn't be older than sixteen—ran into a back room and came back with tiny cubes of cheese.

I could be friendly for cheese. I approached cautiously, ducking my head the first time he tried to pet me. He held the cheese out on his hand. I reached out with a paw to knock the cheese to the floor before eating it. No way was I eating food from someone's hand twice in one day. After I finished the cheese, I leapt up onto the counter, parading back and forth as the clerk petted and praised me. It's always nice to find someone who really appreciated me for me. At the same time, I was able to catch glimpses of the book he had checked for Kestral earlier. The latest updates were mostly about Kila and the mage hunters she had slain. There were two entries regarding Eagan, detailing some fierce-sounding fire magic. I flopped over and rolled on the book, hooking my claws into the pages and pulling them over myself. The clerk laughed in delight. I slipped out from beneath the pages, sat on the book and washed my face. Cats weren't always the most dignified of creatures, but I made it work for me.

The page I'd revealed had several sketches of my brothers and sisters. Reina, the eldest, Cera and myself were absent from the page. I didn't recognize anyone but Velyn, with his cumulous-like hair style. I fought the urge to tear his face out of the book; just looking at it filled me with rage.

The door to the commander's office opened and both I and the clerk froze as if we'd been caught doing something wrong. My ears flattened under Kestral's glare, my body lowering itself to the counter.

The commander sighed. "What have I told you about pets in the office, son?"

"I didn't bring it in," the kid said quickly. "It came in by itself."

My tail twitched in annoyance. I was not an "it."

The commander rolled his eyes and turned back to Kestral. "I'll send runners to share your information with the other mage hunters in town, as well as messengers to the capital. Thank you for bringing this information to light as quickly as you did."

"That's my job." Kestral's arm twitched, as if about to give a military salute.

The commander nodded formally and turned back to his office. Kestral let the counter door swing shut behind himself with a bang.

I used the noise as an excuse to startle, run to the edge of the counter, and leap through the window I had entered through. I slunk around the side of the building until I saw Kestral untying Shan from his post.

The other two horses were gone already.

Kestral's eyes narrowed as he saw me trotting over to him.

"What part of 'stay out of sight' was confusing to you?" he growled, voice low. "I have a room at the Sleep and Stew, top floor. Go wait for me."

I flicked an ear at him. Like dust I would.

Kestral narrowed his eyes dangerously.

I flicked the other ear.

"At least turn in to something else," Kestral growled. "I don't want anyone seeing me talking to a cat."

Which was why I should have just stayed human, I thought, glancing around quickly before shifting. Kestral jumped as I scaled his pant leg as a rat, then tucked myself into a belt purse. The neck of the bag was open enough for air, but I couldn't see much besides Kestral's arm. I heard a sigh, then bounced around a bit as he walked to the inn. I hooked my claws through the cloth and held on. It was a short walk to the inn, followed by a stop at the stable. Kestral tossed some hay at his carnivorous horse before returning to the inn. He walked up three flights of stairs to the top of the inn, bouncing me in the belt purse with each step. The door clicked shut before the belt purse was unclipped and gently set on the room's writing desk.

"You really paid money for this room?" I asked, disappointed that my sudden shift didn't startle Kestral at all. "This is an attic."

"It's cheap," Kestral replied. "Unless you happen to be hiding a stash of gold coins somewhere, it's the best you're going to see."

"Ugh." Wix didn't even rent out her attic rooms; they were miserable. Low slanted ceilings, hot in the summer, cold in the winter, all the noise from the lower floors coming up through the floor. I dragged my finger through a layer of dust on the desk. "So . . . you know those other mage hunters?"

Kestral nodded, looking away. "We served in the army together."

"They called you 'captain,'" I recalled, taking a seat on the bed. I sneezed. Even the bedclothes were dusty.

Kestral nodded.

"So, you can either answer my questions with satisfactory answers, or I can go see if your old army buddies are more willing to talk." I leaned forward, setting my chin in my hand. "Your toss."

"They would mark you as mage-born by your eyes. I doubt the conversation would end well for you."

I shrugged. "You marked me, but I was able to charm you until those pigoblins attacked. Unless I'm mistaken, your friends are looking for a diversion at The Coop and I can be . . . diverting." I flashed him a wicked grin. Kestral glared back darkly.

"If I answer your questions, will you stay in the room all night?" Kestral glanced out the window, marking the hour. "Morro and Wen will want to talk to me after the runner finds them."

"Sure thing." Dust, no. Wherever Kestral went, I'd be there.

Kestral jumped, his arm jerking as if it had been burned. He glanced down at his left wrist then looked at me. "That's the first time you've actually lied to me."

"What?" Surprised, I looked at his wrist, too. A mark I had never noticed before glowed hot and red. "Cheater! A liar's brand? Really?"

Kestral rubbed the mark, glaring at me. "What will it take to keep you from following me?"

"Doesn't it take a mage to etch a liar's brand?" I asked, tucking my legs beneath me and folding my arms. "Did you kill him after he etched you?"

"The army had it done. You're going to follow me no matter what, aren't you?"

I refused to answer, laying back to stare up at the ceiling instead. Really, a liar's brand? It was pure luck I had gotten along this far without being caught in a lie. Wix's fairy-speak must have rubbed off on me. At least I knew about the mark now, so I could keep my answers vague going forward.

Boots crossed the floor and I felt a slight pressure on the bed. Kestral leaned over me, one hand supporting his weight on the bed.

"Reshi."

A shiver ran through me; it was the first time he had called me by my name. Why was that such a thrill?

"I know these men," he continued, his voice soft, deadly. "If they figure out who you are, they will kill you without a second thought."

"Like you tried to do?" I challenged, looking up at him. "I don't recall a whole lot of second thoughts happening when that crossbow bolt was flying at my face."

Kestral stood then turned to sit on the edge of the bed. He rested his elbows on his knees, staring at the floor as if trying to work something out. I rolled over, propping myself up on an elbow to watch him.

"You already know I was in the army in Beramin, under Duke Allaran?" Kestral began.

"Yeah, I remember."

"I was discharged under . . . dishonorable circumstances."

"Did they catch you in bed with the duke's daughter?" I laughed; I couldn't picture anything more absurd.

Kestral glanced back over his shoulder, eyes dark.

"No!" I gasped.

"Close enough, anyway." Kestral dropped his eyes again. "I turned to mage hunting after. Some of the men who served with me did the same. It's a blemish on my service and I'd rather you not hear about it from someone else."

I didn't know what to say to that. There were dark parts of my past I wasn't ready to share either, so I couldn't hold it against him. At the same time, waiting around in an empty room would be boring.

Kestral turned, placing a hand on the bed to do so. "You asked what I was doing, passing through your village. The truth is, I was looking for you. After four years of hunters failing against the mistress's mage-born, I decided to search for the youngest child, the one with the least amount of known information."

That new fact sent a completely different thrill through me, but at least I recognized this one—fear.

"I'm not the only hunter trying to find the younger children," Kestral continued. "Morro and Wen, those other hunters, they're here because they were closing in on Cera. Once they know she's dead, they're likely to start looking for you. I'm trying to keep you safe."

"Why?" The question was out before I realized I'd asked. There was no good reason for Kestral to protect me. If the story of his dishonorable discharge was true, it would only dishonor him further to be caught harboring me. By the way he kept staying in cheap inns and walking in worn boots, he could use the money my bounty would bring him. Truly, what advantage was there in letting me live?

Kestral met my eyes then looked away. "I promised I'd help you get your vengeance. After that, I don't know, Reshi. Maybe I'll kill you."

He stood, checked his belt pouches and sword, then walked to the door. "There's food in the travel bags. Stay put if you value your life."

I was torn. Truly. He had seemed vulnerable for the first time as he talked about his past, which made the request for me to stay put sound sincere. As if he were actually worried about me, not just about my bounty. On the other hand, I could learn a lot more about him and his past if I followed him out to The Coop. And that would be a lot less boring. I fell back on the bed with a sigh.

That liar's brand dusted me off, but it wasn't as big a game changer as I had made it out to be. I had spent enough time with Wix to learn all sorts of ways to tell half-truths or distract from the question. The struggle now was to keep answering vaguely without Kestral catching on. I could still follow him tonight and probably tell enough of the truth to hide it, but if he found out after the fact . . .

He'll never trust you again, a tiny corner of my mind whispered.

I sighed and kicked myself up into a sitting position. I guess I'd just be bored, then. I should have at least asked him to send a washbasin up.

Preening and cat baths only got a body so clean. It would have been nice to take an actual bath. The room did have a full hand basin as well as some soap, though, so I decided to make do. I stripped to the waist, making sure my belt was tight enough to keep my pants from slipping, then used a cloth to lather up, taking the extra time to clean under my nails where I found flecks of either dirt or blood. The soap was a little harsh on my face, but it felt better for the scrubbing. Finally, I untied my hair and dunked it in the water, finger-combing soap through it. I had to wash it twice as a surprising amount of sweat and dirt came out on the first wash.

I was patting my hair dry when the lock on the door clicked open. I froze, considering a split-second shift, despite the fact that I wasn't wearing my cloak. Kestral couldn't be back this soon, could he? Was someone coming to clean the room? Did I have enough time to shift?

Kestral looked just as surprised to see me as I was to see him. He was carrying a covered bowl in one hand, the room key in the other.

"I thought you would be waiting at The Coop already," Kestral said, locking the door behind him.

"I was just on my way there now." I smirked as Kestral's arm burned at the lie. He glared at me, but it only made me laugh. "Why are you back so soon?"

"I don't want to see them." Kestral turned his face away as he spoke. "I can wait outside if you need to finish washing."

"Nah, I'm done." I sniffed; something smelled delicious. I stepped closer to him, eyeing the covered bowl. "What is that?"

Kestral thrust the bowl into my hands. "Dinner. I got it in case you hadn't snuck out."

I snorted. "Like a reward for staying put? You can't just keep me like a pet, Kestral."

"Sorry." Kestral looked down at the floor. "Can you move? Or put your clothes on?"

"Hm?" Was that a faint blush on Kestral's cheeks? "Why do you need me to put clothes on?" I sidled a step closer, trying to see his down-turned face better.

Kestral backed up—he actually backed away from me! Like I was the scary one! But then his shoulders tensed, and his hand came to rest on the hilt of his sword. His eyes snapped up to mine, driving me back half a pace. No blush colored his cheeks now. He shoved past me, heading for a chair across the room. He pulled a hand cloth from his pocket, unsheathed his sword and sat down. He began cleaning his blade as I peeked inside the covered bowl.

Large chunks of chicken and diced vegetables dotted a mound of rice covered in a broth. I pulled up the writing desk's chair and dug in. It was only after several mouthfuls that I remembered Kestral hadn't bought a single meal at Wix's inn. Why the sudden splurge? I glanced back at him only to find him staring at me. We looked away at the same time.

An awkward silence suddenly cloaked the room. It should feel awkward all the time, really, but mostly it was . . . well, it was hard to define what it was. We weren't friends; maybe we could have been, under different circumstances. But I wasn't exactly his prisoner either. I had plenty of opportunities to leave if I wanted to. Allies? Was that the right word? We were allied against Velyn. Maybe that's what this slightly-awkward-but-mostly-okay feeling was.

"Did you want a—"

"Thanks for the—"

We started talking at the same time then cut ourselves off. For a long moment, no one spoke. I broke the new silence first. "Sorry. I was just thanking you for dinner."

Kestral nodded, eyes down on his blade. "I can have a full washbasin brought up, if you want."

I shrugged. "I'm fine. It felt good to wash some of the road off me."

Kestral's eyes flicked up to mine then away again. "I don't mean to keep you as a pet. I'm trying to keep you from being discovered. Some hunters have more powerful talismans than a liar's brand."

"I get that, but you can't just order me—" A sudden pounding at our door made us both jump.

Kestral was on his feet in an instant, naked sword in hand.

"Captain! Come on out of there!" The pounding continued, along with loud, drunken laughter. "Come on and have a drink!"

"Yeah, come play in the hen house with us," a second voice chimed in. "We'll buy the first—Whoa!" The cheap wood along the doorframe splintered and cracked, the door falling in under the drunken pounding it had received. I jumped to my feet, trying to put some distance between me and the fallen door.

"Oh, wow, we're sorry about that, Captain, we'll pay . . . Hey, hey, who's this?" The taller man grinned at me, his eyes roaming over my half-naked body. "You really do like the pretty boys, don't you, Captain?"

I set my hand on my hip and smiled suggestively. The hunter leered, and I winked, letting one hip drop lazily.

Kestral stormed towards the door, sword glinting. "Get out." The snarl drove the two men back on their heels.

"Sorry for interrupting. We didn't know you already had—"

"We didn't mean for the door to break, honest—"

"Go." He didn't raise his voice, but it lost all its humanity, as if he wouldn't lose any sleep over running both former comrades through with his sword. "Tell the innkeeper about the door on your way out. Don't come back."

They scrambled away. I didn't blame either hunter for being scared. When Kestral spun and pinned me with his ice blue stare, I felt absolutely petrified.

"What was that?" he asked in that deadly soft voice.

"What was what?"

I suppressed a shudder and tried to hold my ground as he took a step towards me. "They thought I was a cockerel, so I played along. A whore is better than a mage, right?"

Kestrel stopped advancing but his eyes were still dark with anger. A muscle ticked in his jaw and I got the impression he wanted an excuse to attack something. I stayed perfectly still, doing my best not to provoke him. It was difficult, because all I really wanted to do was ask what they had meant about Kestral liking pretty boys.

Footsteps pounded on the stairs outside the room and Kestral sheathed his sword. "Either hide or shift or do both." He turned towards the door.

I swept my cloak up around my shoulders and shifted to my cat form, slinking easily under the bed. Even I understood that now wasn't the time to stand up to him about being ordered around.

Kestral railed against the innkeeper about using cheap wood for doorjambs while the innkeeper apologized obsequiously. Money eventually exchanged hands, Kestral pocketing some of his own coin back. He agreed to jam the door shut with a chair in exchange for the innkeeper keeping any other guests away. The innkeeper scraped and bowed a bit more before leaving, then Kestral dragged the nearest chair in front of the door and sat back in it, exhaustion clear on his face.

I crept out from under the bed, eyeing Kestral warily. When he didn't look up, I leapt on to the writing desk without a sound. My dinner still sat on the table, but instead of shifting back to finish it, I pawed the chicken chunks out and ate them. I wanted to be able to make a quick getaway in case Kestral was still angry with me. He finally looked around, noting me on the writing desk. I froze but he merely stood, scratched my ears and returned to the chair where he had been cleaning his sword. I kept an eye on him as I continued eating. Cleaning his blade seemed to be a ritual to him; he appeared to calm with every swipe of cloth over the steel.

I finished eating and leapt from the desk to the bed. Kestral seemed to have fallen into a trance, staring into the clean blade. I mewled at him, calling him back to the real world, instead of whatever battle his mind was waging. Surprisingly, Kestral smiled at me. He set the blade down on a clothes chest within arm's reach of the bed, then stripped quickly out of his leathers. He sat on the edge of the bed and reached out to pet me. I arched into his fingers, enjoying the neck and back rub.

"Sorry," he said, voice soft. "Seeing my old squad . . . it brings back more bad memories than good."

I purred in response. Kestral sighed. He stretched out on the bed, carefully, so I could move around him. I climbed onto his chest and gently rubbed my head against his jaw. His hand on my shoulders was warm and comforting with just the right amount of pressure. I dropped my shoulder and rolled across his stomach and chest; I felt the chuckle more than heard it, and for some reason that thrilled me. Kestral doused the candle and rolled to his side, tipping me on the bed. I set my back against his chest and fell asleep with his arm over me.

Kestral woke up before me, as usual. I had drawn from him that night, so I was feeling refreshed. Apparently, so was he, what with how quickly he climbed out of bed and began exercising. Just watching him made me sleepy; I crawled into the warm spot he'd left and curled up, half dozing.

I perked up when he pulled his shirt off and washed himself. Water ran in tiny rivulets between the muscles of his chest and stomach. I was envious of the musculature, but not enough to want to exercise before the sun rose. He'd taken his belt off before bed, so his pants rode a little low, giving me glimpses of a tan line. He barely ran a soapy hand through his hair before rinsing it, almost as if hair-washing was an afterthought.

I shifted, nearly choking as my cloak twisted around my neck. I unfastened it, letting it fall to the floor. Mid-stretch and hoping to surprise Kestral, I called out, "I think I left the drying cloth near the writing desk."

Kestral glanced at me over his shoulder, disappointingly unsurprised. He blinked, his expression staying neutral, but his hand slipped, and he knocked the basin of water and suds over. He scrambled to find the cloth and keep the water from seeping into the floor below.

"What? Did I drool or something?" I pulled myself into a sitting position on the bed, checking to make sure my pants hadn't slipped down to reveal my right hip. After a relieved breath, I checked my face for blanket creases, drool and eye crusts. Yes, I'm vain, I admit it. It was when my hands reached my hair that I grimaced. "Ugh, I forgot to tie it before shifting. It must look like a rat's nest."

I finger-combed my hair, trying to get it to lay flat. Some men could pull off messy hair, I couldn't. Kestral finished cleaning up the spilled water and dressed, peeking at me from the corner of his eye as if he'd never seen sleep-mussed hair before. While I struggled with my hair, Kestral counted out a coin purse. He didn't look too happy with the total.

"I'll go buy supplies in town," he said finally, tying the purse to his belt. "Stay here and—"

"What supplies?" I asked. "You just bought a lot back in my village and you took all of Cera's food."

Kestral scowled at me. "I only have the one bedroll, so you'll need your own. You should also have your own flint, soap and salt, in case we get separated." He held up my shirt from where I'd draped it over the back of a chair. "And maybe a set of clothes that don't make it look like you're about to rob all the inns in town."

I blinked at him. "I don't need any of that."

Kestral eyed me darkly. I shrugged.

"You're just going to make me shift every time we get to a village, right? So why bother with different clothes? And if we get separated I can fly to you. Or away from you, on the off-chance that I'm running. As a cat, I have night-vision and fur, so I don't need to build a fire at night. Which also solves the bedroll problem, really."

Kestral narrowed his eyes at me. "You're planning on drawing every night?"

"Well, yeah." I shrugged, smiling. "Isn't it better to draw a little each night than a lot all at once? Do you even feel tired this morning?"

Kestral rolled his shoulders and flexed his arms and chest. "Not particularly. There's a little fatigue like I ran drills yesterday but that's it."

"See? It's not so bad." I swung my legs over the edge of the bed, searching for the clothes I had discarded the day before. "The important thing on the road is food."

"We can always hunt," Kestral replied.

"I'd rather fish." I smiled, thinking of the last time I had fresh fish. "I'm not much of a hunter."

"Really?" Kestral's voice was dry. "I hadn't noticed." He walked to the door, removing the chair that had been our temporary lock.

"You're still going shopping?" I asked, surprised.

"Yes." He glanced back. "Two of Shan's shoes are loose, thanks to chasing you. He's not going anywhere without seeing a blacksmith."

"You should have just told me that from the start," I said, sitting back on the bed. Kestral turned a little more, his face quizzical. "I don't want to be anywhere near that beast for as long as I can avoid it."

Kestral chuckled. I loved seeing his face when he laughed. One day he might kill me, but until then I'd like to keep making him laugh. He pulled the door shut behind him and I dragged the chair over to block it.

Waiting again. Ugh, I hated waiting. Waiting was boring!

I opened the shutters of the room's tiny window and looked out at the street three stories below. The village was still just waking up so hardly anyone was out and about yet. One lone man pulled a cart full of hay from one inn's stable to the next, chickens pecked in the street and the delicious smell of baking bread wafted toward me. I considered digging through Kestral's bags to find some breakfast but forgot the idea as the man himself came into view, leading Shan to the blacksmith. The horse moved with an uneven gait, most likely due to a bent or lost shoe. I tried to feel bad for the monster but couldn't.

As Kestral passed an inn across the street, the door was flung open and one of the ex-soldiers from yesterday greeted him brightly. Kestral stopped and the two of them spoke for a while. I itched to fly down as a crow and listen, but Kestral would recognize me in a wingbeat. It seemed like the other mage hunter was trying to get Kestral to enter the inn, but Kestral waved him off.

I leaned back from the window, thinking quickly. If the blacksmith was already up and running and if they already had shoes perfectly matched to Shan's hooves, it would probably take at least an hour to properly shoe him. But that was a serendipitous scenario; it would most likely take at least twice that much time. As long as Kestral would be occupied, I could take the chance to learn a little more about him.

I swept my cloak tightly around myself before shifting to my crow form. A quick hop to the window sill and I was in flight. I circled the other inn until I found an open window in a room without occupants. Another shift to rat and I crept through the room, under the door and into the hallway. I spied Kestral's old comrades in the common room eating breakfast at a table. I looked around carefully before shifting into my human form. Out of sight at the top of the stairs, I mussed my hair and untucked my shirt. I made my way down the stairs as if trying not to be seen, hugging the far wall with my eyes on the exit.

"Hey there!" And that was my cue. I paused, looking around in confusion. The blond ex-soldier waved to me. I pretended to look surprised. "Shouldn't you have been up to crow at the sun?"

A rooster joke. How original. I smirked and shrugged. "Sometimes doing a thing right takes longer than the sunrise." I looked over their faces and frowned, pretending not to remember them. "Have we met, sirs?"

The men exchanged a look, then laughed. "You were with our captain last night, remember?"

I cocked my head to the side. "Lots of my customers like to be called captain. I don't remember servicing anyone in a military uniform, though."

"Well, he's not a captain any more." He pulled a chair out. "Join us for breakfast, won't you? As an apology for breaking down your door last night."

I laughed. "Now that's something I remember." I ran an appreciative eye over the taller man. "I think I'm remembering you now, too. Weren't you both off to enjoy The Coop's services?"

"I would have enjoyed your services more if you hadn't already been occupied." He leered at me.

I leaned in, smirking suggestively. A barmaid appeared, and I ordered breakfast, taking advantage of the offer.

"I'm Morro," the taller man said once the maid took my order. "My partner is Wen. We're mage hunters."

"That sounds . . . strenuous." I put emphasis on the last word, turning it into a suggestion. Morro grinned; Wen shifted in his seat. "And the other one, he's your captain?"

"He was when we all served under Duke Allaran," Morro explained. "He's a mage hunter too, now."

"Ah, I see." I sipped my wake-tea, running the tip of my tongue over the rim of the cup to catch a drip. "I just have to ask. Was he just as uptight in the army as he was last night?"

Both men chuckled. They waited to answer until the maid finished setting my breakfast in front of me, then Morro leaned in close. "He was even more uptight, if you can believe it. He never would have hired a cockerel back then, right, Wen?"

Wen snorted. "Can't imagine he would have. He was the youngest captain ever. Strongest, too. Bravery bordering on stupidity sometimes."

"But he always led the charge from the front, never asked his men to do something he wouldn't," Morro added. He reached one hand out, tracing a line on my sleeve. "But ah, I imagine a man like that might be a little boring for someone with your experience?"

"A cock may crow, but we never tell tales." I winked at Morro before pulling back from him. "If this captain of yours was so strong and brave and everything, why did he leave the army at such a young age? Is he just that passionate about killing mages?"

Wen chuckled. "I don't know if he's passionate about anything. He was always such a reserved guy."

"There was a charge brought against him." Morro hesitated. "We really shouldn't be telling tales, but if you're free tonight, maybe we can trade stories."

I rolled my shoulders in a slow shrug. "I'll have to check with the coop master. If I don't get home to roost soon, he'll worry." I slathered a piece of toast with jam. "Not to make you tell tales at all, but did this business have something to do with the duke's daughter? I heard a rumor of that nature some odd couple of years ago."

Morro and Wen shared a glance. They were silent for a long moment before Wen said, "The duke doesn't have any daughters."

I paused, trying not to betray my shock. Had Kestral lied to me? But then why had he left the army? The men stared at me, waiting for a response. I took my time, licking jam from my fingertips, before looking up at Morro. "Well, that shows the quality of rumors we get way out here. Thanks for breakfast, fellows."

"Wait." Morro grabbed for my hand, but I moved it just beyond his reach, shifting my weight to make the movement appear natural. I didn't want him touching me. "If I speak to your coop master, who do I ask for?"

"You ask for me." I winked over my shoulder as I continued to the door. On the street, I turned to walk towards the brothel called The Coop, but once I found enough shadows I shifted and flew back to the open window of our room. Kestral wasn't back yet, which was lucky. I sat on the edge of the bed, trying to think.

When I had asked him about his discharge from the army, he'd admitted it was "something like" being caught in bed with the duke's daughter. Had it been the duke's wife instead? Or maybe another soldier? I didn't know enough about the army to make any educated guesses. Kestral hadn't really lied, but he hadn't told me what had happened, either. My curiosity was like an itch somewhere out of reach. If I asked more questions about it, would he figure out that I had been talking to Morro and Wen?

Admitting that would only get me into trouble. Besides, I had things in my past I didn't want dug up, either.

The sound of wood scraping wood made me jump, and I looked over to the door. It was being pushed in, sliding the braced chair across the floor. My heart pounded as Kestral shoved his way inside the room, cursing mildly at the chair. He held a wrapped bundle in one hand while he wrestled the chair out of the way with the other. Once he had the door propped closed again, he looked up at me.

"Were you just staring at the floor the whole time?" he asked.

"No," I replied, thinking fast. I couldn't lie; his brand would tell him. "I stared out the window, too."

Kestral set his bundle on the writing desk. "Some fruit and bread. Whatever you don't eat for breakfast we can take with us to eat on the road."

"Great. Thanks." Was my voice always that high? What did natural sound like? I picked through the fruit, selecting a bunch of grapes. I wasn't hungry, but if I didn't eat he might get suspicious.

Kestral sat on the edge of the bed, bracing his elbows on his knees. He gave me an intense look.

Stars, did he know? Could he have guessed? Would he kill me here or drag me to the military outpost first?

"Where are we going?" Kestral asked, voice as even as ever.

I choked on a grape. After a minute of coughing, I rasped, "What?"

Kestral leaned back, grimacing. "When I met with the commander, I tried asking about nearby storm reports, or strange weather, as that seems to be Velyn's magic. He hadn't heard anything of note except for the lightning out near your sister's cottage. If we wait for Velyn to make a move, I'm worried he'll kill another of the mage-born and become even stronger. We need to figure out where he's going and get there before him. So." Kestral looked at me again. "Where are we going?"

That was probably the longest set of words I had ever heard Kestral speak all at once. Which was lucky as it gave me time to recover from choking. "He wanted to target the weakest siblings first. He would probably come after me again if he knew where I was."

"Who is the next weakest?" Kestral asked.

I shrugged. "I don't know any of them, remember? But I doubt he would go after Kila or Eagan, not with just Cera's magic added to his. Reina—I think her name is Laureinaqin—hadn't been seen for years even before the bounties were announced, so he would have to find her first."

"She's the eldest. In theory, she would be the strongest." Kestral shook his head. "I don't see him going after someone he thinks is strong."

I skinned a grape, turning over a thought in my head. "Laki."

"He isn't weak. He's turned away every hunter who ever came after him."

"Right, but he's never killed one, has he?" I leaned forward, rolling the grape between my fingers. "When we talked about our siblings, Velyn scoffed about that. Letting the hunters live. He probably considers Laki weak for not killing them."

Kestral fell silent, deep in thought. Finally, he nodded. "Laki isn't hard to find. The ledger at the outpost listed his general location. We can be there in a week if we ride hard."

"So that's decided." I tossed the grape up and caught it in my mouth before asking, "When do we leave?"

The answer was "right dusting now." Kestral packed his bags swiftly then gave me the option of flying down to the stable as a crow or riding down in his belt purse as a rat. As tempted as I was to shift to my spider form just to dust him up, I chose crow form. I perched on the stable roof as Kestral prepared Shan for the ride then flew out ahead of them, waiting until they made it to the open road beyond the village.

It was late enough in the morning that farm carts were on the main road, making it impossible for me to ride on Kestral's shoulder without attracting attention. I flew on ahead of him, hassling farmers hauling bags of grain. Real crows were out in force, so I played a few chasing games with them until a tree rat chewed us out. When Kestral turned off the main road, I lost my sources of amusement. Instead, I flew from branch to branch, weaving in and out of trees ahead of the slow-moving horse.

Just before midday, hooves pounded along behind us. Kestral turned, one hand on his hilt. I landed on a branch set back from the road, wondering who would chance a horse's leg on this uneven trail. A moment later the tall, blond ex-soldier rode into view, drawing up short as he saw Kestral ahead of him.

"I came after you when I heard you'd left." He tossed sweaty hair out of his face. "The commander's runners only found us this morning. Why didn't you tell us Hacerathan was dead? You knew we were searching for her."

"You chased after me for that?" Kestral relaxed his grip on his sword. "I gave all the information I had to the outpost. The way hunters are supposed to."

"Yeah, but, we go way back." He smiled charmingly. "You could have told us about the fight and the brother called Velyn."

"I left an accurate accounting. I'm sure the runner relayed it." Kestral's voice was as even as ever, but something felt wrong to me. Where was the other hunter? Was this one just the faster rider or was there another reason he was alone?

Following a hunch, I swooped out of my tree for a look around. Nearby forest creatures were all silent, which prickled my pinfeathers. It didn't take me long to find the shorter mage hunter padding silently through the trees, strung bow in hand. I landed on a branch behind him and considered my options.

If they killed Kestral, I was free of him. These new hunters didn't know me; I could escape back to Wix and my old life. My bounty information would be safe too, provided Velyn didn't rat me out. Granted, I didn't stand a chance against Velyn without Kestral if he came for me again, but maybe I'd be lucky, and another sibling would kill him for me.

But was I really going to bet against Kestral? He had taken down over half the pigoblins without taking an injury and these were only two men. If they failed to kill Kestral and I didn't help him, he might suspect that I had plans to run soon. Not that I did, but until I had a solid plan in place, I needed him to trust me.

I decided to toss the dice on Kestral.

The short, squat archer was taking careful aim, while the tall blond kept Kestral's attention. I waited until he drew the arrow back to his cheek, then dove at him, cawing loudly and smacking his face with my wings. The man cursed as his arrow went wide, shattering against a tree on the far side of the road. He swatted at me with his bow until I flew to a high branch and cawed again. Kestral turned in his saddle, instantly marking the hidden archer.

The blond man cursed. "Well, there goes that plan. What happened, Wen? You never miss."

"A dusty bird got in the way," Wen growled, stomping out into the open, a new arrow to his string. "It can still be painless, Captain. Don't move."

Shan sidestepped, turning slightly so Kestral could keep an eye on both men. He was silent for a moment before asking, "Why?"

Blondie—I had already forgotten his name—made a show of leaning over his saddlehorn with a sigh. "Well, it's a real shame, honestly, Captain, but you know mage hunting has always been competitive. Especially since the only good bounties are the seven—six now, I suppose. And Wen and I figured out you weren't entirely truthful in your report to the command outpost."

Kestral narrowed his eyes and said nothing.

"You see, after we met with the runner, we went back to the outpost and studied the report you made. You detailed Velyn's weather magic, but ultimately Cera was killed with an ice dagger at close range. It got us thinking: why so much power for such an up-close kill?" He rolled his shoulders, subtly preparing for a fight. "That's when Wen and I remembered you weren't hunting Velyn or Cera. You were hunting the youngest, Jereshin."

A shiver ruffled my feathers.

"Your report didn't mention him at all, despite your hunt. And then there was that pretty little cockerel in your room last night." The hunter smiled wolfishly. "He really had me fooled, I admit. I went so far as to ask for him, but you know what I found out? They don't keep cocks at The Coop. Shame, really, but pickings are slim when you get this far out into the backwoods. So, either you're under an enchantment or you've bound the mage-born, either way, you're between us and a bounty, so—"

The blond leaned back, just as the other hunter loosed his arrow. I never saw Kestral unsheathe his sword, but suddenly it was out, shattering the arrow mid-flight. The rider cursed and charged, sword clearing its sheath. The archer whistled sharply and a moment later his horse crashed through the undergrowth to be at his side. He swung himself up into the saddle with surprising ease and prepared another arrow.

While I could hold my own in a fight, I wasn't about to tangle with ex-soldiers on horseback. I didn't have a form big enough to take on a horse, and daggers would be next to useless if I fought as a human. Kestral would understand that this wasn't something I could help with.

Horses.

The thought flashed through my mind like lightning. At first, I was confused, but gradually the thought fleshed out—take the horses out of the fight. I had made the pigoblins run, hadn't I? There must be a way to do that now.

I had never been formally trained in my magic—shifting came to me as easily as breathing, but the rest of my power was a mystery to me. It often only pulsed through me when my life was in immediate danger, without proper channeling or control. I stoked the golden well of light that lived in my chest, willing it to connect me with the hunters' horses. After a few tries, I found myself connected to all three of them and found the same thing: battle-tested warhorses trained to resist magical interference. Huh. Guess that's why Shan hated me so much. It was easy to find the part of the mind that wanted to spook and run—much like cats, horses startle easily. The harder part was disconnecting from Shan. I didn't want to toss all three riders—Kestral would probably kill me later if I made Shan dump him.

Finally, I managed to disconnect from Shan but kept the connection with the other two. I stoked their fear, trying to get them to panic and rear. Their eyes rolled, and their ears pinned, but neither broke. I felt a grudging respect for the horses' trainers. These horses were too well trained to dump their riders. They needed an extra kick, something to really light a fire under their tails.

Luckily, I happened to have a form that could strike fear in the hearts of all horses.

I dove from my tree to the roadside bushes, shifting quickly. As a snake, I undulated towards the closest horse, hissing and flaring my hood. Wen's horse screamed its terror the instant it saw me, rearing and kicking wildly until the archer tumbled free. The second horse caught the first's fear and bucked like a barely-broken colt, freeing itself from its rider to run after its partner. Shan reared but Kestral stayed in the saddle, soothing his mount back to four feet with a word. The blond hunter landed with a curse but was back on his feet in an instant. The archer, however, landed face to face with me, horror-stricken as my tongue flicked his nose.

"Morro," Wen whispered, as if afraid a loud noise would make me bite him. The swordsman, busy blocking Kestral's downswing from horseback, ignored him, even as a desperate, strangled whine twisted itself from the prone man's throat. "Morro!"

I could have killed him in an instant, but I wasn't sure if Kestral wanted them dead. They were former comrades, after all. Then again, they had just tried to kill him with an arrow in the back. I held off, waiting for a clear signal from Kestral.

The taller soldier managed to stagger back from Kestral and Shan long enough to shoot a look at his fallen partner. "It's not real," he said, swiping sweat from his eyes. "It would have bitten you by now if it was. It's an illusion, Wen."

An illusion, am I? I snapped at Wen's face as he scrambled to his feet, rising as he did and wrapping my powerful long body around his. I pinned his arms and flicked my tongue against his neck as that horrible whine continued to rise from his chest.

"Doesn't look like an illusion to me," Kestral noted calmly, his eyes on the swordsman. "He might need your help."

Morro's eyes flicked to me for an instant before coming back to Kestral. He licked sweat off his upper lip, keeping his sword in a guard position. "And catch a sword from you in the back? I don't think so, Kes—" Kestral swung, forcing the hunter to block high. Kestral kicked, landing a solid hit in the center of the tall man's chest. He just about flew backwards, his sword slipping from his hand. Kestral dismounted and stalked after him, the very image of death.

"When I kill you, Morro, you will be facing me." Kestral's boot pinned an outstretched hand, fingers straining to brush his sword's hilt. "Unlike you, I give my opponents an honorable death."

"Honorable?" Morro twisted to look up over his shoulder at Kestral. His hair was wild and sweat-soaked, his breath came in gasps. A light sheen of sweat glistened on Kestral's skin, as if he had just finished his morning exercises. Only his eyes betrayed him: empty and devoid of all pity. "You can still talk about honor? After what happened to our troop because of you? Allaran still—ouff!"

Kestral kicked the man in the ribs, flipping him over onto his back. The tip of his sword leveled at Morro's throat, drawing out a strangled silence. Wen struggled against me but a hiss and a dart at his face stilled him again.

"Did you think I didn't know about your testimony?" Kestral asked, his voice so soft I could barely hear it.

Morro paled, and the pitch of Wen's wail rose an octave.

"I was trying to save my own skin." Morro swallowed, the ball in his throat brushing Kestral's sword as it bobbed. "There was no reason for the whole troop to face death because of you. You dragged us down, Captain! All for tickling the wrong tailfeathers!"

I saw the waver in Kestral's eyes the same time Morro saw it. I tried to call out, but all I could do was hiss. Morro flung a handful of dirt up, obscuring a kick to Kestral's knee. Kestral grunted and missed plunging his sword into Morro's throat by inches. The taller man rolled to his feet, clearing a heavy dagger from its sheath. His sword lay behind Kestral who had already regained his stance and his resolve.

"I make my peace with that every day," Kestral said, softly. "I'm still working to keep the kingdom safe, every day of my life, the same way I did as a soldier. Can you say the same?"

Morro backed away a pace, keeping his knife up and between himself and Kestral. He licked his lips and looked around quickly. "Wen! Stop playing with that snake and help me!"

Wen whimpered and struggled against me. I pulled my coils tighter, circling his neck and flexing slightly. I wished Kestral would hurry up and give the kill-order already. It was getting tiring, holding this sweaty cretin still.

"I really don't want to have to kill you," Kestral said, his voice passionless. "I haven't bonded a mage-born."

Nervous laughter bubbled out of Morro's mouth. "You expect me to believe that? With that unnatural snake holding Wen?"

"I think he's on to me, Kestral." My sudden shift caused a scream of fright from my captive. I held one fae dagger to the man's throat, the other hovered near his midsection, his back pressed to my chest. Kestral turned his head just enough to glare at me. I shrugged as much as possible without giving my victim the space to struggle in. "I'm pretty sure we're going to have to kill them."

"Hey, pretty boy." Morro winked at me, trying for a charming smile and failing. "If he's got you bound, help us kill him. We'll take the bond off."

"Right before you kill me?" I replied. I had no idea what bond they were talking about. It didn't sound good, whatever it was.

"Well, not right before." His eyes flicked down my body. I rolled my eyes; it was unbelievable that he had the capacity to imply a dust up while facing death.

Kestral shifted his stance slightly, drawing our attention back to him. With a small smile on his face, Kestral said, "He's not bound."

He lunged, Morro parrying poorly with his dagger. Wen managed to get his elbow under my arm and into my ribs, freeing himself enough to draw his sword. I dragged my fae blade across his body, trying for disembowelment but instead catching his hip. It must have hurt, but it didn't stop him from turning his sword on me. I flipped one dagger around in my fist, holding it so the tip pointed back. The other I held as a guard, slipping under the bigger blade and diverting it to the side. Wen was clearly a practiced swordsman. But swordsmen rarely fought against dual-wielding opponents. While he watched my parrying blade, the other slipped past his defenses, burying itself deeply into the elbow of his sword arm. He cried out as his sword tumbled from his hand, leaving himself open. I rammed my shoulder into his chest and snaked my ankle around his. He went down hard, gasping for breath. I looked around for Kestral just in time to see him throw Morro towards me. A quick shift to cat got me out of the way but I still pinned my ears in annoyance at Kestral.

Morro landed on Wen, both struggling to get back to their feet. Kestral stalked up to them, blood-tipped sword held almost casually before him. I twined between his feet mid-stride, putting myself safely behind him. He kicked Morro's wrist, sending his dagger flying before placing his sword against the man's shoulder and digging it in.

"What did you tell the outpost commander before you came after me?" Kestral spat.

Morro's face contorted in pain, hands grasping the blade as he tried to free himself. Wen twisted free of his partner and rose to his knees, holding empty hands up. "We didn't say anything. We didn't know for sure and we didn't want anyone coming after us in case we were right."

Kestral's eyes narrowed. "Good." An easy flick of his blade took it from Morro's shoulder and through his neck. A quick step to the side avoided the worst of the blood spray. Wen scrambled backwards, then came back up on one knee, hands clutching the bow he had dropped when his horse dumped him. He didn't take much time to aim as Kestral was barely ten paces from him. He also didn't notice that I had shifted back to my human form.

At least, he didn't notice until the hilt of my dagger sprouted from his chest. He looked down in surprise, arrow tumbling from his fingers as he swiped at the dagger in vain. A cough of blood burst from his mouth before he fell backwards. Kestral glanced back at me, one eyebrow arched.

"What? Was I not supposed to kill him?" I stepped past the mage hunter, picking my way over bodies to collect my dagger. It was strange; such a wickedly-shaped dagger should not have flown so true, but as I'd thrown it, I thought I had seen its shape change. Once in my hand again, it appeared the same as it always had. Blood rolled off the blade like rain off a waterbird, allowing me to slip both daggers back into their hidden sheaths.

"They had to die." Kestral crouched beside Morro's body and wiped his blade clean with the dead man's shirt. He faced his former comrade in silence for a moment, then reached out to close his eyes.

"Don't do that," I chastised. I was already searching Wen's body for a coin purse. "Bandits wouldn't close their eyes."

"Bandits?" Kestral looked up and saw what I was doing. "No."

"No?" I jingled the purse I'd found; it was significantly heavier than Kestral's was this morning. "They'll get robbed anyway if we leave them here. And someone will have to answer for their deaths. Is that going to be you?"

Kestral shifted uncomfortably. I found myself wondering if he had ever killed someone off the battlefield before. "They came for my life. I was justified."

"I get that, sure." I plucked a ring from Wen's finger and pocketed it. "But will a justice get that? You don't have a witness. Don't forget, I'm a wanted man."

"How can I?" Kestral asked dryly. "You're planning on robbing the bodies and making it look like bandits did it. You'd be a wanted man even if you weren't one of the mistress's seven."

"Six." I felt a pang in my chest. "We're after Velyn, remember? I'm not waiting around for a justice to clear you of a murder charge."

Kestral turned his sword in his hand, appearing to think deeply. My heart sank as I considered a different story for a justice, one involving a dangerous mage-born killing two mage hunters but falling to the third. I waited with held breath as Kestral slowly dragged his gaze from the blade to me. He held perfectly still for a moment, then sheathed his sword. I released my breath in a rush.

"You're right. We don't have time to waste on amoral opportunists." Kestral tugged on Morro's belt purse, snapping the ties. He whistled, calling Shan to him. "What are you doing?"

"Hm?" I looked up from tugging Wen's boots off. "It's not enough to just take their purses; bandits take everything." I held the boot up against mine, sizing it. "Shame. I think these are too small for you and the others are certainly too big."

Kestral raised his eyebrows. "What are we going to do with boots?"

"Ideally wear them." I stepped on one end of Wen's bow and bent the other half back, snapping it to give a reason for leaving it behind. "Your boots are barely worthy of the name any more. If you're opposed to selling their gear, then we can toss it in a river. We just have to make it believable that bandits did this."

Kestral stood back and watched me strip the bodies of anything useful. I even went so far as to check their teeth for gold fillings. I heard him shuffle his feet a few times, but I didn't look back at him. Two of his former comrades were dead at his feet and I couldn't begin to understand how he might be feeling.

"Have you stripped bodies like this before?"

I turned back and arched an eyebrow at him. "Are we asking about our pasts now? I have some questions I could ask."

Kestral turned his head. "Forget it."

Dust. I had a feeling his story would be better than mine. His troop had faced death because of him? Whose tickled tailfeathers had caused that? My skin itched from all the unanswered questions. Morro and Wen had created more curiosity than satisfaction in the end. I finished gathering up their valuables and wrapped everything up in one of their cloaks, slinging it over my shoulder like a pack. Kestral took Shan by the bridle and led him forward, continuing along the trail.

"That was good work with the horses," Kestral said after several long moments of silence.

"It was, right?" I grinned. "Wasn't sure if I could pull it off at first. Aside from shifting, I don't use my magic much."

Kestral glanced sidelong at me. "If I ask a question, are you just going to ask the same question of me?"

"Seems fair, doesn't it?" I shrugged. "Actually, you get the better end of that deal since you can tell when I'm lying. So, you better give me more than one-word answers. Got it?"

Kestral thought for a moment, then nodded. "Where did you learn to fight?"

I groaned. "That's not fair. If I ask you that, you'll just say the army."

"That's the truth."

"Yeah, but it's boring." I rolled my shoulder, adjusting the makeshift bag I carried. "I never really trained to fight. Most of it is just instinct. Someone taught me how to throw knives when I was young, though."

Kestral paused, waiting to see if his liar's brand would burn. When it didn't, he asked, "Who taught you?"

I hummed. "That's a lot longer of a story than I'm willing to trade."

Kestral nodded. I thought he would ask more questions, but instead we relapsed into silence. Which was boring. I wondered if he would answer me if I asked him a question. Maybe we could learn more about each other. But then, if we were exchanging answers, what question could I ask that wouldn't give too much of me away? It was a dangerous game, but I really wanted to know more about him.

"Can I ask what made you want to join the army?"

"I'm a good fighter and it pays better than any other job." Kestral turned to look at me. "What were you doing when you were sixteen?"

"That's not a fair question."

"Neither was yours. But I enlisted at sixteen, so it's close enough."

I rolled my eyes. This is what happens when I try being clever. What could I say without lying? "My magic came in when I was sixteen. That's also when the bounties were announced, so I went into hiding." There. No lies.

"Does your magic only work on animals?" Dust, he was good at picking questions.

"I don't know. So far, that's how it's worked." I thought for a minute before asking, "How good are you with weapons besides the sword?"

Kestral glared at me, considering the fairness of the question. "I'm equally strong with a longbow. I ranked higher than the other soldiers in my squad with spear, axe, hammer, shortsword and unarmed combat. I can use any weapon given to me skillfully. I'm also a fair tactician."

"So that's why you were made captain?"

"Yes." Kestral stopped, checked one of Shan's hooves, then faced me. "Were you ever a roadside bandit?"

"Unfair—"

"My last answer was better than your last answer."

Dust, why was he so good at this?

"No," I said firmly. "I was never a roadside bandit."

Kestral glanced down at his left wrist, as if checking that the liar's brand was still there.

"But I did travel with an all-female theater group, performing as a woman in villages from Heston to Kibernia and ate nothing but the rarest chocolates and exotic fruit with—"

"Stop." Kestral shook out his left arm, grimacing. He picked up Shan's reins again and continued along the trail. "You're a good fighter. I just want to know where you got your skill."

I shrugged. "Orphans pick up skills to survive or they die. That's all."

"But you're not an orphan," Kestral reminded me.

"I didn't know that for sixteen years." I looked away into the trees at the side of the trail. "Even if they're not dead, they're not really my parents. Either of them."

Kestral nodded, the contemplative look in his eyes indicating that we were going to fall silent again, and I didn't want that. "Do you have family?"

Icy eyes glared, but I was rapidly becoming immune to them. "What, I can't ask? You know more about my family than I do."

"No. I don't have family." His voice was flat, emotionless. Dangerous. As much as I wanted to learn more, I took the hint and didn't ask.

In the silence that followed, I heard running water up ahead. Before long, we arrived at a short bridge spanning a river. When we were halfway across, Kestral stopped and held his hand out for my bag of loot.

"Some of this stuff could be valuable," I argued. "We could sell it in a village."

"We're not passing through any villages." Kestral gestured sharply. "Better to dump it than get caught with it."

I handed the tied cloak over with a sigh. "Really? No villages at all?"

Kestral untied the cloak and tossed items into the river—boots, food pouches, belts. "We need to avoid other mage hunters, which means no villages. Inns are expensive anyway."

"But we've got money now." I jingled the stolen coin purse on my hip. "We could even eat really well and have our clothes washed and—what?"

Kestral held his out to me again. "The purse."

"Wha—no!" I gripped the bag and took a step back. "You're just about broke. What if Shan needs more shoes? What if I need to eat?"

"I can hunt. Hand it over."

"But we can use this money," I whined. "They tried to kill you; you earned this money."

"They were dishonorable at the end, but they were both good men once. If this is the only tribute I can give them, I will." Kestral gestured again. "The purse."

Foolishly the thought to fight crossed my mind, but when I realized that option had only one possible outcome, I reluctantly handed over the purse. Besides, what Kestral didn't know was that I had slipped almost half the purse into different pockets and pouches already. As any street kid knows, it's foolish to keep all your coin in one easily-stolen purse.

Kestral removed the purse he had stolen from his belt and upended both bags into the river. I wanted to cry as I watched the coins sink, but Kestral raised his eyes to the sky and mouthed what looked like a prayer. After he was done, we cleared the bridge and Kestral swung up into the saddle.

"Are you riding with me?" he asked.

I considered it for a moment. I could ride on his shoulder as a crow, or I could ride in a belt purse as a rat. In fact, his bags were packed in such a way that I could perch on them as a cat. But I shook my head and shifted to my crow form, taking off ahead. Maybe when I tired of flying, I'd ride with him, but I'd had my fill of surly silence.

"What do you know about Laki?" Kestral asked as he turned Shan loose to graze. Our campsite was a simple affair—a ring of gathered stones, a single bedroll and a small pile of bags. I found myself hoping they held a lot of food; I was tired from flying all day.

"Only what Cera and Velyn told me." I attempted to light a fire with Kestral's flint. I had only built a fire once or twice before in my life, and I felt Kestral's judgment heavy on the back of my neck as I failed. "Cera says we all have a stubborn streak. Velyn said Laki's power is something about life to the lifeless."

Calloused hands gripped my wrists and adjusted my hold on the flint. Kestral crouched beside me, watching as I struck the flint again. "The reports I've read said he can manipulate plants. Give them a sort of sentience. They also said he's dangerous when he gets scared."

"But he's never killed anyone, right? He seems like the complete opposite of his twin." Sparks flew but failed to catch my kindling. I tried to pass the flint over to Kestral, but he pushed it away, gesturing for me to try again.

"Laki may never have killed anyone, but there've been some near misses." Kestral grabbed my wrist again and dragged my hands closer to the kindling. "One hunter was so badly concussed that he barely made it back to town for treatment. A few hunters were found tied up in thorny vines for days and nearly starved. Just because he doesn't kill doesn't mean he's weak. Stop flinching from the sparks."

"Animal instinct," I muttered, striking again. "We don't like fire as a rule."

Kestral sat and leaned back. "The sooner you get that fire started, the sooner we eat."

"Dust and ashes," I growled, drawing sparks again. The kindling caught this time, but quickly started to burn out. I added more, trying to keep it going. "You ever go after Laki's bounty?"

"No." Kestral handed me several sticks he had gathered earlier. "Yours was the bounty I chose after I left the army." His eyes flicked to me, then away. "If I'm honest, I wasn't really expecting to find you. It was more of an excuse to stay on the road."

"Do you just not like settling down?" I asked, only half paying attention as I fed the fire. There was food on the line and for once I was more interested in that than learning more about Kestral.

Kestral rolled his shoulders in a shrug. "I'm a soldier. I like to fight. A lot of remote villages aren't worth the army's attention, so they get plagued by minor mages, cruel fairies or dangerous beasts. Fighting for the kingdom was all I wanted to do."

I sat back, grinning. The fire had finally caught. Kestral reached back and dragged his bag of cooking supplies closer. "Wait," I said as Kestral set up his cooking tripod. "If you didn't think you'd find me, are you still going to kill me?"

Kestral was quiet a moment, setting the poles of his tripod together and suspending a shallow pan from them. He slid the tripod over the flames then rummaged through his packs for food. "You are a dangerous mage-born, aren't you?"

"That's right. I forget sometimes how dangerous small cats and spiders are to the kingdom."

Kestral tried to suppress a shudder at the mention of the word spider, which made me laugh.

"I may be one of Laurana's kids, but I'm not exactly dangerous. Not like Kila and Velyn."

"Kila's not really dangerous. She served honorably in the army until the bounties were announced."

"Really?" That surprised me. "Did you ever meet her?"

"No, I heard she was stationed to the west, defending against Viaparaiso. She had an impressive battle record, was even on track to become a high-ranking officer." Kestral poured a little water in the pot, then dumped a package of rice and dried vegetables into it, stirring with a long wooden spoon. "Her squad turned against her the day the bounty was announced. She slaughtered each and every one of them."

I shuddered. "And you say she's not dangerous?"

"She's never gone looking for a fight and she makes her location known." Kestral shrugged. "If people stopped trying to kill her, I doubt she'd be a threat. To our kingdom, at least. She's not like Velyn, looking for a fight or a throne."

"I'm not looking for a fight or a throne," I muttered. I searched through Kestral's bag until I found an oilcloth wrapped around some kind of meat. I held it out to be added to the pot. He stared at the offering for a moment as if considering whether to add it, but finally he took it and cut the meat up into small pieces before feeding them into the pot. "How did Kila serve in the army without anyone knowing she was one of Laurana's children?"

Kestral looked up at me, his eyebrows disappearing beneath that messy mop of hair. "You really don't know anything about your family, do you?"

I shrugged, trying to look as if I didn't care. Because I didn't. "It's not like I knew I had a family until four years ago. Dear old Dad is trying to have us killed and Ma is in prison."

"But you didn't try looking into your family after you found out?" Kestral asked, still surprised. "You weren't curious?"

"My only interest was in survival," I replied, leaning back, resting one hand on a bent knee. "I went into hiding and hoped no one would figure out who I was."

Kestral shook his head as he stirred the pot. "I only know what they told the hunters, but it seems that the king took an interest in his older children. At least until the queen finally bore a live heir."

I nodded. Everyone knew the queen was sickly and had had several failed pregnancies before finally giving birth to the realm's only prince. He was a few years older than me, but that was all I knew about him. The queen barely survived the birth and hadn't been seen for years afterward.

"The two eldest were adopted by noble families. Your sister stayed in the capital, but your oldest brother's family took him to their keep in the south. Neither has been seen by their families since the bounties were announced." Kestral paused to taste the food, then continued stirring. "When the twins were born, the king wanted one to go into the military and the other into the Order of the Great Canvas."

"He took that much interest in us?" I asked, mildly surprised.

Kestral shrugged. "The prince was born a year after the twins and after that it seems he stopped caring about where the queen sent you all."

"How paternal," I replied dryly. "Wait, if he wanted one twin in the military and the other in the Order, then why did Kila end up in the army? Shouldn't they have sent the male twin?"

"You would think so. The queen says it was a mix up." He took another small taste of dinner. It smelled good to me, but Kestral kept stirring. "Laki was sent into the Order and Kila entered the military."

"So, is Laki a priest now?"

"Monk. He entered the Star-Strewn sect. It's possible he's no longer practicing religion, though." Kestral glanced over at me. "It doesn't seem as if the king took any interest in Laurana's three youngest children. Velyn went north to a fishing village, Cera was given to traveling performers. The queen claims she has no memory of where you were sent."

I chuckled. "She didn't want to admit to sending me to Giltner, did she?"

"Most likely not. It's not a place anyone would have thought to look, though." Kestral pulled a bowl out of his bag and tipped the cooked rice and meat into it. He passed it over to me without a spoon, so I sipped from the rim. Halfway through my bowl, I looked up and realized Kestral wasn't eating.

"Not hungry?" I asked. I had been starving half the day.

"I only have the one bowl," Kestral replied. "I'll eat when you're finished."

"Why only one bowl?"

"Why would I need more?"

I shrugged and finished gulping down dinner. When I passed the empty bowl back, Kestral poured the rest of the meal into it and indicated that I should break down the cooking instruments. I set the pot and rods aside, allowing them to cool off.

Kestral glanced up, opened his mouth, then shook his head and continued eating.

"What?" I asked. Now that I'd eaten, I was interested in learning more about him again, so I wouldn't mind resuming our question-for-question game.

"Nothing." He tipped his bowl back. I slid over so that I sat right next to him, hoping to surprise him when he lowered the bowl. No luck, just a glare.

"What is it? More questions?" I grinned, leaning close. "I don't mind trading answers."

Kestral stared for a moment. "What was growing up in Giltner like?"

I forced a laugh and drew back. "It'll take more than dinner to get that story out of me. A keg of Wix's darkest ale isn't enough for that."

Kestral set his empty bowl down and rummaged through his food satchel again. He pulled out a waterskin, sloshing the liquid inside before he uncorked it and took a sip. "What about for Goldwater Whiskey?"

I leaned forward despite myself. I took the skin by its neck and sniffed. A heady aroma of woody liquor burned my nose. I had only sipped it before, but it had been wondrous. I pushed the skin back into Kestral's hands, letting go with difficulty. "It would take more than you have there."

Kestral shrugged and took another sip before tucking the skin away. "I'll remember that."

I forced another laugh but this time it sounded bitter. "Why do you care if you're only going to kill me?"

"I will kill you if you don't finish cleaning up dinner." Kestral nudged the dinner bowl over to me with his foot, then stood. He whistled to call Shan in from grazing.

I grumbled as I scrubbed out the bowl and dinner pot, wiping them clean with a small cloth. After everything was dry enough, I packed them into Kestral's food bag. I glanced over at him as he set up his bedroll with his back to me. Did I have time to sip his whiskey while he wasn't looking?

"Oh, I do have a question," Kestral called without looking back at me. I lifted the skin, hoping to sneak a quick sip. "How much liquor would it take to make a cat drunk?"

I pulled a face at him and put the whiskey back in the satchel. "I don't have to sleep as a cat, you know. I can draw from you in any form."

That earned a glance back at me. "If you want to draw, you'll do it as a cat. If I even catch you thinking about another form, I'll crush you."

I laughed before slipping into my cat form. Cats were the best sleepers anyway.

4

The forest was dense and ancient with trees so tall their dark green summer leaves cast deep shadows, making midday feel like early evening. Thick layers of leaves and grasses made the trek arduous. My sneak-thief boots weren't helping matters either. The grips for climbing became easily matted with dead leaves or clumped with mud. For the first time, I wished I had a pair of simple leather boots like Kestral's. Of course, Kestral was nowhere nearby. He had wanted to hang back so we wouldn't appear to be ganging up against my brother.

How anyone could find a Star-Strewn monk in the middle of this dusty forest was a mystery to me, but Kestral assured me we were on the right path. Or, at least, the right lack-of-a-path. Laki might be easy to find but he wasn't easy to approach. Spotting sunlight up ahead, I eased my back against a wide elm and leaned around it, peering into the clearing.

My brother sat on a stump in the middle of the clearing, whittling a block of wood. Behind him stood a dead, hollowed-out tree that appeared to be his home. A cloth was strung across a doorway and a tall carved bear stood outside of it. The clearing was dotted with carved nymphs, animals and shaped bushes, many out of wood, several out of clay or stone. Laki himself wore a dirty, dark green robe, giving him a shapeless look. He had rounded cheeks and a squared-off jaw. While seated it was hard to tell, but he appeared to be a few inches shorter than I. His head was bald and his eyes downcast, focused on his whittling.

"Come into the clearing, Reshi. It's rude to linger out of sight," Laki said softly without glancing up. Only my half-expectation that he knew I was there kept me from jumping. I tossed my cloak back over my shoulder and stepped lightly into the clearing.

"How did you know it was me?" I asked, mostly for the sake of being polite.

Laki looked up, a sad smile on his face, eyes the dark green of leaves in midsummer. "The elm you were standing beneath is a friend of mine."

"Ah. Well, I hope I didn't stomp on any of his roots." I glanced back, giving the tree a friendly wave. "I wasn't trying to sneak up on you."

"Speaking of 'sneaking up,'" Laki said, lowering his head to continue whittling, "Call your hunter friend in where I can see him."

"Hey Kestral!" I called over my shoulder. "Laki says come on out!"

I shifted my weight from foot to foot, waiting in uncomfortable silence. Kestral had stopped much farther back, hoping not to scare Laki into a fight. It would take him a while to lead Shan through the nearly impassable forest around us, which was probably by the design of the brother in front of me.

"Nice carvings," I said, pointing to several that looked like a family of foxes. "Did you make all of these?"

Laki nodded, working silently on his block of wood.

I wandered slowly around the clearing, looking at each carving with interest. "You're really detailed. I couldn't do anything like this. I don't have the—"

"Patience?" Laki interrupted. He looked up, smiling again. "You don't like waiting, do you?"

I laughed nervously. "What makes you say that?"

"You pace like a wolf." Laki tilted his head, his eyes never leaving mine. "No, more like a nightblack cat. Caged and waiting. But what are you waiting for, little brother? To fight? Or to flee?"

"Are those the only options?"

"Generally speaking, yes." Laki put his head down but this time he only stared at his block of wood. "My twin and I are good examples of this natural law. She fights. I flee."

"Are you and Kila close?" I asked. I had never met Kila, but I imagined her to be a little like Kestral—a warrior always looking for the next battlefield.

"Not particularly." Laki shivered. "Hers is a star of blood and pain. Mine is of peace and growth. We met once. We didn't get along well." He looked up at me again, eyes catching mine. "What star is yours, Reshi? A violent star? A timid star? Which star draws you when you gaze upon the Great Canvas?"

Oh stars, he really is a monk, I thought, suppressing an eye roll. "I never learned the names of the stars. I prefer the darkness in between the stars, anyway."

"A shadowed star." Laki stared at me for a long while before nodding slowly. "It suits you."

Before I could ask what he meant, booted footsteps drew near, and a horse's neigh rang out. Kestral and Shan could be deathly silent when needed, so I imagined Kestral was taking care not to surprise Laki in any way. A moment later Kestral stepped into the clearing. He left Shan just behind him, grazing at the edge of the clearing.

"Telakishin." Kestral nodded his head to my brother.

"Mage hunter." Laki only flicked his eyes up at him. "Do I have reason to fear you this day?"

"Not this day," Kestral assured him. He held his hands away from his sides. He still wore his sword, along with other weapons, on his belt but he kept his hands clear of them. "We came to talk."

"About Sister Cera." Laki sighed. The knife flashed in his hands as he resumed whittling. "May she find the rest she deserves, cradled in the star that burns only for her."

"You already know about Cera's death?" I asked, surprised. I doubted Laki received many guests out here and not many knew of Cera's demise just yet.

Laki nodded, his eyes on his whittling. "I'm certain we all felt her passing. She was our link to each other. Our guiding star." He glanced up briefly. "Why don't you sit? I feel this may take some time."

A number of stumps littered the clearing. I selected one near Laki. Kestral glared grimly at a few stumps before choosing to lean against an unshaped boulder. He crossed his arms over his chest, keeping his hands away from his belt. Honestly, if he was so worried about scaring Laki, why hadn't he left his weapons with Shan?

"What do you know of Cera's death?" Kestral asked.

Laki sighed, his knife pausing in its work. "When I felt her slip through the Canvas, I read the stars. A star of chaos and storms eclipsed Cera's star of light and when it passed, her star had burned out. I couldn't see what made Velyn's star lose its balance, its alignment, but I can see it is still raging as it burns among its brethren."

I blinked. This was all just a little too mystical for me. I had never been very religious; most of what I knew about stars came from gambling games.

"I am sorry now that I did not go to Cera when she urged me to," Laki continued, his knife slowly resuming its task. The lump of wood was beginning to take shape as slivers of curled wood pooled around Laki's feet. "Once, she allowed me to divine her stars and I found that our values were closely aligned. But Cera wanted us to stand united against the hunters and I . . . I just wanted to hide."

"I understand that." I said, relieved to find we agreed on something. "That was why I didn't join her either. At least not until—"

"Not until the hunter was upon you." Laki glanced up at my silent partner. "And now the both of you would like me to fight our brother Velyn. Is that right?"

"Not exactly." I leaned forward on my tree stump, bracing myself with my hands. "We think Velyn might be targeting you next. Kestral has agreed to help me kill him, for what he did to Cera. Your help would be appreciated, but we're mostly here to keep Velyn from killing you."

"And to keep him from stealing my power."

I nodded.

Laki turned to look up at Kestral. "And then what?"

Kestral met his eyes and said nothing.

"Will you collect Velyn's bounty?"

Kestral remained silent, meeting Laki's gaze calmly.

"And after that?" Laki continued. "Will you kill Reshi and collect his bounty?"

The hunter stared back, unperturbed.

"And after you kill him," Laki asked, "Will you kill me?"

Bright blue eyes stared into deep green. The silence grew until it was deafening. I shifted in my seat, trying to avoid antagonizing either of them. Stars, this wasn't easy! I nudged a nearby wooden carving of an angry badger with the toe of my boot. Someone say something, I begged silently.

Kestral finally took a breath and uncrossed his arms. "I have no plans to harm you or Reshi until well after Velyn has been dealt with. My promise to Reshi is that I will give him a head-start before I renew my hunt for him. It was never my intention to hunt you, Laki."

"Not your intention," Laki repeated. "Yet here you are, a strong mage hunter on the verge of collecting three large bounties. What holds you back, ice star?"

Kestral flinched. I almost thought it was his liar's brand, but it didn't originate from his left arm. Instead, his shoulders hunched, and his gaze dropped to the ground.

"Yes, I see the ice in your eyes. My twin's is a hot violence, quick to flare up but also quick to burn out. But yours . . . yours is enduring, cold and long-frozen." Laki narrowed his eyes at Kestral. "You have had your stars divined before, haven't you, exiled warrior? What can you offer that would make me trust one such as you?"

"Laki," I cut in, no longer able to sit quietly. "I don't know dust about stars or religion or anything, but I've spent a lot of time with Kestral. He's had a lot of opportunities to kill me, but he hasn't. He's been . . ." I almost said he was like a friend, but I wasn't sure how Kestral would react to that. "Honorable."

For some reason, Kestral's eyes flicked up to me then dropped just as quickly. Had I offended him somehow? We had traveled together for just over a week; we were still a little awkward around each other, but each night Kestral allowed me into his bedroll to draw a little of his life force as he slept. That took trust, didn't it? On both our parts, really. It wasn't fair for Laki to judge him without knowing him.

Laki continued staring at Kestral, who was now avoiding his gaze.

"Look, Laki, how can we trust you?" I asked. "Cera and I trusted Velyn and look where that got us. I'm taking a risk here, too."

Laki blinked, glanced down, then shyly met my eyes. "I suppose you're right. It wouldn't be hard for me to turn on you as Velyn turned on dear Cera. But you have nothing to fear from me, Reshi. I desire neither power nor a throne. The stars and my solitude are enough for me."

Laki caressed the roughly shaped carving in his hand lovingly. He glanced around at his clearing, a fond smile on his face. "I should hate to leave this place."

"So, you'll help us with Velyn?" I asked.

Kestral was still looking away, almost as if he felt out of place.

Laki shook his head and stood slowly. "I am not one for confrontation. For that, you need my twin."

"Kila?" Kestral asked, turning back to us. "Is your sister coming here?"

"No. In truth, I was going to go to her for protection. But my forest warned me of your approach and I decided to wait for my little brother." Laki smiled softly at me.

"Have you spoken to Kila somehow?" I asked, surprised.

Laki nodded. "Ever since Cera's death, the bond between my twin and I has strengthened. In the time before we sleep, our thoughts connect, and we converse. Haven't you noticed changes in your power, brother?"

"No, I—" I paused. Wait, had I noticed something different? A voice, or thoughts that weren't mine? I would have to pay more attention in the future. "Kila is going to protect us?"

Laki tilted his head, eyes considering. "It is not Kila's way to protect. But it is her way to fight. She is looking forward to the confrontation with Brother Velyn and sees my arrival as a means of hastening it. She is expecting me shortly and I will bring you along, Reshi."

Kestral shouted out suddenly. I spun, hands reaching for the hidden daggers at my back. At first, I couldn't see what had happened but as Kestral struggled I understood. The rock he had leaned against had somehow grown and closed around his right wrist, trapping it. As I watched, the rock seemed to ooze around him like mud, though it was clearly solid from the way it held him.

"Don't worry. Your hunter will be freed once we are away." Laki picked up a small travelsack from behind his stump. He slipped his carving inside it before shouldering it. "Come, Reshi."

"I'm not leaving him!" I stared at my brother in shock. "He's been protecting me since Velyn—"

"I can protect you." Laki turned his back on Kestral, walking towards the trees. "You don't need him any more. You're with your family now."

"I was with my family before, too," I reminded him, standing halfway between Kestral and Laki. Kestral had stopped struggling against the rock, his eyes on me. "Laki, I can't just leave him."

"Why not?" Laki stopped and looked back over his shoulder. "He's a hunter, Reshi. The only thing he needs from you is the price on your head."

I looked back, meeting Kestral's eyes. "I need him."

"You need him?" Laki asked, voice soft.

"Yes!" I spun to face my brother, relieved to have found a good reason to keep Kestral. "My magic—I don't know how yours works, but for mine I need to draw life force from sleeping humans."

Laki grimaced. "We can get a more compliant human for that, I'm sure. Come now, Reshi. Kila won't wait forever."

I turned back to Kestral, trying to find another reason that would keep him with me. Laki walked away; in a moment he would be out of sight. My heart twisted in my chest as I thought of just leaving him there, alone, for what might be days.

But why? I wondered. He'd told me that he'd kill me. He was hunting me specifically. Why do I care? I should have been relieved. I should have felt free.

But I didn't. Laki had reached the edge of the clearing by the time I made my decision. Before I could take a single step, Kestral cleared his sword from its sheath with his left hand. He reversed his grip and slammed the hilt against the rock gripping his right arm. The rock shattered as he yanked his wrist free and stepped forward, transferring his sword to his right hand.

I froze in surprise. Laki turned, an expression of terror on his face.

Oh no.

We'd done the very thing we had wanted to avoid from the beginning.

We'd scared Laki.

I turned to face my brother, hands held wide as I backed towards Kestral. There was a plan in place for this, it just wasn't very elegant: run.

Laki beat us to it. He dropped the bag he was carrying and lit off into the trees. Before I could make my way to Kestral, a bellowing roar shook the trees around us. In horror, I watched as the enormous, carved wooden bear in front of Laki's home began to move. It dropped down to all fours, rolling powerful shoulders, flexing dagger-like claws. On its head were wide, curling horns, like a ram. It took a step, roaring again and showing rows of vicious teeth.

"So, when you read the reports of Laki's magic, did they mention anything like this?" I asked Kestral, my voice high-pitched and wavering.

"No." How could he sound the same as he always did in a situation like this? "Can you scare it away, like the horses?"

I shook my head, still backing towards Kestral. "That's no animal. It may look like a horny bear, but it's still just a lump of wood. My magic can't do anything to it."

Kestral stared at the bear-carving for a moment then suddenly sheathed his sword. "Keep it busy." He turned to walk away.

"What?!" I cleared my daggers, but I turned back to look at Kestral. "Hey, you're the warrior! I'm barely—" The ground shook as the bear charged in earnest. I dove to the side with a roll, narrowly avoiding a swipe from sharp wooden claws. "Kestral!"

I heard a whistle, then hooves pounded across the clearing. Kestral had called Shan. He wouldn't run away and leave me, would he? I didn't have time to look; the bear had reared and was attempting to crush me. I dodged again, this time swinging one of my daggers, scoring a hit against its flank. Silver scraped against wood, gouging a shaved ribbon free but otherwise causing no damage. How do you kill something made of wood? I ducked another swipe and rammed my dagger into the beast.

The blade bounced, sending shockwaves of pain up my arm. I flinched and a heavy backhanded swing from the bear sent me flying across the clearing. Luckily, I avoided crashing into any of the smaller carvings and was able to roll to my feet.

What was Kestral doing? I could barely see him with the wood-bear between us. It looked like he was stringing his longbow, but what good would that do? A dagger at close range couldn't leave a mark.

No time to think about that. I leapt as the wooden beast charged again, landing lightly on its back. It spun, perhaps thinking I had landed behind it. I slammed a dagger between its shoulder blades and hung on as it tried to shrug me off. The bear glared at me over its shoulder, sightless eyes full of fury. It reared, standing at its full nine feet of height.

"Reshi, get clear!"

I kicked off, ripping my dagger free and landing several paces away. I heard a thunk, and as the bear turned to chase me, I saw an arrow had pierced its chest. Wait, was that an oilcloth bag suspended from the arrow? I darted in close, ducking a swipe before lighting off towards Kestral. He stood with an archer's perfect form, an arrow sighted on the bear.

A flaming arrow.

As I reached Kestral's side, the arrow flew, perfectly hitting the little bag the first arrow had carried. The bag split and as I watched, liquid fire rolled down the bear's chest and stomach, quickly growing and spreading to its head, back and limbs. The beast roared its defiance and charged at us, flames and smoke pouring off it as it ran. My heart beat fit to burst but Kestral stood firm, watching its approach. Before it could fully reach us, it collapsed in a heap of shapeless, burning wood.

"Wow." My knees buckled as the air in my chest left me all at once. "Wow. What was in that bag?"

"Cooking oil." Kestral set his bow down against his foot. "I'm sorry that Laki didn't—"

"Uh, Kestral?" I set my hand on his bracer, stopping him before he could unstring his bow. "I think you're going to need that."

All around the clearing Laki's carved creatures were coming to life. None were as big as the bear, but the fox family had sharp teeth, the boars had long, pointed tusks and the winged critters stretched their wings and took flight. Not all were wood, either, but stone and clay as well. And each one of them turned their lifeless eyes towards Kestral and me.

Kestral swore darkly as he quickly nocked another arrow. A clay rivercat shattered as an arrow shot through it, but a stone boar barely noticed as his second arrow glanced off its hide. I stood shakily, unsure that my fae daggers would be of much help against wood and stone.

"You need to do something," Kestral said, backing up a step to shoot another arrow at a clay beast. It crumbled to dust as he sighted on another clay carving.

"Me?" I asked. "I distracted the bear. The rest is on you."

"I used all my cooking oil already and the stone ones wouldn't burn anyway." Another clay figure burst but now the animals had drawn too close. I kicked at a stone fox, driving it back as Kestral dropped the bow in favor of his small crossbow. "There must be something you can do."

"I'm the mistress mage's youngest, remember?" I kicked again, this time the fox caught my boot and hung on. I slapped it away with the hilt of my dagger. "All I can do is shapeshift and . . ." I trailed off, a thought occurring to me.

"Whatever it is, do it." Kestral loaded the crossbow with an armor-punching bolt and shot down a stone falcon that had been diving for his head. He stepped down on its wing, then crushed the bird beneath his heel, snapping the wing off. It thrashed at his feet as he stepped coldly over it. "I'll distract them."

I wanted to find a safe corner to hide in while I attempted magic I had never performed before, but with my brother able to control any inanimate object at will, there didn't seem to be any safe corners left. I put my back to Kestral and tried to keep pace with him while I reached for the well of golden magic in my chest.

Animals had instincts. The instinct to eat, the instinct to sleep, the instinct to flee from hunters or to chase prey. The instincts varied with each individual species, but some were very nearly universal. For instance, almost all species would flee a fight they have no chance of winning.

Unless they had something to protect.

The closest animals to the clearing were all small—songbirds, rabbits, tree rats and the like. Nothing like that would help us in this fight. Instead, I sought predators, waking them from their dens and stoking their instinct to protect their young. It wasn't easy, trying to convince strong-minded carnivores that they should come to my aid, but I prodded that protective instinct and they came.

Wow, did they come.

The first to arrive were the hunter-birds, unsurprising as they were already awake and hunting, unlike most furred hunters. They dove into the clearing, scattering Laki's flying critters. A heavy hawk drove its talons into a stone pixie, sending it spiraling to the ground where it shattered. An eagle pierced a wooden dove with its beak, severing the dove's neck. Bits of wood and stone began raining down as the raptors tore the lifeless flyers to pieces.

"What's happening?" Kestral called. At some point he had switched to his sword, using the hilt to rap a stone badger over the head.

"I found help for us," I replied, focusing fully on the fight once more. "There's more coming but it might take—Uff!" A wooden ram charged into my side, driving the air from my body. Pain—hot and white—blurred my vision as my right arm dropped, hand barely still clutching my dagger. Kestral was there in an instant, slicing off the wooden creature's head.

"How bad?" Kestral asked, cutting off the ram's front two legs as it continued staggering about.

I grunted, trying to remember how to breathe. My side was on fire, my arm tingling and numb. I was pretty sure I'd heard something snap but before I could fully explore the injury, I had to drop my left dagger and throw a knife through a clay winged-rabbit with tiger's teeth. Seriously, did Laki just make creatures up as he carved them? That just wasn't fair.

"Reshi, are you—" Kestral cut himself off. I finally caught a breath and turned to see what he saw. "What did you do?"

Wolves streamed into the clearing, their hackles raised, lips peeled back in dangerous snarls. Kestral took an offensive stance, his sword glittering before him. With a gasp of pain, I reached up and grabbed his arm.

"Don't." So much pain. I gripped his arm tighter. "Friends."

Kestral paused long enough for the lead wolf to snatch up a stone fox in her jaws. She shook her head violently, the fox crying out soundlessly. When she let it go, it slammed into a tree trunk and shattered. The other wolves snapped at the carved creatures, driving them back from us, forming a half-ring around Kestral and me. Kestral kept his sword up, but refrained from attacking. Around us, wood snapped, and claws scraped on stone, but for the moment we could catch our breath.

For me that was a little more literal than I would have liked. I drew air into my chest, despite the searing pain in my side. Kestral dropped to one knee, his sword still in front of him but his free hand checked my ribs, the light pressure making me see stars.

"Broken ribs," Kestral reported, standing up in a guard position again. "Try not to move your right arm."

It was hard to move anything at all, but I staggered to my feet, keeping my right arm pinned to my side. I had broken bones before, sure, but never had they felt as intense as this. Every breath was agony, but I didn't have time to waste complaining about it. A stone boar charged through the ring of wolves, overly-large tusks drawing a yelp from one of them. The boar closed with Kestral, who reversed his grip on his sword and slammed the hilt into the stone beast's head. It diverted the boar to the side and sent a spider web of cracks through the stone, but the boar turned and charged again. As Kestral turned to face it, a delicate stag with mighty stone antlers leapt over the wolves, coming at us from the opposite side of the boar.

"Any more friends coming?" Kestral asked, turning the boar aside again.

Seriously, he expected me to be chatty now?

"One," I wheezed. "Far."

The stag lowered its head and tried to gut me from groin to neck. I ducked its antlers and kicked at its finely-carved legs, hoping to break them. The stag merely shifted its weight so the kick glanced off, leaving me off-balance for another blow. It swung its head again, but this time I grabbed its antlers and yanked, toppling it on its side. It righted itself quickly enough, but that was enough time for me to back away.

"Shift," Kestral called to me, still trading blows with the boar. It had scored a hit while I'd been distracted—blood ran down Kestral's pant leg. "Fly away."

I shook my head, unable to use my breath for both combat and speech at the same time. The stag charged. I dove recklessly, simply trying to stay away from it. I landed on my injured ribs, my breath rushing out of me as starbursts of pain blossomed before my eyes. The stag reared and spun, ready for another pass.

A bloodcurdling scream echoed through the clearing. Even the fake creatures stopped and turned towards the source. I finally got to see Kestral's look of shock as a nightblack cat slunk into the clearing. He moved like a shadow, paws padding soundlessly across the ground, tail lashing, teeth gleaming. He pounced, leaping nearly thirty feet to land on the stag attacking me, ripping its stone head from its shoulders in one sharp motion.

"Your friend?" Kestral asked.

I was a little proud to hear the tremble in his voice. All I could do was nod as the cat swatted the boar into a tree, finishing the network of cracks Kestral had begun. From there, the predator targeted the larger carved animals while the wolves finished off the smaller ones. I looked up for the hunter-birds, but it seemed they had already considered their contribution over. I rolled up to my knees, wrapping one arm around my ribs, gasping for air with Kestral at my side, guarding my right. Each movement a fresh wave of pain, I forced myself to my feet, dagger in hand in case of another attack.

Once the lifeless attackers had been broken beyond repair, the nightblack cat faced down the wolves. He screamed a challenge and the lead wolf snarled a response, her hackles raised and ready for a fight.

"Reshi?" Kestral's voice was low, eyes focused on what was about to be an epic fight.

I closed my eyes, leaning my right shoulder into Kestral for balance. It was harder now to reach that well of golden fire than it had been earlier. It was still just as bright as before; I hadn't used a lot of it. But concentrating through the pain in my side kept me from grasping it fully. I had to hold my breath to dull the pain as much as possible before I could grip my magic and reach out to the cat and wolves. I soothed away their protective instincts and instead made them think about sleep, conserving strength for the next hunt, and healing from their wounds. The animals continued to posture for a moment until one of the male wolves scored down his flank from a stone tusk, whined softly and tucked his tail. The other wolves shrunk in on themselves too, seeming to ask the lead wolf's permission to leave. The cat pinned its ears, then turned and slunk back into the forest. Once its tail disappeared into shadows, the wolves turned as one and trotted silently in the opposite direction.

Kestral's arm was somehow already around my waist as I lost my balance from holding my breath too long. He lowered me gently to my knees and whistled for Shan. The horse came running, eyes still rolling in fear of the predators. Kestral reached into a bag, pulling out a jar of ointment and a roll of bandages.

"Lift up your shirt," Kestral ordered, crouching beside me.

I wanted to make a quip, but the pain overwhelmed me. Groaning, I lifted my shirt high enough so Kestral could smear ointment over it.

"No bleeding, that's good." Kestral wiped his hands on the grass then wrapped the bandage so tightly that I gasped. "Looks like three broken ribs, maybe some fracturing. Binding them will help. The ointment should numb it a bit."

The wrap hurt as he pulled it tight, but a moment later I noticed some relief. I was able to draw shallow breaths without wishing for death by the time Kestral tied the bandage off.

"I think we scared Laki," I panted, lowering my shirt again.

Kestral laughed as he tucked his ointment back into its bag. "This may be difficult for you but try not to—"

The rest of his words were drowned out as the trees surrounding the clearing began moving. Not just branches shaking, or leaves rustling, but actually *moving*. The trunks groaned and creaked as roots lifted themselves. Branches snapped and waved as if reaching for us. Shan reared and might have bolted but I pressed my hand to his flank, reaching for my magic to soothe him. It was easier to reach his mind with my magic through the physical contact. It also helped that over our last week of travel, Shan and I had come to an understanding of sorts. The horse stilled under my hand as Kestral stepped in front of us, his hand on his sword.

"I knew you were dangerous from the moment you stepped into my forest." Laki's voice came from somewhere above us.

I gripped a stirrup and pulled myself to my feet.

"We don't want to fight you, Laki!" Kestral called. "Your brother is injured. We just want to leave."

"I won't let you leave."

I spotted Laki in a tree to my left, perched on a high branch, one hand wrapped around the trunk.

"You've taken my protection from me by killing all my friends. You die here today, hunter."

"Die?" I tried to shout but it only came out as a wheeze. "You don't kill hunters, Laki. You never have."

"Dear Reshi, the only thing that will stop an ice-hearted hunter like him is death." Laki shook his head sadly. "For some, it is a mercy. Step away from him, Reshi. Let him be crushed by my friends."

I drew closer to Shan and to Kestral. Kestral took a step towards Laki.

"What happens to Reshi if I stand aside?" Kestral called.

"What?" I turned, the pain in my ribs burning at the movement. "Kestral, what are you—"

"Reshi comes with me," Laki replied, his voice soft. "If we make it to Kila without running into Velyn, he'll be safe."

"And if Velyn catches up to you before you reach your sister?"

Laki shrugged, his tree mirroring the movement.

"You would use him to buy your own freedom, wouldn't you?" Kestral asked, his hand going to the hilt of his sword. "Either you would trade him to Velyn for your own safety or you'd kill him for his power. Isn't that right?"

Laki dropped his gaze. "It is unfortunate times when brother turns on brother. I don't want to fight, but I will preserve my own life. The stars guide—"

A sudden roar and a powerful wind cut Laki off. The tree he rode burst into flame so suddenly that I barely heard him scream before the whole thing was charcoal and ash. The tree crumbled, showering the clearing with dust and smoke. Coughing was agony; I fell to my knees, eyes watering and lungs fit to burst. A hand found my shoulder and a wet cloth was pressed to my mouth. Breathing through the cloth helped me find my breath again and when I could see, I found Kestral at my side, wet cloth in hand. His skin and clothes were black from ash. Shan shook violently, dusting us with another layer of soot.

"What happened?" I coughed again, my throat raw. Kestral only shook his head, staring ahead where Laki had been not a moment before.

When the ash finally settled, and the smoke cleared, I saw Laki's charred remains at the edge of the clearing. Green mist rose from his body, twining through the smoke still rising off of him. A figure in a long cloak stepped out from between the trees and knelt

beside the body, holding its hand in the middle of the mist. When its hand closed, the mist became a glowing ember. As Kestral and I watched, my oldest brother stepped forward, clutching the ember of Laki's magic.

"Little brother Reshi! Such a pleasure to meet you." His voice was cheerful enough to make the greeting sound genuine. He was dressed stylishly, like a noble, with embroidered leather boots, black hunter's leggings, a dark grey tunic over a red silk shirt and a black cloak edged in a shining orange ribbon. For the first time I saw myself in one of my siblings: the same face shape, the same quirk of the mouth, the same impertinent raised eyebrow. We were even within a few inches of the same height. The biggest differences were in hair and eye color: his were flame-orange with his hair long and brushed back. His eyes seemed to flicker like candle-flames. As I watched, he pulled the ember close to his chest and crushed it, drawing Laki's power into himself.

"Eagan," Kestral said, rising to his feet and starting forward.

"Hunter." Eagan inclined his head politely. We could have been meeting at a dinner party, the way my brother was acting. "I don't mean to be rude, but if you'll just stay right there." Eagan raised a hand and a circle of waist-high flames sprung up around Kestral. "I have a few matters to discuss with my baby brother before I get to you."

"I hope one of those matters is about where you commissioned those boots," I said, leaning casually against Shan's shoulder to hide my injury, a careless smirk plastered on my face. "Or maybe that you have an extra pair to lend? It looks like we might be the same size."

Eagan's smirk was a mirror of my own. "They are a beautiful pair, aren't they? I doubt you could afford them. But if you manage to kill me, they're all yours."

"That sounds fair." It didn't sound fair at all, not with me unable to shapeshift and Kestral held captive by fire, but I had the seed of a plan beginning to sprout. If he was anything like me, it should be easy to keep him talking.

"You see, Laki was kind enough to demonstrate his powers for me, so I was kind enough to grant him a quick death." Eagan flipped his cloak back, revealing a narrow sword belted at his waist as he began walking towards me. "You, on the other hand." Eagan reached out to me, but Shan lunged, snapping at my brother's hand. The fire mage backed up a step, glaring at the horse while I hid a gasp of pain with laughter. Eagan looked over his shoulder at Kestral. "What do you feed this thing? Untempered steel and small children?"

"Mages," Kestral replied. He stood ready to draw his sword, flames licking at his boots, blue eyes promising a swift death. I had seen that look before.

Eagan tossed his head back and laughed easily, like a courtier at a ball. "Pretty and terse. We have similar tastes in more than just boots, Reshi."

My chest tightened inexplicably at the comment, but I kept my smile in place. "I'll trade him to you for the boots. The horse is part of the deal, though."

"Well, that's a deal breaker." Eagan turned his back on me, walking towards one of Laki's unshaped boulders. The same boulder that had grabbed Kestral earlier, in fact. He placed a hand on it and my stomach rolled as the boulder's shape twisted and changed. Part of it flattened out into a seat, the back part rising in what appeared to be flat, shallow mountains, or perhaps misshapen flames. "Hm, that didn't quite work out the way I had hoped."

"If it helps, I think Laki carved the stones by hand and only used his power to enliven them," I explained.

"It does help, thank you." Eagan smiled brightly. Dust, we had a lot of similar mannerisms. He sat back in the chair, crossing his ankle over his knee and placing his chin in his hands. He looked the part of a prince preparing to pass judgment. "As I was saying, I found Laki's demonstration of power quite helpful. Reshi, if you would be kind enough to do the same, I promise you a quick death."

"You know, as tempting as that is, I think I'm going to decline." I gave him a one-shouldered shrug.

"Oh no, you haven't heard the whole offer yet." Eagan held up a finger to halt me. "You get a painless death and your hunter friend here gets to walk free. And before you give me the whole 'I don't care what happens to him' farce, I saw how he patched you up after that last fight. You care, and I know it." Eagan laced his fingers together and set his chin on his hands. "Or I can begin burning him slowly, letting him scream long and loud for you until you show me everything you can do. Which will it be, baby brother?"

"That is a much better deal, I'll give you that." I kept one arm wrapped around my ribs while I scratched my head with the other, pretending to consider the deal. Eagan watched me patiently. I had a feeling that throwing a knife at him would only hasten the second option. "I'd like to take you up on it, but I'm afraid I can't."

Eagan narrowed his eyes and the circle of fire drew tighter on Kestral. I could smell the leather of his boots burning.

"It's not about him, Eagan, it's about my condition." I raised my shirt to show the bandages. "I'm a shapeshifter, but I can't physically shift while I'm injured. I'm not able to show you anything, even if I wanted to."

"Hmm." Eagan glared at me over his fingertips, mouth pursed while he considered. "All right. Just this once, I'm going to let you tell me all about your powers. You still get a quick death and he still goes free." He flipped his hands up in an elegant shrug. "You're getting a real steal here; I'm the one losing, really."

"You are generous." I nodded my thanks. "It makes this request sound selfish, but can I also ask a question?"

"Ah, well, if you make it quick."

"Why come for Laki and me in the first place? Why not hunt down Velyn? He collected Cera's magic so he's a much better catch than I am."

Eagan tipped his head to one side, eyes narrowing. "So, it was Velyn who killed little Cera?"

"Yes," I said quickly, hope catching in my chest. "He stabbed her through the heart with an icicle dagger, then he gathered her magic. I was too far away to help. He tried to kill me next."

Eagan stared at me over his hands for a moment as if trying to decide whether he believed me or not. "While I'm grateful for this information, it doesn't change the fact that I need your magic. Take heart in the fact that I will use your strength to take revenge for sweet Cera."

That wasn't the response I was hoping to hear, in all honesty. "Why not join us and fight Velyn? I won't fight you for his magic once he's dead. I don't have any designs on taking the throne or stealing magic or anything."

Eagan chuckled softly. "What makes you think I need your help to kill Velyn? I'm the second oldest of Laurana's children; I could kill any of you any time I like."

I struggled and failed to keep the smirk from my face. "Any time at all?"

Eagan narrowed his eyes. "What are you—"

The rain started so suddenly that for a moment I thought I had been dropped into a lake. The flames around Kestral went out and though Eagan tried to fling more, the rain simply doused them. Kestral and Eagan both looked around in surprise, then Eagan cursed, rising to his feet and looking around.

"My brothers. So nice to find you all here." A patch of mist solidified into my brother Velyn, smiling darkly at the both of us. "Looks like I'm too late to meet Laki. Shame."

Seeing his face rekindled my rage over Cera's death. While Laki's death was sad, he had been trying to kill me. Cera had been innocent. The false humor I played at with Eagan vanished, replaced by a cold fury. I flicked my left hand, a throwing knife falling into place. Before I could throw, Kestral's hand was on my wrist, holding it back. He shook his head, then tilted it towards Shan. Did he want to run?

"So, you're the one who killed little Cera, are you?" Eagan looked Velyn up and down. "I hope you still hear her voice every night before you fall asleep, as I do."

"Only some nights." Velyn shrugged, trying to look callous, but his white-blue eyes flickered with something like shame.

"Let me relieve you of that burden, brother." Eagan shoved both hands out before him, fire curling and raging forward. Velyn simply raised a hand, palm up, and the rain increased, dousing the flames.

"I was going to come for you sooner or later, but now seems as good a time as any." Velyn reached to the sky, calling down lightning. Eagan leapt back, but the lightning singed the edges of his cloak. The playfulness had left his face now, anger and fear replacing it.

Kestral looped one arm around my waist and reached for Shan's saddle with the other. Before he could grab it, lightning struck the ground in front of us, sending grass and dirt flying. Shan reared, his eyes wild in panic. I gripped his mind with mine, gritting my teeth as I willed him not to bolt. The boom of the following thunder rang in my ears, making it difficult to hear Velyn speaking. "Stay right there, Reshi. If you rush me, I won't be able to properly coalesce your power. Just wait until I finish dealing with Eagan."

"By all means, come deal with me, rainy-day mage." Eagan tossed his cloak back over his shoulder before raising his palm towards Velyn. Tree branches whipped against the wind, one striking Velyn in the gut, tossing him roughly to the wet ground. Green vines pulled free of their trees, twining themselves around Velyn's arms and legs, pinning him in place. He struggled, but the vines refused to break. "You were right, Reshi. This power is more about manipulation than creation. I knew I'd get the hang of it."

"Glad to help," I muttered, reluctant to take sides as the winner would most likely attempt to kill me next.

Kestral leaned low, still holding me around the waist. "How did you know Velyn was near?"

"The sky," I replied, briefly looking up. "It never got bright again after the smoke cleared."

Kestral nodded, his expression grim as he watched Eagan advance on the fallen Velyn. A vine snaked its way around Velyn's throat, bringing a vicious smile to our oldest brother's face. Velyn's eyes flashed just before he was struck by his own lightning, burning away the vines and singing his clothes. He stood, unharmed but faintly smoking, and raised a hand towards Eagan. The fire mage snarled, throwing his hands out in front of him.

Kestral gripped my right wrist, turning it over, his fingers scrambling beneath the cuff. I tried to help him without revealing my own plan. My light-fingered left hand untied the small crossbow from his belt. It was still loaded from our fight with Laki. All I had to do was aim.

"Tell me, did Cera cry at the end?" Eagan asked, eyes hot with fury.

"She never saw it coming," Velyn hissed. "And neither will you."

In the midst of thunder booming and trees lashing, Kestral whipped one of my throwing knives free, hurling it at Velyn's neck. I fired the crossbow over his shoulder, aiming for Eagan's chest. A lightning bolt redirected itself, blasting the knife out of the air and a roar of flame leapt from the ground, consuming the crossbow bolt, but before either brother could react, Kestral vaulted into Shan's saddle, hauling me along with him. Shan took off like a hunter's arrow, racing through the woods at a reckless canter. I nearly tumbled free at the sudden start, but Kestral tightened his grip around my chest. Every step the horse took was pure agony. Pain lanced through my ribs, making it difficult to draw a breath. It all became too much, and my vision slowly faded to black.

5

Consciousness came back to me slowly, like water seeping through wood. The smell of old manure and hay guided me back from the realms of sleep. I was flat on my back, something soft cushioning my head. I forced my eyes to open and found myself looking up at wooden planks high above me. Rays of light filtered through the tiny gaps between the planks. Motes of dust and hay danced in the light, dizzyingly fast, and I shut my eyes again with a groan.

"Don't sit up," an emotionless voice ordered.

I ignored him and tried to sit up. My right side burned as if on fire and I lay back down.

"I told you not to sit up."

I twisted to my left this time, getting one arm beneath me to push myself up into a sitting position. "Where are we?"

"Abandoned barn." Kestral sat somewhere to my right.

I struggled to turn without hurting myself. Near the back wall of the barn, Shan sifted through windblown piles of leaves, picking out pieces of hay.

"You should lie still."

I was naked to the waist, except for the bandage wrapped tightly around my broken ribs. I had been lying on my cloak with my shirt balled up beneath my head. A familiar fear crept up on me and I checked to ensure my pants hadn't slid down my waist. Reassured, I looked around. "How did we get . . . are you—" My stomach rolled, and I begged myself not to vomit; that would surely only cause more pain to my ribs. "Are you stitching your own leg?"

Kestral glanced up from his seat on an old crate. Soot was stuck to his face where blood had dried, though a fresh trickle seeped through his messy hair. He had slipped out of one of his pant legs and was, most definitely, sewing up a long wound on his outer thigh. "Lie back down before you hurt yourself."

This time I listened, lowering myself carefully and lying on my left side, right arm hugging my aching ribs. I took a few moments to catch my breath and swallow down the urge to be sick. Of course Kestral was sewing himself back up. That was probably battlefield injury treatment lesson one. I simply couldn't bear to watch. Once my stomach settled and I heard the rustle of clothing, I lifted myself carefully again. After lacing up his pants and pulling his boot back on, Kestral walked steadily over to me, betraying neither pain nor limp. He stood over me, looking down at me as I rested on my left elbow.

"Was it true when you told your brother you can't shift while injured?"

Shrugging was difficult and a little painful. "Did it set off your liar's brand?"

"You lived with a fairy. You know there are variable degrees of truth."

I sighed. "I can't shift with broken bones. Superficial injuries don't bother me, but broken bones tear me up if I try to shift."

"So, you're stuck like this?"

"Don't sound so disappointed." I grinned up at him. "This is my prettiest form, after all."

"Hm." Kestral walked back to the box he had been sitting on, where he'd set up an array of ointments, bandages and jars of powder. "Are you injured anywhere else?"

I did a quick inventory. I had accumulated several cuts and bruises that I couldn't recall receiving, but nothing that required attention. I was grateful that Kestral hadn't tried to fully undress me to check for injuries. After relaying this information, Kestral began packing away his supplies.

"What about your head?" I asked. Fresh blood oozed down his face, but Kestral merely swiped at it in annoyance.

"What about my—" Kestral stopped, noticing blood on his hand for the first time. "That's not mine."

"Dust it's not yours, it keeps coming out of your hair." I grunted, forcing myself to my feet. "One of the flying critters must have fallen on you at some point in the fight."

Kestral wet a hand cloth and scrubbed the side of his face. He grimaced as it came away covered in ash and blood.

"Let me get it," I offered, placing a hand on his chest to press him down onto the box. I didn't press hard—I couldn't—but Kestral sat. I used the wet cloth to clean his face. As I wiped away some of the congealed blood around his hairline, more dripped down. "How does this not hurt?"

Kestral shrugged. "None of it hurts much any more."

"Some day you'll have to tell me what types of battles you've been through so that head injuries don't hurt any more."

"Some day you'll have to tell me about growing up in Giltner."

I shook my head, holding his head still so I could peer through his thick hair. "Goldwater Whiskey, remember? Lots of it. Sorry if this stings." I found the cut and pressed the cloth to it. Kestral didn't flinch, merely grunted and withstood the paltry amount of pressure I could apply. "What do you have to clean it with?"

"Here." He held up a bottle of brown liquid. "Does it need stitching?"

"If it does, we're going to have to find a priest. Can't help you with stitches." I poured the brown, acrid liquid over the cut. "It's not that big, really. It is bleeding a lot, though."

"Head wounds usually do. Use this." Kestral held up a bottle of clear liquid and a small brush, the kind women used to paint their lips.

"What is that?"

"It's like a glue. For skin." Kestral pushed the bottle at me. "Just smear it over the cut while holding the skin together."

"Ugh, I did not sign up for this." With a grimace, I wet the brush and painted it over the cut, trying to ignore the blood still oozing from the wound.

"You didn't expect injuries on your path to vengeance?" Kestral asked. It seemed like I was more bothered by his head wound than he was.

"I expected that once I found vengeance, I'd be too dead to worry about injuries." I held the cut closed, giving the liquid time to dry. "So where are we on the whole vengeance thing if Eagan kills Velyn?"

"It looked far more likely that Velyn would kill Eagan. In either case, the one who walks away will be all that much more powerful."

"Yeah, they both have double powers now, so one of them could have four times the power." I ruffled Kestral's hair and stepped away. The glue appeared to be working, which was good. I really would have been sick if he tried stitching his own head wound closed. "If Laurana's kids keep killing each other, there aren't going to be any bounties for you hunters to collect."

Kestral tossed his head back and laughed. Just like on the first day I met him it was long and loud and hard. I would have found it more amusing if I wasn't half-worried it was caused by his head injury. I found Kestral's waterskin on the floor, took a long draught and waited for him to stop. When he finally caught his breath, Kestral's eyes were bright and clear, still smiling as he met my eyes. Slowly, the smile faded.

"Can your family find you?"

I shrugged. "Velyn has Cera's far-sight, so maybe. If he can use it like she did."

Kestral nodded, thoughtful. "Eagan had some trouble using Laki's power. Velyn could be struggling with Cera's."

"Maybe." I touched my hair with my left hand, dismayed at the mess it was in after our battle and subsequent escape. I pulled the tie out and tried to smooth it back one-handedly. "Why do you ask?"

"We probably need to keep moving." Kestral watched me for a moment. "Hopefully their battle continues awhile so we can get farther away. Stop. You're going to hurt yourself."

"Breathing hurts me, but I'm not going to stop doing that," I countered, painfully raising my right arm to fix my hair.

Kestral stood, striding right to me and taking my elbow. "Sit down."

"Don't tell me what to—Ugh!" Kestral barely turned my arm before the radiating pain through my ribs cut me off. With light touches, Kestral turned me and pushed me back to sit on the box he had been using. I curled my arm defensively around my chest while Kestral stepped behind me, smoothing my hair back. "I don't want it to look like yours."

"It already does," Kestral replied. "I couldn't make it worse if I tried."

A clever response came to me, but I swallowed it. He hurt me even when he was trying to be gentle; goading him while in a vulnerable position just seemed like a poor idea. After a minute or two, he held out his hand for the tie. I passed it over and he tied off my tail. It sat a little higher than I usually liked, but overall it was better than I could have done with only my left hand.

"Thanks," I said, patting at my hair.

Kestral shrugged, looking away. He gave a soft whistle and Shan trotted up, looking fresher after his rest. As he prepared Shan for a ride, I went to my pile of clothes and pulled them back on, awkwardly tying on my cloak using only one hand. When I looked back, Kestral was holding Shan by the reins. "Mount up."

"Me?" I chuckled, gently rubbing my side. "I can't ride like this. And you said he can't carry us both."

"He can't. I'm going to lead. You're going to rest your ribs." Kestral had his usual expressionless face back. "It's going to take months for you to heal completely. Walking will only stress your injury."

"No, I can probably get over this in about a week." I eyed Shan warily; his ears were half-pinned even though he stood perfectly still. "Less, if you let me draw deeply."

Kestral backed Shan up a step to glare at me. "What?"

I shrugged. "I heal quickly. In my sleep. Life force is restorative. It restores me."

Kestral blinked, then stared off for a moment, thinking deeply. "All right. There's a chance then. Mount up."

"Um . . ." I stared up at the saddle, wondering just how I was to get up without hurting myself. With a sigh, Kestral led Shan to the box, which was much easier to climb. A quick hop had me in the saddle, one hand down to steady myself, the other holding my side. "So where are we going?"

"For now, just away." Kestral led Shan to the entrance of the barn, looking around carefully before stepping out. "I want as much distance between you and them as possible."

"Aw." I grinned down at Kestral. "It's almost like you care about me."

Kestral glanced back quickly, then looked ahead again. "Keep quiet. Laki could talk to trees, remember?"

"Yeah, but Eagan—" A dark look from Kestral shut me up. With a grumble, I agreed to the silence. Talking hurt anyway. So did riding. And everything, really. How could normal people allow injuries to heal naturally? It seemed so inconvenient. To keep myself from talking, I rooted around in Kestral's saddle bags until I found an apple. Shan rolled an eye back at me as I crunched into it. I grinned and taunted him with the fruit wickedly. The horse responded by intentionally tripping over a root, jarring my ribs. Well played, beast. Well played.

Two of my siblings were dead and two others were murderers. Cera's death still weighed on me, an ache in my chest different from the broken ribs but just as sharp. She had been the only one I had known before this whole adventure began, even if I had only known her as a voice in my dreams. All she had wanted was for Laurana's children to stand united. And now two of us were dead.

Maybe three, after Eagan and Velyn's fight ended. Or four, if they killed each other, but I probably wasn't that lucky. Who was left, then? Just my sisters, Kila and Reina. I didn't know anything at all about Reina. I could probably pass her in a tavern and never recognize her. But Kila was easily found, a hardened warrior who slew all who came against her. Should I try to find her next? If what Laki said was true, she would be willing to fight whichever brother emerged victorious from this latest battle. But what if she turned on me? There was no way I could stand against someone who killed without even using her magic.

But I've got Kestral, I thought, watching him walk along beside Shan. She couldn't be stronger than him, right? So far no one has been stronger than Kestral. Not without magic, at least.

I considered the idea of asking Kila for help as Kestral eventually led us back to a path wide enough to be called a road. The sky was still darkly overcast, but it wasn't raining on the road. Towers of smoke rose up between the clouds. I supposed the battle was still raging. A powerful feeling hit me hard enough to make my ribs hurt. It was like a cross between relief and gratitude at Kestral for getting me away from my brothers. If not for him, I would have been dead at Velyn's feet over a week ago.

Kestral led Shan along the road well after sunset. I nodded off in the saddle, nearly slipping off at one point until Kestral prodded me awake. I started as I realized we had left the woods and were on a fairly open road between farms. My chest tightened as I frantically searched for a hiding place. As a shapeshifter, I could usually hide in plain sight, but while stuck in my human form, I needed something more substantial than a bedroll under an open sky.

"Kestral, where—"

He pointed. "Empty grain silo. Farmers are in for the night, they'll never know."

It was a little creepy the way he had just read my mind like that. "How do you know it's empty?"

Kestral glanced back at me. "Anything from last year would have gone bad by now. It's not the right season to fill it again yet."

"Ah." I had lived in a village of farmers and never learned so much about grain and silos. Kestral led Shan off the trail, cutting across a field towards the tall wooden structure. The door wasn't locked, but if it was empty, why bother locking it? With a hand from Kestral, I dismounted and helped set up our camp for the night. Kestral unsaddled Shan and turned him loose for the evening while I laid out the bedroll. I wasn't even hungry. Just eating the apple earlier had hurt and I was more tired than anything else. With a yawn, I curled up inside the bedroll.

"What are you doing?" Kestral asked, glancing over at me.

"Sleeping." I tried to only stretch the half of my body that didn't hurt. "I told you, I heal in my sleep."

Kestral stared for a minute before asking: "Where am I supposed to sleep?"

"There's room." I scooted over and patted the blankets.

His blue eyes narrowed. "No."

"What?" I looked up, surprised. "Kestral, I have slept with you just about every night I've known you."

"As a cat."

"Yeah." I blinked. "What the dust is the difference?"

Kestral loomed over me, icy eyes glittering. "Unless you are a cat, we are not sharing a bedroll."

I sighed, rubbing my side. "Look, I can't turn into a cat until I heal. I can't heal until I draw enough to fill my well. I can't draw at all unless you sleep next to me. But you don't want to sleep next to me until I'm a cat again. You see where I'm going with this?"

A muscle in Kestral's jaw ticked. "You want to share a bedroll for the next week in order to heal yourself?"

"Less if you let me draw more deeply." I shrugged. "It's up to you."

"If you draw all you need, how long until you're healed?"

"Maybe three days? Four? I've never broken ribs before, but if I can draw a lot I can heal fairly quickly."

Kestral rubbed his leg where he had stitched it earlier that day, as if preparing himself for something just as distasteful. "Fine. Take what you need, just heal as quickly as you can." He shrugged out of his leather armor and removed his belt, setting his sword within arm's reach of the bedroll. "Roll over." He settled into the bedroll carefully, setting his back against mine.

I grinned, pressing back against him. Honestly, it was the weirdest argument ever. He knew who I was even as a cat and he knew I'd been drawing from him. The only difference was a little less space in the bedroll. His back against mine was a warm, familiar presence and I found myself dropping towards sleep. I had to remind myself to stay awake until Kestral nodded off, so I could draw from him.

After three failed attempts to draw from his life force, I tipped my head back towards his. "You know you have to be asleep for this to work, right?"

"Shut up," he growled. "I'm trying."

"Are you hungry? I didn't see you eat."

"Not hungry, stop talking."

I shifted, trying to get comfortable again. I waited, then tried to draw again but failed. "Is your leg hurting you? You still have that numbing ointment, right?"

"If you keep moving and talking, you aren't going to get the chance to heal."

"Why not? You going to sleep somewhere else?"

"No. I'm going to kill you."

I sighed, moving once more to get comfortable. Forget him; I was mostly full of magic anyway, so I simply let myself drop off to sleep.

When my well of magical energy drained completely, I awoke. My ribs still throbbed painfully, but the ache was less than it had been. Somehow Kestral had rolled onto his back, throwing one arm wide and pillowing my head with it. This wasn't too strange, as he normally slept with one arm over me as a cat. I shifted a bit closer, resting my head on his shoulder then drawing deeply of his life force. Instead of feeling the magic gather in my chest, it trickled directly into my side, healing the broken ribs and torn muscles. I drew as deeply as I dared, staying awake until I couldn't any more. I drifted off with a smile, wondering how upset Kestral would be in the morning to find me cuddled against him.

I never found out what his reaction was. Kestral was out of the bedroll the following morning before I woke. A cold breakfast of cheese and fruit had been left beside the bedroll but Kestral's bags were gone. I ate, rolled up the bedroll and stepped outside the grain silo. Shan was picketed and waiting, but I didn't see Kestral nearby. After tying the bedroll to the saddle bags, I stretched, testing my side. Definitely still some broken bones but moving was a little easier than it had been. I eyed Shan warily.

"If I untie you, are you going to take off or let me mount?"

Shan swished his tail back and forth, the picture of equine innocence.

"I'm not buying it, murder-horse." I stepped back and looked around for Kestral again. The field surrounding the grain silo was open and empty. If he was near I should have seen him. "Okay, horse of death, here's the deal. If you let me ride you, I'll give you an apple when we find Kestral. Got it?"

Shan snorted and shook his head. I took that to mean he accepted the deal. After releasing him from the ground tie, I mounted clumsily. My side was still in pain, but I had enough range of movement to pull myself up. Shan started trotting before I was fully settled, so I grabbed a handful of his mane and held on, hoping he knew where he was going.

I hadn't noticed that a small stream cut across the farm, a tiny furrow in an otherwise flat field. Shan slowed as he approached the edge of the stream and whickered softly. Kestral looked up from his fishing line, wet hair shading his eyes.

"Are you two friends now?" Kestral asked as I carefully climbed down from Shan's saddle.

"I think friends is too strong a word." I rooted through Kestral's food satchel and found an apple for the monster horse. "More like we've come to an understanding."

Kestral nodded. "You look like you're moving better."

"Still hurts." I rubbed my side, grimacing. "Catch anything good? I love fish."

"Nothing." Kestral wound in his line and wrapped it in a small leather pouch. "I came down to wash and wait for you to wake up. I was going to hunt, but I'm still tired." A glare accompanied that last comment.

"You said to take whatever I needed to heal." I rolled my good shoulder in a shrug. "Mind if I wash up?"

"Go ahead." Kestral stood, stretched, and walked up the small embankment to Shan. I kept an eye on him, making sure his back was turned before stripping down. It's not that I'm shy or anything, I just didn't want him seeing the marks on my hip. I waded into the waist-deep water, leaving my clothes and weapons on the shore. Above me, Kestral combed out Shan's tail with his fingers.

"So where are we going now?" I called, checking to make sure the water obscured everything below my waist. "Any sign of Velyn or Eagan?"

"No sign of them," Kestral called, his back still to me. "I think we should follow Laki's advice and go to Kila."

"I thought about that, but . . ." I hesitated, dunking my head underwater to think before responding. "Kila's really strong. What if she decides to kill me for my magic?"

Kestral shrugged. "If Kila wanted to kill her siblings for magic, you would all be dead by now. Laki said he met with her once, but he walked away unscathed."

"Do we know that for sure?" I asked, wringing water from my hair. Dust it, I would need his help to tie it back again. "Maybe Laki escaped. Or maybe she didn't know about the whole power-stealing thing."

"I doubt Laki could have gotten away from her if she wanted him dead. Also, the one report that always comes back from hunters who survive Kila is that she doesn't use magic. You might be safe if we use you as a lure so that Kila can kill whichever brother comes for you."

I stepped onto the bank of the stream, swiping water from my limbs with a corner of my cloak. Something drew my eyes to the west and a sigh escaped my lips.

"What?" Kestral glanced over his shoulder. I lifted the cloak as a shield until he looked away again.

"Every time I've met one of my siblings, they've either been murdered or turned into a murderer. It's like I'm heralding their deaths."

"You don't have to worry about that with Kila."

"What makes you so sure?"

"I doubt Kila would die as easily as Cera or Laki. And we already know she's a killer."

"Somehow that's less than comforting." After tugging on my pants and boots, I climbed the stream bank and held out the roll of bandages to Kestral. Without a word, he rebound my ribs. "Can you pull my hair back, too? It still hurts to raise my arm."

Kestral's mouth twisted as if he had swallowed something sour, but he nodded.

I turned around and gentle fingers gathered my hair back before tying it into a tail. I pulled my shirt on, checked my weapons, then turned back to face him.

"I can walk today, if you want."

"No. You'll heal quicker if you ride. Mount up."

I considered arguing even though I knew he was right. He had to be tired, considering how much I had drawn from him last night, but he wouldn't appreciate any sympathy from me. I climbed up carefully and this time Shan held still until I was firmly seated. Kestral led us back to the road, heading west.

"How do you know where Kila is?" I asked.

"Everyone knows where Kila is." I could hear the smirk in his voice. "She's on the bloodiest battlefield in the kingdom."

"That bodes well for me," I muttered, leaning back in the saddle. I looked around for signs of Velyn's storm or Eagan's fire but saw nothing obvious. Strangely, I didn't think either one of them was dead. I wasn't certain of it, though. Without Cera, I had no psychic link to the rest of my siblings, but somehow, I thought I would know if one of them had died. Laki had mentioned an awakened link between himself and Kila after Cera's death, which seemed to mean that although Velyn had taken the majority of her power, some had dispersed to the rest of us. Now that Laki was dead, I thought I felt an increased sentience from the plant life around me. It was a little like my ability to communicate with animals, but different. As if I could hear the plants but they were speaking another language. As Kestral was content to walk in silence, I spent the day trying to listen to the plants along the side of the road, seeking to understand. When that grew boring, I dug a coin out of my pocket and walked it over my knuckles, switching hands several times throughout the day. Kestral glanced back at the coin once but said nothing, which was lucky as it was one of the coins I had stolen from his former comrades.

After nightfall, Kestral found shelter under a natural rock formation just off the road. A tall, gray rock jutted up high enough to hide the sky and beneath it lay thick, pillowy moss which was perfect for the bedroll. I tried to start a conversation over dinner, but

Kestral just ignored me. The way he kept glancing at the bedroll, I figured he was still feeling awkward about sleeping together. So was I, but for a completely different reason.

In complete honesty, I found Kestral attractive. Highly attractive. If I had met him in a bar, I would have convinced him to buy me a drink and then let him take me upstairs. I mean, with those eyes and those broad shoulders, he was exactly my type. The whole "I'll kill you" thing had put me off him for a while, but since we had grown closer, the attraction was getting harder to fight. For stars' sake, we were sleeping together! How could I not be attracted to him?

And then there were those comments from Kestral's former soldiers, about "pretty boys" and "tailfeathers." Even if Kestral didn't feel the same as I did, sex was sex, right? Maybe I could loosen him up a little, get rid of some of the awkward feelings between us. And if he felt differently about killing me afterwards, so much the better.

"Hey Kestral," I started, carefully stretching my left arm luxuriously. "How about a little of that Goldwater? Just a taste?"

He glared at me, brows furrowed.

"It'll help me sleep through the pain." I rubbed my right side, trying to look innocent. "It'll probably help you sleep, too."

He considered my argument, then shook his head. He cast another shifty glance at the bedroll, then stared into the fire.

"I'll trade a question for a sip," I offered. "I won't ask you one in return. Just not about where I grew up."

Kestral sighed. "Are you going to keep pestering me until I give in?"

I shrugged my good shoulder. "Yeah, that's about the size of it."

He rummaged through his satchel until he found the waterskin. He took a short pull and corked it, pulling it away from me as I reached for it. "Who taught you to throw knives?"

Of course, he would ask a question I'd avoided earlier. I sighed, taking a moment to get my story in order without lying or revealing too much. "I forget her name, but she was a caravan guard. I used to watch her spar with the other guards and I asked her to teach me, but she laughed at me. Said I was too skinny to hold a sword, never mind use it. Instead, she taught me to throw knives."

"How old were you?"

Ugh, had I told him he could ask follow-up questions? "I don't know. Twelve, maybe. Something close to that, anyway."

"How long did she train you?"

I bit my lip. Kestral locked eyes with me as he took another short pull from the waterskin. I exhaled in exasperation. "Less than a year. Nine months, probably."

"How long were the two of you traveling in the same caravan?"

"No, that's all you get." I leaned forward and pulled the waterskin from his hands. He could have resisted, but he let it slide through his hands. I took a long draught, making up for the extra answers he'd pulled from me. The liquor was smooth and heady, burning a trail of fire down my throat. I felt it light a comfortable fire in my chest. After a moment, Kestral tugged the waterskin back from me.

"Did she train you in anything besides knife throwing?" Kestral asked. He shook the waterskin, indicating I could have another sip. This plan was completely backfiring on me, but stars did I want more of that whiskey.

"Some dagger grips and stances. That's it." I reached for the waterskin, brushing Kestral's hand with mine as I took it. I took a shorter sip this time and passed it back. I was hoping Kestral would drink more, as he needed more loosening up than I did, but he secured the cork and put it away. While he was turned away, I unfastened my cloak and skinned out of my shirt, unwrapping the bandages around my chest. Kestral turned back and blinked, almost appearing surprised.

"What are you doing?" he asked.

"Getting ready for bed." I wound the bandage around my hand, so it would be easy to put back on in the morning. "It's hard for me to breathe with this on. And I think it's cutting off some blood flow."

Kestral frowned but said nothing. He watched as I stood and sauntered over to the bedroll, preparing to lie down. After putting a boot through the fire to reduce it down, he followed. I curled up on my left side, pillowing my head with my arm. Cloth rustled as Kestral stripped out of his travel leathers before he lay down with his back to mine.

"You sleep better on your back," I said, facing away. I could feel him glaring at me, though. "I'm pointing it out because you had trouble sleeping last night and my wellspring is completely dry right now. I can't start healing until you fall asleep."

Kestral grunted, then shifted carefully so he didn't jostle my ribs. He tucked the arm closest to me under his head, which was perfect. I shimmied back towards him, tucking myself under that arm. Under the pretext of moving my hair out from under me, I lifted my head and settled it on his shoulder. Kestral tensed but said nothing. I let a moment pass in silence before rolling back against him, turning my head so I could smell the whiskey on his breath. With my right hand, I reached for the laces on the front of his shirt.

Kestral's hand caught mine. "What are you doing?"

"Relieving some of the tension between us." I gave him a lazy smile. "You'll sleep better for it. I promise."

"No." Kestral pushed my hand back and tried to pull away. I rolled with him, pressing against him from hip to shoulder and wrapping an ankle around his.

"Why not? It won't change anything between us." I gripped the top blanket and pulled it taut, smirking as I glanced down the plane it made against our bodies. "And that doesn't look like an objection you're raising."

I gasped as Kestral shoved me away roughly, pushing against my injured ribs. I saw stars and blinked back tears of pain as Kestral kicked free of the bedroll and stood. By the time I could see clearly again, Kestral had pulled his boots and leathers back on and was walking away from the campsite.

"Where are you going?" I asked, my voice tight from pain.

"Hunting." Kestral scooped up his bow and strung it in the faint firelight. "I'll be back after you fall asleep."

"But I—"

Kestral turned and walked away quickly, disappearing into the trees.

I wrapped my arm around my side, holding back a whimper. I needed to be awake to be able to fill my well, Kestral knew that. Stars, but I must have really dusted him up to get him to react like that. He couldn't really hunt in the dark anyway; most prey animals were in their lairs by now. My ribs ached, keeping me up for long hours into the night. I wondered what would happen if Kestral returned before I fell asleep, then decided I didn't want to find out. I tossed and rolled, trying to find a path to sleep.

This would be when Cera would reach out to me, I realized with a sigh. I used to hear her voice right before I succumbed to sleep, urging me to join up with her and our siblings. I felt a pang in my chest different from the ache in my ribs. It was still strange to think I'd never hear her voice again.

I drifted off thinking of Cera, trying to remember the sound of her voice in my dreams. By the time the horizon turned a hazy gray, I awoke to find Kestral's back to me. Greedily, I soaked up whatever I could, willing my ribs to heal faster. The gold magic gathered in my side, easing the pain and knitting my bones back together. I lay awake, soaking it in and watching the stars slowly wink out. The sky brightened slowly, turning pink, then orange. Taking great care not to wake Kestral, I wriggled out of the bedroll and gathered up my clothes. Shan eyed me from his ground tie as I slunk off to dress.

Kestral will be mad when he wakes up, I thought, struggling to tie my own hair. My ribs were feeling a lot better. They still twinged when I turned, but at least I could turn now. Should I make breakfast as an apology? Knowing him, he would probably wake up before I could get the fire lit.

Why did I have to apologize anyway? He was the one who overreacted and used my injury against me. I had only been trying to be nice to him. And, being completely honest, the worst part was the rejection. I didn't hear the word "no" very often and I had it on good authority that I was attractive. It stung that Kestral didn't seem to think so. Okay, so I was a little vain. Or maybe a lot. I was a cat, I was allowed to be vain.

I pondered over how to put the situation behind us, and my mind kept going back to breakfast. I must have been hungry. Kestral had left his flint on the stones surrounding the fire, so, with one eye on Kestral, I tried lighting a cooking fire. It took a few attempts, but I was proud to see a spark catch. I kept the fire low, then rummaged through Kestral's bag for something to cook. My search yielded thinly sliced pork belly, cheese, a potato and a small packet of herbs. We'd have to stop in a town soon or else we'd starve. I arranged the stones so I could set Kestral's cooking pan over the fire and began frying the pork belly.

I lost track of time as I cooked. By the time I began cooking the potato in pork grease, I completely missed Kestral waking up. I jumped when he stepped up across the fire from me. Our eyes met for a moment and I searched his for any remaining anger over last night. He looked the same as ever—emotionless and implacable. After a moment, he sat down and helped himself to some of the pork. I finished the mashed potatoes and scooped half of it into his only bowl. Too hungry to wait, I ate from the pan.

"How are your ribs?" Kestral asked, not glancing up from his breakfast.

"Better." I twisted, showing him my range of motion. "Not completely healed, but nearly."

Kestral nodded, still not glancing up. "You should walk today. Give Shan a break."

"Sure." I finished the last sliver of pork and began cleaning up. "Looks like you're running low on food. Maybe we should stop by a village."

He shook his head, swiping out his bowl with a cloth. "I don't want bystanders caught in the crossfire if one of your brothers catches up to you."

"What about food?" I asked, my voice low.

Kestral finally glanced across the fire at me. "Any idea which of your brothers survived the fight?"

I shook my head. "This is going to sound weird, but I don't think either of them is dead. It's just a feeling I have."

Kestral nodded as if that made perfect sense. "We've put a lot of distance between us and them. Regardless of who wins, he'll be magically drained for a while. I suppose you also don't know how they regain their magic?"

"Yes, in the ten minutes I spent with Eagan, he decided to tell me all his deepest, darkest secrets." I rolled my eyes. "I'm pretty sure Velyn recovers magic by drowning puppies, or something else horrible."

Kestral glared at me. "Is it ever possible for you to give a one-word answer?"

"Where's the fun in that?" I replied.

Kestral's mouth turned up in a tiny smirk before he looked away. "How many more nights until you're fully healed?"

I flexed and twisted. "Probably just tonight. Maybe two."

"Make it one." Kestral stood and began loading Shan with satchels. I cleaned up breakfast and the campsite, trying to stay out of Kestral's way as much as possible. I still wasn't sure how upset he was with me.

Once Shan was loaded with our supplies, Kestral took him by the reins and led him back to the road. I followed a distance behind them—a wide distance, in case Shan got it in his head to try and kick me. Kestral didn't bother to check if I followed or not, which made me think he was still fairly upset with me. I hated awkward silences, but I was too afraid to try speaking to him, so I occupied myself by rolling coins in both hands simultaneously. It was difficult enough that it kept me distracted for a number of hours, especially when I dropped a coin and had to chase after it. For all that, Kestral still didn't glance back or speak to me.

It was barely past midday when Kestral veered Shan off the road. I started to speak but one sharp look from Kestral snapped my mouth shut. I followed as Kestral wended his way through trees until he found a clearing sheltered from the wind by a wide, moss-covered boulder. He pulled the bags down from Shan as if preparing to set up camp before turning to face me.

"We're stopping so I can set some snares and sleep," he explained. "We're nearly out of food and I'm exhausted from you drawing from me."

I shrugged. "You wanted me to heal quicker."

"I still do. But I need a few hours of sleep without you draining me." Kestral slipped a small leather pouch from a bag and tossed it to me. "Find a stream and catch us some fish for tonight. I'll go set snares."

I peeked inside the bag and found a few fish hooks and fine string. The thought of fresh fish for dinner put a smile on my face for the first time that day. "Too bad I used the last of the herbs on breakfast. They would have been perfect for fish. Do you always wait until your food runs out before catching more?"

"I'm not normally between villages for this long."

I flinched. It was my fault he was sticking to back roads and forest trails.

"Reshi."

I looked up slowly, meeting his eyes.

"I don't care that we're out in the back hills. I enjoy hunting for my food and sleeping out in the open. But if you try anything like you did last night, I will serve you up to your brothers like a meal."

I laughed darkly. "Don't worry, your message was painfully clear last night." I rubbed my side. "I don't get it, though. Don't soldiers normally kick up dust at hen houses, or with each other, or whoever happens to be nearby?"

"Some do," Kestral acknowledged, sifting through his bags for small animal traps. He took a deep breath before continuing, "I know you don't want to talk about Giltner. There are things I don't want to talk about either."

"And one of those things is why you don't want to kick up the dust with me?" I snuck a glance at him as I threaded a fish hook. His eyes were shadowed, his movements slow and deliberate.

"Yes."

"Fine, then." I shrugged as I tucked the hook back inside the bag. "But if you ever change your mind, the offer's open."

Kestral glanced up at me, his eyebrows raised.

I smiled coquettishly. "I wouldn't mind the diversion. And it's not like it'll change your mind from turning in my bounty."

Kestral opened his mouth then shut it and looked away. I shrugged and turned to leave the clearing. "Do you want me to wake you for dinner, Kestral?"

"No, let me sleep. I'll check the traps in the morning."

"Suit yourself." I pushed through a hedge of bushes, listening for the sound of rushing water.

"Reshi."

I glanced back.

Kestral was still crouched over a satchel, his blue eyes watching me. He seemed hesitant for some reason. "Be careful. We don't know where your brothers are."

I nodded, acknowledging his words even as I discarded them. For some reason I knew, beyond a doubt, that neither Velyn nor Eagan were close by. Even if they were, they were probably still magically drained. And I was still hoping they had killed each other, despite how unlikely that was to be true.

It turned out to be a perfect day for fishing. The afternoon was hot enough to make me drowsy as I lounged in the shade of a large tree, watching the three hooks I had set in the river. By sunset I had caught four good-sized sharp-spine trout, so I made my way back to the campsite while I still had enough light to find it.

Kestral had built a small firepit and tied Shan to a ground stake before falling asleep, it seemed. He was curled up in his bedroll, one arm across his eyes to block the light. I set a fire as quietly as possible and began cleaning my trout. When I was halfway finished, Shan snorted at me. I paused to toss an apple at him and scrounged around for several long sticks to cook the trout on. Dusk covered the clearing by the time the first fish was ready to eat.

As predicted, the fish was bland without herbs, but I ate anyway, hungry from missing lunch. I wrapped the other fish in oilcloth from Kestral's food satchel, sneaking a quick sip of Goldwater Whiskey as I did. After circling the campsite to ensure it was as secure as possible, I stirred the fire to reduce it to embers. I approached the bedroll slowly, noting Kestral's sword within arm's reach, as usual.

I sighed. I was lucky he had only hit me. With that thought, I loosened the ties on my shirt before skinning out of it. I placed my weapons beneath it, easily within reach in case I needed them. I stepped out of my boots and eased into the bedroll as gently as possible, taking care not to jostle Kestral. I put my back to him and tepidly drew on his life force. More than anything, I looked forward to sleeping as a cat again.

I awoke as the blanket pulled around me, rolling me from my side to my back. I blinked sleepily, the world slowly coming into focus.

Or, I should say, Kestral's looming form above me coming into focus.

"What . . ." I started to speak but cut myself off as Kestral's hand skimmed down my side. I drew a sharp breath, half scared, half aroused. He stared at me with such intensity that I found myself wondering if he was taking me up on my offer. The breath burst from my chest violently as Kestral pushed against the ribs on my right side. I flinched but the pain I expected didn't come.

"Looks like you've healed." Kestral withdrew his arm and turned so he sat beside me in the bedroll. "Can you shift again?"

"Wait. I'm still just waking up." The sky showed hints of the coming dawn—far, far too early for rational thought. I shook my head to clear it, then checked inside for my magic.

It was there, but dimly. The golden magic glimmered like a shrouded candle, light without heat.

"Yes, I can shift again." A glance at Kestral showed him watching me expectantly. "Don't you need to go check traps or feed Shan or something?" I lay back down and turned away from him, hoping he wouldn't notice the heat I felt on my cheeks.

Kestral snorted. He slid free of the bedroll and moved away from it, and me. Mornings were usually an uncomfortable time for me and waking up to Kestral hovering over me hadn't helped matters at all. I took deep, calming breaths as Kestral dressed, rustled through bags, then left the clearing. Once I was sure he was gone I kicked free of the blankets to go handle my body's needs. I made it back to the clearing before Kestral did, so I packed up the bedroll and prepared two of the fish for breakfast.

Kestral came back to camp, carrying three unfortunate rabbits along with his traps. He laid them beside his boots as he sat down and helped himself to a fish.

"I caught one more than you," I said with a smirk. "How does that feel, Sir Hunter?"

Kestral snorted. "Do you use your magic when you fish?"

I furrowed my brow, taken aback. "What? Why would I?"

"You talk to animals, right? Do you call them when you're fishing?"

"No. And it's not really like talking, it's more like encouraging natural instincts. Nothing gets caught on purpose." It disturbed me that Kestral would accuse me of using my magic in such a way. "Even if I could catch fish that way, it wouldn't be very sporting, would it?"

Kestral shrugged. "You're always so focused on your next meal that I didn't think you would care whether it was sporting or not."

"It's not that I'm always focused on the next meal, I just like knowing that there is a next meal," I grumbled, working a fish bone out of my teeth. "You're always so skinflint, I worry you can't afford the next meal."

"If you keep complaining, I'll just turn in a mage-born for his bounty." Kestral arched his brow at me. I chuckled as I tossed the remains of my breakfast into our cold fire pit.

"Don't think I'll make it easy for you." I glanced up at him. "You'll honor that head start, won't you?"

"I will." Kestral grinned. "You're going to fight me, Reshi?"

"Of course, but that's not exactly the plan." I smiled back. "No one runs and hides better than I do."

Kestral laughed. "I found you once. I can do it again."

"We'll see." I watched as Kestral tossed the rest of his fish on top of mine. He picked up one of his rabbits, flipped his belt knife out of its sheath and began skinning it. I watched him work for a minute before he noticed my gaze on him.

"You ever skin a rabbit before?"

I shook my head.

He threw one into my lap. "Cut the fur at the neck and tear."

I made a face and attempted to follow his instructions, making more of a mess than he did. To distract him from my disastrous skinning attempt, I asked, "How far are we from meeting up with Kila?"

"Hard to say." Kestral tossed a handful of viscera into the fire pit. "She should be on the Viaparaison front, but that's almost our entire western border. When we get close, we'll probably hear where she is."

"I still don't understand how everyone can know who she is and where she is, but no one has killed her yet."

Kestral shrugged. "I'm sure we'll understand when we meet her. She had a superb military record before the bounties were announced."

"And if she tries to kill me?"

"I don't think she will." Kestral skinned the last rabbit while I still worked on my first. "But if she does, I'll kill her."

I cocked an eyebrow at him. "No other hunter has succeeded in killing her, but you think you can?"

Kestral met my eyes. "You think I can't?"

I shivered despite the warm morning sunlight, remembering what Laki had said about Kestral's cold, enduring violence. If Kila really burned as hot and fast as Laki said, wouldn't she be a perfect counterpoint to Kestral?

"Dust if I know. I've never met her."

Kestral wrapped his two clean rabbits in oil cloth, then took my half-mangled rabbit from me, cleaning it up as best he could. Once he tucked it away, we broke down the campsite and tied the bags to Shan's saddle.

"Are you flying or riding?" Kestral asked once we were ready to go.

"Riding, if it's all right. I'm still tired." I rubbed my side. While the ribs had mended, I still felt a little sore. Kestral waited as I shifted, shrinking down into my rat shape. Kestral crouched, holding his palm flat. I scurried onto it, digging my claws into his sleeve as he mounted up. Once settled, he opened a belt pouch for me and let me duck inside.

"Ready to go meet your sister?" Kestral asked, turning Shan back towards the road.

Why was he always so much nicer to me when I was an animal? With that thought, I turned in a circle in preparation for sleep.

It's because you're quieter.

Was that Kestral's voice inside my head? No, I must already be dreaming.

I awoke to the world shaking around me, tossed about like a leaf in a tempest, or a raft on the waves.

Or like a rat in a belt purse as someone dismounted a horse.

When the movement became less violent, I poked my head out of the pouch. I couldn't see very much, but it seemed Kestral was walking and leading Shan. By the light it couldn't have been much past midday. With a clawed rat-paw, I tugged on Kestral's leather overshirt to get his attention. He glanced down after a moment a faint smile on his lips.

"I thought we might make camp early." Kestral looked up, facing forward. "I haven't recovered from all you've drawn from me these past few nights."

Maybe you'd feel better if you would sleep in once in awhile, I thought to myself, still grumpy about being awoken before dawn this morning.

Kestral frowned down at me. "Did you just—" He shook his head, looking ahead again. "There are some farms nearby. Sometimes farmers will sell soldiers some food or let them spend a night in their barn. A lot of young men pass this way to join the army, so it wouldn't be strange to the farmers if I were to ask—"

With difficulty, I scrambled out of the belt pouch and down Kestral's pant leg as he spoke. Something didn't feel quite right. I hoped I was wrong. The second my feet hit the ground, I shifted back to my human form, turning and looking back behind us.

"Reshi, what—"

"Look." I pointed back the way we had come. "You spend a lot of time out in the elements, right? Is that normal?"

Kestral stopped and looked back. Purplish-gray storm clouds hovered over the forest where we had camped the previous day. They hung low and thick and seemed to be moving, sprawling like the tendrils of a sea-beast searching for prey. Kestral stooped, picked up a handful of dirt, then scattered it.

"Those clouds are moving against the wind. Definitely not natural." Kestral cursed softly.

"That's Velyn's magic. He's using the storm clouds to search for us." I couldn't be certain, but it seemed like the perfect combination of Velyn's weather magic and Cera's far-sight.

"It could be Eagan," Kestral replied, patting Shan's neck before lightly climbing back into the saddle. "If he's killed Velyn, he'll have both weather magic and far-sight."

"No." How was I so sure? There. The answer was in the shape of the cloud. "Velyn once made a joke about fishermen and krakens. Is that—"

"A kraken. Eagan wouldn't have shaped it that way." Kestral cursed. "Shift and climb up. We'll make a run for it. Even magic like that has limits."

I shifted, this time taking my crow shape. I wanted to be able to see the clouds coming up behind us. I perched on Kestral's shoulder, clinging to the protective leather over his clothing as Shan took flight. I had to flare my wings to keep my balance. Shan could really move when he wanted to. I turned back to look over my shoulder, watching the oncoming clouds. The trees on either side of the road were growing further apart, gradually changing from forest to farm land. Soon we wouldn't have cover to hide under.

"At least now we know that Velyn killed Eagan," Kestral said, leaning up and over Shan's neck, urging the horse on faster. Very carefully I changed my grip to face backwards.

Not necessarily, I told myself. I couldn't shake the feeling that both of my brothers were still alive. I felt more than saw Kestral shoot me a strange glance over his shoulder. The clouds were coming too fast. We needed to find cover and hide, if cover worked against far-sight. I couldn't be sure. Cera had been able to speak to me wherever I had slept.

We have to hope far-sight and far-speech work differently.

I blinked and cocked my head at Kestral. That sounded like something he would say. What was going on?

"If we can get enough distance between us and those clouds, maybe we can take shelter in a barn. With the farmer's permission." Kestral faced directly ahead, without looking at me. "Or you could take off and hide yourself. I doubt even far-sight would distinguish you from any other crow."

That gave me an idea. My magic was still barely a shimmer in my chest, but I was only playing on creatures' natural instincts, which made the magic easier to work. I reached out magically, touching the minds of hundreds of crows in the surrounding forest and farmland. There was certainly no shortage of the black birds in these parts.

Once I had their attention, I showed them the images of both Velyn and Eagan, since I couldn't be completely certain which one of them was wielding this far-sight magic. In particular, I showed the crows Eagan's golden earrings, the shining thread on his cloak and the rings on his fingers. For Velyn, I showed them the buckles on his belt and boots, as well as the glittering necklace that held a sea-creature's tooth. For good measure, I showed them bags of food that either brother most likely carried with them. It didn't take much to earn a crow's persistent interest.

All around us, crows suddenly took wing, like a black wave cresting over us. Their wings beat the air down on us, their caws a deafening din. Crows in the forest had already found one or both of my brothers and they called to their kin, drawing them in to harry the humans into handing over their shinies and their food. As the murder soared towards the calls, the wind from their flight slowly tore apart the storm clouds, shredding and scattering the sight-magic until it winked out.

"That was good thinking," Kestral said, slowing Shan down to a less reckless pace. "It should give us time to find lodging for the night."

I cawed in agreement, settling down on Kestral's shoulder. The thought of crows converging on either of my brothers was a comical one. I only wished that I could see it.

An hour later, Kestral secured us shelter in a half-empty barn as well as a large bowl of vegetable stew. Shan munched happily on a pile of fresh hay in one stall while Kestral unrolled his bedroll in the stall next door. I watched from atop a stack of hay bales, eyeing the single bowl of stew.

Kestral sighed, seeming to guess at the source of my annoyance. "You know I couldn't ask for two bowls. It would have seemed strange. Are you going to shift so you can eat?"

I leapt down from the hay bales, my tail lashing behind me. I only had enough magic to shift once; if I had shifted human, I would have had to sleep that way and I didn't want to dust off Kestral. So instead I used my last shift to take my cat form. It was my most comfortable form anyway. I sat down near the bowl of broth, lowering my head to give it an appreciative sniff. Kestral picked up the bowl and sat down on his bedroll.

"I'll leave you the broth," he said before tipping bowl back. My tail lashed of its own accord; broth was well and good—vegetables tasted strange to a cat's palate—but what I wanted was meat. While Kestral sipped from the bowl, I reached a paw inside his food satchel and dragged out the wrapped rabbit by its oilcloth. Kestral caught me before I could wrestle the packaging open. "Wait, stop. I'll cut some up for you." He set the bowl down and used a belt knife to slice off a few slivers of rabbit. "Do you need it cooked?"

I shook my head before pouncing on the meat greedily. Kestral chuckled softly before returning to his own meal. The benefits of shapeshifting made it so I could eat any food natural to the form I was in. The downside was that I could never quite eat enough to feed my human body. Otherwise I might have simply lived my life as a city cat. My family would never find me that way.

By the time I finished the rabbit, Kestral had set the bowl of broth down for me. It was still warm and well seasoned; a nice contrast to the meals we had been eating lately. When my cat belly felt full, I looked up at Kestral, licking my lips to let him know I was finished. He shoved the bowl away before settling into his bedroll.

"So, you think both Velyn and Eagan are alive?" Kestral asked.

I blinked back at him. As cats know all things, they have no translation for a shrug.

"It would be nice to know for sure which one is chasing us." Kestral stretched beneath the blankets. "It's hard to develop a strategy without knowing the enemy."

That made sense. Fighting a storm was different from fighting a fire. Hopefully, they were both still magically drained, wherever they were. I curled up on top of the bedroll, laying against Kestral's side. He scratched my ears before settling his arm around me and falling asleep.

I dreamt that Eagan and Velyn sat on the deck of a small sailing boat. The boat appeared to be anchored, barely bobbing as it rested against its tether. The boat seemed to be on a wide river, but the dream didn't give me a broad enough perspective to be certain. Velyn sat on a deck railing, fiddling with something in his hands. His perch should have appeared precarious, but he looked as comfortable as if he sat in a plush lounge. Eagan sat across the deck from Velyn on a low box. He leaned back against the railing, one arm looped over it, the other holding his cloak in his lap.

Both looked slightly worse for wear. Threads had been pulled from Velyn's vest and one of Eagan's ears was caked in dried blood. They looked as if they had jumped hastily into the river and their hair was only just drying. In fact, both were barefoot with their boots set in the middle of the deck to dry. The boots themselves made a strange picture together—Velyn's thick, plain leather with deck grip along the bottom beside Eagan's calf-high, calf-skin ornately decorated boots. What were they even doing in the same dream together?

". . . think they went west?" It took me a minute to realize that Eagan's mouth had been moving.

"That's the direction I was searching in before we got attacked," Velyn replied, not looking up from whatever he fiddled with in his hands. "Reshi must have noticed the cloud and used the crows to flee."

Eagan made a rude noise and turned to look back over the deck railing. "Cera didn't use clouds for her far-sight. She just Saw."

"Cera had years of practice." Velyn's cheeks flushed red. "It's easier for me to partner her magic with mine until I learn. How is mastering Laki's magic going for you?"

With one hand extended over the railing, Eagan twirled his wrist. The water beneath it churned for a moment, a single tendril snaking up towards his hand before it dropped. Eagan scowled. "It works fine on some lifeless things, like trees, but not on others. I am not learning a trade like carving to make this magic work; I'll just kill another sibling."

Velyn glanced up, glaring at our oldest brother. Eagan smirked easily back.

"Relax." Eagan pulled his hand back from over the railing. He held up his cloak, turning it over in his hands. "I can tell you've regained more of your magic than I have. And I find our deal to be advantageous at the moment."

Velyn grunted as he looked back down at his hands. The dream seemed to focus a little, letting me see that he was threading fishing line through the links of a delicate chain, like a necklace. With a start, I realized he wasn't wearing his tooth necklace.

"Of course, our deal is contingent upon you finding out where our baby brother went." Eagan flicked his candle-flame eyes up at Velyn. "You think they went west?"

"It's the only thing that makes sense." Velyn smiled to himself as he held the necklace out, the links now rejoined by the thread. He took a moment to fasten it around his neck. "Besides, you said you overheard them talking about Kila and we know she's in the west."

"Hm, which one of their powers do I want more?" Eagan mused. His face twisted distastefully as he found a large, white splotch on the cloak. He reached for a cloth in a nearby bucket of water and scrubbed until the white splotch was clean. "Shapeshifting seems like fun, but not very powerful."

"You could roll the dice on Kila's magic," Velyn offered, leaning back with a wide stretch. I hoped he would fall off the railing, but he appeared too practiced for such a folly. "I've seen all of Reshi's forms. I can handle his magic."

"And leave me with the unknown, possibly useless magic of the older sibling?" Eagan mused for a moment as he searched the cloak again for more white splotches. "Honestly, it's a dice-roll for me. You say Reshi is the easier kill, but this is the second time he's gotten away from you, isn't it? Or is it now the third?"

Velyn flushed red again. "It's that hunter of his! I'd already have his magic if not for that rusting warrior."

"I had the warrior well in hand before you showed up and spoiled it," Eagan replied, wiping up a newly discovered splotch on his cloak. "If I kill the hunter, I should get Reshi's magic."

"How about this?" Velyn hopped off the railing, bare feet padding confidently over the slick boat deck. "Whoever is close enough to coalesce Reshi's magic gets to keep it. The other gets Kila's magic uncontested."

"And then Reina's magic?" Eagan asked, glancing up.

Velyn shrugged. "Every mage-born for himself."

Eagan chuckled and continued cleaning his cloak. "And then that's the end of our alliance, isn't it?"

Velyn turned, hiding a shark's grin. "You should clean your ear. It's been bleeding this whole time."

Eagan grimaced as he checked his ear, his hand coming away with dried blood. "Well, you've had crow shit in that nest you call hair for hours now."

Velyn made a disgusted noise before opening a door to belowdecks, presumably to check his hair.

I started awake, leaping to my feet so quickly that Kestral's arm fell from me. Could that dream have been . . . wait, what had Cera said? I scrambled over the blanket towards the stall door. I hissed as a hand closed around my tail.

"Reshi?"

I shifted, impatient for answers and thinking that in my human form I would have the strength to pull free of Kestral's grip. I don't know why I thought that; not only was Kestral still stronger than me in my human form, but as I shifted his grip changed from my tail to my hair.

"Let go!" I swung my arm into his, startling him into releasing me. I shoved the stall door open and stumbled out of the barn, looking up into the sky.

As I expected: a full moon. I leaned against the doorframe, staring up at the silver orb. The memory of sitting on Cera's roof beside her came to me unbidden. My chest became tight, my throat threatened to close. I blinked furiously, driving back tears. I found the tiny wooden lyre in a belt pouch and turned it over in my fingers, willing it to take my sudden grief away from me.

A shuffling step was the only warning I got before Kestral stood beside me, following my gaze up to the moon. "A dream about Cera?"

"No. A dream because of Cera." I looked down, trying to master my emotions. "She told me that her powers became stronger during the full moon. I think I just had a vision."

Kestral remained silent as I described the dream in as much detail as I could. It was really the reference to the crows that made me feel as if it might be real. Kestral was quiet for a moment before nodding slowly.

"So, the both of them are coming after you. Together."

I nodded. "If it wasn't just a dream."

"Hm. We better find Kila soon, then." Kestral turned to walk back to our shared stall, then paused, looking back at me. "Did you know that if I'm holding you while you shift, I'll be holding your new form?"

I shrugged. "I never went out of my way to shift in front of people before. I certainly never stood close enough to be grabbed during a shift before."

Kestral nodded slowly before adding: "I think I have been hearing you inside my head."

I felt my jaw drop in surprise. "Really? It's not just me?"

"You're not doing it on purpose?"

"No, how would I do that?" I glanced back up at the moon. "That's never been my magic."

"But it was Cera's," Kestral pointed out. "Laki said that he and Kila established a bond after her death. Is it possible that you did, too?"

"Maybe, but why with you?" I slipped a coin out of my pocket and rolled it across my knuckles, the familiar action helping me to think. "Kila and Laki were twins, so it made sense. You and I aren't related at all."

"I've been thinking." Kestral turned his head, looking down at the barn floor. "I only hear you when you're shifted. Is it the same for you?"

"Yeah. Usually only when I have something to say to you," I mused, trying to recall all the instances of strange thoughts popping into my head. "You put the idea of spooking the soldiers' horses into my head."

"That wasn't intentional," Kestral explained with a small shake of his head. "But I remember wishing you would scare the horses, the same way you scared the pigoblins."

"It didn't come across as a clear thought, more like flashes of an idea. I don't know, it was strange." I hummed, mulling it over. "I'm not close with any of my siblings. Since Cera's death, you're the person I've spent the most time with. Maybe that's why the bond formed with you?"

Kestral shrugged. "Can you speak with me now? In your mind?"

I took a moment to try it, starting with a simple thought about our paltry dinner, then slowly ramping up to a lewd suggestion. Kestral continued to stare at me blandly. "No, I don't think so. It must only happen when I'm shifted."

"Great," Kestral said dryly, turning to walk back to the stall serving as our bedroom for the night.

"You don't sound like it's great," I said, following behind him. "We can communicate while I'm wearing a form, now. That's got to be useful in battle or over distances or something. Right?"

"All it means is that I'll never have another moment of peace and quiet any more." Kestral stretched and yawned before ducking back into the stall. He glanced back once more: "Don't drain any more energy tonight. I have to be alert to run Shan."

I didn't respond, having already shifted back to my cat form. My tail lashed at the minor offense of his comment. In any event, I was too tired to stay awake and draw more from him.

6

I had never stood on a battlefield before. The stench was overpowering—blood, excrement and desperation. Footing was treacherous; it was hard to tell if I was stepping in mud or viscera, or if the crunching beneath my boots was metal or bone. I constantly felt as if I was being watched. All in all, it reminded me of growing up in Giltner.

Kestral and I picked our way carefully over bloated corpses and rusted weapons. Shan had been left at the closest village, which was more like a military compound than a proper village. I had stayed hidden in animal forms while Kestral asked around for Kila's location, posing as just another mage hunter come for her bounty. It wasn't too much of a stretch for him, really.

As we crossed the battlefield to Kila's last known position, Kestral filled me in on the war with Viaparaiso, our country's western neighbor. Viaparaiso was one of the few sorcerous capitals of the world remaining, and its army consisted primarily of war mages. As our army was still fresh from the Great Mage Hunt, they employed all the latest magic-inhibiting weapons and tactics, keeping Viaparaiso from gaining a foothold across the wide river that separated our nations. Kestral believed that if our country defeated enough of Viaparaiso's mages, we would invade the country and annex it, or at least topple the magical government.

"But why?" I asked. "I mean, I get that war mages are dangerous, but most of us aren't. How am I a danger to anyone?"

Kestral glanced at me, seeming uncomfortable by the question. "I keep forgetting how little you know."

"Well, the way you keep asking about my childhood in Giltner, I figured you already knew what the education system was like." I smirked. "It wasn't exactly all book-learning in glass-windowed towers."

Kestral chuckled softly. "One day, I will find a few skins of Goldwater Whiskey, so you can tell me about it."

I laughed. "Try a cask of it." I squinted off into the distance. "I see someone."

Kestral loosened his sword in its sheath.

Our strategy for approaching Kila would be almost the exact opposite of how we had approached Laki—a show of strength instead of a timid approach.

"Remember, if it gets too intense, shift into something small and run."

"Why? You said you were a match for her, right?" I glanced sidelong at Kestral. I knew he hadn't slept well, despite the fact that I had barely drawn from him at all. He had spent a long time down in the bar, drinking with battlefield soldiers. I had crept out and heard a few of the stories they told of Kila. I remembered my fur standing on end until I slunk back to our room. If half the stories were true, I was in more danger here than I was facing both Velyn and Eagan together.

"Just be cautious." Kestral faced forward, taking half a step in front of me. I gulped back a lump of fear. If Kestral was nervous, I was terrified.

The figure ahead turned to look back at us and stood slowly, a dangerous smile on her face. I nearly fled when I realized she had been sitting on a pile of fresh corpses.

She stood almost a head shorter than Laki, putting her a head-and-a-half shorter than me. I could see some of her twin in her features, though—rounded face, blunt chin, pale skin. She wore skirted chainmail over a red tunic, which I hoped was dyed red and not turned red from blood. Black leggings disappeared into leather boots laced high over her knees, which looked flexible and battle-tested. Long leather gauntlets covered her hands and halfway up her arms, but her belt drew the eye—at least three swords, a heavy dagger, a war hammer and several belt purses were lashed to it. Over her shoulder the hilt of a monstrous bastard sword rose, almost as long as she was tall. Her red hair was coiled around her head in a braided crown, her eyes gleamed the color of fresh blood.

Kestral stopped several paces away, close enough to speak without shouting but far enough that a sword couldn't bridge the distance. For a moment, the two warriors simply sized each other up, saying nothing.

Kila grinned.

Kestral glowered. "Tekilashan." Kestral barely inclined his head to her.

"It's Kila to hunters." Kila set a hand on her hip and raised her chin. "Come to test me? I'll let you walk away up until you draw steel. After that, your life is forfeit."

Kestral set his hand on his hilt but didn't draw. "I'm not here to fight you. I've brought your brother Reshi to you for protection against your brothers."

Kila tilted her head. "Brothers? I had one of those once. He's dead now." She flicked her blood red eyes to me before looking back to Kestral. "I don't know any other brothers worth protecting."

"Kila, I'm your youngest brother, Jereshin." I took a step forward but halted under her intense stare. "We met with Laki just before—"

"You killed him?" Kila's grin turned to a sneer. "No, I doubt someone as scrawny as you killed Laki. He was stronger than he let on."

"He was ambushed by your brother Eagan. The fire mage." Kestral held perfectly still, prepared to draw at any moment. "Eagan and Velyn have joined together to hunt both you and Reshi."

Kila laughed joylessly. "You think that scares me, hunter? Have you heard nothing about me? I'm not afraid of a fire-starter and a lightning bug. Let them come."

"They are coming. For each of us." I held my hands out to the sides, trying to show her I wasn't a threat. "We stand a better chance facing them together than separately."

Kila shook her head, chuckling. "Does it look like I need your help?"

"No, but . . ." I hesitated. "I need yours."

She narrowed her eyes, sizing me up. "That's seems true enough." Her eyes glimmered before they snapped back to Kestral. "All right. I'll make you a deal. Fight me. Perhaps then I'll listen to your pleas for help."

"What is it with your family and deals?" Kestral asked me, though his eyes stayed locked on Kila. "Is your father a king or a merchant?"

"Kila, we don't want to fight you," I protested, ignoring Kestral. "I mean, what would be the point? If we could beat you, we wouldn't need your help against Eagan and Velyn. Besides, no one beats you."

"Then amuse me." Her teeth flashed in an evil grin. "Prove you're worth protecting."

"Can't we do that over drinks in a bar?" My eyes lit up. "What if I beat you in a drinking contest? That's really my battlefield."

"A skinny blade like you?" Kila snorted. "You couldn't outdrink me. Sit down and let your hunter's sword do the talking, little brother."

"Are we starting then?" Kestral asked, his monotone voice barely above a whisper.

"Sure." Kila widened her stance, hand to hilt. "A word of warning, though. Don't hold back."

Kestral charged in a sudden fury, mud flying from his boots as he raced across the battlefield, sword whipping from its sheath faster than belief. Kila faced the charge with an uncanny calmness. She drew her own blade, a thin longsword, but as Kestral brought his sword down in a powerful, two-handed swing, Kila merely raised her other arm above her head.

I gasped, certain I was about to see my sister lose her arm. Instead, the ring of steel on steel reverberated in the air as she caught Kestral's blade on the back of her wrist.

Kestral's eyes widened in shock.

Kila smirked. "Last warning against holding back." Kila turned her wrist and flung her arm wide, sending Kestral staggering. "It's no fun if you're not fighting for real."

Kestral regained his stance, turning to face her again. Without taking his eyes from my sister, he called back to me, "Reshi, forget the plan. Stay out of this."

"No worries!" I called. Kestral glanced back, doing a double-take as he realized how far off I had moved. I wasn't stupid. My sense of self-preservation was strong enough to let me know I wasn't about to win against this apex predator.

Kestral waited on Kila's charge this time, bracing himself to meet a testing side-slash. Instead, Kila pivoted at the last second, changing her slash into a thrust. Kestral barely countered in time, stepping back to avoid the tip of her longsword. Kila pressed her advantage, slashing upwards, spinning her blade in a circle to counter Kestral's attempt at a strike, then thrusting for his left side. Kestral parried again, backing up another step.

I had never seen anyone push Kestral back on his heels like this before. He was usually the one to charge, press and keep advantage during a sword fight. This defensive fighting didn't really seem to suit him. He couldn't really lose, could he?

Finally, as Kila drew back for a thrust, Kestral caught the tip of her blade along the flat side of his, throwing her off balance. Quick as a nightblack cat, Kestral leaned back and slammed his boot into her stomach, tossing her back several paces. Kila only grinned, pulled her sword back, and charged.

Kestral darted to the side, his hand sneaking into a belt pouch. Kila moved her free arm, intending to block whatever Kestral might throw, but instead of aiming for her head or chest, Kestral tossed something small and low—a bolo. Steel balls connected by a wire. Kila hadn't been expecting that. The bolo wrapped around her boots, sending her crashing to the ground. Kestral darted in, driving his blade point-down towards her throat. From where I stood, I could just make out Kila's wild grin as she turned her sword, bracing the blade with her left hand and caught the point of Kestral's sword in the groove on hers. She spun the sword, ripping Kestral's blade from his hands and sending it flying. With both her hands on the naked blade of her sword, Kila thrust the pommel up into Kestral's chest with enough force to toss him backwards—all from the flat of her back.

Before Kestral could regain his feet, Kila made a sharp motion with hers. The wire snapped, freeing her ankles so she could leap to her feet. Blades. Blades on the instep of her boots, between the leather and the grip. They were narrow enough to be nearly invisible, but sharp enough to slice wire. I shivered, out and out terrified, as she advanced on Kestral. He had recovered his stance but not his sword. He unsheathed his heavy dagger, holding it behind him with one hand ahead, presumably to block a blow.

Luckily, that blow never came. Kila spun rapidly to deflect the four knives I threw at her back. I *was* stupid. Not stupid enough to get close, but stupid enough to draw my sister's attention. I gaped at the pure art of her movement to deflect the knives. As she spun with a dancer's grace, she drew a second sword in her left hand, holding both swords and spinning them in a windmill of death, fast enough to knock the knives from the air.

And then she advanced on me.

With a gulp, I stupidly stood my ground, fae blades in hand.

As Kila stalked towards me, a grim visage of a painful death, she stabbed her longsword into the ground and drew her second shortsword. Just my luck; my sister could dual-wield weapons just like me. At least she came at me slowly, not the same vicious charge she used on Kestral. Her first strike was a testing strike, meeting my blade hard enough to make it ring.

"Oh, those are pretty." Kila eyed my daggers the way most women eyed diamonds. "Fae made?"

I grunted, turning her shortsword off my dagger. "Yes."

She wasn't even slightly winded from her fight with Kestral, which I found disconcerting.

"Have you figured out their secrets yet?" she asked, knocking both daggers to the side and trying for a thrust to my neck. I crouched low before slashing at her with both daggers, forcing her blade back.

"What does that mean?" I asked, trying to find an opening.

"This." Kila feinted left, making me dodge right. She tossed one sword to the ground and grabbed my wrist in the same fluid motion. She twisted my wrist behind my back until I thought it might break. As my dagger dropped from pain-numbed fingers, a boot slammed into my back between my shoulder blades, sending me crashing into Kestral, who had been attempting to retrieve his sword while I had Kila distracted. Not only did he not recover his sword, but it took precious moments to untangle ourselves from each other. By the time I could look up at Kila, she had my dagger in her hands and both shortswords sheathed.

"Absolutely beautiful." She smiled at her reflection in the silver. "You don't know anything about these weapons, do you?"

"Ah, well," I hesitated. "It's not like I'd tell you if I did."

Kila glared at me darkly. "There's nothing I hate more than seeing a beautiful weapon in the hands of a fool." She held the dagger in one hand and placed the palm of her other hand against the blade near the hilt. She slid her hand up the blade, somehow elongating it into a stiletto blade. I think I would have sat there gawking while she stabbed me with it if Kestral hadn't thrown me clear of her thrust. Kila came after me, despite Kestral racing to recover his sword.

"If you can't use them, you shouldn't have them." Kila came at me in truth this time, stiletto whistling through the space where I had been standing. It was all I could do to keep dodging backwards, still amazed at what my dagger had become. As Kestral prepared a strike to her back, I attempted to keep her attention.

I darted forward, catching the delicate blade on my remaining dagger while Kestral charged with a sideways slash. Her eyes locked on mine and she smiled. Using her left hand, she drew the shortsword on her left hip, but only halfway. Braced against her hip and its sheath, the sword blocked Kestral's blow, the recoil setting him back a pace.

"You're a demon!" I gasped.

Kila laughed.

I captured the stiletto within a pointed-wave of my dagger and yanked it free of Kila's hand. She released it easily enough, rocking back a step to grip the hilt of the bastard sword over her shoulder. The stiletto spun, and I grabbed it by the hilt. Instinctively, I clanged the blades together near their hilts and the stiletto snapped back into its original shape. Kila released her shortsword, gripping the hilt of the bastard sword in two hands.

"Come," Kila said, settling into a defensive stance.

Kestral came at her from the left, I slipped a step behind her. In a beautiful display of swordsmanship, Kila defended against the both of us, wielding a sword that I was sure I would have trouble lifting, never mind using. She turned Kestral's sword aside time and again, and neatly sidestepped each of my attacks, sometimes with the barest margin for error. A few times my blades scraped her chainmail, but they never found flesh.

Finally, Kila managed to shove Kestral back far enough to turn to me. I ducked her first swipe but caught the backswing. Luckily, she had turned the blade, using the flat side to slam me sideways into Kestral. With an irritated grunt, he elbowed me behind him, holding his ground between my sister and me.

Kila smiled, spun her blade then sheathed it over her shoulder with a flourish. "Well, I'm amused. I'll buy the first round of drinks tonight." She turned her back on both of us, walking calmly to collect her longsword from where she had left it stabbed into the earth.

Kestral and I exchanged a startled glance.

"So . . . you're going to help us?" I asked, mind reeling to catch up.

"I said I'll listen to you try to convince me over drinks." Kila twirled her longsword, leaned it back against her shoulder and looked back at us. "You coming?"

Kestral looked at me and shrugged. "Quick to flare, quick to burn out."

"Right. Star of fire and pain." I took a breath and sheathed my daggers. "Drinks sound great. But . . ."

Kestral sheathed his sword before addressing Kila. "Velyn has Cera's power of far-sight. If Reshi moves in the open, he'll be found."

Kila shrugged. "Isn't that the point? Dragging the others out into the open so we can kill them?"

Kestral frowned. "What about other hunters?"

Kila gave us a feral grin. "No one will kill him for his bounty while he's with me. The soldiers and townsfolk all know me here. They won't touch one of mine without my say so."

"You mean I can actually walk into a town as me?" I ran up beside my sister before Kestral could protest. "He's been keeping me in a shapeshift form every time we even get near other people. Stars, I miss real conversation!"

Kila laughed, sheathing her sword as she led the way back to town. "That's probably what kept you alive until now. Right, hunter?"

"It's Kestral." He followed just behind us. "Are you sure he'll be safe?"

"Sure." Kila shrugged. "As safe as any of us are."

"So, no one tries to kill you any more?" I asked, keeping pace with Kila. "When Kestral asked around for you, they told him where to find you."

"Oh, they won't get in the way of a hunter." Kila grinned. "They trust I won't die so easily. And the villagers and the army both like having me here. I am keeping foreign invaders from crossing the border, after all."

"Even the army knows you're here?" Kestral asked.

"Know? Rust, they pay me to be here!" Kila laughed. It sounded bright and cheery, which somehow seemed wrong, considering the splashes of blood on her boots. "I can't fight in the army because of my bounty, but that that doesn't stop them from paying me as a mercenary. They can't turn down a single fighter on this front or Viaparaiso wins."

Kestral grunted before falling silent. This was probably a lot of information for him to consider. He lagged a step behind Kila and I, deep in thought.

"Hey, if you've been here awhile, do you know where I can get more of these?" I flicked a throwing knife from my sleeve and showed it to her. "I'm down to my last two."

"Sure, but wouldn't it be better to use these?" A triangular dagger no longer than her palm appeared in Kila's hand as if summoned by magic. "You could keep almost three times as many in the same space as those long knives."

"Well, sure, but the tiny ones are harder to aim and don't cause as much damage," I replied, trying not to appear put off at how quickly Kila had armed herself. "I don't have to aim as precisely with the long ones."

"Suit yourself." Kila shrugged and the tiny dagger disappeared. I think I saw her tuck it beneath her leather-and-steel gauntlet, but the motion was hard to follow. "Afterwards, you should let me teach you how to fight."

"Teach?" I sputtered. "I held my own just fine!"

"No," Kestral called from behind us. "She went easy on you."

My mouth gaped and I turned to Kila's smirking face.

"Your hunter—Kestral was it?" Kila glanced back over her shoulder to see Kestral nod. "—is right. I only used testing strikes against you. I had to hold back to keep from accidentally killing you."

I looked away, hiding my embarrassment. "Why not just kill me then? Why play with us?"

"I was only playing with you, little brother. Your hunter is quite good." Kila tossed a smile over her shoulder. I don't think Kestral looked up to see it, though. "But if I killed you here, your power would disperse. I didn't want that to happen."

"You don't like magic, do you?" Kestral asked, voice soft.

Kila stopped and looked back at him.

"It's the only thing that makes sense." Kestral met her blood-red gaze and held it. "You never use yours. You don't want Reshi's magic. I would wager you've gained more power than you wanted with the deaths of your two siblings."

Kila's jaw tightened, as did her grip on one of her swords. "It's true. I hate magic. That will be part of the deal I make with the both of you." She turned back towards the village-turned-military-outpost. "But let's discuss it over dinner. That last fight really worked up my appetite."

"That's the first thing you've said that I've agreed with." I grinned and trotted alongside her, Kestral following behind.

I imagined that at one point this village had looked as prosperous as the village where Kestral had found me. Now it was ringed by a log palisade with three gates, each manned by several uniformed soldiers. Beyond the wall were barricades of sharpened logs to stop a cavalry advance. Banners flew at every corner of the wall, noting which noble families had troops in residence. The village had been enlarged to encompass the army storehouses and barracks. Kestral had only been allowed entrance by his credentials as a former soldier and current mage hunter seeking Kila's bounty. Anyone other than local farmers or licensed merchants were usually turned away.

Which was why it surprised me when the army commander himself greeted Kila at the gate.

"How many did you slay today, Killer?" the commander asked affectionately.

"More than I could count." Kila grinned and gave the commander an off-handed salute. Behind me, Kestral took an at-rest military stance.

"There was a hunter looking for you last night. Did he . . ." The commander trailed off, puzzled, as he noticed Kestral and me standing behind her. "Are you taking prisoners now, Kila?"

Kila laughed. She reached out and dragged me forward. "This is my brother, Reshi, and his mage hunter. Former eastern-front soldier, if I'm not mistaken. They'll be staying with me for a short while."

"Ah, well," The commander shifted uncomfortably, grimacing as he met my eyes.

"If any hunters come looking for him, just direct them to me." Kila let my arm go. I rubbed the spot where she'd held me; I was sure there would be bruises. "They won't stay long, and I'll keep them from causing trouble."

The commander sighed. "I guess having two mage-born in residence is just as bad as having one. I'm not protecting you, you understand?" He turned to address me directly. "My men won't stand between you and a hunter."

"That's fine." I grinned and pointed to Kila and Kestral. "That's what I have them for."

"Maybe," Kila added. She held her hand out to the commander. "My wages?"

The commander unclipped a leather pouch from his belt and tossed it to her. "Thanks for the help today, Killer."

"It's a pleasure. Really." Kila tied the bag to her belt and led the way into the village. "I stayed at the Rickety Stool yesterday, so tonight I think I will stay at..." She turned slowly, glancing up and down the town's main street. "The Drunken Fish. If you want to keep Reshi safe, you should stay there tonight, too."

I nearly wept. The Drunken Fish was one of the nicer inns in town. The night before we had stayed at a single-story inn off the main road and I thought we would die from the terrible food alone. The Drunken Fish would have music and dancing and I wouldn't have to hide in an animal form.

Kestral held his hand up, drawing Kila and I to a halt. "We don't have the funds to stay there. Besides, my horse and belongings are still at the Dark Iron Inn."

Kila laughed. "If they haven't been stolen already. I wouldn't stay at the Dark Iron for all the stars in the Canvas."

Kestral glared at her. I shrank behind my sister. I did not want to stay in that dismal, creaking inn another night.

"Look, you want to keep Reshi safe? You'll want to lodge with me. People here know me, and they know not to dust me off. Once they know who Reshi is, someone might take a chance at his bounty." Kila flicked here eyes up and down, taking in Kestral's worn out boots to his battle-worn leather armor. "If you really can't pay, I can cover you both for the night."

"We graciously accept!" I wasn't going to let Kestral take this chance away from me. It had been too long since I had interacted with anyone besides him. "Let's go get Shan and your stuff and we'll—"

Kila reached out and caught the collar of my shirt, stopping me in my tracks. "Didn't you need knives? I'll take you to my weapons merchant." She hooked a thumb at Kestral. "You go get your horse and bring it to the Drunken Fish."

"No." Kestral's voice was like ice: cold and unmoving. "Reshi stays with me."

"Why? Afraid he's not safe with me?" Kila grinned tauntingly. "If I wanted him dead, I would already have his blood on my sword. I can keep him safe for you."

Ice blue eyes locked with mine. Was he asking me what I wanted to do?

"I do need more knives," I said, trying to twist my shirt out of Kila's grip. Failing that, I tried to look casually comfortable. "And Shan hates me anyway. You'll probably have an easier time collecting him without me."

Kestral met Kila's eyes. "If anything happens to him . . ."

"Ooh, I'm starting to wonder if this isn't just about his bounty." Kila smirked. "He's safe with me. Stars' Honor."

"You're not in the army any more."

"Neither are you." Kila arched a brow at Kestral.

After a beat, he nodded, and with one final look at me, he walked back to our inn from the night before.

"He's a bit over-protective, isn't he?" Kila asked, finally letting me go.

"Well, he has kept me alive until now." I fixed my collar, trying to get it to lie flat again. "Were you just trying to get me alone?"

"Yes." Kila grimaced, meeting my eyes. "Do you need me to kill him? Has he bonded you?"

"What?" I started. "No. What is bonding?"

Kila crossed her arms, a pensive look on her face. "Are you traveling with him because you want to? Or are you being forced?"

I hesitated. "It's a little of both. I'd be dead without him, but he's also supposed to kill me, so it's a tough question to answer."

Kila remained silent a minute, then said, "He'll be a good asset in the fight against our brothers. If you need me to kill him afterwards, I could."

"No, I . . ." I frowned. It was the perfect way out. If Velyn, Eagan and Kestral were all dead, no one would be chasing me. I would be completely free again. Isn't that what I wanted? "I don't know, Kila. We've sort of become friends, I think."

"You think?" Kila arched her brow. "That man could really use a bounty or three, based on the wear on his equipment and the inn he chose to stay in. Isn't he just using you to draw out our brothers?"

I sighed and looked away. "Let me handle Kestral, okay? He's honored his word and I'd like to stick to mine. He's said he'll give me a head start before he hunts me."

Kila shrugged. "It's your pyre, I guess." She turned and started walking away. "Let's get those knives you wanted. Maybe some armor as well, so you're not just a target."

"I can't shapeshift with metal armor," I explained, trotting to catch up to her. "Or at least, once I shift I won't be wearing it any more."

Kila groaned. "Magic is more trouble than its worth. What about leather armor? Not that it's good for much, but maybe it could save you from a scratch or two."

"I like my range of motion." I shrugged. "I'm a close-quarters type of fighter, so I need flexibility."

"You're not any type of fighter," Kila scoffed. She stopped at a small shop set up beneath a tarp. She and the merchant exchanged pleasantries before she explained what was needed. The vendor sold me two full bracers of throwing knives as well as a roll of extras. I paid him with the money I had stolen from Kestral's former soldiers, grateful that Kestral wasn't around to question the money's source. By the time we left the merchant's stand, Kestral and Shan were waiting for us outside the Drunken Fish Inn.

"Do you switch inns every night?" I asked Kila as we approached the waiting hunter.

Kila nodded. "I don't mind hunters coming after me; they usually find me on the battlefield like you did. Assassins, though—I don't like making their job too easy, so I pick my inns randomly every day."

"A determined assassin would find you anyway," Kestral pointed out, tying Shan to a post outside the inn.

"They do, on occasion." Kila shrugged, as if assassination was merely a mild inconvenience. "One might get lucky one day. That day hasn't come yet."

I suppressed a shiver. Hopefully no one in this town would find out that I was one of Kila's brothers.

"Hey Darren, you old fool!" Kila announced, shoving the inn's door open. "Three rooms for the night, for me and my brother and his hunter."

I groaned inwardly.

"Two rooms," Kestral corrected, close at my side. "Reshi rooms with me."

Kila rolled her eyes at him. "You really can't let him out of your sight, can you? Fine. Two rooms, Darren."

A wizened innkeeper, who barely appeared able to keep up with the conversation, slowly accepted the coins for two rooms and passed over two sets of keys. I glanced around the room. In the corner, musicians tuned their instruments, and the scent of dinner hung in the air. A real inn, at long last!

"Have a tub of warm water sent to my room," Kila ordered, sliding over another coin.

"Mine too!" I cheerfully slapped down another coin. "And soaps! Lots of soaps!"

"And someone to bring his horse around," Kila said, tipping her head towards Kestral. "We'll all want dinner as well."

"That was bath water, soap and . . .?" I swear a puff of dust left his mouth as the old innkeeper spoke.

"A runner for the horse," Kila repeated slowly. "And three dinners later."

Darren nodded, his neck popping as it moved.

"Is Laryssa around?" Kila asked. She leaned over the counter and shouted, "Laryssa! Get out here, wench!"

Tinkling laughter floated into the bar from the direction of the kitchen. A moment later a young woman followed it, smiling and dusting her hands on her apron. She was pretty with large brown eyes and dark hair covered by a scarf. "Kila, are you staying with us tonight? I'll charge you extra if you scratch up the floors with your weapons again."

Kila laughed, pulling up a stool to the bar. "That's your fault for making such a potent light ale." She turned to Kestral and me. "The Drunken Fish brews its own ales. They're all excellent, but I like the palest one." She turned back to the bar wench. "Can we get three mugs while we wait for our tubs to be filled?"

"Sure thing, Killer." Laryssa winked at Kila then looked over at the innkeeper. "Grandpapa, have you sent a runner for the tubs yet?" When he shook his head, she set her fists on her hips. "Honestly, Grandpapa, why do you still work? You should be out on a bench enjoying the sunshine. I'll send a runner then get your drinks." She caught my eye for a moment and I offered her my best smile. She winked at me as she had at Kila before ducking back inside the kitchen. I caught Kestral glaring at me. I shrugged the glare off. It had been too long since I'd been able to wink at a pretty bar wench for me to care what Kestral thought of it.

"Here you are. Three mugs of Fish Piss." Laryssa reappeared, setting the tall mugs down on the bar. "Can I get you anything else?"

"Would you mind sending a runner to the Rickety Stool for my things?" Kila asked as she gathered up the mugs. "And let me know if anyone comes looking for me."

"You got it, Killer." Laryssa smiled fondly at my sister. Kila led us to a far table, away from the few scattered patrons enjoying mugs of ale.

"Fish Piss?" I asked skeptically as Kila set the tankard down in front of me.

"It's stronger than it tastes." Kila slid another mug towards Kestral before tipping hers back for a long sip. "Mmm. If you like darker ales, they have Murky Water and Watery Grave. Both good, but not to my taste."

I sipped at the pale ale and hummed in appreciation. It certainly was better than other pales, but I looked forward to sampling the darker varieties later. But probably not as much as I looked forward to a bath with soaps.

"So." Kila set her mug down with a clack. "You want me to slay my kin when they come for dear Reshi. Is that right?"

Kestral nodded. He took a short sip before speaking. "Velyn and Eagan have each taken the life and power of one of your siblings. Now they have formed a partnership, if the dream Reshi had is true."

"Dream?" Kila looked at me sharply. "Was it during the last full moon?"

I nodded, coughing as I tried to speak while swallowing a mouthful of ale. "Velyn tried to find us using sight-magic bound to storm clouds. I sent crows to attack him, and later I had a dream—"

"Were they on a boat?" Kila asked. "The gray-haired one was fixing a necklace?"

"And the flame-haired one was cleaning a fancy cloak." I nodded. "You saw it too?"

"Ugh, more magic I don't need." Kila took a long drink from her mug. "I didn't mind being connected to Laki, but the rest of this is just . . . ugh. I hate magic."

"Can I ask?" I leaned closer to her, dropping my voice conspiratorially. "What is your magic?"

Kila shook her head. "You'll probably see it before this is over, but I'm not saying. I hate it. Which brings me to my half of this deal: when we kill those two, you will have to take their magics. I don't want any piece of them."

"What?" I sat back, startled. "I don't want them either. I never set out to hurt anyone or steal their power."

"If Reshi takes both their powers, it makes him a bigger target," Kestral pointed out.

Kila shrugged. "I don't care. If we kill them and let their magic disperse, I'll end up with even more powers than I already have. It took me years to control my magic. I'm not wasting my time learning new magic."

I exchanged a glance with Kestral. He grimaced then dropped his gaze to his ale. I didn't want Velyn's or Eagan's magics. Nor did I want Cera or Laki's magics. Aside from shapeshifting, I barely used the magic that was mine. What would it be like to have the magic of four of my siblings?

I glanced over at Kestral, who was still staring into his mug. A new thought occurred to me. With the powers of my siblings combined, I might stand a chance against him and any other hunters who came after my bounty. It wasn't the worst idea ever. And as long as our oldest sister wasn't hunting us, I could be free again.

"What about it, Kestral?" I asked, dragging his gaze up to meet mine. "It's better than letting Velyn or Eagan take my power, isn't it?"

Kestral held my gaze. "You're really asking me what I think?"

"Of course." That surprised me. "I only made it to Kila because of you. And we'll need your help fighting them. Won't we?" I glanced at Kila. She shrugged.

"I've killed plenty of mages, but it always helps to have allies." She smirked at me. "I'd rather have his help than yours, based on how you fought today."

I ignored the jibe. "Well, Kestral?"

The mage hunter took a deep breath, letting it out slowly. "I don't like it. But if that's the price, that's it. If Reshi is close enough to either body when it releases its magic, he should be the one to coalesce it."

"Great. Glad we worked that out." Kila tipped her mug back, finishing her ale. "I figure the best way to draw them out is to just sit tight, spread the word that little Reshi is here, and wait for them to meet us on the battlefield. You can tell me all about them and their powers over dinner tonight." She pushed her chair back and stood. "Right now, I'm going to take a bath."

"Me too!" I leapt up, knocking my chair over. I scrambled to set it aright as Kila laughed at me. Kestral rose soundlessly, following us upstairs to the rooms. Kila's room was across the hall from ours. I was more excited to see steam rising from the tub than I had been by the chance to drink ale in a tavern again.

"Me first!" I called, nearly tearing the laces off my shirt in my haste to jump in the water. "I'll make sure there's still some heat left for you, Kestral."

He eyed me warily. "Do you need me to leave?"

"Yes, unless—" I stopped, spotting a folded screen leaning against the wall. "No, you can stay. Whatever you want." I set the screen up, shielding the bath before I finished undressing. I didn't mind being seen naked, except for those little marks on my hip. Kestral would know what they meant, and I didn't want to talk about them. If the room had been darker, I would have chanced it, but it was still early in the evening and the room was bright with sunlight.

The tub was wide enough for me to sit in and just a little hot, so I eased in gently with a relieved sigh. I sat for awhile, simply enjoying the heat. Beyond the screen, a chair scraped the floor before I heard the familiar sound of a sword clearing its sheath. I imagined Kestral was cleaning his sword, as he did every night.

"Kila isn't what I pictured," I said, selecting a sweet-smelling soap from the basket that had been left near the thick drying-cloths.

"What were you picturing?" Kestral's voice came from beyond the screen.

"I don't know. Someone taller." I sighed as I scrubbed a layer of dirt from my skin. "She isn't even as tall as Cera was."

"None of you seem to look anything like the others." He paused for a moment. "Except for maybe you and Eagan."

"Kila and Laki looked a little alike," I countered. "But then, I guess twins are supposed to look alike. Is Kila what you were expecting?"

"She looked like the portrait on her bounty," he replied shortly. "I was expecting a fight. Weren't you?"

"Not really. Well, I was half-expecting her to try and kill me, so maybe. All my other siblings have tried to kill me so far." It was hard to keep the bitterness out of my voice.

"Except Cera."

"Except Cera," I agreed. I dunked my head under water before scrubbing my hair with soap. "I wonder what Reina is like. Do you think she knows what's going on with us out here?"

"If Kila saw the same vision as you, it's likely Reina did too." I heard Kestral sheathe his sword, followed by footsteps across the floor. It sounded like he was pacing. "If Velyn and Eagan hear that you're here with Kila, they might decide to pursue Reina instead."

"Maybe." I rinsed my hair then soaped it again. "But they have to find her first. Kila and I are making ourselves easier targets. Eagan strikes me as the type to like easy prey."

Kestral chuckled softly. "Is that because it's what you would do?"

"Don't lump me in with that noble bastard," I growled, rinsing my hair for the final time. "The easiest thing to do is to not go around killing siblings."

Reluctantly, I finished bathing, drying off quickly with a cloth. I really wanted to sit in the water until it cooled, but Kestral deserved a warm bath as much as I did. I stepped past the screen after knotting the drying-cloth high above my waist. I smirked as Kestral eyed me, pausing in his pacing across the floor.

"Like what you see?" I dropped my chin, looking up through my lashes. "The offer's still open."

Without replying, Kestral pushed past me to the bath. I heard him kick off his boots and set his weapon-laden belt down on the floor. As I began finger-combing my hair, I heard him slip into the water.

"It's still warm, isn't it?" I called.

Kestral grunted a reply. "How much of this soap did you use? The bath is more foam than water."

"The soap isn't going to hurt you." I rolled my eyes. As Kestral grumbled about the foam in the water, I checked over my clothing. It was a little worse for the wear, especially after my battle with Kila. I rummaged through Kestral's bags until I found a small sewing kit then curled up on the bed to stitch my clothes. It wouldn't do to look like a scruffy traveler on my first night in real civilization in weeks.

Kestral finished his bath before I finished darning my clothes. After he dried himself, he dunked his clothes in the soap-foamed water of the bath, wrung them out and draped them over the screen to dry. With a cloth wrapped around his waist, he searched through his bags for a fresher set of clothing. He barely glanced at me on the bed as I stitched my clothes. There went my theory of him liking what he saw. Dust him. I was going to dance tonight.

A weight on the end of the bed made me look up. Kestral sat there clad only in a pair of loose brown pants as he scrubbed at his hair with a drying cloth. My mouth watered as tiny rivulets of water traced paths between the muscles of his chest and stomach and along the lines of old scars. My needle paused in its work as I imagined running my fingers over his warm, tan skin. He glanced back at me and I quickly tried to appear as if I hadn't just been staring at him.

"You don't mind that I'm using your thread, do you?" I asked, holding up my stitching.

"No." Kestral looked away, then back again. "Finish up. Kila might be down at dinner already."

I shoved away lewd thoughts, replacing them instead with thoughts of real food with butter and seasonings. Food was another one of life's greatest pleasures, after all. It shouldn't be approached like a chore, as Kestral did. I finished stitching the cuff of my shirt before pulling it on. After making sure Kestral had his back to me, I slipped into my pants, belting them snugly over my hips. By the time he looked back, I was lacing up my boots. With a tilt of his head, Kestral indicated that I follow him downstairs to the bar.

Kila was there ahead of us, leaning over the bar and talking to the wench from earlier, a tankard already in hand. No longer armored for the battlefield, Kila wore a simple tunic over leggings, boots stopping at mid-calf rather than over her knees. She still wore more weapons than necessary on her belt, but only one full sword. Her wet hair was pulled back in a simple braid reaching nearly to her sword belt; I hadn't realized it was so long before.

When Kila saw us approaching, she ordered three meals and beckoned us to the corner table we had sat at earlier. The bar wench took drink orders—Fish Piss for Kila, Murky Water for Kestral, and Watery Grave for me—before ducking back into the kitchen. Soldiers from the army kept stopping by to chat with Kila and each time she introduced me as her brother—spreading the word, as she put it. I was sure that by the end of the night, everyone in town would know who I was.

When dinners arrived at tables, the soldiers settled down to eat, leaving us in relative peace. The musicians strummed their instruments softly in a corner of the room, creating background noise for the diners. I hoped they would play something livelier for dancing later.

"This has got to be the best mutton I have ever had," I announced, wiping my chin. It helped that it had been rolled in spices before being cooked, and that the bread was fresh, crusty, and heaped with butter. The ale was so stiff and dark that it could nearly stand on its own. I think I caught Kestral holding back a laugh at my enthusiasm for the food, but by the time I could look properly the moment had passed.

"So, which of my darling brothers killed Laki?" Kila asked, setting polished lamb bones down on her plate. Somehow the lack of armor and weaponry didn't make her look any less intimidating.

"Eagan, the fire mage," Kestral replied. "Laki was focused on Reshi and me. Eagan took us all by surprise."

"So, the fire-starter has Laki's life-magic?" Kila asked.

"Yes, but from what we saw, he was having trouble using it." Kestral seemed happy to fill Kila in on the details, so I just let him talk. The musicians were beginning to ramp up their tune and I scanned the room for possible dance partners. "Velyn also seemed to be having some trouble with far-sight."

"Serves him right, going after little Cera." Kila slammed her empty ale tankard down, summoning the wench with a refill. I tried to catch her eye to see if she was interested in a dance later, but she seemed too busy to notice. "Cera was a weakling, but she didn't deserve to go like that."

"I would like to hear your strategy for fighting your brothers when they arrive," Kestral said, pausing for a sip of his ale. "Both may have grown stronger since the last time we faced them."

Kila nodded and leaned forward on her elbows. She and Kestral drew on the table, using the condensation from their mugs to indicate patterns of attack and positions. I tuned it out as the music swelled, drawing dancers out onto the floor.

"Reshi."

"Hm?" I was half out of my seat when Kestral called me.

He glanced towards the dancers, then back at me. "Stay alert for assassins."

"Isn't that what I keep you around for?" I winked at him. Before he could stop me, I was on my feet, weaving and swaying with the other dancers in the corner near the musicians. It wasn't long before I had a new mug of ale in my hand and a lovely on my arm. When the room continued spinning longer than I did, I paused, considering going back to sit with Kestral and Kila. As I looked back towards the table, Kestral threw his head back in one of his rare fits of laughter. He smiled at Kila before they banged their mugs together and drank deeply. My mood soured instantly; they barely knew each other. How could Kila draw that laughter from him so easily when I had to work so hard for it? I called for another mug of ale and found a new pretty girl to dance with. Forget Kila. Forget Kestral. The music was good and so was the ale. I didn't need them right now.

Hours later, the room tilted around me instead of just spinning. It really had been far too long since I had had a proper drink. Someone laughed shrilly and a small hand on my arm dragged me up the stairs. I was trying to follow but the stairs twisted and turned, making footing treacherous. I tried a step and stumbled. It took me a minute to realize I hadn't fallen because a strong arm had me around the shoulders. There was a conversation full of giggles and a steady monotone voice that I couldn't follow, and then I was being towed up the stairs into a mercifully dark room.

I wrapped my arms around broad shoulders, closing my eyes and willing the world to stop spinning. When it did, I blinked up into ice blue eyes.

"Of course it's you." I pushed away from Kestral, staggering towards the bed. "Couldn't let me have one night of fun, could you?"

"From the look of it, you had plenty of fun." Kestral stayed near the door, watching me make my way across the room.

"Would have been nice to dust up with a sweet armful," I muttered, flopping onto the bed. I had to grip the blankets as it tried to buck me off. When it finally settled down, I fumbled with the lacings on my boots. "What did she say that was so funny?"

"That girl? She was drunk. She thought everything was funny." Kestral crossed his arms, leaning back against the door.

"Not her. Kila. My sister." How had these laces become so knotted?

"Nothing. We were talking strategy for your brothers."

"Liar," I accused, thumping my heel against the floor. Could I just pull the dust-ridden boots off? "I saw you laughing with her."

Kestral was quiet a moment. "Oh, that. It wasn't really that funny."

"Liar," I repeated. I wasn't all that witty when I was drunk. I fought with my boot again but suddenly large tan hands were there, untying the laces and pulling the boot free. Without a word, Kestral unlaced the other boot. I fell still, watching him. "What did she say, Kestral?"

"You'll see tomorrow." Kestral rocked back on his heels to look up at me. "Can you shift?"

I grumbled about how I wouldn't have to shift if I was dusting up in another room. Kestral only watched me silently, waiting. It took a bit longer than usual to make the shift from human to cat. When I did I was unsteady on four feet instead of two. Kestral moved me to the middle of the bed before undressing and climbing in after me. I'd never admit it, but his arm made me feel safer as the bed continued to spin and tilt beneath me as I drifted off.

Kestral was up the next morning before me, as usual. I heard him moving around the room, but as no sunlight was yet filtering through the window, I hooked a claw through the blanket and pulled it up over my head. My magic helped me avoid the worst of a hangover, but it had still been a late night after an intense day, and I intended to sleep in. An unexpected knock at the door had me growling and tucking my face beneath a paw.

Boots crossed the floor and soon I heard my sister's voice. The tones were low, so I figured the matter couldn't be too important. I tried to fall towards sleep again when the blanket was rudely pulled off me.

"Aw, is that my baby brother?" Kila vigorously ruffled my fur, brushing it backwards and causing my skin to ripple and itch. I hissed in irritation. "Aren't you just the cutest little meal on four feet? A little skinny though." A finger prodded my midsection. I swiped at it, but she quickly withdrew her finger.

"Are you ready to warm up?" Kila asked, addressing Kestral. I sat up and tried to smooth my fur without shifting back to human shape. I wouldn't be able to go back to sleep so long as Kila remained in the room.

Kestral nodded as he finished tying his sword onto his belt. "Let me warn you, Reshi drew from me last night so I'm feeling tired this morning."

"Not to worry. They have black tea here." Kila's eyes fluttered shut and she shivered with delight. "It'll wake you right up."

"Southern black tea?" Kestral's voice held a note of interest. That was odd; nothing ever seemed to interest him. "I haven't had any in over a year."

"The army stockpiles it, so the inns here can serve it." Kila scooped me up despite my yowl of protest. I struggled to free myself, but my sister's arms were like iron, especially while encased in her leather-wrapped-steel armguards. With a grumble, I settled back against her chest, letting her carry me down to the common room. Why couldn't she just leave me in bed? And just what the dust is black tea?

Kila set me down on the bar in the common room and placed an order for two black teas. I blinked sleepily at the room. Were we the only fools awake at this hour? Why were we awake at this hour? It felt as if I had only gone to bed an hour ago. Was this punishment for having fun last night? My tail lashed as I eyed Kestral. He chuckled at me before inhaling deeply over a steaming mug.

Kila cradled her own mug of black tea lovingly, sipping slowly despite the torrent of steam pouring off of it. I wandered over and stuck my nose over the rim. Kila swatted at me but I was already backing away. The aroma was thick and heady, searing sleep from my mind as cleanly as fog wiped from glass. It might taste good on a human palate, but it was overwhelming to my cat sensibilities. Kestral actually smiled into his mug as he drank. For some reason, that irked me more.

"Kila." A chastising voice came from the kitchen doorway. "A cat on the bar? Really?"

"Oh, right." Kila turned to me. "Do you need milk or something? Do cats drink tea? Or do you hunt?"

I flicked an irritated ear at her.

Kila looked up at the bar mistress. "A saucer of milk, I think. Thanks, Laryssa."

"That wasn't what I...oh, fine." Laryssa threw her hands up and went to fetch a bowl of milk for me. She set it down with a clack, refusing to acknowledge my adorable meow for affection. "Do you know what inn you will choose tonight? I can have your belongings sent ahead of you."

"I haven't decided yet," Kila replied, stretching her arms over her head. She wore studded leather armor with her hair once again coiled around the top of her head. "Do you mind if we use the inn's back courtyard for training?"

Laryssa made a face. "Are you going to damage anything?"

Kila shrugged. "Not intentionally."

Laryssa rolled her eyes. "Do whatever you need to do, just know you'll pay for anything you break."

Kila shrugged, setting her empty mug down with a sigh. "Ready?"

Kestral nodded. This time he picked me up, slinging me over his shoulder and ignoring my cry of protest.

You could always shift, came Kestral's mental voice. I chose to ignore it. As soon as I could, I would bound back to our room to sleep.

Once outside, Kestral set me down on the packed earth. He secured the door to the inn behind him, giving me a glance to make sure I understood that if I wanted to open it, I would have to be human. I turned my tail on him and trotted to the stacked hay bales near the barn. I leapt to the top of the stack, turned a circle, then curled up into a tight ball. I didn't have to sleep in a bed, after all. Kestral shrugged at me then stretched his arms and back. Nearby, Kila did the same.

Is that what she meant by "warm up?" Were they going to spar? They both stretched before moving to a few strength exercises. I drifted off but came to abruptly at the hiss of steel being unsheathed.

"Two out of three bouts?" Kila asked, wiping imaginary dirt from the blade of her slender sword.

"One sword only," Kestral added, eyeing the other weapons on Kila's belt. "Three touches. No head strikes."

I tried to make a quip, but it came out as a meow. Dust it, if I shifted they would rope me into training somehow.

Kestral brought his sword up into a guard position. Kila held hers back behind her, balancing in a long stance. Her lips curled up in a secretive smile; Kestral's face held no expression at all. For a long moment, no one moved. I nearly jumped when both swordsmen burst into motion, flying at each other in a fury of sword strikes.

It was over before I could blink. Kestral's armor was scored across his leather glove and his side. Kila's was marked along her shoulder, sleeve and hip. She bowed her head briefly, acknowledging Kestral's win, then fell back into a defensive stance. The bout began all over again.

Kestral won two of the three bouts, to which Kila protested the use of a single sword. If allowed her normal range of weapons, she never would have lost. Kestral agreed with her as they shared a waterskin. My tail lashed. I was in a foul mood which I decided to blame on my lack of sleep.

"Come down, Reshi," Kila called. "It's your turn."

I shook my head, fluffing up the fur around my neck and shoulders.

"You need proper training," Kestral added. "Unconventional tactics will only get you so far."

I turned around, lashing my tail at both of them.

Kila sighed dramatically. "Well, Kestral, I think we'll just have to split that flask of Goldwater between the two of us."

I turned back to peek over my shoulder.

"That could make this a nice evening," Kestral said, leaning back against the inn's barn, wiping down his sword with a cloth. "Exchanging war stories over good whiskey."

"It's good and aged, too," Kila added. "The soldier I won it from swears he got it from a cask stored over twenty years."

"I see what you're doing," I called down from the hay bale. At least Kila jumped at my sudden shift. Kestral merely eyed me coolly.

"Come down and train, Reshi." Kestral sheathed his sword. "Kila says she'll share the flask."

I narrowed my eyes at my sister. "Has it really aged twenty years?"

"At least." Kila shrugged. "Could be longer. I only had a taste of it; nearly knocked me straight over."

"You're small so that's not saying much."

Kila narrowed her eyes at me. "Come down here and say that, skinny blade."

Kestral set a hand on Kila's elbow as if to hold her back. "We'll just go over stances and a few movements. No sparring today."

I groaned, then slid carefully down the stacked hay. I had never particularly enjoyed training. It was boring and often it hurt. The Goldwater Whiskey had better be worth it. Kestral dropped my boots in front of me and I tied them on, refusing to ask when he had gotten them. I didn't have my throwing knives on me, but my fae daggers were in their usual hidden sheaths.

"We just want to make sure you survive the fight with our brothers," Kila said. "This is all useless to me if you die and I end up getting all five powers."

"We could accomplish the same thing if I just hide and you two kill Velyn and Eagan," I pointed out. "Since you've both decided I'm useless in a fight."

"Not useless," Kestral said. "You're impressive for someone without formal training. Kila and I just want to give you an edge."

I grumbled, but I allowed Kestral to show me several stances, most of which I had thought I knew already. He ran me through a few drills, which involved getting knocked out of stance and recovering it. That got boring fast. Afterwards, Kila drew two daggers about the size of mine and showed me several different paths of attack, only a few of which were new to me. At least with Kila's training there was a real possibility of getting hurt, as she didn't seem to care whether she cut me or not. Dodging her strikes held my attention, if nothing else.

By midday I had worked up a sweat, which I despised. I could often get away with only washing my clothes out every once in awhile, thanks to Wix's cloak and my shapeshifting. Today would be a different story entirely, especially if I wanted to dance again later tonight. Would my clothes even dry in time for that? Maybe Kestral had been right and I should have a second set of clothes. I took a long draught from a waterskin, finishing in time to see Kila accept a tray of food from the bar mistress. It was a plate of cold foods, pieces of bread, thinly sliced lamb from the night before and slabs of cheese. It seemed a small feast, considering I had only had a little milk for breakfast.

"You looked like a better fighter yesterday," Kila commented, layering lamb and cheese on top of a slice of bread. She topped it with a smear of jam before biting into it. "Everything you did today was wrong."

"Told you I'm not much for training," I replied, rolling slices of lamb up inside a piece of cheese. "I can fight to the death, no problem. Training is just boring."

"You should be trying harder," Kestral admonished, folding a piece of bread in half over slices of lamb. "Drills are what train you to react when you get distracted in the middle of a fight."

"You never see a nightblack cat get distracted in the middle of a hunt," I replied with a shrug. "Or stags forget why they're jousting each other. Animals don't train and neither do I."

Kestral looked over at Kila. "There's a little truth to that."

Kila rolled her eyes. "Nightblack cats also don't stay up all night drinking ale and tripping over bar stools. If nothing else, training will make you stronger, Reshi."

"She's right," Kestral said, assembling another folded-bread meal from the tray.

"You're awfully agreeable today," I commented, snatching the last piece of cheese. I felt like I could eat another whole tray of food. "Did you get to kick the dust off your boots last night while I wasn't looking?"

Kila laughed. "He never took his eyes off you, Reshi. Stars, it was like he expected the flutist to blow a dart at you, or every serving wench to slip poison in your drink. I thought he was going to flip the table over when you tried to dust up with that drunk girl."

Kestral looked away sharply, almost as if embarrassed, but before I could tease him, several uniformed soldiers rounded the inn, calling out to Kila.

"Hey, Killer!" The lead soldier called out. "Commander said you weren't in the field today, but I didn't believe it."

"Yeah, I'm taking a few days to get to know my little brother." Kila grinned at the soldier, but her hand went to her hilt. "Don't get any ideas, now."

The soldiers laughed nervously. "Not as long as you're with him, anyway," another soldier said. "We wanted to ask where you're staying tonight. You owe us a dice game."

I noticed a smaller hooded and robed figure standing behind the soldiers. I couldn't see the face beneath the hood, but by its height I judged the figure to be female. She hovered behind the soldiers, saying nothing, face turned down. The robe she wore looked old and had been frequently patched. Was she a villager who had taken a liking to one of the soldiers? Maybe a message runner of some sort? She flinched each time one of the soldiers made a broad gesture as they chatted with Kila. I couldn't say why, but something about her held my attention.

"Just look for me somewhere along the broad street," Kila said, waving off the soldiers. "I won't decide where I'm staying until later."

"Not even a hint, Kila?" one of the soldiers whined.

"If you ask me again, ask with steel." Kila gave him a feral grin. The soldiers laughed, some with an edge of nerves, before they waved and departed. They were well out of sight before Kila released her hilt. "They were probably just here to size you up, Reshi. Rust, those bonded mages give me the shivers."

"Is that what the girl was?" I asked, turning back to Kestral and Kila. "What is a bonded mage? Are they captured mages from Viaparaiso?"

Kila's jaw dropped. It seemed I could surprise my siblings as much as they surprised me. She turned to Kestral who looked away, refusing to meet her eyes. "How does he not know? I thought . . ." She looked at me, eyes wide in shock. "You really don't know?"

"I asked you yesterday," I reminded her.

"Yes, but . . ." She shook her head slowly before rounding on Kestral. "How could you not have told him?"

"He's been a flight risk since day one," Kestral replied shortly. "I thought knowing would scare him off."

"But that's just like you've been lying to him the whole time!"

Kestral looked up sharply, locking eyes with her. "It doesn't make a difference. I never bonded him."

Kila shook her head, still in shock.

"Excuse me, but I'd like to be filled in at some point," I said, drawing their focus back. "What is bonding? Why does the army have mages working for it since the Great Mage Hunt ended?"

Kestral looked away again, refusing to answer.

Kila took a breath before answering. "Army officers can use a specific rune to bind a mage's power. It . . . well, it basically turns mages into slaves. During the Great Mage Hunt, powerful mages were killed, the weak ones, too. But any mage of average strength was captured and bound by the army for their battle magic."

"And healing," Kestral added softly. "The Order of the Great Canvas kept any mages skilled at healing."

"They mostly work for the army, too, though," Kila replied. "Battlefield clerics."

"I don't understand." I looked from Kila to Kestral. "The Great Mage Hunt was supposed to kill all the mages, or at least drive them out of the country. No one in any village I've ever visited has ever talked about bonded mages."

"It's the great, dirty secret of the kingdom," Kila said with a bitter chuckle. "The king says mages are dangerous, a threat to normal citizens and gets them to turn in their mage neighbors, their mage friends. The people feel safer and the army gets powerful slaves to fight their wars for them."

"But you're fighting, too," I pointed out. "You agree with this war, don't you?"

"As a soldier, I didn't question orders. But as an officer, I also refused to use or to bond any mages. Using magic is like fighting dirty." Kila grimaced. "I like meeting my enemy eye-to-eye on the battlefield in a true contest of skill. Nothing magical about it."

"But, wait." I turned to face Kestral. He met my eyes, but there was something different in his gaze. Was it shame? "You were an army officer."

He nodded.

"So you could have . . ." I trailed off. I wanted to ask the question, but I didn't want to know the answer. If he could have bonded me at any time, why hadn't he? Or if he had, would I have known? Dust, I could easily have become nothing more than a piece of property again. I shivered and drew closer to my sister.

"I was never going to bond you, Reshi," Kestral said, shifting his gaze between Kila and me.

"But you have bonded mages, haven't you?" I asked. "You said you had helped the army take down minor mages before."

Kestral jaw tightened, but he nodded. Icy fear traced a trail down my spine; I really knew nothing of the man I had been traveling with. After a tense silence, Kestral stood.

"I don't blame you if you don't trust me any more," he said, turning to walk away. "Just stay close to Kila until your brothers get here. After that . . ." Kestral trailed off. He took a breath, letting it out slowly before he walked the long way around the inn, disappearing from sight. I let out a breath I didn't know I'd been holding.

"I didn't know," I said, voice barely above a whisper. "Stars, he could have had me powerless, couldn't he?"

"But he didn't," Kila replied, something strange in her eyes. Respect, maybe? "Do you know why he left the army?"

"Not really." I shrugged, trying to shake out the fear that had settled in my bones. "Something about a dishonorable discharge and someone's 'tickled tailfeathers.' That's all I know."

Kila nodded, still staring at the space where Kestral had disappeared from view. "Maybe there's more to it. The lies about the Great Mage Hunt have turned more than one officer against the army. I think it might be all right to trust him."

"What?" I asked, incredulous.

"He's never hurt you, has he?"

"He fired a crossbow bolt at my head."

"Before or after he knew you? Never mind, I've known you half a day and I could see myself shooting you with a crossbow." Kila waved off my outrage. "My point is, he didn't have to protect you. If I were him, I would have used you as bait, drawing in the others and then killed you either during or after the battle. But he's always run with you, hasn't he? Putting himself at more risk?"

"He—I . . ." I considered Kila's argument. "Even so, why didn't he bond me? What would you have done if it were you?"

"If I was him, I would have bonded you the first chance I got." Kila nodded firmly. "It would keep you from using magic against him, keep you from running away, it would just . . . keep you." Kila looked at me quizzically. "So why did you stay with him?"

I dropped my gaze, puzzling it out. Why? Why stay with Kestral after all this time? I struggled with the question before meeting Kila's gaze.

"I'm going after him."

Kila nodded, as if that was the answer she had expected. I stood up and ran after Kestral, stumbling on legs numb from sitting on the hard ground. He couldn't have gone too far; Shan was still stabled at the Drunken Fish. I didn't see him anywhere along the village's main road but there were shops up and down the street. He could be in any one of them.

Come on, I thought to myself. He wasn't that complicated of a guy, or maybe he was, but at least he was predictable. What did he do when he was agitated or upset?

He went hunting.

I looked around for a fletcher's shop and found one just across the street. I raced up to it, grabbing for the door just as it swung open, bringing me face to face with the man I was looking for.

Kestral blinked at me, eyes wide in surprise. He had a package of unfletched arrows in one hand, a bag of fletching in the other. Thank the stars for predictable habits.

"I don't care," I said it in a rush, the words tripping over each other. Kestral's brows drew close together. "I mean, it doesn't matter. You're right. You're the only reason I'm still breathing right now and whatever you could have done, you didn't. So I don't care. Don't leave, or just don't leave right now, okay?"

We stood in that doorway for what seemed like forever. I got the sense that the shopkeeper wanted to say something, but held back, probably due to the intensity of the moment. I caught my breath while Kestral held my gaze.

"You don't want me to leave, even though you think I'm going to kill you one day?"

"At least I'll live until that day." I tried for a charming smile. "And who knows? Maybe by then I'll be strong enough to put up a decent fight."

Kestral dropped his gaze and shook his head. "Your whole family is crazy."

"At least we're good looking." I started to reach out to him but then drew my hand back. My ribs still remembered what happened the last time I'd tried to touch him. "Come back to the inn with me and Kila. We still need you to help us with Velyn and Eagan."

Kestral nodded. "I was always going to stick around for that. It's not as if either of you can turn in their bounties."

"It's not as if either of us needs the money from the bounties." I cast a disgusted look down at his worn-through boots. "Maybe after we kill Eagan we'll steal his boots for you."

Kestral actually laughed at that. "Noble's boots aren't good for soldiers. They would look better on you, anyway."

"Speaking of things that look better on me." The sweat from earlier had dried on my clothes, leaving them stiff and wrinkled. "I have a few coins and I need clothing I can dance in tonight. Did you want to guard me against assassin-tailors while I go shopping?"

Kestral rolled his eyes but agreed to accompany me. The whole bonding thing was still pretty scary, but somehow not having Kestral near me was an even more terrifying thought. Kestral kept me safe. That was more than anyone else had ever done for me before and it was something I didn't want to give up.

"Are you sure you couldn't have found clothes that aren't all black?" Kestral asked later as I was tucking a wrapped package under my arm.

"I was afraid that if I picked something fancy and brightly colored, you would mistake me for my brother Eagan," I replied tartly. "Wouldn't want you killing me by accident. That would just embarrass us both."

"There you guys are." Kila trotted up to us as we exited the tailor shop. "Everyone happy? No one dead? Good. We're staying at the Pluck and Courage Inn tonight. I got our rooms already."

I cheered but Kestral frowned. "You know we can't—"

Kila waved him off. "Don't worry about it. I've got a lot of credit built up in this town, it's not a problem. We just have to buy lots of drinks to make it up to the innkeeper."

"Best deal ever made!" I linked my arm through Kila's. "Lead on to the Pluck and Courage, good sister."

Tonight's inn proved to be as nice as the Drunken Fish, with a different set of musicians and a fresh set of pretty partners to dance with. Once again Kestral caught me before I could kick the dust up with anyone and once again the morning was dedicated to practicing stances and weapons. Kestral got it in his head that I needed to learn the sword and Kila insisted on playing with my fae daggers to learn their secrets. The days continued cheerfully, the only thing that changed daily was our inn. Getting to know my sister without worrying about her trying to kill me was refreshing, but it was shadowed by the fear that Velyn and Eagan would eventually show up and ruin it. Kila and I didn't have very much in common, but it was nice connecting with family.

Even nicer than connecting with Kila was connecting with non-relatives after a night of drinking. I managed to drunkenly sneak away from Kestral's watchful eye three times, dusting it up with a dance partner for the night. Kestral always left the door to our room open so I could slink in later, though he barely spoke to me the mornings after. His training sessions those mornings were always a little more grueling too, but it was worth it. Maybe he would be happier if he kicked the dust up once in a while. He seemed to find Kila agreeable enough and she didn't seem to be dusting up with anyone, but before I could try to work something out between the two of them, storm clouds gathered on the horizon.

Velyn and Eagan had finally caught up with us.

7

Kila picked the battlefield where we awaited our brothers' approach. The border river here had recently swelled then retreated, leaving the ground too murky for soldiers in heavy armor to defend. The ground had dried enough such that leather boots treading lightly could walk unhindered. Kestral and Kila had both donned chainmail armor— Kila's skirted beneath her belt, Kestral with steel plates stitched to his leather-armored leggings. Kila was as heavily armed as always. I was impressed she could carry so many swords; the overall weight had to be greater than her own. Kestral wore only his normal sword and heavy dagger, along with a pair of gauntlets I had never seen before and my bracers of throwing knives looped through his belt.

I didn't feel the need to overdress for my brothers' arrival. I wore my usual sneak-thief's garb and fae-made cloak. The one addition was a pair of gloves for better grip; Kila said sweaty palms were the number one death for dagger-wielders and she drove the point home by painfully disarming me a number of times.

Kila and I both felt Velyn and Eagan's approach, not just in the rolling fog that preceded them, but as a constant tug in our minds. I figured it must be a weak combination of Cera's sight and speech magic. The closer they got, the more we could sense them. I could feel them like I was sitting too close to a hearth fire, or as if I were caught in a tempest. I often caught Kila glancing in the direction of their approach, her jaw tightly clenched. She still wouldn't talk about anything magical, but it was clear that she also felt their presence.

The three of us stood in the middle of our chosen battlefield, watching thick fog roll in from the east. They would be on us in a matter of minutes. Kestral stood firm, hands on his belt. Kila paced, running her hands over her weapons and muttering to herself. I tucked my hands in my pockets and slouched comfortably. I wished there was something to lean against, but the field was barren of trees and boulders. That was half the reason Kila chose it, I suspected.

"Remember, the fire-bug is mine," Kila said, tugging at her gauntlets for the hundredth time. "I need to pay him back for Laki."

Kestral nodded. "All yours. Reshi, you remember—"

"I know, I know." I waved a hand dismissively. "You made me listen to the plan a dozen times. I got it."

Kestral frowned but said nothing. The wall of fog hit us, rolling over our battlefield and obscuring everything but each other. Kila looked up, baring her teeth in a reckless grin. I smiled lazily. Kestral stared ahead, face betraying no emotion.

Velyn and Eagan stood in the fog just ahead of us. Eagan smiled charmingly, tilting his head to the side, one hand on the sword at his belt. Velyn scowled darkly, hands open at his sides, pushing the fog forward.

"I think they were expecting us, little brother," Eagan said, inclining his head towards us.

"I knew they would be." Velyn smirked at me. "Found more people to hide behind, little Reshi?"

"Hiding is what I do." I shrugged easily, meeting his smirk with mine. "Come to kill another of our sisters? Because I don't think it'll work out for you this time."

Kila laughed dryly, drawing out the sound like steel on bone.

"Mage hunter," Eagan called. "This is your last chance to walk away."

"Raleagan." Kestral met his eyes evenly. "This is your last chance to step away from that murderer."

"Says you," Kila replied. "I'm avenging Laki, with or without you."

"Oh, he knows that," I said, tucking my hands behind my head and stretching as if we were having a casual conversation. "Kestral is saying you don't need our help with that spoiled noble."

Eagan chuckled and rolled his shoulders. "Well, I did warn you." The hand opposite his sword came up, and with it came a ring of roaring flames, closing around Kestral, Kila and me. Kestral stood calmly, still meeting Eagan's flickering orange eyes. I flinched back from the flames; I couldn't help that reflex. Every animal fears fire.

Kila grinned. Her movement was subtle, easily missed, but flinching as I was, I saw it. She raised her heel very slightly, then slammed it back down. The ground shuddered then rippled outward, dropping away beneath Eagan's fire and swallowing it whole. Smirking at the stunned faces of our brothers, Kila drew her sword and began a slow advance, a predator closing in on stunned prey.

"Earth magic." Kestral nodded. "It had to be something like that."

"You expected that?" I asked, still awed by Kila's casual use of such a powerful force.

"No, but something like it." Kestral drew his sword. "Are you ready?"

Ahead of us, Eagan and Velyn recovered from their shock, Velyn cursing and drawing back, Eagan drawing his sword to meet Kila.

I smirked. "Always. Hey, Kila!"

"What?" She didn't turn back, just kept advancing calmly.

"Give me a boost."

She halted, turning back to smile at me. "Ready when you are."

I raced forward, picturing the speed and grace of a nightblack cat on the hunt. As I passed Kila, she lifted her foot slightly, then slammed it back down. A patch of earth rose at an incline before me, giving me a height to leap from. I heard Velyn curse distantly before a lightning bolt sheared the air before me. By the time I could see again, I was in my crow form, arrowing down towards him.

The plan was to draw Velyn's lightning so that by the time Kestral closed with him, he would have spent most of his magic. Nearby, Kila and Eagan had begun their fight, swords clashing, the earth swallowing more fire magic as quickly as it could take form. Kestral would be picking his way across the battlefield, using stray magic as cover. I had to wear Velyn down before Kestral could strike.

"I see what you're doing," Velyn called up to me. A lightning strike tried to sear me from the sky. As I angled my wings to avoid it, a surge of wind tried to sweep me back into its path. I shifted to my human form, using my increased weight to counter the wind, then shifted back, wings catching me before I fell too far. "You can't wear me down, Reshi. Both of you die today."

Hail rained down on me, clipping my wings and tail feathers. It was harder to dodge than the lightning bolts, and a direct hit would probably kill me. Dust it, Velyn had learned some new tricks since the last time we fought. I swooped low, shifting to human and somersaulting with a kick that glanced off Velyn's shoulder. In at instant, I had my daggers out, closing the distance between us. Velyn's white-blue eyes widened with shock and pain, but before I could connect with my daggers, a pike of ice formed in his hands. Instead of being capped by a blade, this pike had two prongs at the end, like a fisherman's spear turned to a weapon. He jabbed wildly, driving me back a pace. Daggers weren't great against pole-weapons. He must have worked that out with Eagan.

"Kill any more helpless girls, Velyn?" I asked, keeping my voice steady as I turned his spear aside. Velyn gritted his teeth, fury on his face.

"I had to kill Cera. There's no way you could understand." Velyn swiped at me with haft of his ice-weapon. He wasn't very good, but that didn't matter so much when it came to a long-arm weapon against daggers. If I'd had my throwing knives, I could have ended the fight in an instant. "It has to be me, Reshi. If you knew what I knew, you'd understand."

"You think I'd go around killing our brothers and sisters?" I laughed bitterly. "For what? A throne?"

"It's not about a throne!" Velyn thrust viciously. "It's about—" He stopped, his speech turning to a cry of fright as I turned the thrust aside on one dagger and slammed the hilt of my second dagger into the haft, shattering the ice-weapon in his hands. I slashed at his throat, but his body turned to mist before coalescing several paces away from me.

"I'm so tired of that trick," I hissed, turning to face him again.

"Not all of us are so limited in our magic." Velyn smirked as he reformed the ice-spear. "Must be terrible, being the youngest of us all."

I grinned, flipping my dagger to reverse my grip. "You're forgetting that I'm not fighting you on my own."

Velyn's eyes widened and he turned just in time to avoid Kestral's sword sweeping down on him. The spear shattered again, sending shards of ice flying. A dozen tiny cuts appeared on Velyn's arms, neck and face before he faded to mist. I was ready for his mist tactic this time, though. A quick shift had me in cat form, racing for the spot I expected him to reform in. By the time he became solid, I was there with a sideways slash. Velyn got his arm up in time to protect his throat, but I tore his arm open from wrist to elbow, grinning wildly. Before he could form another ice weapon, Kestral was on his other side, sword drawn back for a powerful thrust.

Lightning roared down on us. Kestral dropped his sword and dove to the side. I dropped down into rat form, scurrying away as the smallest target possible. The lightning cleared, revealing Velyn holding his arm and panting, trails of smoke rising from his clothing. A quick roll had Kestral up and armed again and a rapid shift had me coming up behind my brother.

We might have had him, but the rushing sound of fire sent us dodging again. Velyn spun, facing the flame head-on through a sudden downpour of rain. He sneered at Eagan, who rolled his shoulders in a shrug, seeming not to care whether he had caught his ally in the inferno or not.

Kestral and I backed away, looking for Kila. She walked calmly towards us, drawing a cloth along the length of her blade. The cloth came away bloody. I looked back at Eagan, noting for the first time that he had lost his cloak and held his left arm close to his side. As I watched, Velyn encased the arm I had cut in a sheath of ice, sealing in the blood.

"My battle isn't going as well as I anticipated, brother." Eagan sheathed his sword, taking an easy stance next to Velyn.

"Mine isn't either," Velyn growled, white-hot hatred in his eyes for both me and Kestral. I smiled and waved at him, earning an enraged snarl. Eagan laughed as he hooked his hands around his belt.

"Kila, are you injured?" Kestral asked, his eyes never leaving our enemies.

She chuckled softly. "As if that feather-fingered noble could touch me."

"This feather-fingered noble still has a few tricks." Eagan gave her a tight smile. "Courtesy of your twin, as a matter of fact."

Kila gritted her teeth. The leather of her hilt crackled as her grip tightened.

"That is, if you're prepared, dear Velyn?" Eagan glanced sidelong at his ally.

"Do you ever shut up, you rusting fool?" Velyn asked, raising his arms to the side, one still encased in ice.

"Hm." Kestral shot a look at me.

"What?" I asked acidly.

"One more thing you have in common with that one."

"Rude, Kestral. Just rude."

Kila laughed but stopped abruptly as freezing rain showered over us, wind whipping it up and around, forming strange shapes that froze in place in the middle of our battlefield. The wind died but the air stayed cold, our breath puffing before our faces. I barely got a look at the strange ice-sculptures—like giant, headless preying mantises, each nearly half as tall as a building—before Eagan threw his arm out dramatically. The ice-mantises scuttled towards us, swinging their fore-arms like ice-bladed scythes.

"Gotta say, I did not see that coming," Kila called to us, meeting an ice-blade-arm with her sword. She turned it aside, shattering it, but freezing rain swirled around it, reforming the blade. Kila cursed and backed away.

"I'm sure I said we should have a contingency plan in case of giant ice bugs," I called from behind Kestral. He crushed a mantis arm with a powerful swing then countered the second arm, ice screeching as it slid along the metal blade. I ducked as ice shards went flying. There were five of these giant ice bugs, all slowly converging on the three of us.

"Kila, what can you do for us?" Kestral shouted as his mantis slowly recovered its forelimbs.

Kila took a minute to respond, tapping her foot against the now-frozen ground. "Not much. I could punch through, but it would take a lot from me."

"Reshi, anything?" Kestral asked, countering a flurry of strikes.

"Yeah, I think maybe . . . no. I got nothing." I shook my head, still half-cowering behind the mage hunter. "There aren't any animals big enough to fight these nearby, and even if there were, I doubt I could convince them to fight something so obviously unnatural."

"Right." Kestral spun suddenly, grabbing me and throwing me flat to the ground, narrowly missing a scissor of ice-blades. He raced forward, ducking the swings of the headless ice-bug to get beneath its long body. He dragged his blade along the belly of the beast, then thrust up at its center, twisting his blade as he did so, causing the abdomen to crack along its vertical axis. The two halves fell away from each other, spindly legs thrashing. I picked myself up out of the frozen mud, half annoyed, half grateful. Kila whooped joyfully as she used her twin shortswords to scissor off a bladed forelimb.

"Kila, I need two things," Kestral shouted as he engaged the next ice-bug.

"And they are?"

"A boost." He turned aside a stab and pointed with his free hand. "This is taking all their concentration. If I can get close, I can kill them."

Kila grunted acknowledgment, driving a sword into a bug's chest and twisting it as Kestral had. A large chunk of ice fell free, but the bug didn't fall. "And what else?"

"Keep Reshi safe." With a crashing swing, Kestral disarmed both forelimbs then darted forward, racing between the ice-bugs coming at him.

Kila switched her swords to one hand, spinning them to ward off a flurry of ice-blades. She stomped one foot firmly down into the frozen ground, cracking the ice beneath it. Just as it had for me, the ground rose beneath Kestral, giving him an earthen spire to leap from, landing well behind the ice bugs. Eagan moved to meet him, but I lost sight of Kestral as an ice bug skittered up to me, swinging those deadly bladed arms.

I slammed my fae blades together and drew them across each other, elongating the daggers into stilettos, giving me a little more reach to block the ice-blades. Nothing I had would cut through them anyway, might as well keep my distance. Kila retreated from her bug until she could put her back to mine.

"Does he always do that?" she asked, crushing a blade between her swords.

"Run off like a big, dusty hero?" I asked, catching a blade along my stiletto and redirecting it safely to the side.

"Take command," Kila panted though she looked more exhilarated than exerted.

"Oh, throw around orders and expect absolute obedience? Yes, he always does that." I grunted as the flat of a forearm caught me, slamming me into Kila, who was surprisingly solid for someone so short.

"You must have something helpful here," Kila said. She craned her neck trying to see through the shifting, skittering ice-legs. "It looks like Eagan is able to fight while he controls this magic."

"Dust, rust and ashes," I cursed. "Yes, I have something."

"Something not suicidal?" Kila glanced back at me over her shoulder. "I don't need your hunter coming after me if you die."

I grinned, baring more teeth than necessary. "No, not suicidal. Kestral doesn't know all my tricks yet. But I could use one of your little throwing knives."

Kila switched her swords back to one hand, running the other through the braid in her hair. It came out clutching a tiny triangular knife between her fingers. She tossed it to me casually, then darted beneath the body of her ice bug, driving both blades up into its stomach. Her arms trembled for a moment, then tore the blades free, causing the bug to break in two pieces, aft and fore. With a fierce battle cry, she threw herself at the next beast.

After turning my stilettos back into daggers, I slipped one away to hold onto Kila's tiny dagger. I crouched low, leaping as the ice-bug slashed at me. I landed on the flat of the ice-blade and ran along it, skidding as I reached the bug's body. Dropping to one knee, I drove my fae blade into the ice to keep from sliding off. As the bug tried to contort itself to slash at me, I unwound a thin copper wire from around the top of my boot: garrote wire. Bracing my foot against the dagger, I quickly tied off one end of the wire to the loop on the end of Kila's throwing dagger. Ducking beneath an ice-blade that nearly gave me a haircut, I slid along the beast's back until I could brace my feet against the joints of its legs. Using the dagger as a weight, I looped the wire around the spindly limb and pulled the wire tight, sawing once before the limb snapped clear.

The bug staggered, spilling me off its back. I threw the wire around the next leg, catching myself before I could fall. The second leg snapped clear, the final leg on this side of the beast buckling. I shifted to my crow form, snatching the knife and the wire in my talons as the ice-mantis crashed to the ground. Lying on its side as it was, the spindly legs couldn't reform properly.

I flew over to Kila, appreciating how she played the final two ice-bugs against each other, dodging so they struck each other's forelimbs off. At some point she had lost her shortswords and switched to her bastard sword, using it more as a shield than a weapon.

I landed on one bug's scythed forelimb, balancing precisely on the raised joint to loop the wire around it before snapping it clear. Before it could reform, I slid down its arm to its back and repeated my trick, sawing off its legs with the wire. As my beast crashed to the ground, Kila's shattered, an earthen spike driven up where its midsection had been. As one, we turned towards Eagan and Kestral, Velyn standing a-ways back, pale and out of breath.

Kestral backed a step up, disengaging from Eagan as the last of the ice-bugs fell. Eagan looked worse for the wear, blood staining his tunic and trickling down his arm. His hair was matted with sweat and his eyes had lost that look of amused disdain he usually wore. Instead, they blazed with an intense hatred, as if they could scorch Kestral where he stood.

Kestral had blood running down his side, coloring the left side of his leggings. Red welts covered his sword arm and one shoulder of his armor had turned black and brittle, the shirt beneath burned away. The ice in his eyes as he stared down Eagan was enough to make me shiver.

"Stand down, Kestral." Kila stepped in front of him, bringing her longsword up into a guard position. "I can finish these two in a single attack."

"We don't have time for that." Kestral sheathed his sword, turning slightly to the east. Kila and I glanced up. Her jaw tightened but mine fell open.

"Is that the army?" I asked, voice pitching higher than I intended. "But why—?"

"That's not the eastern army," Kila said softly. "Those banners . . ."

"The southern houses." Eagan slid his sword into its sheath, squinting at the banners in the distance. "House Clarion, House Hazen." He chuckled darkly. "My old house, too. What an honor."

There was a curse from behind us before Velyn scrambled closer, putting his back to Eagan's. "Over there. Viaparaiso."

Kestral turned, glowering at the forces gathering west of us. "I should have expected this," he said, speaking softly. "With Kila telling the whole kingdom where we were, it only made sense for the king to send forces to crush us."

"But the southern army?" Kila asked.

"It's because you're too friendly with the eastern army," Kestral guessed. "The king probably thought they would let you run."

Kila cursed in a soldier's colorful tongue.

"Our king mobilized a foreign country's army, too?" Velyn asked, sounding as panicked as I felt. I slid back a step, putting myself slightly behind Kestral.

"Most likely he offered some concession to them if they could kill you four." Kestrel turned, sizing up the battlefield.

"I think I would like to extend to the three of you a temporary truce," Eagan said formally, nodding to each of us. "Dying here would defeat the purpose of killing you."

Kila laughed darkly. "Like you weren't already losing."

"I could still kill you," Eagan said, shrugging casually.

"Try it, fire-starter."

"I think a truce might be in our best interest," I said, carefully putting my hand over Kila's sword. "Those are two really big armies coming at us from two directions."

Kila snorted dismissively, but she lowered her sword.

"So we have an agreement?" Kestral asked, still speaking quietly. He looked first to Eagan and Velyn, each nodded, though the latter appeared reluctant. He glanced back at Kila and me. I nodded eagerly. Kila barely inclined her head. "How full are your wellsprings?"

"Mine is a depthless inferno," Eagan replied, smirking.

"I've been keeping the storm at bay." Velyn rolled his wrists, sparks of lightning dancing between his fingers.

"I've got magic for days," I bragged, raising my chin at the others.

Kestral paused, meeting each of our eyes once. "So you three are lying." He turned towards our sister. "Kila?"

"I barely used any magic," she admitted, sounding as if the words were dragged from her. She pointed to the southern army with her sword. "And each soldier who falls only feeds my wellspring."

Eagan breathed deeply, as if smelling something sweet. "Soldiers are always so passionate. I can already feel myself regaining my power."

Dust it. Why can I only gain magic from sleeping people? Judging by a quick look at Velyn, though, I doubted he was regaining power here, either.

"All right." Kestral took a moment to size up each army. "The plan is to break through the center of the southern army's line."

"The center—" Eagan started to interrupt. He froze under Kestral's intense glare.

"The foremost tactic of the southern army is a pincer. The cavalry on the sides will close in, hemming us to the center anyway. We charge straight through." Kestral unhooked the gauntlets from his belt, never taking his eyes from the army's lines marching steadily towards us.

"They'll have bonded mages," Kila said, also watching the approach of the army.

"Leave those to me." Kestral pulled the gauntlets over his hands, snapping them tightly around his forearms. Eagan eyed the gauntlets warily, Velyn backed away from them. Kila laughed as she noticed them.

"Anti-magic wards." She shook her head, grinning. "You've been holding back."

"Everyone knows they only work against bonded mages," Eagan sneered, though he still looked nervously at the gauntlets.

"Or mages I've already encountered." Kestral gave the fire mage a dark look. Hatred rekindled in my brother's eyes.

"We don't have time to fight with each other," I reminded everyone. "Viaparaiso's army is getting closer, too."

Kestral nodded, turning so he faced the southern army squarely. "Kila and Eagan, you two are going to break through the first ranks of the center. Don't get held up, just push through. I'll be right behind, grounding the mage spells." He ran a hand over the steel of his gauntlet, runes glimmering where he touched. "Reshi, you're going ahead. Get in the middle of their ranks and hide. When Kila and Eagan crash into the front, carve us a hole." He glanced over at me. "No flying. They'll have archers."

I nodded, trying to look confident. I was afraid if I spoke I would throw up.

"What about me?" Velyn asked, voice small.

"You." Kestral glared darkly at the weather mage. "Give Reshi cover until he gets behind the front lines. After we break the first two lines, you'll protect our backs. Got it?"

Velyn dropped his gaze to the ground, shifting his weight back and forth nervously. "If any of them fall, I'll risk it all to coalesce their power."

"Go ahead. I'll cut you down before you can reach them." Velyn shivered at the ice in Kestral's voice.

Eagan rested a hand on Velyn's shoulder. "In case you don't die, meet me where we anchored the Silver Minnow."

Velyn nodded.

Kestral glanced back at Kila and me. "If we get separated, meet back by Shan. Reshi, whenever you're ready."

I took a step forward, gritting my teeth and trying to keep my knees from knocking. We were still out of arrow range, but how far could the mages strike? I knew dust about war magic. Movement behind me made me look back. Kestral had Velyn by the collar, tossing him forward next to me. For a moment we eyed each other with open disdain before turning to face the oncoming army.

"What do you need?" Velyn hissed.

"Fog would work." I turned back towards the army. "A nice thick burst of it should do."

Velyn nodded. I took a deep breath then ran, charging a whole army all by myself. I could hear Kestral mustering the others behind me, but I lost all sight and sound as Velyn's thick, cold fog rolled over the battlefield like a blanket. Hidden as I was, I shifted to my cat form for speed. I saw the army well before they could see me, shifting again as I drew close. They would be looking for a full-sized mage, not a scurrying black rat. I dodged plated boots and horse hooves, driving for what I judged to be far enough in to carve out a hole. Shivering, I hid in the shadow of an armored horse, already reaching out with my magic for all the army's horses. They were going to regret bringing cavalry here.

I heard steel crashing against steel, the screams of men and my sister's terrifying war cry. I could almost see her leaping the front line of pikemen, soaring into the second line. Instead of trying to catch a glance back, I focused on the army's horses, stirring up their natural urges to flee. Once I had them stomping and snorting nervously, I used the same tactic I had used on Kestral's former soldiers—I shifted to my snake form.

The nearest horse screamed in pure terror, rearing repeatedly until it threw its rider free. The other nearest horses mimicked it, fear catching like fire. I shrank back to my rat form, dodging trampling hooves as horses turned and fled, turning the battlefield into complete chaos. I ran further ahead into the lines, where men still stood in ranks, trying to figure out why the horses were breaking. Behind me, thunder rolled. Beneath me, the ground shuddered and shook. My siblings were giving our escape attempt everything.

My turn.

I shifted human, slashing outward with my blades, taking two soldiers in the throat before they even saw me. Others reached for their swords, but I was faster, striking forward, darting backwards, carving out that hole Kestral had asked for. I lost myself in the rhythm of the fight, diverting strikes into near misses, sliding through blood as I dodged. I wasn't one for practice drills, but give me a good life-or-death battle any day.

"Reshi!" I turned as Kestral shouted my name.

He tossed me the bracers of throwing knives before turning back to ram his sword through a soldier's gut. He and Kila fought back-to-back, getting closer to where I fought. Velyn and Eagan were just behind them, protecting them from being surrounded.

I caught the bracers and shouted, "Kila, I need a distraction!"

I couldn't see her move, but the ground rippled, rising to ankle height and tripping the soldiers around me. I took the moment to strap the bracers around my wrists before throwing three blades simultaneously. Three soldiers never stood again. I pushed forward, dancing lightly through mud, blood and bodies. I had to be nearing the last ranks, right?

A large man appeared in front of me, swinging a long battleaxe. I leapt backwards to avoid it, but slipped in viscera, dropping to one knee. I watched the blade descend in horror, paralyzed like a stag before an archer.

Lightning flashed down like fire from the stars, catching the axe before searing the soldier. I stood shakily, looking back over my shoulder.

Velyn sneered at me before turning back to his own fight. He wasn't saving me, only prolonging my life until he could kill me himself.

Once my heart climbed out of my throat, I pushed forward again, silver daggers sliding through flesh or scraping armor. Two soldiers came at me from the side and went down with knives through their faces. Was that light filtering between the soldiers? Had I reached the end of the ranks?

I spun, ducking sword blows as I did. From a crouched position, I reversed my daggers and sliced through ankles, knees and hips as I rose again. Hot blood hit my face; I swiped it away with one arm as the other turned a sword aside. As I buried my dagger in the soldier's armpit, I saw Kestral behind me. For some reason, he smiled as he met my eyes. I grinned back; something about the thrill of battle could really make a man feel alive.

As I scanned the battle for Kila and my brothers, I saw Kestral's smile drop. He struggled to get clear of his opponents and was driven back by a spear haft. He shouted my name, but I was already turning to see it for myself.

I had breached the last line of the infantry and faced a line of archers. A throwing knife fell into my hand, but even I knew it was futile. Each arrow was already nocked and drawn. I had seconds to live.

As I drew what was certain to be my last breath, every bow in the line suddenly went up in flames. With smoke searing my lungs, I turned. Eagan stood amid a pile of grotesquely burned bodies. He shot me a wink. I flipped the knife in my hand, grinning as his eyes widened. I threw the blade, narrowly missing my brother, but catching the soldier behind him full in the throat. After he understood what I'd done, Eagan flipped his hand in a kind of salute. I smirked at him before turning back to my own fight.

I threw all my remaining knives, keeping the archers from recovering and reaching for their swords. Kestral finally burst free of the final line, charging the line of archers so that they scattered. I ran to his side, taking a moment to catch my breath.

"Where's Kila?" I asked between breaths. My limbs shook with battle-energy but I knew the longer I stood still, the quicker that energy would turn to exhaustion.

"Took off," Kestral said shortly. He pointed at a distant officer, struggling with a horse that was trying to bolt. "Can you get that horse to come here?"

"I can try. Watch my back." I reached for the horse's mind. It was used to coming at the call of its master's whistle, just like Shan. The most difficult part was convincing it that it was with the wrong master. When it pranced uncomfortably, I told Kestral to whistle.

After knocking aside the blade of a recovered soldier, Kestral let loose a sharp whistle. The distant horse reared, freeing its reins from the grounded officer, then charged at us, sliding to a stop in front of Kestral. He had its reins before it came to a full stop, vaulting easily into the saddle and turning the horse in a spin, warning the soldiers back.

"Up," Kestral commanded, holding a hand down to me. I considered shifting but found my magical wellspring barely above a trickle. I gripped Kestral's wrist, letting him yank me up behind him. Before I was fully seated, the horse charged off at a full gallop, carrying us away from the battle.

I let my forehead fall against Kestral's back, breath finally catching up with me. The muscles in my arms and legs felt like softened butter. My bones popped like fresh kindling in a fire. I might have another shift or two left in me, but that was it. I had to force my eyes open to keep from falling asleep.

Kestral drew the horse up just outside the city walls of Kila's village. I hoped she had gotten back safely, if she had gotten free of the army at all. Kestral climbed down from the saddle then reached up to help me down. His eyes burned as they met mine and for a moment I thought he was angry with me, but suddenly his lips were on mine, a hand on the back of my head pulling me closer.

A muffled yelp of surprise caught in my throat, unable to free itself from the hungry kiss. I clutched at his battle-worn chainmail, pulling him closer still. He broke the kiss for a breath, blue eyes searing into my soul, before he leaned in for a softer, longer kiss. I wrapped one arm around his waist while my other hand fumbled at the side of his armor, trying to undo the binding links that kept it on.

Kestral finally pulled back, breathing hard. He pushed my hand away but kept a grip on the back of my neck. My knees trembled as he shook his head. "Not here." His voice was deeper, his eyes a darker blue than I had seen before.

"Tell me where," I begged. Stars, don't let this be all! I needed so much more after that kiss.

Kestral laughed softly, gently untangling his hand from my hair. "We need to find Kila."

I groaned, stumbling back a step. Logically, I knew Kestral was right, but the blood surging through my body protested. It took a minute for my body to listen to my mind again. Kestral waited silently for me to catch up before leading the way through the unmanned gate into the village.

Torches were lit along the main boulevard. I was surprised to note that it was night. Had we really been fighting for that long? Ahead of us, Kila stood, talking to a group of soldiers, her expression dark. Kestral pushed me behind him protectively as he stepped forward to hear what was said.

". . . can't stay here anymore," one of the soldiers said, staring down at his boots apologetically.

"But I'm the best fighter you have against Viaparaiso!" Kila protested loudly. She didn't appear injured at all, despite the new blood spatters on her armor and boots. Her hair was half pulled down from its braid, as if someone had grabbed it during the fight. Blood was smeared across one side of her face, but I couldn't tell if it was hers or not.

"It's not the commander's decision," a different soldier explained, a pained expression on his face. "We're supposed to arrest you on sight."

"Try it." Kila's face grew dark as she reached back for her sword. The group of soldiers drew back, holding their hands up defensively.

"No, we wouldn't. Not for anything, Kila." The soldier shook his head firmly. "The commander took a patrol to a fort north of here, claiming he received a report that's where you were. He's giving you time."

"Time?" Kila repeated, her hand still on the hilt of her massive sword.

"Time to run." Kestral stepped up beside her, meeting each of the soldiers' eyes. "Is that right?"

Each man dropped his eyes and nodded solemnly.

"We're sorry, Kila."

Kila spat at their feet before spinning on her heel, striding towards the last inn we had stayed in.

"The commander won't be back until late tomorrow," a soldier explained to Kestral, watching Kila's back regretfully. "He wanted to give her time to heal, if she needed it."

Kestral nodded. "I'll see that she makes use of that time. Thank you, soldier."

The group of soldiers started to salute then stopped, realizing Kestral wasn't actually an officer. As one, they skulked off, shooting glances back at Kila as she disappeared inside the inn. Kestral glanced back at me before moving to follow Kila.

"Are you hurt?" he asked, eyes sweeping up from my boots to my face.

"Not badly." I had already taken inventory of my injuries: several cuts and bruises, possibly a pulled muscle in my back, a deep ache in one knee. Overall, though, I thought I would make it. "Are you?"

"I'll be fine." Kestral pushed the door of the inn open, light spilling out to reveal the bloodstains down his pant leg I had forgotten about. Eagan had gotten him earlier, and not just with the cut, but with fire, too. And unlike me, he couldn't just heal overnight. It probably wouldn't even be good for me to draw on him strongly for a few nights. I sighed; there went my hopes for the evening.

The inn was warm and loud, but not loud in a good way. Patrons cowered behind the bar as Kila raged around the room, grabbing heavy wooden chairs and hurling them into tables laden with food. She cursed and shouted, terrifying the poor staff who had been trying to calm her. Kestral stepped in front of her, catching the chair she held, but before he could speak, her eyes flashed, and she whipped the chair sideways, knocking him to the floor before dropping the chair on him. I darted in, grabbing her wrists. Not the smartest move, I know, but I couldn't let her cause further injury to Kestral.

"Kila, stop. Listen." I met her eyes, pleading. "I'm sorry. Really, I am. This is my fault. All of it. If I never came here, none of this would have ever happened."

"It *is* your fault!" Kila raged. Her arms shook as I held them, her skin hot to the touch. "If you hadn't come, I would still have a home here!"

"I know." I tried to sound consoling, understanding. "I lost my home, too. I get it, Kila. I do." Her bright red eyes shimmered; Kila wasn't going to cry, was she? "But there's always another battlefield, right, Kila?"

Kila stared up into my eyes, the trembling in her arms starting to fade. Right. Fast to flare, fast to burn out.

"Come find that battlefield with me, Kila." I gave her a small smile. "Or at least, let's stop terrorizing the villagers, okay?"

Kila gave a watery chuckle before pulling her arms away from me. She lowered her chin, swiping at her face with her hands. "Do you think they'll let me stay here tonight?"

"I think they'd be stupid to tell you otherwise," I replied. I glanced around, making eye contact with the innkeeper. He nodded and made a shooing motion with his hand towards the stairs. I put an arm around Kila's shoulders and led her away from the bar, mouthing an apology to the innkeeper. Kestral had shoved the chair off himself and climbed to his feet. He followed behind us, one hand pressed to his side where fresh blood leaked through his fingers. I grimaced. He would probably need stitches again.

"Are you hurt at all, Kila?" I asked when we stopped in front of her room.

She shook her head. "I healed already. Battlefield injuries are nothing . . ." She trailed off, noticing Kestral hanging back. "Come in. Let's see that." She ducked inside, leaving the door open for us to follow. I glanced back at Kestral. He seemed hesitant, or perhaps just pained, before following Kila inside.

"Here. Burn ointment." Kila tossed me a glass jar full of pus-colored cream. "Get his armor off and start with that." She rummaged through a large satchel as I helped Kestral unfasten his chainmail. It had been ravaged over his left shoulder, almost like a nightblack cat had taken a bite out of it. The shirt over the shoulder had been completely burned away, leaving red, blistered skin behind. Kestral gritted his teeth as I pulled the shirt off. So much for injuries not causing pain any more. I smeared the cream on his shoulder thickly—at least it smelled better than it looked—while Kila finally found her medic kit.

"Did he get your hip?" Kila asked, setting up small bottles of disinfectant out, along with needles and thread.

Kestral nodded.

"Lucky. If he'd had better aim, he could have really opened you up." Without pretense, Kila gripped the edge of Kestral's pants and peeled them down. I shouted a protest; Kestral grunted and flinched away. She looked up at both of us, disgust on her face. "Do you want it cleaned and stitched or not?"

I looked away, trying to hide the flush creeping up my face. It wasn't the stitching I was objecting to. At least she only had to slide his pants down a few inches to find the sliced flesh, exposing that tan line I always found so tantalizing. I used a wet cloth from the hand basin to clean dried blood and soot from Kestral's face and neck while Kila disinfected the wound on his hip.

"Maybe five inches long, not exactly a straight cut," Kila noted, her voice calm. "He's not a great swordsman, is he?"

"Eagan?" Kestral clarified, smearing more of the burn ointment over his arms. "The impression I got is that he's a skilled duelist. Not a warrior."

Kila nodded as if that made sense. She threaded a needle and pierced the flesh just below the laceration.

The room tilted around me, and I must have turned pale because suddenly both Kestral and Kila grabbed me by an arm, steadying me on my feet.

"Reshi, are you okay? Are you injured?" Kila's voice was filled with concern.

"You should go back to our room and get cleaned up," Kestral advised. To Kila, he added, "He doesn't like stitches."

"No, I'm fine," I protested. "It's been a long day and . . ." My stomach turned traitorously as I noticed the needle hanging from a thread through Kestral's skin. It took everything in me not to faint or sick up.

"Kestral's right, you should get cleaned up, too." Kila took my arm and guided me to the door. "Or at least lie down before you fall down."

I glanced back at Kestral, considering another protest, but he looked away. I let Kila push me gently from the room and close the door behind me. I stood in the hallway for a moment, feeling sick as well as rejected. Did I really need to remind Kestral that I couldn't handle very simple medical treatment? He probably thought I was weak. And I was. I felt like I'd spent more time during that battle hiding behind him than fighting.

Wouldn't he prefer someone like Kila? Someone strong? A warrior? Not afraid of stitching up a wound he only got because he'd been defending me. I had thought they would make a good match before. It had bothered me a little, but not much. Now it caused a deep ache in my chest, like an open wound slowly leaking lifeblood.

I made my way back to the room I had shared with Kestral the night before. The maids had been through it, making the bed, lighting candles and refilling the hand basin. No big washbasin, which would have been nice. At least if Kestral stayed with Kila, I wouldn't have to sleep in an animal form tonight. It was better for him not to come back. If I drew from him it would slow his own healing process, and that wouldn't be fair after everything he'd done for me today.

I unlaced my boots, taking care not to look too closely at them, caked as they were with battlefield detritus. I unfastened my cloak, letting it pool on the floor before unlacing my shirt and dropping it as well. The room didn't have a looking glass, which was just fine. I didn't want to see what I looked like. Using the hand basin, I cleaned myself of dried blood, sweat and soot. After letting my hair down, I ran the cloth through it, not really cleaning it but at least getting the blood out of it.

The sudden memory of Kestral's hand in my hair, his lips pressed against mine, hit me hard enough to make me dizzy. I gripped the edge of the hand basin, swaying as I tried to regain my balance. Stupid, I told myself. His blood was up after the battle, that was all. He hadn't been interested in me before. What made me think anything had changed?

I stared into the rippling water of the hand basin, slowly getting my body under control again. Maybe I really did need to lie down. Before I could, there was a sound at the door. I looked up as Kestral walked in, shirt and mail in hand, fresh stitches gleaming above rolled down leggings.

"Kestral." I swallowed and stared back down at the hand basin. "I was just getting ready for bed."

I heard him drop his mail on the floor. There was a soft click and then the sound of his sword and belt being set down gently.

"About earlier." I swallowed nervously. What could I say about earlier? "Don't worry about it, all right? I know it was just, you know, the heat of the battle and . . . winning, I guess, if you call it that."

His footsteps sounded on the floorboards. I stared into the water, watching it ripple with each step.

"I just wanted you to know that I'm not expecting anything. Because of that . . ." That kiss. I couldn't say it. I didn't even want to think about it too much.

He stopped right behind me, the heat of his body enveloping me, the caress of his breath fluttering on my neck. He was probably waiting for me to shift. I wanted to explain that I couldn't draw from him, not while his own wounds had to heal, but the arm wrapping around my waist and pulling me backwards stilled the breath in my chest. He pulled me so that my back rested against his chest, his warm breath on my shoulder sending a thrill down my spine.

"Reshi."

"Yes?"

"Come to bed."

"Yes."

8

What the dust do you say to a lover the next morning?

I had never before woken up beside a lover. My dalliances usually ended around midnight, with both persons going their separate ways. Not once had I ever had to exchange words the following morning.

Kestral was up before dawn, as usual, moving around the room and packing his bags. He made a noise of disgust over his burned and torn shirt before tossing it in a corner, giving it up as a lost cause. On any normal morning, I would have pulled the blankets over my head and tried to fall back asleep. Now, however, I felt I finally had permission to watch him walk around half naked. Our eyes met and he smiled softly.

I was at a complete loss for words.

Seriously, that had never happened to me before.

Slowly Kestral's smile faded and his eyebrows drew together. Dust! Was he expecting me to say something? What should I say? My heart beat a frantic tattoo as Kestral walked over to the bed. Was I supposed to compliment him? Make a joke? Offer to go another round?

Kestral peeled back part of the blanket. I snatched at it, keeping it above my hips.

"You didn't heal," he said, revealing the myriad of cuts and bruises marring my skin.

"No," I replied, pulling the blanket back from him. "Drawing from you takes away your own body's ability to heal. You're worse off than I am right now." I gestured at the cut on his hip and the burns on his arms and shoulder.

"Are you still able to shift?" Kestral asked.

I checked the golden ball of magic in my chest. "Yes. I've got two, maybe three shifts in me."

"Good." Kestral resumed pulling clothes on. "We'll be traveling today. Maybe late into the night, too. We need to put distance between us and the army."

"What about Kila?" I asked.

"If she wants to join us, she can." Kestral glanced over at me. "We can discuss it with her over breakfast if you'd get dressed."

I stretched luxuriously, smiling slyly at Kestral. "Are you sure that's what you want me to do?"

Kestral chuckled, sitting on the edge of the bed to pull his boots on. "No time, Reshi. We need to gather whatever supplies we can and get moving. There's no knowing how long the western commander can keep the southern army away from here."

I waited until Kestral left the room to kick off the blankets and get dressed. Last night it had been too dark to see those three tiny marks along my hip, but the room grew lighter as the dawn approached and I didn't want to risk it. Especially not now. My clothes were still caked in battlefield gore, now congealed from having been balled up on the floor overnight. Instead I dressed in the outfit I usually reserved for drinking and dancing before fastening my fae-cloak over it. After swiping the mud and blood from my boots, I balled up my dirty clothes and stuffed them into one of Kestral's packs. I'd wash them out in the first stream we stopped at.

Downstairs, I found Kila and Kestral sitting at an unbroken table in a corner, each holding a steaming mug of black tea. The room still held the vestiges of Kila's rampage—broken tables and chairs had been pushed to one side, along with shards of broken dinnerware. It seemed the staff knew better than to confront her about it, though. As I sat down a wench set a mug of black tea down in front of me, along with a carafe of cream and a bowl of sugar. I had hated black tea at first, but once a wench taught me how to mix it up sweetly, I had become as addicted as my companions.

Kila looked up at me over the rim of her cup. "Kestral says I should travel with you both. He thinks I'll be safer from our brothers and armies and mage hunters and every other rusting thing trying to kill us."

I laughed as I stirred my tea. "I'm sure what he really means is that you'll keep us safer from brothers and armies and whatever else is out there."

Kestral grunted a sort of agreement as he sipped his tea.

"Assuming I agree," Kila hesitated, circling the rim of her mug with a finger. "Where are you going?"

I paused with my mug halfway to my mouth. I hadn't considered that yet. All I knew was that wherever Kestral was going, I was going. I looked over at him, wondering if he already had an answer.

"I think," Kestral said slowly, setting down his mug, "that it's time to involve your oldest sister."

"Reina?" Kila and I asked in unison.

Kestral nodded.

"How can we involve her when we don't know where she is?" I asked, staring off vaguely as I considered Kestral's idea.

"Even if we did find her, would she take our side? What if she sides with Velyn and Eagan?" Kila tilted her head as her eyes turned distant.

Kestral looked from Kila to me and back again. "You two don't even realize you do that, do you?"

"Do what?" we asked together again.

"First, stop talking together," Kestral said firmly. "Reshi, do you still want revenge for Cera's murder?"

"Of course, I do." My head snapped around and I glared darkly across the room, picturing Velyn and all the things I'd like to do to him if I had him in front of me.

"And Kila, you're still set on killing Eagan for murdering your twin?"

Her red eyes flashed as her head turned, the promise of death glinting behind them.

"Do you both realize you're staring in the same direction?" Kestral asked, taking another sip.

I blinked and looked at Kila. She did the same to me.

"What are you saying, Kestral?"

"I noticed it a while ago. Whenever we discuss one of your siblings, your gaze turns distant. Reshi used to stare west when we talked about coming to meet you, Kila."

"Oh." Kila frowned then slowly looked up, her eyes sliding to the north-east corner of the room. "You think we have an unconscious connection to each other?"

"So, when we talk about Reina . . ." I trailed off, realizing I was once again staring in the same direction as Kila.

"Let's hope your brothers are at least as dense as the both of you." Kestral pushed his empty mug away. "We should get on the road as soon as possible, before the southern army realizes we're still here. Kila, do you have a mount?"

"Yes. He's stabled at the military barracks."

"Think you can get him without any trouble?"

Kila grinned, showing far too many teeth. "I'm sure I can."

"Good." Kestral stood. "Reshi, let's get Shan prepared for a journey. It looks like we may be headed for the capital."

Traveling with Kila was both a blessing and a curse. She was easier to talk to than Kestral and she could even keep Kestral talking as they shared war stories back and forth.

Her horse, Bruiser, was a friendly piebald gelding who didn't try to bite me every time I got too close. The soldiers who were sad to see Kila leave had gifted her with more supplies than she could carry on her own—clothing, armor, pillows and even spices and soaps, which made traveling a bit more comfortable for me.

The biggest curse to having her along was the sleeping arrangements. She knew I slept near Kestral to refill my wellspring, but she didn't know we had crossed the line from traveling companions to lovers. I wasn't sure if Kestral didn't want her to know or if he merely didn't want her as an audience, but either way, it meant I wasn't getting any satisfaction. For weeks.

So, it was an understatement to say that I was excited for our upcoming night at a village inn. Supplies were running low after nearly two weeks on the road, even supplemented as they were by Kestral and Kila hunting in the evenings. Kestral tried to insist we could push on a bit further, but when one of his boots finally gave up and fell apart, he agreed we could pass through the next village.

"We don't need to stay overnight," Kestral said as he used bandages to tie his boot together. He grimaced at how ugly it looked.

I tried not to laugh at it.

"If I have to spend one more night talking only to the two of you without a full wineskin, I'm not sure either of you will wake up in the morning," Kila warned darkly. Her last wineskin had run dry four days ago. She had been cranky ever since.

"Come on, Kestral," I bumped his arm with my elbow as I stirred our last helping of rice over the fire. "It would be so nice to sleep in a bed, just for one night."

Kestral arched his brow skeptically.

I failed to hide a smirk.

"I think it would look more suspicious to pass through without stopping," Kila added, cleaning one of her swords in the firelight. "It's not as if we can reach another town before nightfall tomorrow. Townsfolk know that much."

Kestral sighed, leaning back from the fire. "And what do we do when you're recognized, Kila? Kill everyone in the village?"

"Are you saying I couldn't?" Kila asked, turning her sword so it glittered.

"I think he's saying it wouldn't be very polite," I said, leaning back so I would be out of any line of attack. "Kestral is right, though. You do stand out, Kila."

"Is that the only objection?" Kila asked, leaning forward.

"No, it's just the biggest problem," Kestral replied.

Kila rolled her eyes. "We really need to kill one of our brothers and get you a bounty, rust-cheap hunter."

I laughed, ignoring Kestral's icy glare. The rice was nearly cooked, so I stirred in some mushrooms, chunks of waterbird and spices. Somehow, I had become the cook, since Kila and Kestral did all the hunting.

"If I can blend in, can we stay at an inn tomorrow?" Kila continued, testing the edge of her sword. "I'll pay for the rooms and your boots, too. I mean, I was probably paying in the first place, but now I get to act like I'm—what's the word, Reshi?"

"Noble?" I cocked my head to the side. "Not that nobles act that way, but that's what that word means, doesn't it?"

Kestral snorted. "And how many nobles have you met?"

I laughed, trying to keep the bitterness out of it. "You'd be surprised."

"Kestral." Kila rapped her knuckles against her blade, drawing his attention. "I can blend in. You gotta let me drink at a real bar tomorrow."

Kestral heaved a sigh, looking from me to my sister. "How did I get to be in charge of this group? I'm not even one of the mage-born."

"You just have that 'do what I say or I'll kill you' quality." I spooned a portion of dinner into Kestral's bowl, then into Kila's. I still didn't have my own bowl yet, so I ate from the pot.

"Kestral," Kila warned, eyes glinting through the steam coming off her bowl.

"Fine, Kila. If I think you look unremarkable enough not to be noticed, then fine. We'll stay at an inn tomorrow." Kestral speared a piece of waterbird so hard, bits of rice flew into the air.

Kila smiled, apparently proud of herself as she dug into her dinner. Kestral and I exchanged a glance. How would the most visible of Laurana's children simply blend in with normal townsfolk? I shrugged. It was a question for tomorrow, not tonight.

As always, I hoped Kila would turn in early and fall asleep before Kestral and I finished cleaning up dinner, but just like usual I was disappointed. She was always sharpening a weapon or fixing something. She never seemed to be still. As I scrubbed out the dinner pot, she meticulously cleaned her horse's hooves, digging dried mud, twigs and stones out so she could paint a type of salve on the bottom of the hoof, then fan it until it dried. The process appeared to take forever. And it was all made worse by...

"Kila, can I use that salve when you're finished?" Kestral asked after he finished laying out his bedroll. "It's been awhile since I've gone over Shan's hooves."

"Sure thing." Kila shoved the jar over to him with her foot.

I stifled a moan and fed the fire, so they would have light to work by. Then I shifted and curled up inside Kestral's bedroll. No satisfaction tonight either. Kila had better look the part tomorrow so I could sleep with Kestral in a real bed.

When Kestral woke me the following morning, Kila was gone. Her bedroll was neatly rolled and packed on her horse, as were her saddlebags and her weapons. Even I got suspicious at that point. Kila never went anywhere unless she was visibly armed. After packing up the campsite and putting down a cold breakfast, Kila returned. At least, a girl who looked like Kila returned.

She had let her hair down and tied it back with a simple scarf. She wore an old-fashioned but well-kept brown dress tied with an apron, giving her a hint of a figure that I had never noticed beneath her armor. With her eyes downcast, she looked like a completely different person.

"Well?" Kila asked, a faint blush coloring her cheeks.

"You still walk like a soldier," Kestral commented, straight to the point.

"Yeah, but if she sticks her chest out a little more, no one will notice that," I replied, waving him off. "You should get a dress that shows a little more cleavage, then no one would even look at your eyes."

Kila's face turned a bright red. "Thanks, Reshi. I was really hoping to hear my brother talk about my breasts today."

I shrugged. "I was trying to be helpful. Well, Kestral? She's good, right?"

"Fine. Just keep your eyes down."

Kila glared up at Kestral, which looked a little funny, considering the difference in their heights.

"Mage-blood eyes are a give away. At best they'll think you're fae. At worst we might get to meet the local mage hunters."

Kila turned her head and spat, but she lowered her chin.

"Reshi, when we get to the village, turn in to something small and stay out of sight." I rolled my eyes as Kestral went over a plan I had heard a hundred times. "I'll say I've just left the army and I'm traveling home with my betrothed, which will be—"

"What?" Kila and I shouted, shocked.

Kestral took a breath. "What other feasible story would you two like me to tell the innkeeper? We don't look alike, so we can't be siblings and even if we could sell that story, it's possible the innkeeper might try to put us in the same room. As a betrothed couple, we're obliged to stay in separate rooms."

"Couldn't you just say you and Kila are friends, or something?" I asked weakly.

"If I could just go as myself, we could just be a couple of soldiers returning from the front lines," Kila sulked, crossing her arms and leaning back against her horse.

"We need a story that doesn't attract attention. Red-headed female warriors attract attention, Kila. Every mage hunter in the country has your description. And 'friends,' Reshi?" Kestral raised an eyebrow at me. "I'm sure Kila doesn't want a whole village thinking she's a camp follower."

"She's not showing enough bust for that," I muttered. Kila narrowed her eyes at me, but I got the impression she didn't hear the whole thing clearly. Or else she might have broken my face.

"This village thing is turning into more trouble than it's worth." With a sigh, Kila swung herself up into her saddle. "Almost. Once I have wine again, it'll all be worth it."

"I think we all feel that way about you getting your wine," I said as Kestral also mounted up.

"Keep talking, baby brother. I carved some new crossbow bolts and I'd love to check their range."

Instead of taking crow form as usual, I leapt up into Kestral's lap as a cat, keeping the mage hunter between me and my sister.

Ah, family.

We arrived in the village just before midday, set up some rooms at the inn and took a small lunch in the inn's common room. And by small lunch, I mean Kila slipped a piece of cheese and some bread into the pocket of her apron for me, as I had shifted to a rat just before we entered the village. Kestral paid using Kila's gold, which seemed to annoy them both. Kestral hated being treated; Kila hated having to rely on someone else, even in a pretend betrothal. She kept her head down meekly and kept her mouth shut, which I could tell was hard for her. Probably hard for any of my siblings, really. She still walked like a soldier with a wide, strong gait and I caught her standing in a military resting stance more than once. I rode in her pocket, so I could squeak at her when she began behaving too aggressively. Honestly, I could have been a better girl than her.

She'd probably kill me if I said that out loud.

After Shan and Bruiser were comfortably stabled and taken care of, Kestral went to the local tanner to purchase new boots. When my suggestion to consider embroidered boots like Eagan's was met with derision, I decided to stay with Kila at the inn. She ordered a large lunch up to her room and had her washbasin filled with warm water. Once she was behind the changing screen I shifted out of my rat form to finish her lunch and wait my turn for the bath.

Water sloshed as Kila washed, some splashing over the edge of the basin. Kila swore, displacing more water as she reached for a drying cloth to mop up the spill.

"Leave some water for me, sis," I called through the screen. It was made of thin wood connected by hinges so that it could easily be folded and stored when not in use. With the window on Kila's side of the screen I could make out shadows through the wood, but Kila and the washbasin were appropriately obscured.

"The water isn't the problem." Kila's voice was full of mischief. "The soap on the other hand . . ."

"Don't tease about the soap. That's not funny," I chastised her. "It's bad enough I wake up with dew in my fur every morning. Cat noses are a lot more sensitive than you would know."

"How did you find out you could shapeshift?" Kila asked. It was a strange question coming from her. She didn't often like talking about magic, whether it be her own or the magic of others.

I shrugged even though she couldn't see it. I picked up one of Kila's daggers and picked at the filth under my fingernails. "I was running away from someone and needed a place to hide. Ended up getting myself cornered. Suddenly everything just . . . I don't know, there was a flash and I was smaller, faster. The people chasing me caught up, so I ran through them back the way I had come, but they didn't chase me. Didn't even try to stop me. I didn't figure out I had turned into a cat until later when I found a hiding place."

Kila hummed to herself for a moment, water sloshing gently against the side of the tub. "Do you use daggers because they're like claws?"

I smiled. That was more like the sister I knew. "I learned to use daggers before I knew I could shapeshift. It was the most easily concealed weapon for an orphan to carry."

"That's right. I forget most of you went to orphanages." Through the screen I could see Kila stand in the tub, her arm outstretched for a drying cloth. "Laki and I grew up in the capital before we were sent to different schools."

"Really?" I asked, surprised. "You and Laki grew up together?"

"Just until we were five. The Order and the military schools won't take younger children." Water sloshed onto the floor again as Kila stepped out of the tub. "Laki cried when they separated us, but I was kind of excited to be getting away from that house."

"House? Not the castle?" I leaned forward, the knife in my hand forgotten. "Do you remember our mother?"

"No, Mother didn't live with us. At least, I don't remember her living there." There was a pause as Kila scrubbed water from her hair. "I remember we couldn't live in the castle because of something about the prince's birth. Mostly we had the queen's nursery maids looking after us. It was boring. We were never allowed to leave. The thing I remember most about the house was the garden out back. Laki was always talking to the plants." Kila chuckled. "He used to get mad when I climbed the trees to get over the fence."

I found it impossible to picture either Laki or Kila as a child. Had Laki been red-headed as his twin? What had he been like before swearing to the Order of the Great Canvas? Would they have become different people if Kila had entered the Order and Laki the military?

"Laki mentioned that the two of you met once," I recalled, picturing my first and only meeting with Kila's twin. "He said you didn't get along well."

Kila laughed as she stepped out from behind the changing screen. One cloth wrapped her from shoulders to knees, another bound her wet hair. "Didn't get along? The fae get along with iron better than Laki and I got along. But still . . ." Kila trailed off for a moment, her eyes distant. "He was the only brother I knew."

"At least you got to know him," I offered. It was hard for me to miss Laki. I hadn't known him the way I had known Cera. And, also, he had tried to kill me. But I could see how hard it was for Kila to miss him. "When did the two of you meet as adults?"

"It was just after the bounties were posted and I had to leave the army," Kila replied, holding her cloth tightly to her chest. "It was Cera's fault. She kept talking to me at night, saying we should meet. I didn't know her, but I remembered Laki. She helped us find a place and a time to meet. I'm sure she hoped that once we were together, we would want to join up with our other siblings." She paused, almost as if she wanted to say more.

When Kila didn't continue, I pressed: "Did you guys fight?"

"We were such different people by then." Kila smiled sadly. "I barely recognized him and I'm sure I disgusted him. We probably would have parted on worse terms, but a group of bounty hunters found us, and we had to fight our way free."

"That's terrible luck, having your reunion ruined like that."

Kila met my eyes, grinning. "Actually, it was probably the best thing that could have happened to us. Instead of fighting with each other, we fought a common enemy together. It was easier to part ways, knowing he could handle himself."

I suddenly remembered the bathwater, which was growing colder as we spoke. I kicked off my boots and removed my belt as Kila searched through a leather pouch. "Did you and Laki keep in touch after that?"

"Not really. I would ask Cera about him sometimes, but we didn't exchange letters or anything. He did give me this." Kila pulled a small wooden object from the pouch and held it out to me as I passed her on my way to the bath.

"A sap-sucker?" It was a tiny carved bird with a long, pointed nose, no bigger than the palm of my hand. Sap-suckers beat their wings so quickly that they appeared to blur; somehow the carver had captured that motion within the wood. It was a beautifully worked piece. "Did Laki carve this?"

Kila nodded. "I tried to give it back to him, telling him I didn't keep anything that wasn't a weapon. He laughed at me and said he wouldn't have given it to me if it wasn't a weapon."

I shuddered, remembering Laki's life magic. This beautiful carving could easily become a weapon in his hands. I handed the bird back to Kila. "You've kept it all this time?"

She shrugged. "I'm not really sentimental, but it was from my twin, so yes, I kept it. I'm glad I did now." She curled her hand around it, holding it close a moment before putting it back in the leather pouch.

I placed a hand on her shoulder. "I'm really sorry about Laki, Kila."

Kila smiled up at me before shrugging me off. "I've got other brothers now. And Laki is probably happier on the other side of the Canvas. Go wash before the water gets too cold."

I finished undressing behind the screen, considering everything I had just learned about Kila and Laki. The water was still lukewarm as I eased into it, relaxing for a moment before picking over the nearly used-up blocks of soap. Beyond the screen, I heard Kila dressing.

"So, you regain magic by killing people?" I asked, curious. She had started this conversation by asking about my magic, so it only seemed fair that I ask.

"Not killing necessarily. Freshly spilled blood, that's all."

"Oh. That's not morbid at all." I dunked my head back in the water to wash my hair. "Have you heard that you were supposed to be the twin sent to the Order of the Great Canvas and Laki was supposed to grow up in the army?"

Kila snorted. "Like he would have survived in the army."

"Well, I'm just thinking." I lathered up my hair and sat back to let it sit a moment. "If you had gone into the Order, how would you come across freshly spilled blood for your magic?"

The sound of laces being tied stopped. "I never considered that."

"Right? So how is it decided how we replenish our magic? Is it set when we're born, or does it develop as we age?"

"You never wondered before?" Kestral's voice through the screen made me yelp. I hadn't heard him come in, but it might have been when my head was underwater. "How have the two of you lived this long without knowing anything about magic?"

There was a thunk of metal hitting wood and I imagined Kila throwing a dagger at Kestral and missing. That meant she was still playing nicely, then.

"Well, why don't you enlighten us, Oh Great Mage hunter?" I said it sarcastically even though he had piqued my curiosity.

"Hunting is about knowing your quarry," Kestral said from behind the screen. "The good hunters study magecraft before setting out to kill or bond mages. Did you both come into your powers in your teenage years?"

"I was sixteen." That memory would never leave me.

"That sounds right." Kila sounded thoughtful, as if she wasn't quite certain.

"Generally speaking, most mages gain their power as teenagers, unless something traumatic draws it out earlier."

When had Kestral started sounding like a scholar? I used a pitcher to pour water over my head, rinsing the soap from my hair.

"By then, your personality is generally set, so your magic can manifest and replenish in a way that suits your lifestyle."

"Really?" Kila asked. "So, if Laki were in the army, he might have gotten my powers instead?"

I heard the hesitation in Kestral's answer. "More likely he would have developed a different method of replenishment. As would you, if you weren't constantly surrounded by freshly spilled blood. But your powers would be the same."

I said nothing, considering how my upbringing would have gifted me with the ability to draw life force as someone slept. It fit. How much had Kestral put together about my past? Unconsciously, one hand slipped beneath the water to cover the marks along my hip.

"So now that Eagan and Velyn have each stolen new magic, does that change how they replenish their wells?" Kila asked, sounding surprisingly thoughtful. "I mean, does each magic replenish separately from the other?"

I did a final rinse and stepped out of the wash basin, giving myself a cursory swipe with a drying towel. "I don't think that's how it would work. The magic all goes into the same well, doesn't it?"

"But it's still two different magics," Kila insisted. "Right?"

"I've been wondering about that, too," Kestral admitted. "You seven seem to operate on a different level from ordinary mages, so it's hard to say."

"How are we different?" I asked, using the silvered glass near the basin to tie my damp hair back.

"Most mages aren't as specialized as you all seem to be. What I mean is, most mages have a spark of power in everything—fire, earth, water, the whole range. Usually what they study becomes their specialty." Kestral stopped, staring as I stepped out from behind the bathing screen, wearing only a loosely knotted drying cloth at my waist. I smirked at him and rolled my hips as I crossed the room—a preview of things to come later, I hoped.

"So, even though most mages can use a wider variety of spells than us, they still only use one method of recovery?" Kila asked, her eyes flicking to me before looking back at Kestral. Some people just didn't appreciate beauty.

"That's what I have come to understand about magical wells." Kestral coughed and looked away from me. "Of course, it's hard to be certain since the seven of you defy normal magical metrics. It's possible that your mother Laurana bound each of your powers as children, to protect you from the Mage Hunt."

"I guess that was nice of her," I said, rolling my shoulders in a shrug. I hid a smile as the motion caught Kestral's eye.

"It was probably all she could do for us," Kila commented, eyes down on the whetstone in her hand. "I can't imagine living like she did—a slave to the king, forced to give up each of her children, hiding her magic. I'd have fallen on my sword long before they could have imprisoned me."

I paused, holding my clothes in front of me. I had never pictured my mother's life like that before. I had been so concerned with preserving my own, I never thought what Laurana must have gone through, how she must feel knowing her children were being ruthlessly hunted across the realm. Or if she even knew we had taken to hunting each other.

After an awkward moment of silence, Kila returned to sharpening her knives and I resumed clothing myself. Kestral stayed quiet, eyes shifting between the two of us.

"Ready to go down to dinner, Kila?" Kestral asked finally.

Kila nodded, setting aside her knives. She ducked behind the wash screen to fix the scarf in her hair.

"What about me?" I asked, nearly finished dressing.

"I'll send some dinner up to the room. You should stay out of sight until it arrives."

"But what about ale?" I whined.

"I can bring a tankard up later," Kestral offered. He pushed himself away from the wall he had been leaning on as Kila folded up the wash screen and set it against the wall.

"That's not fair," I protested. "Kila's going to get more than one tankard."

"Jealous, brother?" Kila smirked at me.

"Yes," I snapped testily. "You're not the only one who has been missing civilization."

"Reshi, I can't send ale up to the room, it would appear suspicious. The food will be strange enough, but at least I can explain needing it as extra for the road." Kestral opened the door and peeked out. "The hall is clear. You can cross to our room."

"Don't you wish you could slip into a dress and be anonymous?" Kila asked me, winking smugly.

"Give me an extra dress and I'll show you how it's done," I challenged.

Kestral dropped his face into his hand and shook his head. "Children. I'm not hiding a pair of mage-born, I'm traveling with children. Reshi, get across the hall. Kila, stop taunting your brother."

My sister and I sneered at each other for a moment before doing as Kestral demanded. Using Kestral and Kila as cover, I darted across the hall to Kestral's room. I already missed Kila's town, where I could walk around as myself, having conversations with people who weren't Kestral or Kila. Dancing and drinking and simply enjoying being me.

Of course, that had resulted in two armies arriving to kill me, so that hadn't exactly worked out in my favor.

Once the door was shut behind me, I shifted to my cat form and ducked beneath the bed to wait. I could smell venison cooking downstairs, as well as bread and onions. I hoped Kestral would send something warm. I would be disappointed if the cook only sent up bags of dried rice and uncooked vegetables.

The door to the room opened and someone set something down on the writing desk. When the door shut with the lock clicking into place, I slunk out from beneath the bed, shifted, and whipped the cover off the steaming plate of venison and vegetables. Kestral had been thoughtful enough to send up a hot meal, as well as a few bags of provisions. I cut into the venison steak enthusiastically as the room slowly turned dark with the setting sun.

After dinner, I closed the shutters and lit the candles around the room. I could hear music through the floor, but instead of a group of instruments, it was just the sound of a lute. At least I wouldn't be missing out on too much dancing, then. I paced the room, trapped and bored. How long would it be until Kestral came back? If I finished eating, then he should have as well.

Oh, dust, rust and ashes.

Kestral wouldn't come back to the room until Kila turned in for the night. He couldn't rightly leave his "betrothed" down at the bar by herself. That wouldn't be properly chivalrous. And Kila wasn't one to leave a bar until she'd emptied a whole cask. Dust it all, I was in for a late, boring night. Why had I fought so hard to stay at an inn, anyway? This didn't feel all that different from camping when Kila and Kestral went out hunting together. At least then I had chores to do instead of nothing.

I practiced rolling coins across the knuckles of both hands, a skill I hadn't completely mastered yet. When that bored me, I played with my fae blades, trying to get them to take different shapes. I had found out that, when thrown, they elongated into a long, straight shape but I hated to think about throwing them; so often thrown blades were lost to the battle. Since the battle with Eagan and Velyn, I hadn't been able to replenish my bracers with new blades. I felt a bit naked without them.

When that became dull, which didn't take long, I took to searching Kestral's bags for anything remotely amusing. I found his skin of Goldwater Whiskey and helped myself to a tiny sip. The skin was nearly empty, so I couldn't steal much without getting caught. Kestral had a few neat toys, like bolos and caltrops, both of which I toyed with before setting aside. Mostly everything was utilitarian, just the basics of what he needed for the road. Near the bottom of his clothes satchel, I found a few old cloth-bound books along with an inkwell and a brush. I squinted at the titles of the books, slowly piecing the letters together into familiar words. *Common Magics of Zarapheth, The Battles of General Menneth,* and *Rune Magic.* Not even a work of fiction or a saucy romance. I grimaced as I shoved the books back into their bag. Reading was one of those things my education had missed, though I had picked it up well enough to read signs or price lists. Reading a book would be abject torture for me. Better not ever let Kestral learn that.

In another satchel, I found Kestral's magic-grounding gauntlets. I poked at one cautiously before picking it up and slipping it over my hand. Why had these made my brothers so nervous when they saw them on the battlefield? I had been too busy during the battle to see how Kestral had used them, but I also didn't remember seeing any magic that wasn't cast by one of my siblings. The gauntlet was mostly leather with steel plating on the back of the hand, wrist and around the forearm, so it wasn't quite as heavy as it looked. Different runes were carved in the steel with plenty of space for more. In fact, I had seen Kestral etching new runes just recently. I picked up the second gauntlet, seeing that the newest rune stood out in sharp relief against the older, more worn runes.

The lock in the room's door clicked, making me jump. Would Kestral be mad that I was playing with his gauntlets? I cringed nervously as Kestral stepped through the door and set a large tankard of ale down on the writing desk. He blinked down at my spot on the floor, surrounded by his haphazardly opened bags and scattered belongings, his gauntlets still in my hands.

"I, ah . . ." I looked around at the mess I had made. "I got bored."

Kestral laughed, erasing the nerves I had felt about him finding me going through his things. He sat on the edge of the bed to remove his new boots. "Did you want to learn how to use the gauntlets?"

"No, they're a little big for me." I slipped my hand free of the one I was wearing. "I was just curious about how they worked."

Kestral held his hand out and I passed him a gauntlet. "There are a few common runes used when bonding a mage, so those are all etched on the top row of the gauntlet." He pointed to a series of runes around the wrist of the gauntlet. "If I activate a rune, I can ground out any spell cast by a mage bound by that particular rune."

"So, it only works on bonded mages?"

"No." Kestral hesitated, eyeing me for a moment. He turned a gauntlet in his hand, showing me the newest etching he'd made. "I'm trying to create runes against your brothers' magic. It's harder because they aren't bound, so the rune has to be magic-specific. This is a fire rune."

"An anti-Eagan rune?" I asked, tracing my finger over it. "And you'll make a rune against weather magic, too?"

Kestral hesitated. "I'm trying to. The rune has to be activated just prior to the cast spell. I know that when Eagan throws his hand out, he's always casting a fire spell. Velyn, though . . . he throws lightning and rain and hail and fog, each of which require a separate rune. And then I would have to know which rune to activate as he's casting his spell."

"Ah." I turned the gauntlet over in my hands, looking from the runes up to Kestral. Why did he look so uneasy? The answer occurred to me a moment later. "Could you make a rune against my magic?"

Kestral nodded again, turning the gauntlet over and over in his hands. "I could, but your magic is complicated. It's not typical battle-magic, so the only rune I think might work would be an anti-nature rune. It would only block your connection to animals, though. I don't think it would work on your shapeshifting."

"Huh. Well, I guess that's the advantage of having weak magic." I shrugged as I set the gauntlet aside.

Kestral locked his eyes on mine. "I haven't etched a rune against your magic. And I don't plan to. So, don't go running away."

I laughed, pushing myself off the floor. "How can I run away when you bring me ale?"

"Are you going to help me clean this mess up?" Kestral asked.

I cocked an eyebrow at him. "How are you going to make me?"

Kestral's smile was just a tiny bit devilish.

The mess and the ale remained forgotten the rest of the night.

Kestral kept us to a schedule, which allowed for a stop at an inn once every two weeks of travel. This kept Kila in full wineskins so she didn't murder us in our sleep and gave Kestral and me a little privacy. It gave me something to look forward to after long days of travel. Seriously, how big was this kingdom? It hadn't felt so large back in my caravan days. The one thing I missed, even at our inn stops, was contact with people other than Kila and Kestral. While they got to drink and carouse with the locals, I was stuck in the room alone. One night when Kestral was particularly late in coming up to the room, I made friends with an owl roosting outside my window. I found myself wondering how owls could see at night when almost no other bird could. Even after Kestral came back to the room and distracted me, I found myself wondering about animal night-eyes and how they differed from daytime creatures. It became a common distraction for me to muse over while waiting for Kestral to come to bed.

It didn't take long for my scholarly musings to bore me and I once again began petitioning that Kestral allow me to socialize at an inn. I argued that since no one had recognized Kila and she was by far the more recognizable of the two of us, I should be able to go about incognito as well. Kestral crushed this argument beneath his heel, saying having Kila in the open was risky enough; having two people with unusually colored eyes in our party would have every mage hunter within a three-village radius descending upon us.

I hated admitting it, but at the next village stop he was proven right.

"What's with all the black lace in the windows?" Kila asked, riding her gelding side-saddle and trying to keep her head down even as she looked up and down the village street.

I stuck my head out of her apron pocket to see it for myself. Every window, signpost and shop flew a bit of black lace. The villagers we passed all wore a bit of black tied at their wrist, ankle, or neck as a scarf. They spoke softly to each other in small groups, glancing up as we passed on our way to an inn.

"Probably the death of a noble," Kestral replied, glancing around. "Take care here . . . Darling."

Kila and I both grimaced at his monotone use of the term of endearment. She dropped her eyes, if only to make a face at me. I squeaked a laugh before crouching low inside her pocket. Kestral took care to help Kila down from her saddle and tied both horses up outside the inn. Inside Kila stood back, eyes down, while Kestral negotiated rooms for the night.

"We've been on the road a while," Kestral told the innkeeper. "Has one of this region's nobles just passed?"

The innkeeper's eyes grew wide and she shook her head. "Not one of our nobles, no. Our good queen has passed on. Stars light her way." The innkeeper bowed her head reverently. Luckily, she missed Kila's eyes flashing up as she gasped in surprise. Kestral mimicked the innkeeper's posture, shooting a look back at Kila. She quickly dropped her head.

"How long ago did our queen pass into the Canvas?" Kestral asked when the innkeeper raised her head again.

"Oh, we only got the news here a few days ago. Runners have been visiting all the villages, so it's not surprising you didn't hear." The innkeeper rustled some papers beneath the bar. "Here's the original announcement. It appears she died about a month ago. The capital is in full mourning. If that's where you're headed, you should buy yourself some mourning lace."

"A wise suggestion. Thank you." Kestral scanned the written announcement quickly. I noticed the paper crinkle in his clenched fist. "What is this part about Laurana's mage-born? Has there been new information released about the seven?"

"Five now, if you can believe it." The innkeeper shook her head. "I don't know all the details, but the outpost here received new postings with more portraits. I heard the bounties were doubled! Can you believe it?" She laughed nervously. "It almost makes you want to become a hunter, doesn't it?"

Kestral remained silent a moment longer, staring at the page. He finally set it down, smoothing it where he had wrinkled it. "Could you please send our dinners up to our rooms tonight?"

"No trouble at all." The innkeeper passed over a set of keys before calling stablehands to bring the horses around back. Kestral ushered Kila ahead of him up the stairs to our rooms. After pulling the door shut and testing the lock on it, he held up a hand to indicate we should stay silent. Kestral crossed the room to close the shutters, then rolled up a drying cloth, placing it against the crack between the door and the floor. I climbed down Kila's apron, shifting to human before fully reaching the floor. We both watched Kestral nervously as he made the room as soundproof as possible.

Finally, he nodded and waved for us to sit down.

"I am going to the military outpost," he said, voice soft. "We need to know how accurate the new sketches are."

"Isn't that reckless?" Kila asked. She had pulled her hair over her shoulder and was braiding it rapidly.

"Yeah, Kestral, think about it." I tried to keep the fear out of my voice, but it crept in anyway. "You fought alongside us against the southern army. They could have your description, too."

"It's a risk, but I have to take it." Kestral looked from me to Kila. "Can you tell where Reina is?"

Kila scowled. "We're not a couple of pigoblins, sniffing out fairies." Regardless, we both shifted our eyes to the east.

Kestral shook his head. "We're getter closer and closer to the big cities. There will be more mage hunters with more advanced methods for finding mages. We need to know what they know so we can hide from them."

"But we're not heading straight for the capital," Kila protested. "That would be straight north from here. We're heading somewhere east of there."

I shivered. Giltner was one of the eastern cities outside the capital.

"We're going to end up in one of the cities near the capital. That's bad enough. It's like walking into a dragon's den with only wooden weapons. I need to see the new bounty information."

"What if I go instead?" The suggestion surprised me, even though I was the one who made it. Kila and Kestral gaped at me, clearly shocked. I gulped before continuing, "Even if they have my face, they can't know my powers. No one would have seen me shifting, either in the town or at the battle. I can sneak in, see the bounties, then sneak out."

Kila looked to Kestral. "You know, they'll have the bounties posted on the wall at the outpost. It's not the worst idea."

"No." Kestral's eyes might as well have turned to ice chips. "You're not going out alone."

"Why not?" I challenged, sounding more confident than I felt. "I'm used to sneaking through shadows and no one even knows to look for me."

Kestral narrowed his eyes dangerously. I knew he was trying to come up with a better plan, so I barreled on, "What happens if they do have your description, Kestral? If they catch you, they'll know Kila and I are here. We'd have to fight our way out and find Reina without you. That's if Velyn and Eagan don't catch us first."

"Reshi is right," Kila insisted. "There isn't anyone who knows about his forms who could have reported them. Even if they did, Reshi has the best chance of escaping capture and warning us if hunters come looking for us."

"How would he warn us?" Kestral asked.

I laughed. "That's easy. I'd have Shan kick down the barn. Would that be a clear enough signal for you?"

Slowly, reluctantly, Kestral nodded. "If you're not back in two hours, I'm coming after you."

"It won't take that long." I stood, tossing my cloak tight over my shoulders. "Just don't forget to order an extra dinner for me."

Kestral opened a shutter for me and I fluttered outside, perching on the sill so I could look around for the military outpost.

"Reshi." I turned back, meeting Kestral's eyes. Was he concerned? Scared? His eyes betrayed nothing. "Be careful."

I gave him a bird's jerky nod before taking wing. I circled the village once, noting the outpost near the road that would take a traveler towards the capital. I landed on its roof and spent a handful of minutes observing the people who entered and exited the building. Most were simple workers—post carriers, peace keepers, a stablehand. I followed the stablehand around the back of the building, sneaking into the military's stable behind him as a rat. At least two of the horses stabled here appeared to be mage hunter horses, or possibly soldiers on leave. Either could prove problematic if I ran into them. I climbed to the hay loft above the barn, shifted back to crow, then flew around to the front of the building. When I judged that the outpost was mostly empty and possibly closing up for the day, I shifted to cat form, sneaking around the side and leaping through an open window.

Luckily, almost all military outposts followed the same layout. A long counter was set up between the waiting area and the business area, so I was able to slink beneath the counter unseen. The bounty board was on the far side of the door, blanketed with pages and pages of sketches. After looking around carefully and noting that this side of the room was empty, I took a long, hard look at the bounty board.

My own face jumped out at me first. It was just a black-and-white sketch, the kind meant to be churned out rapidly rather than precisely, so it wasn't a perfect picture. It was close enough, however, that my human form would certainly be recognized. I memorized the bounty number, though it meant nothing to me. I had long since forgotten exactly how much my head was worth. It took me longer to puzzle out the words beneath my portrait. They had no information on my magic but detailed that I fought with daggers. That was an unfortunate note.

I found Kila's picture next, along with portraits of Velyn and Eagan. My tail lashed as I tried recalling all the numbers beneath the faces. Velyn, Eagan and I shared the same number, Kila's was a bit higher. Probably owing to the number of mage hunters she had slain previously. There was also an announcement proclaiming Cera and Laki officially deceased.

I couldn't find a portrait of Kestral anywhere on the board. After a bit of searching, I noted a page that said an ex-soldier might be traveling with the mage-born, but it didn't say who he was traveling with, nor did it mention him by name. A warm feeling of relief filled my chest; they didn't know about Kestral yet.

I heard voices and cowered in my dark corner. The door in the middle of the counter swung open and a pair of heavily booted feet tromped out, stopping to lock the front door as they left for the day. I hadn't noticed the clerks closing up windows and dousing lanterns. How long had I been here? Hopefully Kestral hadn't gotten up to anything stupid. I slunk across the room to the window where I had entered. The shutters were closed too tightly for a cat to fit, but a rat could squeeze right through. Once outside, I shifted again, flying back to our room at the inn.

The shutter to the room was open a crack. I flapped awkwardly outside the window as I tapped my beak against the closed one. The cracked shutter flew open so quickly it nearly hit me. Kila stretched out her arm, letting me land on it so she could bring me inside.

"I told you he would be back soon," Kila told Kestral as I shifted back to my human form. Kestral was near the room's door, stuffing the drying cloth under it once again.

"Aw, did you miss me, Kestral?" I winked at him. "Or were you just afraid some other hunter would get my bounty?"

Kestral ignored my questions. "What did you find?"

I reported on the bounties and sketches as I uncovered my dinner plate. A thick fish stew with buttered rolls and vegetables. Not one of our better dinners, but the stew was good.

"But they don't have a sketch of you, Kestral," I finished, sipping from a mug of ale. Ugh, it was Kila's pale ale. Better than nothing, I guess. "One report mentions a former soldier, but no description."

"It was probably the gauntlets that gave you away," Kila said, grabbing her ale away from me. "They didn't have time to properly identify you while you were grounding all their spells."

"Probably," Kestral admitted. He leaned back against the wall, arms crossed, deep in thought. "Reshi, you said you think there are mage hunters in town?"

"Or soldiers on leave." I shrugged. "I only saw their mounts."

Kestral nodded, deep in thought. Kila tried to snatch a roll of my plate. I planted my spoon on the back of her hand, pinning it before it could escape with the prize. We sparred silently for a moment. I had to bite her before she released the roll. She made a threatening gesture with her sword. I merely tipped my head towards Kestral with a smirk. She rolled her eyes and leaned back, losing interest in the fight. Sometimes having a sister was kind of fun. If I was honest, though, having a Kestral was a lot more fun.

Kestral straightened. "There's no way to avoid taking some chances, but at least in the cities it should be easier to blend in as long as we avoid running into any mage hunters. Do either of you know where Velyn and Eagan are?"

I shrugged, even as I turned towards the south. Kila, scowling, faced the same way as I did.

"Are they close?"

"We're not scent hounds, Kestral," Kila snapped.

"And they know my forms, so I can't spy on them," I added.

"We have to assume that they're also trying to find Reina. With Velyn's far-sight, it's really only a matter of time before they locate her." Kestral paused, watching me.

At the mention of Reina's name, I stared vaguely eastward. Kestral reached into a nearby satchel and drew out a map. He smoothed it out on the floor and placed a marker over our current village. He then traced a line with his finger northeast, ending up in one of the great inland seas. "Reina should be somewhere along this line. Let's make some guesses."

"She was noble, right? Like Eagan?" Kila asked.

"Yes, and kept in the capital until the prince was born."

"You said she was educated, right?" I shivered. The line Kestral had traced passed right through Giltner. "Like, schools and academies?"

"Yes." Kestral tapped several cities known for their schools. "But she would be recognized at any university she previously attended."

"We can't assume that," Kila pointed out. "We don't know anything about her magic. She could be an illusionist, or even a shapeshifter like Reshi."

"Why would she go back to school, though?" I asked. "Aren't noble ladies raised to get married, keep household accounts and have babies?"

"Right." Kila rolled her eyes. "That's what all women want from life, to raise babies."

"No, Kila, I just meant—"

"Wait." Kestral held up a hand. "You're both right. There are only a few acceptable paths for noble women to take. Marriage, the Order, a queen's attendant, or teaching."

"Teaching?" Kila and I echoed.

Kestral's finger rested over the city of Emlenton, home to the most notable tower of learning in the country.

"Let's bet on that." Kestral tapped his map. "We'll take some risks and travel the main road rather than the backwoods. That means we'll be passing through cities, not these little towns. Reshi—"

"I know, I know," I groaned. "I'm going to live in my animal forms."

Kestral nodded. He took a breath before turning to Kila. "How do you feel about cutting and dyeing your hair?"

"I don't know," Kila mused. "How do you feel about cutting your throat and dying?"

"We don't have to cut it," I said, trying to avoid actual violence. "You need to wear some black lace, right? If you can find a black lace hairnet, we can tie it up, so it looks shorter. And Kila, there are powders that can darken your hair and then wash right out. That's not so bad, right?"

Kestral gave me an evaluating look while Kila considered the compromise. After a beat, Kila agreed, but she wasn't pleased about it.

"I can get the hairnet tomorrow when I get my own black lace," Kestral told me. "But where do you get powdered hair dye?"

I grimaced and tapped a spot on the map. "We're passing right by here, right? I know a shop. I can get new knives, too."

Kestral eyed the city then looked up at me with a raised eyebrow.

I shrugged. "Home sweet home, right?"

Giltner was exactly how I remembered it. The same decrepit buildings, the same fetid odor, the same feeling of despair. I flew overhead, marking the familiar buildings below me. My orphanage had burned down at some point. If I could smile, I would have.

Kestral had refused to let us stay inside the city limits, insisting our throats would be slit merely because we were outsiders. For once, I completely agreed with him, though Kila protested she was more than a match for a city of thieves and assassins. She only relented when I pled with her, saying it was hard enough facing my past alone. It would break me to see pity in her eyes, or worse, in Kestral's. She and Kestral set up our campsite while I went ahead into the city.

Entering the city was another argument I had to win. Kestral wanted to go himself and buy the hair dye. First, I had to convince him that every cut-purse, beggar and street rat would mark him as a soldier and try to kill him, rob him or both. Then I told him the shopkeeper I knew wouldn't sell to an outsider. There were ways to buy and trade in Giltner and, by fate, I knew them all. He knew I was telling the truth, but he still didn't want me going in alone. But there's always one place a person can go, and that's home.

I landed in the shadow of the shop and shifted human. I had borrowed a cowl from Kila and wore it beneath my cloak, pulled low over my face to hide my eyes. Affecting the confident stride of any long-term resident of Giltner, I shoved the shop's door open and stepped inside.

The person at the counter was not the one I was expecting, but of course the shop owner would have changed over the years. The shop had not changed—wigs like great, dusty spider webs blocked out light from the windows, hiding alchemical vials dotting the walls. Weapons gleamed behind the counter and in the hands of the shopkeeper as she eyed me.

"Who's this?" the scraggly-haired woman hissed. "I don't know you. Get ye gone."

"Sorry, Grandmother. I've been away for a time." I rolled my wrist, showing her the old hand signal of a thief. She continued to eye me suspiciously as I approached the counter, but she didn't throw her knife at me, which I took as a good sign.

"What are you looking for?" She leaned forward, trying to peer beneath my hood. I turned my head, keeping my face shadowed. "Lookin' for a job? The Roost is always looking for a pretty face."

"Believe me, I know." I bit the words off a little harsher than I'd meant to. I reached inside a belt pouch and laid my knife bracers on the counter, turning a corner inside out to show her the shop's mark inside. "I need new knives, Grandmother. And some hair dye."

The woman inspected the insignia on the bracers intently before grumbling and grabbing two wrapped packages from behind the counter. She followed this with a tiny jar of powder. I frowned. She set a second jar on the counter. I nodded. She quoted a price and I laughed.

"Grandmother, is that how you treat all your children? Why should we bother visiting at all?"

"If I don't know your name, you're not one of mine," the woman spat. "The price is the price."

"I think you'll remember me, Greta." I reached up and lowered my hood just a fraction, letting her see my eyes.

The woman dropped her knife in shock. "Reshi!"

I pulled my hood back up. "Will you give me trouble, Greta? I promise I can make more than a little trouble for you in return."

"You always did, didn't you?" She chuckled. "I'll never forget how, when the peace keepers came to town, you snuck into their barracks at night and switched all their coin purses. Tied to their belts as they slept, no less! And then—"

"I'm not here for memories, Greta." I rapped my knuckles on the counter. "What happened to the orphanage? How did you end up taking over Coran's shop?"

"Ah, well, Giltner always had too many orphanages, didn't it, little Resh?" She shook her head. "A rival of mine burned it down. Lost half my kids. Sold the others at a steal. Coran died, right about the same time so I bought the shop."

I doubted Coran had died pleasantly by the way she said it. Maybe even ol' Greta had helped him pass on. But it wasn't my business any more.

"I always thought you'd end up a belted whore in a hen house," Greta said mildly.

"I know. I'm sure I'm a disappointment on that count." I pointed to the counter again. "How much?"

"Wait, I have something special for you." Greta started to turn. I lunged across the counter, grabbing her arm. Stars, the woman had grown frail over the years! She used to knock kids twice her size across the yard.

"Easy, Greta." I held Kestral's small crossbow on her. "No tricks."

"I'd be a fool, wouldn't I? Now that you're one of the dangerous mage-born." She cackled to herself, shaking her head and pulling away from me. "Who would have guessed it?" She rummaged behind the counter a moment before coming up with a small alchemical vial. "Eye drops."

"For?"

"Eyes. You never were bright, were you, Resh? Except for your eyes." She gazed up at me for a moment. "I'll let you have the lot for a quick tumble."

I shuddered. "No. Not ever. Not for anything. What do the eye drops do?"

"They darken your eyes, turn 'em brown." Greta batted her eyelashes at me. "Just like mine. If you're looking to hide, which . . ." She picked up the hair darkener and raised an eyebrow. She had to know it wasn't for me.

"No questions, Grandmother." I slipped a few coins onto the counter. "Call it even?"

She shoved the coins back at me. "Not by half, you cheap child."

I leaned across the counter, meeting her eyes. "Call it even for how you sold me." I swept the vials off the counter and into a belt purse before grabbing the bundles of knives. I turned my back on her, striding from the shop.

"Can't blame me," the old woman called. "You were such a pretty child."

A knife tumbled into my trembling hand. I clenched my teeth, adjusted my hood and shoved my way out of the shop. My past was behind me. So far behind me I could only see it when I bathed. Dark reminders of dark days. That woman wasn't even worth killing. Even if she did rat me out, which I fully expected her to do, no one believed anything that came out of Giltner.

The bigger problem was that now I had my knives, I couldn't fly out of the town. I'd have to hoof it. In the shadows of the shop, I pulled my bracers on over my sleeves, slipping each knife into a sheath. The knives were readily visible as my cloak fluttered around me. I wanted them to be seen. Head low, shoulders back, I walked through the town as if I owned it. I remembered that strut from when I'd watched assassins from the rooftops, dreaming of one day when I could apprentice to one. I was sold before that day came.

Probably a good thing, too. I would bet good gold that Kestral would have marked me as an assassin from day one. I chuckled, silently thanking Greta for making the choice that had scarred me for life.

I got a little lost on my way back to the campsite. Everything looked different from a crow's perspective. Darkness was setting in and I didn't want Kestral to worry, so I reached out with my magic until I found Shan. Using him as an anchor, I wended my way back to the campsite.

"Is that dinner?" I asked, startling both Kila and Kestral. The warriors glared at me darkly as I crouched down to eat a cold meal of cheese and jerky. They weren't risking a fire so close to Giltner. Kestral watched me curiously. I tried to act as natural as possible, as if I hadn't spent the last few months avoiding talking about my home town.

"I see you found your knives," Kila said, grabbing hold of my wrist. "What about the hair dye?"

"That, and one more little goodie." I held out the vials of dye and the eye drops. "Supposedly the drops turn your eyes brown. No idea if they've been tested on mage eyes."

"Did anyone recognize you?" Kestral asked.

"Yeah. I don't think we have to panic or anything, but maybe we should try to push on tonight." I met Kestral's eyes and held them. I knew he wanted to ask more, but there wasn't any more I was willing to share. Not without opening old wounds.

Kestral nodded. He seemed to have expected this. The bags were still packed except for the food satchel. He repacked it, nearly grabbing the food from my hands. He had to wrestle a wineskin away from me in order to finish packing.

"How are we going to move at night?" Kila asked, eyeing the jar of hair dye doubtfully. "The horses can't see properly."

I recalled the owl I had met at one of the inns. If there was ever a time to try new magic, this was it. "I think I have a spell that can turn the horses' eyes into cat's eyes. It should help them see in the dark."

Kestral's mouth twisted. "You've used a lot of magic today. Are you sure you're up to working a new spell all night?"

I shrugged. "As long as I get to sleep all through tomorrow, I should be fine."

Kestral nodded. "Let's go."

I shifted to my cat form and leapt into Kestral's lap, working my magic to help the horses see. On to Emlenton.

9

"That has got to be the tallest tower I have ever seen," I said, staring out over the river surrounding one of the greatest centers of learning in the entire kingdom. The windows were all made of pure, transparent glass, the stones a uniform shade of gray. The surrounding grass was clipped short and cultivated flowers decorated the base of the tower as well as many windows. Ivy scaled the walls in the shade. We had walked a wide circle around it, crossing bridges over the river. As we walked, I felt a tug of familiarity. Not to the tower itself, but something inside it. Kestral seemed to believe we had located the first child of Laurana.

"Should we go in and say hello?" Kila asked. It had taken me quite awhile to get used to seeing her as a brown-eyed brunette. She still wore her hair tucked into the lace net at the back of her neck, making her look fairly elegant. Today was the first day I had used the eye drops, and Kestral kept giving me strange looks. If I had to guess, I'd say he wasn't very fond of my new look.

"She might know you're here," Kestral reminded us. "Take caution. We don't know what kind of magic she has."

Kestral took a step onto the bridge leading to the main entrance. Kila and I halted before our feet could reach the stones. He was halfway across before he looked back at us. "What are you doing?"

"Oh," Kila startled. "I don't know." She tried taking a step, but somehow put her foot back down in the same place. She frowned at the bridge, seeming perplexed.

"I think it's spelled, Kestral." I tried tripping forward to fall onto the bridge. I ended up falling backwards, landing on my hands and backside.

Kila gritted her teeth, as if she would charge the bridge, but Kestral held a hand out and had us back up.

"It's probably bloodline magic," he explained, glancing back at the tower. "You're all full-blooded siblings; it would be an easy spell for most mages to manage. I could go in."

"How would you know who to look for?" I asked, reaching up a hand to him.

Kestral gripped my arm and pulled me to me feet. He nodded in agreement.

"We can circle the tower and see if it has any weak points," Kila suggested.

Kestral shook his head. "Unlikely. This type of barrier usually only works on towers because the caster sets the spell at the very top, dropping the spell down like a dome."

"So then what—" Kila started, but I hissed her into silence. "Reshi, what in the rust—"

"Ssh, just stop talking." Something about the tower was not right. I walked a few paces away, dimly aware that Kestral was fighting to get something small and metal out of Kila's hands before she could throw it at me. "There aren't any crows here."

"So?" Kila pouted, crossing her arms petulantly. Kestral tucked a throwing dagger into a pouch, waiting for me to continue.

"There's all kinds of birds, see? In the flower pots and on the grass, birds everywhere, but no crows." I closed my eyes, reaching out further with my magic. "I'm not too surprised that there aren't any snakes, but no cats? There are dogs, kept as pets, mostly. But not a single cat." The final absence made me dizzy, knocking me out of my concentration while I staggered to stay upright. Kestral's hands were on my shoulders, steadying me.

"What is it?" Kestral asked.

"It's—" I shook my head. It was simply unnatural. "There aren't any rats at all in that building."

"That's impossible," Kila scoffed. "Haven't mages been looking for an extermination spell like that forever?"

"Are you sure, Reshi?" Kestral glanced back at the tower. "None of your forms are in that tower?"

I grinned up at him, drawing his eyes back to mine. "I didn't exactly say that, did I?"

Kestral looked confused, but only for a second. Then he shuddered and shoved me away.

"What?" Kila asked, looking from me to Kestral. "What is it?"

"Not here." Kestral held a hand up to his mouth, indicating silence. "It seems that Reina has been preparing for your arrival. We need to plan this out."

Emlenton was a true city—crowded, loud and expensive. On the starry side, that meant as long as I colored my eyes, Kestral didn't mind that I walked around as a human. On the dusty side, Kila's gold was finally beginning to bottom out so we were staying in a pretty rough inn. We left most of our belongings inside Shan's stall rather than our rooms, for security reasons. On returning, Kestral collected a few satchels and carried them up to our rooms. One of the kitchen servers caught my eye with a wink and a smirk. I replied with a coquettish head tilt and side-eye glance. Stars, it was nice to be seen again. Maybe I could even squeeze in a little dancing tonight.

Kila followed us into the room Kestral and I would be sharing for the night, letting her hair loose from its net. It seemed braiding and unbraiding was a nervous habit of hers. Or perhaps, she just didn't like sitting still. She and I had a fight the first time she tried braiding my hair. She'd argued it wouldn't get wind-tossed in a braid. I told her that if she were willing to wear a dress I picked out for her, she would be welcome to braid my hair. After I described the dress, she backed off. She wasn't against wearing tight clothing, but apparently baring skin was something that made Kila the Fierce blush.

"I think our best approach will be tonight," Kestral said, getting down to business. "It's likely that Reina already knows the two of you are here from your attempts to cross the barrier. So tonight—"

A knock at the door made us all freeze in place. Who would be knocking? My breath caught in my throat; a shortsword appeared in Kila's hand and I honestly couldn't say where it came from. Kestral made a quelling gesture at the two of us and crossed the room, loosening the sword at his belt. He cracked the door open and the last thing I expected happened.

Kestral laughed, embraced a person I couldn't see, then stepped out into the hall, closing the door behind him.

"What the rust was that?" Kila asked, still holding her sword.

"No idea." I went to the door, pressing my ear against it. I heard boots on stairs and distant voices that faded as they reached the ground floor. "Hey, Sis, spot me some coins."

Kila narrowed her eyes at me. "You know I'm down to my last silvers, don't you?"

"I know." I grinned at her. "I'm going to turn them all into bright, shiny stars."

Kila hesitated, shaking the coins in her purse. "All right. But before Kestral kills you for eavesdropping and gambling, have a washbasin sent up to my room."

"Sure thing." Kila tossed me the pouch and I tied it to my belt before striding confidently down to the bar below. I stopped at the counter and slid over a coin, requesting Kila's bath. As the innkeeper turned to find a runner, I leaned back against the bar and surveyed the room.

Kestral had spotted me and was leveling a glare so cold it gave me chills. He sat at a table with a tall, dark-skinned man whose black curls obscured his eyes as he turned to see what Kestral was glaring at. The stranger was either a soldier or a mage hunter, based on his military-issue boots. He didn't wear a sword. In fact, I couldn't see a single weapon on him. I felt him studying me as I studied him. Finally, I smiled at them both and gave them a lazy wave. Spying on Kestral wasn't my first priority, after all.

Even though the hour was early, the bar had a handful of patrons. There was a table of sailors drinking loudly and harassing the serving wench, a few patrons sitting by themselves and a pretty little hen sitting at the far end of the bar from me. She tried to catch my eye, but I ignored her. I never paid for my pleasure.

The wench bustled past me in a huff, clearly agitated by the sailors' advances. I caught her attention with a coin and a tilt of my head. She glared at me warily until I whispered what I was after. She smiled and nodded, agreeing to play along. By the time the sailors ran their drinks dry and started looking for the wench, she was leaning over the bar, topping off my drink and laughing at something incredibly clever I had said. Or at least that was what it looked like. She had even scrunched down the front of her dress and let a curl fall loose from her scarf. I'd chosen correctly; the girl really knew how to sell the act.

First, the sailors tried slamming their empty mugs against the table for attention, then they tried hollering for her. With a scowl, the wench ducked into the kitchen and sent a different server to their table, while she continued flirting with me at the bar. Finally, the biggest sailor from the table stood up and swaggered up to me. I had my back to him, so it was the wench who tipped me off to his approach.

"Hey, kid!" The sailor grabbed my shoulder, turning me around. "You're netting up our wench over here! Be a good kid and let her get back to her job."

Across the bar, Kestral stood up, hand on his hilt. Discreetly, I shook my head at him. He paused, apparently trying to decide whether he would ignore me or not.

"You let him go!" the wench cried, swatting the sailor's hand with a bar rag. "Remi is one of our regulars, you can't just go manhandling him!"

"Ah, well, he's probably right," I agreed amenably, rolling my shoulder free of the sailor's grip. "Sorry for taking up your time, stardust. Looks like I'm wasting my time here anyway." I shook my fist, letting the objects inside rattle.

"You a dicer?" the sailor said, suddenly interested. "How many blocks?"

"Hmm." I shrugged casually. "Usually three. Four, on a good day. But I'd be a fool to play with sailors. Knowing the stars is your livelihood, isn't it?"

The sailor chortled. "We're none of us navigators and we've some coins to toss. Come sit with us, friend."

I sighed. "Just a toss or two, I suppose." I winked at the bar wench for her assist as I followed the sailor back to his table. The glance back also showed me that Kestral had sat back down with his . . . friend? Soldier? Former lover? I shoved the questions aside as I sat down with the sailors, grinning as I set my dice on the table.

Clusters was a fairly simple dice game. The roller chose how many dice to toss and the other players tried to guess how many constellations would form from the pips and the position of the dice. Whoever guessed the correct number of constellations won the pot, but if no one guessed correctly, the tosser won. As with any game of chance, the players bluffed each other into both the shapes and names of the constellations; you really had to know your stars to win.

Or if you didn't, you had to be extremely convincing.

The sailors and I started by tossing only three dice, trading coins back and forth good-naturedly. Eventually, we added a fourth die, then much later, I let them convince me to add a fifth. The wench kept my drink refilled at no cost, happy now that the sailors were interested in something other than her. Across the room, Kestral kept an eye on me, probably making sure I didn't lose all our money.

"One more die, Remi!" a sailor begged. "Give us a chance to win our coin back!"

"Your ears have gone swimming! I'm barely staying afloat over here!" I laughed. Of course, I was winning—and by a lot more than they realized, as I had been slipping coins off the table using sleight of hand—but I was careful to let the sailors think they had a fighting chance. The wench had kept their ale topped off, and while I'd slacked on drinking mine, they had become drunk enough not to notice how little coin was left on the table. "All right, one six-dice toss, but everything goes into the pot."

I scooped up the dice while the sailors shoved their coins into the center, forming a ring with the scattered coins. The dice all had to fall within the circle of coins to count as a legal throw. I rattled the dice as the ring completed "What are the calls?"

"Fourteen!"

"Sixteen!" two men called it at the same time. If they were right, they would split the pot.

"Nineteen!" one bold man called.

"Twenty-five."

The table fell silent. We hadn't noticed Kestral or his shadow-skinned friend step up to the table. The stranger reached over the table and dropped three gold coins. It was a high call and a high wager. The sailors suddenly looked nervous. Finally, the big one laughed.

"That's a ridiculous call, but we'll take your money. Drop the dice, tosser!"

I stretched out my wrist, letting the dice rattle. I caught Kestral's eye and casually tapped my inner left wrist, the spot where Kestral had his liar's brand. He stared back at me, quirking an eyebrow. With a shake of my head, I tilted my hand and let the dice fall.

The table went quiet as we counted up the constellations.

"I count fifteen."

"No, sixteen! See here!"

"There're easily nineteen, open your eyes!"

"Twenty-five." Kestral's friend spoke softly, but it immediately quelled the table. He reached over, tracing the pips with his finger. "Selurnis. The Bridge. Blood Way. The Light's River," he continued, tracing each constellation, using only one or two constellations I had never heard of before, listing them off like items on a price list. I noted several of the sailors gaping as he finished with, "The King's Arch."

"Now wait a minute," one sailor challenged. "I've never heard of the Blood Way before. And not the Fae's Wing, either."

"Over the eastern edge," Kestral said, referring to the sky in the far east. "I'm sure there's a star chart we can use, if you doubt it."

"No seas in the east," the sailor grumbled. The others stirred grumpily, unhappy that an outsider had come in at the end to take their money.

"Pardon, sir, but there's at least twenty-six." I leaned over to trace a new shape. "The Beggar's Crown."

The dark stranger nodded once. "I see it now. You're right. I suppose I lost."

The sailors began a wild raucous cheer, as if they themselves had won. The big one patted my back hard enough to leave bruises as I scooped my winnings into my belt purse. Kestral caught my eye and jerked his chin towards the stairs. I was surprised to see how late it had grown while I'd gambled. I let Kestral and his friend ascend the staircase ahead of me before thanking the sailors for a good game and sneaking through the kitchen to take a back staircase. I had to keep appearances as a regular, after all.

Kestral and his companion were waiting for me in the hallway just outside our room. Neither seemed particularly surprised about me coming up the back steps.

"So, do I get to meet your mysterious friend who knows far too many constellations?" I asked, giving them a crooked smile.

"Ammon." Kestral tilted his head back to his friend. He then jerked his chin towards me. "Reshi."

It took me aback, him using my real name. Weren't we keeping a low profile? While I was stunned to silence, Kestral pushed our door open and waved the both of us inside. As I passed him, Kestral held out his hand to me. I arched an eyebrow, playing innocent, but Kestral glared. With a sigh, I handed over the coin purse. Kestral removed his friend's three gold coins and handed them over before tying the purse to his belt. I pushed past the both of them to drop into a chair and tilted it back, looking up at Ammon. Stars, the man was tall!

"So, you're like, what? A scholar? A priest? Do you actually know the lore of all those constellations you named?"

"I'll trade my lore for yours." A tiny smile graced the newcomer's face. "What is the Beggar's Crown?"

"You haven't heard?" I arched an eyebrow. "It's a tale as old as time! You see, a beautiful queen falls in love with a—"

Ammon rolled up his cuff, revealing a brightly burning liar's brand, just like Kestral's.

"Tch." I stared up at the ceiling. "Not allowed to use liar's brands in a game of chance. I should report you to the Order."

"I've never seen anyone so upset over winning." Ammon lounged back against the wall, arms folded. "Kestral seemed to think you were about to lose all your funds, so I helped."

"First, I wasn't about to lose." I leaned forward in the chair, letting it fall heavily on its front legs. "Second, it wouldn't have mattered if I lost that toss because—"

"You were cheating," Kestral supplied.

I glared at him darkly.

Ammon chuckled softly. "Who's bringing whom before the Order, now?"

I looked from Ammon to Kestral. "Who the dust is this guy?"

"Ammon and I enlisted at the same time," Kestral explained as he lit candles around the room. "We served in the same squad until we were both promoted to the rank of captain."

"Oh, so you two go way back?" I grinned mischievously up at Ammon. "If you've got any embarrassing stories of Kestral, like, if he ever cut his foot with his own sword, or tripped during drills, I'll make it worth your while."

Ammon gave me a cool look. "I doubt you could. And anyway, Kestral's already shared more about me than he has about you. Not that I haven't put some of it together."

Kestral's head snapped up. "Reshi."

I spun to face him, eyes wide in alarm. He met my eyes then began cursing. Across the room in a silvered glass, I caught my reflection. The eye drops had run out. My eyes were gold again.

Kestral stared a challenge at Ammon. His hand wasn't on his sword, but the threat was there. Ammon lifted a hand, palm up, seemingly unconcerned.

"I'm not a mage hunter, Kestral. I'm not even on duty. I'm in town on personal leave. I don't care what you're up to."

Impossibly, Kestral relaxed.

I stared at Ammon in wonder. Who could he be to have earned that much trust from Kestral? Kestral didn't even trust me that much and we had been traveling together for months now.

"Are you on leave because of your sister?" Kestral asked, as if he hadn't just been ready to draw steel on his friend.

Ammon nodded. "Her child is due any day and the eastern front has been quiet. It seemed like a good time to take a leave." He glanced beyond Kestral to the open window. "I should get back. Give her husband a break from her for at least a little while."

Kestral nodded.

Ammon shrugged himself away from the wall, moving with a soft, deadly grace. As he turned, he met my eyes. I had thought they were black, but as I looked into them, I noticed a gleam of green.

"I don't know what you two are up to, but if you have need of me, you can find me in the craftsman district. Ask for Zera's shop."

I nodded, as it seemed the only appropriate response.

Ammon glanced back at Kestral. "It was great catching up. Let's do it again sometime."

"Sure thing." The door closed behind Ammon.

Kestral and I waited to speak until the sound of his boots faded down the staircase.

"So, are all your friends just creepily intense like that, or was that your long-lost brother?" I asked.

Kestral shook his head. "Ammon's a good man. You can trust him."

"Such a good man that he didn't speak for you when you were discharged?" I asked archly.

"He wasn't part of that." Kestral scowled. "He would have spoken if I'd asked, but it would have only have stalled his career."

"Do I finally get to know the secret?" I asked, leaning forward. "Why the great captain was dishonorably discharged?"

Kestral met my eyes, expression totally deadpan. "What happened to you in Giltner?"

I rolled my eyes and fell back into my seat. "Maybe I can get your friend to tell me."

"You could try." Kestral crossed the room towards me. He reached out, sliding his fingers into my hair and tipping my face up. "But even you're not that convincing."

I gave him a slow smile. "You haven't even seen convincing from me."

"Is your friend gone yet?" A loud voice from the window made the both of us jump.

Kestral spun, drawing his sword in the same motion. I had a knife in each hand and my heart in my throat. Kila perched on the windowsill, clad entirely in black, including a black scarf over the lower half of her face. She stepped into the room, ignoring the drawn weapons. "I got so bored waiting, I think I drifted off."

"You were waiting on the roof?" I asked. "Wait, you fell asleep *on the roof?*"

Kila shrugged. Her outfit was skintight, like a sneak-thief's, but also studded with weapons. Her longsword peeked up over her shoulder, a shortsword at her belt. The hilts of both were wrapped in black leather. A belt of tiny throwing knives circled her waist and worn, padded boots laced up halfway to her knee.

"Why are you dressed like an assassin?" Kestral asked her, sword still in hand.

"Aren't we breaking into the university tonight?" Kila tugged the scarf so that it dropped beneath her chin. "Or did your old war buddy make you forget why we're here?"

"We can't break in, Kila, there's a barrier," Kestral reminded her.

"Well, then, we bring the quarry out to us, right?" Kila glanced at me. "You can get in, can't you?"

"Of course I can." I slipped my knives back into their sheaths, then slid the bracers off my arms. "Kestral isn't going to like it, though."

Kestral sheathed his sword, refusing to look at me. "Kila, take care of Reshi. I'll meet you both downstairs."

Kestral didn't look for or even ask about me as we walked back to the university tower. Kila loved my spider form. She asked if I had a venomous bite, as if considering me a new, exciting weapon. I rode on the tail of the scarf she wrapped around her face, hiding in its folds as it trailed in the wind.

Clouds covered the moon, so the night was darker than usual. I crept up the scarf to sit near Kila's shoulder, looking up at the Great Canvas. What type of star was my oldest sister? A violent star? A shy star? Why hadn't I thought to ask Laki? Knowing a little about her would have helped me to approach her. I had good reason to feel nervous.

Traditionally, each time I met a new sibling, I ended up in a fight. At least I knew to expect it this time.

"I'm going around to the north side," Kestral said from somewhere on Kila's other side. "Count to one hundred before beginning. Reshi." He didn't look at me, but I crept around Kila's back to peek over at him. "Don't be afraid to run if it goes bad. We'll be just outside."

Without a backwards glance, Kestral set off to the opposite side of the tower.

"He really does have a spider thing, doesn't he?" Kila chuckled softly. "I guess everyone has a thing, right? Where are you?"

Kila raised her black-gloved hand to her shoulder and I crawled onto it. She held me in front of her, so we could see eye-to-eye. Not that it helped. Spiders don't exactly have a variety of facial expressions.

"Kestral's right. Don't be afraid to run," Kila reaffirmed. "Try to draw her out here. I hate sending you in alone." Kila tickled my body with a gloved finger. "I'm sure Kestral hates it, too. Be safe, little brother."

Kila stepped as close to the barrier as she could and held her hand up high. I spun a few threads of silk, connecting them into a sort of sail to catch the wind then stepped off Kila's hand. Tugging on specific strands of the silk carried me to the wall of the tower, where I began to climb. The windows were all glass fit into iron frames and almost all the rooms beyond were dark. It seemed the tower's students stayed in a type of barracks in the city of Emlenton, and only a few staff members lived in the tower. A gentle tug on my consciousness drew me ever upwards, seeking an open window.

I finally found one, open barely a crack. I scuttled into a dark room with a dim line of light beneath a door. Even as large a spider as I was, I could squeeze through some impossibly tight spaces. Once in the hallway beyond the dark room, I saw a soft light spilling down a staircase just ahead. I crawled up the wall and headed towards the light.

Would I recognize my sister? Or would I just have to rely on this shaky connection I seemed to have with my siblings? What would I say to her? Wouldn't she be scared if I simply materialized in a room she felt safe in? I definitely wanted to avoid another Laki incident.

Light spilled from an open door off a hallway at the top of the stairway. I crawled up the wall to the ceiling, deciding that the safest entrance had to be the most unexpected one. I crept into the lit room, ready to bolt at a hint of danger.

A woman sat with her back to the door, hunched over a desk and muttering to herself.

Was it Reina? I couldn't see her face, but I was afraid to get too close. The woman had her dark hair pulled back into a bun with several sticks thrust haphazardly through it to hold it in place. As I watched, she pulled one stick free, revealing it as a charcoal pencil. She scribbled quickly on a piece of parchment before thrusting it back through the bun. I crept a tiny bit closer, trying to hear what she said.

"Too advanced, too much too quickly," she said, scribbling through lines of text on parchment. I was surprised to note that she wrote with the opposite hand she had just written with. "Too complex, won't hold for longer than . . ." She trailed off and flipped rapidly through an open book, stopping suddenly to read a page. "Can't believe a bloodline spell isn't enough, only covers humanoid . . . doesn't help against magic . . . or deception." She took a deep breath and tossed her pen down in frustration. "But I guess that's how you're here, isn't it, Jereshin?"

"Were you expecting me?" I asked, hopping down from the ceiling, shifting seamlessly to land on my feet.

"Yes and no." The woman at the desk looked back at me over her shoulder. "I felt you and Tekilashan test the barrier earlier. I thought my precautions would be good enough. I saw a few of your forms through Cera's dispersal and had to extrapolate on the others. I guessed there was a smaller, less obvious form, but I thought perhaps it was a frog or a toad."

I blinked at the sudden flood of words. "Extra-what?"

She gave an exaggerated sigh. "I guessed. Based on previously collected data."

"Oh." I grimaced. "Why does everyone guess frog or toad?"

"Did you know there's no biological difference between a frog and a toad?" she asked.

"No bio-what-what?"

"So why, if there's no difference, does it take two different spells to banish frogs and toads? One should work just as well as the other."

"Um."

"The spider form was completely unexpected, though. Well done, Jereshin."

"Just Reshi is fine."

"No, no, no, it's not." My sister pivoted in her seat, the chair turning with her like a spinning barstool. She wore a pair of spectacles over unremarkable brown eyes. "You lose the majesty of your name. Don't you understand the power of the names given us?"

I arched a brow. "I can honestly say I have never considered it."

She leaned back against her desk with a sigh and drummed her fingers on the desk. "I knew most of you weren't as educated as myself, but I didn't expect you to be dull as well."

"Well, it's nice to meet you too, Reina."

"Laureinaqin," she snapped. "Do you know what that means?"

"I have a feeling you're going to tell me regardless of what I say next."

"Mother chose to name us as if we were royalty from her home country, where Father met her." Reina pushed on, intent on her lecture. "Laureinaqin meaning, literally, Queen Laureina."

"Really? I might have guessed it meant something else."

She glared at me over her spectacles. "Raleagan would translate to King Raleagh, or Ralean, depending on how he wanted to be called. The rest of you simply had the word 'prince' or 'princess' inserted at the end of your name. Mother had such hopes for the seven of us."

"As the realm has only one prince, I would say that didn't work out for her."

Reina tapped her pen against her palm, staring hard at me for a moment. "Did you know that before the prince was born, I was the kingdom's heir?"

"I'm sure you're not bitter about that at all."

"Yes, after three failed pregnancies by the queen, Father met with my adoptive parents and signed documents naming me his heir. I received a queen's education, attended council meetings, studied foreign relations. There was even talk of an engagement." Her eyes grew distant a moment. "Did you know Mother was supposed to be the queen?"

"Did you know male sea stars give birth?"

"Father wanted to put—No." Reina's eyes snapped into focus, fixing me with a glare as good as any of Kestral's. I laughed, infuriating her more. "No, that is absolutely, unassailably incorrect." She stood, pushing past me to stand before a bookcase, trailing her hand almost lovingly along a few spines before removing the desired tome. "Sea stars disperse genetic material into . . ." She trailed off, eyes snapping up from the page to meet mine, catching on to my diversionary tactic. "Hm. You may not be smart, but you might be clever."

"Thanks?" I gave her half a smile. "If I might interrupt what sounds like a really fascinating lecture, which I didn't even have to pay tuition for, so I'm sure it's a real steal—I'm not really here to learn a history lesson."

"No. You're here to ask my assistance in your fight against our brothers Raleagan and Navelynstra." Reina crossed the room to another bookshelf, selecting a book seemingly at random. She leafed through it before continuing, "I have no interest in helping you."

"First, that's a completely acceptable answer." I held my hands out, trying to look as unthreatening as possible. "I would point out, however, that the last time one of us didn't want to fight, he got roasted before he could finish screaming. I feel like maybe we could be a help to each other until—"

"No." Reina set her book back and selected a different one.

I stuttered to a stop, trying to think of what to say next.

"Jereshin—"

"Reshi."

"It's not that I can't defend myself, unlike poor Telakishin. I simply have no interest in what is currently an all-out brawl between siblings. Once one of you emerges with the powers of the others, then I will go and take what is rightfully mine. The power, and the throne." Without looking up from her book, Reina walked over to an unlit candle sconce. She pinched a wick between two fingers and when she pulled her hand away, the candle was lit. I gulped. Was she another fire-user like Eagan? No, that was something different. I backed up a step.

"You see, Jereshin." She glanced up over her book, those plain eyes somehow wildly disconcerting. "Not only am I the eldest, born with more magic than any of the rest of you, but I am also the only one of us to receive a formal magical education."

"So, you learned magic from books? That's the advantage that'll keep you alive against the fire noble and the lightning lunatic?"

"No." Reina smiled for the first time. She set the book down on the edge of a shelf. As she met my eyes, she slowly removed her spectacles. I gaped in horror as her veil dropped, smoothing her fly-away brown hair into a smooth, precise knot at the back of her head. Her eyes gleamed with violet light. She even seemed to stand several inches taller. "You may even be familiar with this magic, dear Jereshin. I am fae-trained."

I took another step back, stumbling into the desk where Reina had been writing when I entered. When had she put herself between me and the door? There were three tall windows in front of the desk, but they were shut tight. Maybe I could push past her? Or turn into something small and dart around her? When had I missed my opportunity to run, as both Kila and Kestral had suggested?

"Well, I can see that there's nothing I can say to change your mind." I shrugged, smiling congenially. "It seems like you've got a pretty solid plan, so . . ." I took a step forward, hoping to pass by her. "Good luck, I guess, when you face the ultimate sibling and—" I grunted as a solid wall of air pressed me back against the desk.

"Now, Jereshin." Reina smiled as she shook her head. "I have no intention, whatsoever, of leaving my tower and hunting down our brothers and sisters, as some have. But I also can't ignore it when one shows up, uninvited, essentially offering himself up to me. I'd be a fool to let you go. You understand, don't you?"

"I don't. Not really." I struggled against the heavy air pinning me to the desk. "What magic is this? This isn't fae."

"I am, what you might call, a mystic," Reina explained, appearing ready to begin another lecture. "I may be fae-trained, but my magic is human in nature."

My arms and legs were pinned, my chest could barely move to breath. Pressing against the invisible weight was impossible, so I tried throwing my weight sideways. Objects on the desk rattled, something fell and rolled. Reina shrieked, cutting off her lecture and the magic holding me down. She lifted her wide trouser leg and stomped on a lit candle, sent rolling by my struggle against the desk. Parchment beneath the candle barely smoldered before Reina doused the flame, looking more relieved than rational. I smirked as she looked up to glare at me.

"Do you have any idea what a flame could do in here, you ignorant—"

I leaned back against the desk and used both legs to kick her chair across the room. Reina's form shimmered and reappeared, out of the chair's path, but it struck my true target: a standing brazier of tiered candles. The brazier wobbled for one breathless moment before toppling forward, sending candles rolling over stacks of parchment and bundled scrolls. Reina's hands balled into fists, her face contorting with fury, before she raised one hand to the fire and one towards me. I felt, more than saw, an invisible force slam down on the toppled candles, smothering the flames. At the same time, a force slammed into me hard enough to flip me over the desk and through the window beyond.

Not exactly my best plan. Glass and iron shredded my clothes and skin as I fell from a height I had previously thought unachievable by human construction. But at least I had escaped. I shifted to my crow form, wincing as blood drenched my feathers. I set my wings straight out, content to glide to the ground without causing further harm to myself.

"Kestral, I'm landing to the south—" My thought was cut off as an invisible force slammed into me from above. I fell before catching myself, spiraling into an awkward dive. Since I had no night vision in this form, I couldn't tell how quickly the ground was coming up beneath me. Attempting to avoid more solid walls of air, I swerved left and right, trying to trace an unpredictable pattern to the ground.

I cawed a scream as a wall of air slammed into my right wing. I felt the bone snap like a piece of dried straw. My left wing fluttered frantically, trying to control my descent. Air burst from my lungs as I hit the ground, luckily not far below me. My shattered wing flopped uselessly alongside my body, my beak open, panting in pain. I tried reaching out for Kestral, but pain was a white searing heat not only in my body, but in my mind as well. For a moment, all I could do was stand and pant.

There was a faint shimmer in the air ahead of me and then a pure, white light. It took long moments for me to understand what I was seeing—my sister Reina held a ball of witchlight in one hand while the other reached back to the sticks in her hair. She touched one, twisted it, and out popped a long, metal needle. She held the light aloft, walking towards me on slippered feet.

I flapped my good wing and cawed loudly, but I was going nowhere fast. Reina seemed to know it too, the way she stalked slowly forward. Struggling was only making me bleed out faster. I stopped and cowered against the dark grass. Reina smiled down at me, the needle glinting in her hand.

A shadow fell over me. For a moment, I thought I had fallen through the Canvas, meeting the star that burned only for me. Didn't the Order define death as eternal darkness? Had they ever mentioned the ground rolling and rumbling, though? My mind caught up slowly, like walking through ankle-deep muck beneath thigh-high water. The ground rippled and pulsed. Kila stood between Reina and me, a black shadow baring cold steel.

"Out of my way, Tekilashan."

"Go through me." Kila's voice echoed off the tower. "If you can."

Kila charged and was suddenly swept sideways with a grunt. Before Reina could take a step, the ground opened beneath her and she tumbled down. Orbs of witchlight blossomed against the night sky, throwing the grassy field outside the tower into relief. The ground continued to shudder and ripple, each new tremor a fresh wave of pain. I hunkered down in the grass, panting, as Kila and Reina moved against each other.

I cawed in alarm as a hand scooped me up. I pecked, bit, twisted flesh beneath my beak, unseeing in pure panic.

"Reshi, stop!" Kestral's voice, slightly breathless but otherwise calm. "It's me. Calm down."

I resumed panting, turning my head to stare up at him. Kestral grimaced.

"Broken, isn't it? You can't shift?"

More panicked panting.

"Don't worry." Kestral dropped to one knee, glancing up briefly at the fight between Kila and Reina. He pulled a strip of bandages out of a belt pouch and carefully wrapped my body from breast bone to tail feathers, setting the broken wing out straight. The bandages quickly turned bloody, and I had to shove down the panic that accompanied my inability to move. "That will have to do for now. When we get back, you can heal up."

Yet more frantic panting.

"Stay calm, stay down." Kestral lifted me so I could see into his eyes. "Can you tell me anything about her? Her powers? Anything?"

I tried to push past the pain. I think I got one thought out, *"Mystic."*

Kestral nodded and set me down gently. He removed his heavy dagger from his belt and drove the tip deeply into the earth beside me. "Stay near this so I can find you afterwards." His head snapped up as one of my sisters screamed. "Reshi, whatever happens after this, draw as deeply as you have to, to heal. Understood?"

I watched him stand up, wishing he didn't have to go help Kila. What could he do against such a powerful mage? Reina was right. The rest of us were just muddling through our magic, learning as we went. To me, she appeared every inch the master sorceress. Kestral strode away from me. I cawed after him once. He glanced back with a small smile before pressing forward, snapping leather-and-steel gauntlets over his wrists.

Balls of light hovered above what was rapidly becoming a battlefield. Kila's swords had been knocked from her hands and she was charging Reina bare-handed. Reina threw a hand forward, but the earth rose before Kila and she leapt over whatever invisible wall Reina created. Reina shimmered and faded from sight and Kila missed her attack. Just as Reina reappeared, Kestral erupted out of the shadows, sword flashing for her neck. Reina shimmered again, disappearing. Kestral and Kila pivoted in the same instant, turning their backs to each other and keeping their eyes out for Reina.

"Above!" I screamed the word mentally. Reina hovered, impossibly, just over Kestral and Kila, holding her hands palm down. Kestral grabbed Kila's scarf, tossing her forward before rolling out of the path of the attack. Solid air impacted the ground where the two of them had been standing moments before. Reina gritted her teeth and turned her head, searching the dark grass. The hovering witchlights glided through the air, searching for my hiding place. I hunkered down lower in the grass.

Kestral stood, firing a bolt from his small crossbow. Kila swung her arm in a wide arch, throwing her tiny daggers. Reina shimmered and faded. Kestral loaded another bolt, turning a circle with his eyes up. Kila waited a breath then slammed her foot down against the ground, hard. Rocky spears drove up through the earth all over the grassy field, seemingly at random. Someone screamed far too close to my hiding place in the grass. With a bone-jarring hop, I turned to look behind me.

Witchlight illuminated my hiding place, as well as my sister standing behind me. One of Kila's rock-spears pierced Reina just below her collarbone and protruded from her back. Before relief could wash over me, Reina reached up and grabbed the rock-spear, turning it to dust. As I watched, she placed her hand to the wound and it healed beneath her touch. Icy terror gripped my heart as Reina's violet eyes flashed with rage.

Kila and Kestral were too far, I realized. She would kill me. She could stomp me to death or break my neck or . . .

I heard cries from behind me, Kestral and Kila's shouts. I had an idea, but I knew I didn't have the time or the wits to explain it to Kestral. As Reina stalked towards me, I tried showing Kestral Reina's reaction when I nearly burned the papers and books in her tower room. Even if they couldn't set it on fire to save me, it would keep Kestral and Kila safe.

Reina towered over me, lifting her slippered foot above my head. Inwardly, I rolled my eyes; couldn't even get stomped to death by a pair of proper boots. What had happened to her steel needle? At least that would have hurt less.

A resounding crack echoed across the field, followed by the groan of stone on stone. Reina stopped, foot still raised, as she stared across the field. Slowly, she set her foot down, backing up a step.

"You wouldn't," Reina called.

"Wouldn't I?" Kila's voice, but I could hear the strain in it. Another painful hop and I half-turned, peering over the grass to see what had stopped Reina's moment of triumph. In the distant tower, only one set of windows had light behind them. One of those windows had been broken when I was thrown through it. The stones making up the outer wall between the windows had cracked. And the crack was growing.

"That's a bluff. You may slaughter indiscriminately on the battlefield, but you've never harmed innocents."

"I don't have to harm any innocents." Kila grinned, lit by the floating orbs of witchlight. "All stones are mine. I can weaken the stones around your floor and strengthen the ones above and below. The upper floors will drop and settle, as if your floor never existed."

Reina's eyes widened, for the first time, she looked worried. "You have no idea—you can't possibly understand—all my years of study and research! You would set that work back decades!"

Kila shrugged. "I'm just an ignorant soldier. None of that means a thing to me."

"Step away from him," Kestral commanded, his crossbow raised as he stepped forward.

Reina bit her lower lip, eyes flicking to me, then up to her tower. A second crack formed at the far end of the wall from the first. As we watched, the two cracks strained towards each other, like lovers reaching for each other across a void.

"Stop!" Reina shouted. She shimmered, reappearing far across the field, between Kila and the tower. "You cretinous blood-spiller, you do not know what you're doing!"

Kila responded with a vulgar suggestion.

Kestral turned, keeping his crossbow trained on Reina as he continued backing towards me. As he passed, he nudged Kila with his elbow, drawing her back as well.

"We're taking Reshi and we're leaving," Kestral called. "We want no fight with you, Laureinaqin."

Reina narrowed her eyes at him. Perhaps she was wondering if his use of her name was respectful or mocking. She watched the pair of them back right up to me.

Kila removed the dagger from the ground.

Kestral clipped his crossbow to his belt and gently picked me up.

"Fix my tower, you termagant mountain ape!" Reina shouted.

"I will," Kila called. Sweat beaded on her brow, her skin pale and her hands shaking. "After we're safely away. Don't follow us, or it all goes up in dust!"

Kestral cradled me against his chest, one hand holding the broken wing as steady as possible.

"We need to run," Kila hissed softly.

"We can't. He's already bleeding out."

"Kestral, I can't stop the tower from collapsing," Kila whispered, face close to his. "I'm using everything I have to delay it, but those walls are coming down. If she comes after us . . ."

Kestral swore, shifting his grip on me to hold the wing steady. "Double-time, then. We'll disappear into the city."

That first jarring step drew a screaming caw from my throat. Half-closed wounds re-opened. By the second step, I sank into blackness.

I woke up alone in a strange bed, in my human form. I stretched out my right arm, popping my shoulder, elbow and wrist, but the bones all seemed to have healed, which left me wondering: How long had I been here? And where was here? My cloak had been draped over the blankets and I clutched it to me as I looked around, trying to figure out where I was. The window across the room was partially open, showing me a midnight sky.

"There's a pitcher of water next to the bed."

I jumped like a cat at the unexpected voice, reaching for my magic to shift quickly. A deep ache filled my chest, like a pulled muscle, as I found I didn't have even enough magic for a single shift. Once my heart climbed back down out of my throat, I looked around for the source of the voice.

In the shadows off to the left of the bed, Kestral's friend from the bar lounged against the wall. The tall man's arms were crossed and he wore a sword on his belt. I felt his eyes on me beneath those long, dark curls.

I cleared what felt like a week's worth of road dust from my throat. "Where's Kestral?"

"He left a few hours ago with your sister. I find it odd that you asked about him before you asked about her."

"She can take care of herself," I argued, dragging my cloak around my shoulders. Every muscle in my body felt stiff. Moving, even slowly, was difficult. "How long have I been here? And where is here?"

"You're in my sister's house in the craftsman district of Emlenton. Kestral showed up here late last night with your sister, holding a nearly dead bird in one hand and a sleeping draught in the other. He asked to stay the night." The dark man tilted his head, still watching me carefully. "In all the years I've known him, Kestral has never once asked a favor."

I remained silent. I didn't know what to say to that. I couldn't remember this man's name, even though Kestral had introduced us last night. "Is your sister all right? You said she's pregnant, right?"

"I sent her to stay with her husband's family. She'll be fine." Ammon—that was his name—rolled his shoulders in a slow shrug. "Your sister is also fine, by the way. She guarded this room most of the night, even though she looked exhausted. Kestral slept for over a full day and woke up looking worse for the wear."

I flinched at that. I must have unconsciously drawn deeply from him to heal so quickly. It didn't happen often that I drew life force without meaning to, but it had happened before when I'd been one step away from falling through the Canvas. I probably also fell out of my crow form once the bones had healed as I didn't have the magic to maintain the form. "Where did Kestral go?"

"Your sister passed out around mid-morning. I moved her to a bedroom and took up her post outside your bedroom. I'm not complaining, but it would have been nice to know what I was protecting you from." He shifted his eyes to the door before meeting mine again. "When Kestral woke up, he woke her and went out looking for a fight, I believe they said."

I tensed, worried that Kestral and Kila had gone after Reina, but if Kila was drained, that was probably the last thing they would do. Looking for a fight . . . perhaps a bar fight? Kila needed freshly spilled blood to refill her wellspring.

"No one came after us?" I asked, slipping from the bed. Someone had removed my boots, so I knelt to pull them on. "Nothing bad happened after we got here?"

"There was some commotion in the city this morning. Something about the university." Ammon arched a brow at me. I ducked my head, trying not to give anything away. "But no one came here looking for any of you." Ammon paused, watching as I stood, stretched, and adjusted my cloak. "Kestral said you would be hungry."

I opened my mouth to protest, but my stomach growled a warning at me. I smiled sheepishly. "I am. Can I get something small? I should go after Kestral and Ki—"

"Don't." Ammon held up a hand. "Don't tell me her name. I don't want to know one more detail than I have to. Once Zera has her child, I'm returning to the army."

"Oh." I hesitated. "Did Kestral ask you to guard me?"

"And feed you." Ammon shifted his weight away from the wall, moving with a slow, casual grace. This man was every bit the warrior that Kestral was, I could sense it. "And keep you from following him."

"What?" I stumbled over my own boots and tried to cover it with outrage. "He can't just keep me trapped here. I'm not some pet he can—"

"No, apparently you're a half-dead bird he had to rescue last night." Ammon gave me a steady look that was more than a little disconcerting. "Eat something first. If Kestral isn't back by the time you finish, I'll help you look for him."

That sounded like a fair deal. I pretended to think it over, before agreeing and following Ammon to the kitchen. Zera's house had two stories—the downstairs was her clay shop and kitchen; the upstairs had the bedrooms and a sitting room. The shop looked fairly prosperous with beautifully painted plates, bowls, cups and other assorted items.

"Your sister must be quite the artist." I picked up a pitcher shaped like a bell-mouth flower, the handle shaped like its stem. "Or is this her husband's work?"

"Zera does all the sculpting and painting," Ammon explained as he pulled food from a cold box for me. "Her husband runs the shop. They were planning to be closed this week anyway, with the baby coming, so don't worry about inconveniencing them at all."

I grimaced. It was unfair to kick a pregnant woman out of her own home, but then, I had been too unconscious to be part of that decision. I hollowed out a large roll of bread and stuffed the inside with shaved lamb and cheese. I spread butter over the soft inner bread I'd torn out and ate that first.

Ammon stood nearby, watching silently.

"Thanks for offering to come with me to find Kestral," I said between mouthfuls. "You must know what type of trouble he finds when he's not being watched."

"You mean the type of trouble that gets him caught up in a mage-family war?" Ammon asked, eyebrows raised.

I choked on a mouthful of bread. He sure knew a lot for someone who didn't want to know anything.

"And it's not Kestral I'm worried about. I don't feel I know you well enough to prevent you from doing something unexpectedly stupid."

"Oh." I wanted to debate that point but couldn't come up with an argument that wasn't an outright lie. Dust liar's brands and the men who used them! I poured myself a mug of cold milk and set to eating my stuffed roll. After a few minutes of silence, I asked, "Is this why you and Kestral get along so well? You just sit together saying nothing?"

Ammon chuckled. "Most soldiers are loud. Boisterous. The fact that we were both on the quiet side was probably what drew us together."

I nodded. I had a question I wanted to ask but I didn't know Ammon well enough to ask it. He didn't seem the type to talk unless prompted, but he also seemed overly cautious. He probably couldn't be goaded into giving anything away, accidentally or otherwise.

I was nearly finished eating when Ammon drew the chair across from me and sat down. He pushed the curls out of his eyes to meet mine squarely.

"This is none of my business, but as Kestral's closest friend, I have to say this." Dark green eyes bored into mine. "Whatever you've roped Kestral into, I can see it's been good for him. He needed a purpose after the army betrayed him, and it seems like you've been able to provide that for him. However, if you're stringing him along for anything else, personal or otherwise, you need to stop."

I blinked innocently and spread my arms, preparing to deny the charge. Ammon held a hand up, his sleeve slipping just enough to show his liar's brand.

"I'm not accusing you of anything. I don't know Kestral's business. I don't want to. What I do know is that Kestral doesn't enter into anything—and I mean anything at all—without going in all the way." Ammon stared me down, making me feel as big as a rat. "He doesn't trust easily. He doesn't fight for unworthy causes. He doesn't look for a retreat, he charges until every enemy is defeated." Ammon leaned over the table, staring me down. "If he loses his purpose again, he might not be able to pull himself together again. If you're not with him for the full journey, Reshi, you need to release him. Kindly."

I turned my head, staring at the floor. "I didn't ask for any of this. I've been his prisoner since the beginning."

"A prisoner?" Ammon leaned back, crossing his arms over his chest. "So, you're not taking any responsibility for what's happened between the two of you?"

I looked up, thrusting my chin forward stubbornly. "If you know him, you know he doesn't get taken for anything unless he's willing. And how would you even know anything about that? Were you lovers in the past?"

Ammon smiled. "There it is."

"What?"

"I knew you wanted to ask." Ammon met my eyes steadily. "Kestral and I were never lovers. Only good friends."

I gaped for a minute, astounded. I had wanted to ask that question since the first minute I'd laid eyes on the tall, striking man. There was no way I could have asked Kestral and I didn't exactly know Ammon well enough . . . A nervous laugh worked its way up from my chest. This son of a dust merchant manipulated me! I hadn't even suspected him of it. I laughed again, earning a small smile from Ammon.

Ammon stood and started to speak but was cut off as the kitchen door shoved open. Kila stumbled in with Kestral's arm around her shoulders. She looked hale enough, considering the last time I'd seen her she had been pale and shaky. Kestral looked awful. There were deep bags under his eyes as if he'd missed a week of sleep. A bruise colored one of his cheekbones and he was definitely limping.

"Reshi!" Kila cheered, carefully setting Kestral in a chair at the table.

Kestral folded his arms on the table and put his head down on them to rest.

"We were just in the best bar fight ever! We all got kicked out into the street and the fight kept going! I think more people even jumped in. It was glorious!" She picked through the food Ammon had set out. "Is there any honey? I'm dying for some honey."

Ammon eyed her for a moment as if deciding whether to lecture her on ordering people around inside their own homes. He must have realized it wasn't worth it, because he dug through a cabinet and handed Kila a jar of honey. She thanked him genuinely, which seemed to placate him.

"Are you all right, Kestral?" I asked softly, leaning low over the table to speak to him. Kila was cheerfully describing her brawl to Ammon, who nodded politely. I got the feeling he wasn't missing a word I said to Kestral, though.

"I'll live," he growled, as if he could accomplish that goal through willpower alone. "Wasn't sure you were going to survive the night."

"Me neither." I faked a laugh. "Would have been a shame if Kila had to coalesce—"

Kestral reached out and took my hand. I wasn't sure if he meant to stun me into silence, but that's what it accomplished. He tilted his head towards Kila and whispered, "She says they're getting close."

"Who—?" But even as I said it, I visualized my brothers. There was that familiar tug at the edge of my subconscious, drawing my eyes south. Normally, I couldn't judge distance, but it felt as if Eagan and Velyn were only a day's ride away. "What phase is the moon in?"

"Near full. I checked." Kestral let go of my hand and pushed himself up off the table. "Ammon, I'm sorry to impose, but could we stay just one more night?"

"I don't see the harm." Ammon shrugged lightly. "But now that you're all conscious, I must warn you. If you break any of Zera's ceramics, she will charge you three times the price."

Kestral chuckled, wrapping his arm around his chest as if it hurt. "We'll leave before dawn in the morning. Sorry to bring you into this."

"I'm not in this. Don't worry about me." Ammon collected the remains of the food and put it away. "As far as I'm concerned, I've been catching up with an old army buddy. That's all."

Kestral gave the tall man a sleepy smile. "Thanks, Ammon. When this ends, we'll catch up over drinks."

"Good. You're buying." Ammon smiled back.

Kila looked from Ammon to Kestral, a quizzical look in her eyes. She glanced at me and I shook my head. Whatever Kila was thinking, the answer was probably no.

Kestral pushed himself up from the table. "Only a few hours until dawn. We should—
"

A loud knock at the front door found us all suddenly armed and on our feet. Ammon recovered first, sliding his sword back into its sheath. After glancing around at the various blades we held, he reminded us again not to break any of his sister's clay creations. He answered the door while Kestral warned both Kila and I to stay back and keep our eyes down. There was a hurried, almost-frantic conversation at the door before Ammon returned, pulling on a cloak.

"Zera has gone into labor. I expect I'll be out all night. Lock up after yourselves, won't you?"

Kestral nodded. "Stars guide her newborn to a bright life."

"Yeah, good luck," I added.

"Stars all bless," Kila said.

Ammon nodded to us, then left. Kestral finished gathering up the assorted foods and putting them away.

"Reshi, sleep with your sister tonight. I need real rest."

"Yeah, I can, but . . ." I hesitated. "You'll need me to shift tomorrow, right?"

Kestral nodded.

"I need to draw just a little." I held my fingers up barely an inch apart. "Tiny. I promise. I wouldn't ask if I wasn't dry."

Kestral sighed. "Fine. Just don't stay."

"I won't." But I did.

There was no plan for a next move. Approaching Reina had been a failure, but at least we knew she wouldn't take sides with Eagan and Velyn. Small blessing, though. If we ever did manage to kill our brothers, she would probably descend on us like an avenging, bespectacled fairy. According to Kestral, our only move was to pick an advantageous battlefield against Eagan and Velyn and try to kill them again. As Kila and I had never been to the rural northeast before, we let Kestral choose our destination.

Luckily, the others only seemed to travel by boat, which allowed us the advantage of cutting across the countryside. A countryside littered with comfy inns. And with the eye drops from Giltner, I was able to mingle like a normal person. Kestral wasn't thrilled about the situation, but he seemed to think it was less suspicious than sending meals and ale up to the room.

"The stone plain between the ocean and the fae wilds is the best spot," Kestral explained over a map in our inn's common room. We had traveled for four days and I still felt a prickle on the back of my neck, as if one of my brothers were about to slide a knife between my ribs at any second. Kestral was still recovering from the energy I'd drained the night my wing had healed. This was the first Kila and I were hearing of a plan. I'd like to say I was interested, but the inn had a four-instrument band and a lot of enthusiastic dancers.

"Reshi." Kestral pulled my attention back to the map. "I know you've never been here before, but are there animals you can bring in to fight with us?"

"At the edge of the fae wilds?" I hummed, glancing back at the dancers. "I've heard only magical beasts live there. I've never tried controlling one of those before. When we get closer, I can try."

"There are plenty of normal animals," Kestral said. "And some that only slightly differ from mortal animals, like the dire bears. Do you think you could control a dire bear? Reshi?"

"What?" I turned back around, facing the map again. "Sorry. Um, maybe? I don't know."

Kila rolled her eyes. "Kestral, if we're on the stone plains, we have a solid advantage even without Reshi. The steam vents will make Velyn's ice creatures melt and Eagan will have nothing to burn. If we can neutralize their magic, we've got them."

"They surprised us last time. We can't let that happen again." Kestral squinted at the map as if it could tell him the secret to beating Eagan and Velyn. "Would the heat from the steam vents be of any use to Eagan?"

Kila shrugged. "How should I know? He's only thrown around fire before, not heat."

"What do you think, Reshi?"

"Hm?" I blinked, focusing on the map again. "I think . . . I don't think this is really helping right now."

"I think *you're* not really helping right now," Kestral replied with a scowl.

"Battlefield tactics aren't my thing," I replied, leaning back with a shrug. "Just tell me the plan after you've figured it out."

Kestral glowered at me. "You just want to go drink and dance."

"What's wrong with that?" I grinned at him. "Come drink and dance with me, Kestral. You need to relax. You've looked dead-tired for days."

"Whose fault is that?" Kestral asked, eyebrow arched.

Kila pushed back from the table. "If we're not discussing strategy anymore, I'm getting a drink. Might even gamble a little. I've missed gambling."

"No, Kila, wait—" While Kestral tried to convince Kila that gambling might tip off her identity, I slipped away in search of a dance partner. It had been ages since I'd been properly admired.

The band was in high spirits and so were the dancers. I traded partners as quickly as I traded drinks, letting my mind grow pleasantly fuzzy. At one point, I noticed our dinner table had a new set of patrons. I paused, looking around for Kestral and Kila. My sister sat at the bar, talking with a few other women over mugs of ale. Kestral must have succeeded in keeping her away from the gambling tables. I couldn't see Kestral anywhere. I hoped he'd gone to bed; he really needed a night of uninterrupted sleep.

An hour past midnight found me suitably drunk with an arm as thick as a blacksmith's around my shoulders. I stumbled, one hand braced against my partner's chest to keep myself upright. We both laughed, then the big man lowered his mouth to my ear, making an offer. The hearth fire still burned hot, and after dancing for so long, I was sweating. The invitation to step out back was tempting, so when he started leading me through the kitchen door, I didn't resist.

I told myself it didn't mean anything as he pushed the back door open. The cool air felt like a sudden head rush, burning in my chest and causing goosebumps to rise along my skin. Kestral needed to sleep anyway, I'd just be bothering him. Draining him. This was better for both of us.

The stranger leaned down, pushing me back against the wall of the inn. I tilted my head back, inhaling the night air. Hands and hot breath roamed over my body; it had been quite a while since my last tryst under the stars. I felt a tug at my belt, my hands instinctively reaching down to assist his when the back door suddenly crashed open, spilling light from the kitchen into the courtyard. Before my mind could catch up, my partner was thrown several paces back, hitting the ground with rather heavy sounding "thump."

Dust. Dust, rust and ashes.

"Get. To. The. Room." I'd never heard such fury in Kestral's voice, not even when his former comrades had tried to kill him. His blue eyes flashed with a threat of violence. A muscle ticked in his jaw. I felt paralyzed as if he had somehow frozen me with a spell.

"Hey!" My huge oaf of an almost-partner had stumbled back to his feet. "This in't any o' yer business! Git on out o' here afore I put you through a wall!"

Kestral turned slowly. Without his eyes on me, I caught my breath. The sudden scare along with the cool air helped me regain a semblance of sobriety while Kestral exchanged words—among other things—with the larger fellow. As the stranger limped away to lick his wounds, Kestral turned on me again.

"What are you doing?" he asked, voice deadly soft.

"Whatever I want," I replied casually. "I thought you were in bed already and I wanted to dance. So, I found a partner."

Kestral gritted his teeth, hands fisted at his sides. I tucked my hands behind my head, lounging against the inn's outer wall.

"Honestly, Kestral, you can't be this mad about it." I smirked. "Sex is just sex. It doesn't mean anything."

"Doesn't mean anything?" Kestral repeated, voice strained.

I rolled my eyes. "Sex is just something people do. Like when their blood's up, or when they need a release. When they need to feel in control or when they need to hurt someone. You're a soldier, you should know that better than anyone."

Kestral's fist flew at me faster than I thought it could. I flinched, the punch landing on the wall beside my head.

Kestral leaned in close, not quite touching me. "It's never been about any of those things between us."

I swallowed, trying to keep my head clear after that wall-shaking punch. "Look, Kestral, I may be your prisoner or whatever, but you don't own me."

Kestral narrowed his eyes at me. "Is that what this is about? Giltner?" The hand not planted next to my head moved towards my hip. Quicker than a heartbeat, I flicked a knife into my hand and held the blade against Kestral's wrist, his fingertips inches from me.

Dust.

Rusting dust.

Rusting dust and rusting ashes.

I thought I had been careful. I thought I had kept the rooms dark enough, kept the blankets high enough, shifted often enough. I thought I had kept those marks hidden.

But he'd seen.

He knew.

A hysterical laugh bubbled up from my throat as I turned the blade, using the flat side to toss Kestral's hand back. Pushing off the wall, I shoved Kestral a step away from me, knife held down at my side as a ward. We stared at each other in silence. Kestral looked steady, but I felt a slightly manic grin on my face. He knew the truth. He'd known for a while.

"What happened to you in Giltner?" Kestral asked softly, all fury gone from his voice.

I laughed again. "You already know, don't you? Figured out my secret?"

Kestral said nothing, watching me with those emotionless eyes. At least no emotion was better than pity.

If I saw pity in his eyes, I'd probably slit my own throat. "You thought I was a thief, didn't you? A cut-purse or a window-breaker or a lockpick? That's what you thought, right?"

Kestral jerked his chin in a nod.

"Weren't you so glad to find out that I never got the chance to be guilded? Was it a relief when you found out I had been sold as a whore?"

Kestral shook his head but he didn't interrupt.

"The orphanage sold me to a noble when I turned ten. My contract was sold twice more after that. You saw, right?" I sneered at him. "When I turned sixteen, I was too old to be sold as a child-whore, so my master gave my contract to a brothel. That's when I ran." I laughed bitterly. "I might be the only one of Laurana's kids to have two bounties on my head, although I guess the first one doesn't really matter anymore. Well, Kestral? Happy now? That's the secret of Giltner." I bowed mockingly.

"Reshi." He reached a hand towards me. I warded it away with the knife.

"Don't." How long could I keep my voice steady? How long until my hands started shaking? "Don't, Kestral. Whatever you think you can say, it doesn't matter. I may be beholden to you right now, but don't think that means you own me."

I took a step back, preparing to shift. Kestral started to say something, reaching forward for me again but the shape I chose drove him back on his heels. A spider could disappear into shadows quicker than tears into the ocean.

There was nothing quite like being kicked out of bed by your sister to start your day.

"What the—Reshi, is that you?" Kila blinked over the edge of the bed, rubbing her eyes blearily. Her other hand held a sword. I had no idea where it came from as I had checked her bed carefully for sharp objects before sleeping at the end of it.

After finally confessing to my past in Giltner the night before, I hadn't wanted to be alone, but I also didn't feel charming enough to find another partner in the common room. I certainly hadn't been about to go sleep with Kestral, so I had curled up with Kila as a last possible resort. It wasn't an ideal situation as I couldn't draw magical energy from her, but at least I was safe with her.

As Kila stood and stretched, another sword tumbled out of her bed.

Maybe. Maybe I was safe with her.

"Why are you here?" Kila asked, scooping up the fallen weapon. I lashed my tail at her, still irritated to have been kicked off the bed. "Is Kestral still exhausted? I don't blame him. I'd be tired of you too by now." She laughed at her own joke as she searched for something beneath fallen blankets and puddled clothing. "Where did I put . . ."

When camping, Kila was just as organized and self-contained as Kestral. At an inn, Kila's room looked as if she had lived there for a week without doing any laundry. Even I couldn't make as big a mess as hers. But then, I didn't use swords as clothing racks.

I leapt up on to the writing desk and gave myself a cat bath while Kila changed. She wore leather leggings and a tight shirt beneath her dress, in case she needed to skin out of the dress for a fight. With her riding boots and lace hairnet, the whole ensemble looked a little too constrained for me. One day I'd get her in something fun and airy for dancing. Unless she killed me first.

A soft knock on the door came while Kila brushed out her hair. She glanced over her shoulder at me. "Can you get that?" she asked.

I pinned my ears at her.

With an eye roll, Kila let her hair fall and answered the door.

"Morning, Kestral," Kila greeted cheerfully.

"Morning." Kestral peered past her into the room. "Have you seen—" He stopped, eyes falling on me. He nodded and took a step back.

Was it just me, or did he look even more exhausted after a night without being drawn upon?

"I'll order breakfast downstairs."

"Thank you!" Kila called after him. She shut the door and pulled up her hair. "I'd kill for more black tea. Northerners don't know what they're missing. Are you going to shift for breakfast?"

I flicked my ears and looked away.

Kila shrugged and pushed her door open.

I trotted after her on padded feet.

Downstairs, I noted that Kestral had ordered three breakfast plates, but I was still too angry to be tempted out of form. Instead, I crossed the common room and ducked into the kitchen, where I found a discreet corner to shift in. I told the cook I was preparing the horses for the ride, so he gave me a cold breakfast of fruit and cheese with a few extra apples for Shan and Bruiser. By the time Kestral and Kila came outside with their packs, Bruiser was saddled, and Shan was tied to an outside post. The monster horse still didn't like anyone but Kestral loading him up for a journey. I perched on the top of the barn as a crow, waiting for them to finish riding preparations. Kestral glanced up at me but didn't try to say anything, out loud or along our mental bond.

Kila didn't seem to realize anything was wrong. She chatted cheerfully at Kestral, who only grunted back. At lunch time she tossed tiny pieces of jerky into the air for me to catch. She didn't even seem to notice that I only shifted human after dinner was finished cooking, then immediately shifted to my cat form to curl up on her bedroll. Kestral didn't say anything to me either, choosing instead to study maps and develop battle plans. He and Kila stayed up late, discussing strategies while I napped. After Kestral was deeply asleep, I crept out of Kila's bedroll and crouched near Kestral's feet, drawing just deeply enough to maintain my forms for the next day. I doubt he would even notice I'd taken anything. Afterwards, I returned to Kila's bedroll, curling up in the crook of her legs.

What got me the most wasn't how Kestral had chased away my potential partner, but rather that he had seen my tattoos—the proof of my sale—and hadn't said anything to me about them. At some point, he had figured out what I used to be and kept sleeping with me anyway, never letting on that he knew. The three little tattoos were family crests, two had been noble houses, one had been a wealthy merchant. Each time my contract was sold, a new tattoo had been etched on my hip and the previous crest had a line crossed over it. Some whores were sold so many times the tattoos circled their waist like a belt. By the time my contract was turned over to a brothel, my magic had come in and I'd decided to run. I broke into the brothel and drew a line across my last tattoo, indicating my own freedom, but the line had come out shaky and uneven—obviously the mark of a runaway. I had been careful to keep the marks concealed ever since.

Or, at least, I thought I had.

Not that it mattered much. The bounty for being a mage-born was much higher than the return of a runaway cockerel. If Kestral wasn't killing me for my bounty, I doubted he would turn me in to my last owner. I still hated that he had found out. It made my past real to me, after four years of denying it had ever happened. I hated having to face my own weakness, my own powerlessness, the way I had scraped and begged in order to survive another day. The day I escaped was the day I promised myself I would never be made that weak ever again.

Then, of course, my magic developed, and I figured out that the only way to keep my well full was to draw life force from someone who slept. It wasn't as if my life had changed greatly, but at least I could make my own choices. Sometimes good choices, sometimes bad ones. Making bad choices was easier and maybe I would have continued making them if it hadn't been for Wix. A trick of the stars had landed me at her inn, sleeping off a night of bad choices. Wix liked the way my partner woke up stumbling and barely able to form sentences the following morning, and she picked me for a mage. I figured her out as a fairy, so we made a deal—protection for amusement. Best deal I'd ever made.

This was the problem with sticking to forms while traveling. I wasn't speaking to Kestral and I couldn't speak to Kila, so I just brooded in silence. I flew on ahead of the horses, perched in a tree and brooded. At night, while I waited for Kestral to fall asleep, I'd brood. But brooding became boring. Luckily, after only three days, we finally approached a town. Regardless of whatever Kestral said, I would use the eye drops and pick up a new dance partner. He owed me for scaring away the last one.

I stayed in a form until Kila and Kestral finished carrying their bags up to their rooms and went down to dinner in the common room. Kestral shot me a glance before leaving the room, as if he wanted to say something, then shook his head and left. I shifted, changed out of my sneak-thief clothes and used the drops to turn my eyes brown. It wasn't my favorite look, but I could tolerate it for a night of anonymity.

I took a short flight out the window to the barn, so that the innkeepers would think I had been with the mounts while the others checked in. I entered the common room from the kitchen door and saw Kila waving for me to join her and Kestral at their table. I took a breath. Dinner with Kestral couldn't hurt, right? Surely a musical group would arrive soon, and the inn would liven up so I could slip away. With that in mind, I slipped into a chair across the table from Kestral.

Kila kept up a lively chatter as we ordered and ate. Dinner was a simple affair, just river fish on a bed of vegetables. The ale wasn't as dark as I preferred and the only entertainment for the night was a flute player. This inn wasn't shaping up to be at all what I had hoped for. I surveyed the inn's other guests as I picked at my vegetables.

". . .know what really bothered me about Reina?" Kila was saying, waving a bit of speared fish around. "Did you notice that for all that power she threw around, when she wanted to kill Reshi, she had to be really close? Didn't you say she was going to spear you with a needle, Reshi? And then stomp you later? Doesn't that seem strange?"

Kila chomped the piece of fish from her fork and continued talking with her mouth full: "I mean, she kept creating those walls of solid air, right? Couldn't she just have crushed Reshi from a distance? Or any one of us, really. Did you notice, Kestral?"

"Kila." Kestral's voice dragged my attention back to the table. When was the last time I had heard him speak? "Would you mind giving Reshi and me a moment alone?"

Kila paused before glancing over at me, as if asking if I was all right with being alone with Kestral. That was nice of her; it felt like she was looking out for me. I nodded, letting her know it was okay to leave.

"Good. You two better fix whatever broke. I'm tired of being the one who has to do all the talking." Kila shoved her chair back and picked up her empty tankard. She gave us a cheerful wave before heading to the bar. I smiled a little, watching her kick her skirts out of the way with every step. After all this time she still hadn't mastered the skill of walking in a dress.

"Reshi."

I grimaced at the tabletop before looking up to meet Kestral's eyes.

"I . . ."

"Look, Kestral, just forget it." I glanced away. "I'm still grateful to you for saving my life all those times and I guess it's stupid to be mad that you found out. I just don't want to talk about it. Let's just let it be over."

Kestral was quiet as he stared down at his barely-touched dinner. "I don't want it to be over."

"I don't mean over-over," I amended. "I've been listening when you and Kila talk strategy at night. I think you've got a good plan for Velyn and Eagan, and I'll still listen to you. You're the only reason I've lived this long. You know I trust you on the battlefield."

Kestral took a breath, still staring down at the table. "Reshi, knowing about your past—"

"Stop, Kestral."

"—doesn't change anything for me. I should have handled it better—"

"Stop talking about it."

"—but I think I can help you understand."

"I don't want to talk about my past!" I slammed my palm down on the table, surprising Kestral into looking up. "It's over. We're over. Just . . . let it be over."

Kestral shook his head. "I'm not talking about your past. I want to talk about mine."

My breath left me in a rush, leaving me lost for words. I stared across the table, searching his eyes for a lie. When I couldn't find it, I leaned back in my seat and crossed my arms. "Go ahead then. Tell me."

Kestral looked around the common room, for once appearing shy. "Not here." Kestral stood, sliding his chair back gently. "Come to my room tonight."

Every animal instinct inside me screamed out that it was a trap. Set with a very pretty lure, to be sure, but a trap nonetheless. I watched Kestral warily as he pushed in his chair and walked to the stairs, heading up to his room.

Well, if he's gone for the night, I have my pick of partners, I thought, looking around the common room again. Kila was still drinking at the bar, having a boisterous conversation with some soldiers. There weren't many pretty patrons at this inn; they were probably mostly locals, come in for dinner. The flute player wasn't helping me any; she had begun a long, sad ballad that would keep the people drinking, but not dancing. I would have settled for gambling, but I didn't have any coins on me.

I slumped in my seat, weighing my options. I could be bored down here all night until Kila went to bed. Or . . .

With a sigh, I heaved myself out my chair and ducked outside the bar.

Kestral had left his window open, as I'd expected. I perched on the ledge, peeking inside before making my decision. Kestral sat near the writing desk, cleaning his longsword. He had left the door to his room open a crack, just enough for a cat to slide through. He was really hoping I'd accept his invitation, then. I didn't think he saw me as I slipped in through the window, but he looked up as I shifted, leaning against the window frame in case a quick escape was needed.

Kestral didn't invite me further into the room. In fact, he ignored me for a minute as he wiped down his blade. Before putting it back in its sheath, he tested its edge and frowned. We'd probably have to make a stop at the town's blacksmith tomorrow. After setting the sword down, Kestral stood and closed the room's door. He leaned back against it, arms crossed, eyes down.

I waited. Sometimes finding a place to begin was the hardest part.

"I only ever wanted to be a soldier," Kestral finally said without preamble. "It wasn't just the pay. I was my village's best hunter, the best swordsman. Whenever soldiers passed through town, I begged for a sparring lesson. I was good at it. It was all I thought about. I read books about famous generals and battles, I studied army tactics and how to run supply lines.

"I left my home city with a caravan heading to Beramin when I was only fifteen because I couldn't stand to wait for the next caravan to pass through. They wouldn't let me enlist officially until I turned sixteen, but they let me run messages and clean stables, that kind of thing. I used to finish up my duties early, so I could watch the combat training in the afternoon. I never thought of doing anything else. I was born to be a soldier."

Kestral fell silent, a tiny smile on his face. I found myself wishing I had known him then. I couldn't help but picture him as an eager, earnest bright-eyed child. Oh, how time changed us.

"I was promoted to captain two years later. I qualified in one, but the commander didn't think the men would respect me at seventeen years of age. Do you know the differences between the border armies?" Kestral glanced up at me for the first time since he began.

I shook my head.

"The western army has been actively at war for over five years now. They're our biggest standing army and they have the most soldiers, healers, and bonded mages. The southern army is the nation's reserve army. They have the largest cavalry unit, so they're the most mobile. When the fighting gets too intense on either border, the southern army gets called in. Of course, the north has the navy." Kestral waved a hand dismissively. "The eastern army—my army—defends against the fae wilds. So rather than working as one massive force, the army works as a series of small strike forces ranging from ten men up to sixty. Every man in the group is expected to be able to switch from pike to sword to bow as needed. We patrol the fae wilds or respond to villages under magical attack. Sometimes we would find mages hiding in the fae wilds. If we didn't kill them, it was my job as captain to bond them. I didn't really understand what bonding was at the time; the eastern army doesn't keep many mages. Most are sent to the west. The ones we had stationed in Beramin were all healers."

Kestral took a breath, pausing. "Each squad spends a number of days out on assignment, then another number of days back at Beramin for training, rest and reassignment. It was usually about a ten-day cycle—ten days in the field, ten days back in the city. Captains are expected to pick up extra tasks while stationed in Beramin, things like training new recruits, ordering new supplies. General tasks. I worked in the armory, receiving new equipment as it was ordered. Not just weapons and armor, but horseshoes, unworked iron, tools, even some siege equipment. The storerooms were a mess, and no one had been keeping proper ledgers, so every time I was in Beramin I worked to clean out the storerooms and set the ledgers right."

I had to stifle a yawn. I had never pictured working in the army could be quite that boring.

"It took a year, but I finally straightened everything out. And I found a lot was missing from the storehouse. I submitted a list to the commander, letting him know my findings. He blamed it on a lack of organization, saying the equipment had probably been properly assigned but the paperwork had been lost. I accepted his explanation like a good soldier and, moving forward, made sure everything was properly accounted for.

"But then, as new orders came in, the items ordered didn't match up to the items received. I spoke to caravan leaders and showed them the orders placed. They showed me the orders they received, and they didn't match. I made a report to the commander again. He promised to investigate and again I let it go." Kestral flicked his eyes up to me before looking away again.

We had to be getting close to the point of the story now, right? I braced my elbows on my knees to lean forward.

"After I made the report, my platoon was sent on assignment. When we returned, all my new ledgers had been replaced. They said we had supplies we didn't have or misrepresented how many items we actually had stored. I tried telling my commander, but he avoided me. When I could talk to him, he said it was a mistake and it was being investigated. I got suspicious, so I investigated on my own." Kestral scoffed. "I should have just let it go and been a good soldier. I should have just . . ." His hands curled into fists that shook. He was silent for a minute, jaw muscle ticking over clenched teeth. His eyes turned distant. For him, it was all happening again.

I knew that feeling; it still woke me up some nights.

"I found out that Duke Allaran's son, one of the army's sub-commanders, was the one changing the equipment logs. He was the one posting one set of orders to the commander and the crown, but a second set of orders to the merchants and pocketing the difference in cost. Not only that, but he was selling the army's raw iron to the local villages cheaper than they could buy from other cities, but at a significant mark up from what the army paid for it. I couldn't figure out why he was stealing; his father was the duke and he was set to take over as commander eventually." Kestral closed his eyes, fists shaking at his sides. "I followed him into one of the storehouses and confronted him as he changed the ledgers. I told him I knew what he had been doing and I could prove it. I didn't want to report him, but if he turned himself in and returned the money, I was sure he would be pardoned. His father was the duke, so it wasn't as if he would be sent to prison or even get more than a slap on the wrist. It wouldn't even have set his career back, I was certain of that. He listened to me and he agreed. He went to talk to his father about it that same day."

Kestral fell silent. He was breathing rapidly, muscles trembling.

Had he ever told this story before? It seemed so raw to him. I wanted to go over to him, touch him, let him know it was over and just a memory now. I held myself back, biting my lip to keep from speaking.

When Kestral finally looked up, his eyes were overly bright. "Instead of confessing to stealing from the army, he accused me of taking advantage of him."

"No!" I jumped up, surprising myself with the action. "How could . . . there's no way! There must have been a trial?"

Kestral shook his head. "His father said he didn't want to further embarrass his son with a trial, and instead offered me a discharge from the army. Not an honorable one, but not dishonorable either. I refused. I knew I hadn't done anything wrong and I insisted on a trial. He wouldn't. He couldn't let it go to trial. It wasn't just the son who was stealing, but apparently Duke Allaran himself was stealing from the crown as well. Something about house debts . . . I didn't know, I found out later. But they were nobles, so they buried my plea for a trial. Instead, my platoon got more and more assignments with fewer days in between. It got so bad that whenever we returned to Beramin, we were sent out again the very next day. I tried talking to the commander, but he made an excuse about how recruitment was down, and the realm still needed to be protected. Then he sent us into the Ash Flats."

Kestral shuddered. "No troop had ever been sent into the Ash Flats before. We often fought monsters from the Flats, like the fire scorpions or the occasional manticore, but we didn't go in there looking for trouble. But I was still a good soldier, just following orders."

"This is when you killed that slag, isn't it?" I asked softly.

Kestral nodded without looking up. "Have you ever seen one?"

I shook my head.

"I've charged dire bears head-on. I've stayed steady against griffons protecting hatchlings. I've lived through a manticore sting. None of that prepared me to stand against a slag.

"I think we were all expecting to find a scorpion nest. We were looking low, kicking up ash, when the slag rose up out of the ground, a massive golem of flame and molten stone. It must have been nearly twenty feet tall. I was still trying to comprehend what it was when it swiped at my advance team, killing four men at once. The men started firing arrows at it, but they burned on impact without causing any damage. Two men charged with me, but our swords melted on contact. The golem crushed the man next to me, missing me by inches. I called a retreat, but stars that monster moved fast! I couldn't . . . we didn't stand a chance. Only mages can kill slags."

"But you did," I reminded him, barely seated on the window sill anymore. "You told me you killed it."

Kestral nodded. "More by chance than skill, but yes. You can't run in the Ash Flats—the ash is piled higher than your ankles and it's slick under your boots. But you can hide things beneath the ash, like a tripwire. I ordered two groups to go on ahead and set up a steel cable tripwire in the path of our retreat while the rest of us distracted the slag. I lost half my squad that day. Just by trying to run." He drew a shaky breath. I pretended not to notice the wetness on his cheeks. "We retreated when we got the call that the tripwire was set. The steel was strong enough that the beast tripped before it melted. I knew mages would have used water magic to fight a slag, so I grabbed as many water-skins as I could and ran up on the golem's back."

"You ran onto a slag?" I repeated. "I mean, you stood on it. Molten stone and fire and . . . were you stupid?"

"I was mad," Kestral whispered. "At the duke, at his son. At my commander. At myself. It wasn't a smart move, I know, but I was beyond caring any more. If I died . . . maybe my men could get away. I wasn't thinking straight, I know that now. But army boots are made of thick leather and tough to burn, so they held up long enough for me to pour out the waterskins. The skin, I guess, on its neck sizzled, then turned black and hard. I speared my sword through it and twisted, snapping its head off. I wasn't sure if that would be enough, but the beast slowly turned black and cold. My troop dragged its head back to Beramin."

"You were a hero," I breathed, completely taken in by the story.

Kestral shrugged modestly. "That's not how my commander saw it. He said I was reckless and blamed me for the loss of my men. There was going to be a hearing but before that could happen . . ." Kestral shook his head, eyes on the floor. "I don't blame my men for what they did. That day in the Ash Flats would have shaken any good soldier, but the worst part was that we were being sent out again after only two days of rest. When my men heard about the next assignment, most of them went to the commander and gave testimony saying they had witnessed me assaulting the duke's son. That was all Duke Allaran needed to officially release me from the army. Dishonorably."

"Kestral—"

He held up a hand, stopping me. "It actually gets worse. And this is the part no one knows, not even Ammon." Kestral met my eyes and I saw regret in them. "Originally, I had wanted to help train new recruits as part of my captain's duties. I requested to work in the armory because . . ." He drew a deep breath. "Because I was attracted to the duke's son. I noticed that he worked closely with the armory and I had wanted to get close to him."

A strangled sound worked its way out of my mouth. The fact that anyone could falsely accuse Kestral in the first place was unthinkable. That someone he had feelings for had done it was horrifying. "Is that why you gave him the chance to come clean?" I asked. "Because you liked him?"

Kestral nodded. He opened his mouth then closed it and cleared his throat. When he trusted himself to speak, he continued: "I wasn't looking to start anything with him. It was just . . . it was new. I wanted to get to know him. Maybe get closer to him. He was only a year or two older than me, but he had this way of putting everyone around him at ease. He could make anything funny without being insulting. He was . . ." Kestral shook his head. "He wasn't who I thought he was."

I waited for more, but Kestral seemed finished. "What was his name?"

"Lowel." The name sounded like a curse. "Lowel of House Kenton."

My hand had unconsciously dropped to my hip, covering the marks hidden there. I knew about betrayal, sure. But Kestral's story, while sad, didn't parallel mine at all. I looked up to find Kestral staring at me intently.

"I never meant to get involved with you," he said softly. "In bed or otherwise. Everything I ever tried to hold on to . . . I lost it. I lost my squad. I lost my place in the army. I lost . . ." Kestral turned, cutting himself off and looking away. "Becoming a mage hunter was Ammon's idea. He thought if I had a purpose again, I wouldn't feel so lost. I think I just wanted to feel lost. That's why I chose to chase a bounty with no information on it." He looked up to me again. "You were so welcoming, so full of light. You made me laugh that first day, remember?"

I did. It was still one of my favorite memories, despite everything that happened after that.

"After I realized who you were, I tried to kill you before I could stop myself. That's when you ran. I thought if I could back you into a corner and get you to fight back, it wouldn't bother me that I'd killed you. But I couldn't, not after I saw your sister die. Instead, I gave you the chance to run. You were supposed to run, you know that, right?"

I chuckled weakly. "I don't always do what I'm supposed to."

"I know that now." Kestral tried a smile but failed. "I tried keeping you at arm's length. I thought that if I didn't have you, I couldn't lose you, like I lost everything else. But then I nearly lost you when those archers had you in their sights. I thought perhaps it was better to have you before I could lose you." The look in his eyes was intense. As intense as that first time he kissed me. "I couldn't help it. Forgive me, Reshi."

I was across the room before I could stop myself. I drew up short of touching him because I knew if I did, I'd be lost. I didn't know what to say and even if I did, it was too hard to speak past the ache in my chest. Kestral pushed himself away from the wall. We stood close enough to feel each other's body heat, close enough to touch but we didn't. Not yet.

"Kestral, I didn't know."

He looked down, fingertips brushing my hip.

I flinched.

"I didn't know either."

"I'm sorry, but I—"

Kestral took his hand from my hip and cupped my chin, pulling me forward into a slow kiss. My hands reached out of their own accord, but I pulled them back. When Kestral ended the kiss, he leaned back and said, "I'm not trying to own you, Reshi."

I looked away, swallowing fear. "I don't . . . I don't do relationships, Kestral. It's too much like being under a contract. I won't do that again. Never."

We stood that way for a long time, the silence between us growing like trapped heat. I couldn't change. I didn't even want to, not even for someone as wonderful and beautiful as Kestral. I wished I had never made a move on him, wished I didn't have to miss him.

Finally, Kestral stepped back a pace, lessening the intensity between us. He turned halfway away from me and took a breath. "Fine. Then after this battle with Velyn and Eagan, we'll go our own ways. It'll be over." He nodded to himself. "I intend to hunt the other mage-born. Not you or Kila, but Reina, and if either of your brothers survive, I'll hunt him down. You should go back into hiding. After the battle, you should be strong enough to fight off any other hunters that come looking for you."

"Just like that? We'll just be done after we beat my brothers?" I asked. I shifted my weight from foot to foot, then blurted out the question I wanted to ask, "Can we keep sleeping together until then?"

Kestral searched my eyes. "Is that what you want?"

"I mean, might as well make the most of it." I shrugged. "As long as you won't go around beating up my other partners."

Kestral's eyes narrowed. "No."

"What?"

He shook his head. "You're not getting everything your way. If you want to keep on as we have been, you're mine alone. If that's not what you want, you only come to my bed as a cat. The choice is yours." Kestral turned away from me, cracking open the door to the hallway. "I understand if you need time to decide."

I reached around him, placing my palm against the door and pushing it closed. "I already have."

10

"You keep staring at it like you think it's going to creep up and get you from behind."

"I just never imagined it would be so big. Kila's impressed, too."

"You said you'd been around the kingdom, which usually means you've seen at least one of the inland seas before."

"Yeah, but . . ." I couldn't tear my eyes away from the majesty of Piercestra, the smallest of the kingdom's inland seas. The inland seas marked our northernmost border, running right up to the base of the ShearSaw Mountains. I had seen the seas on maps before, but nothing prepared me for the enormity of them.

Or rather, the enormity of the smallest sea. I knew the mountains were somewhere in the distance, but I couldn't make them out over the endless stretch of water. I wished I could get closer to the sea's edge, where the foaming waves struck the stony shore with such intensity, but it was deceptively farther away than it looked. I had to settle for staring at it in the distance.

Kila searched for rocks to throw at it, striving to see one splash in the water. I guess everyone reacts differently to beauty.

I sat on a jagged rock shelf, jutting out over the rock below, giving me a view of the distant sea. Kestral sat down beside me, passing me a waterskin. One sniff and I knew it wasn't water. With a grin, I finished the last little sip of Goldwater Whiskey. I tossed the waterskin aside and settled closer to Kestral, our hips and shoulders touching.

"Sandestra is the nicer sea," Kestral said, looking out over the view as I was. "The shores there are sandy, so you can walk without your boots. I'm told the water is calmer, too."

"It does look pretty fierce, doesn't it?" I asked, watching the waves pound against the rocks. Sometimes when the water retreated, I heard a distant, hollow, sucking sound, followed by a boom. Kestral had said there were caves beneath the rock which caused the sound. "People swim in this? Give me a stream any day."

Kestral chuckled. "I don't know if anyone swims here. I think you'd be crushed against the rocks if you tried. The fishing villages have ports so maybe it's calmer elsewhere."

Kila cheered as one of her rocks finally landed in the distant surf. Maybe. I couldn't be sure if she was actually throwing stones that far, or if a seabird had dropped something, making it seem as if Kila's stone had reached the water.

"You said the sea used to come up higher?" I looked around at the plain of rock all around us. Sharp ridges and brittle shelves of rock were everywhere, most darkly colored, but several showing colorful strata where they had broken over time. The rocks at the farthest edge of the stone plains were almost an orange color, with sparkling bits of quartz embedded in them. When Kestral had picked this as our battle site, I hadn't expected it to be so pretty.

"That's what the scholars say." Kestral shrugged, leaning back on his hands. "All this rock was the sea floor once. They say all three seas were one, once. Over time, Piercestra retreated, leaving the rocks exposed."

"Do they know why Piercestra retreated?"

"They think it has something to do with the steam vents." We both turned to look east, where billowing white smoke poured through a crack in the stone. I had tried to touch the steam yesterday; Kestral called me ten times as stupid as the average fool. The steam vents littered the plains like portals to a demonic realm. We watched the steam curl into the sky for a moment before I asked another question.

"Why is it blasphemy to name a constellation after a person, but it's okay to name the seas after the founders of the Order of the Great Canvas?"

"I don't know. Maybe Laki could have told you."

I shuffled a little closer, resting my head against Kestral's shoulder. It felt easier to be affectionate now that our relationship had a walk-away date. I couldn't be sure how Kestral felt about our ending being so near, but to me it was a relief. No more being hunted, no more worrying about family coming after me, no more being beholden to one person. This whole journey had just been too much for me. I wanted to get back to my simple, quiet life with dancing and drinking and the passionate nights with nameless lovers.

That's not to say I hadn't enjoyed some of it. Kestral had been a stalwart protector and a peerless lover. Getting to know Kila had been an experience. I looked forward to remembering each of them fondly, but I still looked forward to all of this being over.

Because one way or another, it would all end soon. Eagan and Velyn would be arriving shortly and either I would be dead, or I'd have the power of four of my siblings combined. As long as Reina kept to what she had said about waiting for only one sibling to remain before attacking, Kila and I could be safe. Relatively. There would always be mage hunters, but Kila could take care of herself and soon I would be able to as well.

"Reshi?"

"Hm?" I hadn't realized Kestral had been talking. I had been mesmerized by the sea.

"Have you found any animals you could call on out here?" Kestral lifted one of his hands so he could twine his fingers through mine.

It was a little more intimate than I preferred, but I let it happen. I liked running my fingertips over his sword calluses anyway.

"No. The biggest animals here are all in the sea and they're strange." My mouth twisted as I remembered trying to converse with the large silver fish that kept leaping out of the water on the day we had first arrived. "Unless either of my brothers has a shellfish allergy, I don't think I'll be much help."

Kestral tossed his head back in a loud laugh.

I picked my head up from his shoulder to watch him. I would miss that the most, I decided. Wherever Kestral's travels took him next, I hoped he'd find someone to keep him laughing.

But that wasn't my concern any more. I took a breath, pulling my hand free from Kestral's. He let go, then wrapped his arm around my waist, pulling me close. I sighed and put up with it. I was cold anyway.

"Something funny?" Kila asked, climbing over a rocky ridge, obscuring our view of the sea.

"Yeah, Kestral thinks we should invite our brothers to dinner and see if they have any food allergies. Just in case we can resolve this without fighting." I expected Kestral to pull away from me as Kila approached, but his arm stayed wrapped around me. Well, that was fine with me. Kila didn't seem to care one way or the other.

"We better not resolve this without fighting, or why the rust am I here?" Kila sat down on my other side, close but not too close. She drew her knees up to brace her elbows on as she looked out over the sea. "They'll be here tomorrow, right?"

"Should be," Kestral replied. "If they're following the Whistling River as we expect, they should arrive tomorrow."

"Does that river empty into the sea?" I asked.

"No, it ends in a fresh water lake near the fae wilds," Kestral replied. "The northern part of the eastern army gets its supplies that way."

"After this, do you think the western army would take me back?" Kila wondered aloud. "I mean, not as a soldier, but as a mercenary? I miss the war."

"I don't know, Kila," Kestral said. "Can't hurt you to try. The king only sent the southern army because you four were bunched up and his wife had just died. Maybe when more than half the mage-born are dead and the pain of his loss dulls, he won't care so much about the survivors."

Kila sighed, setting her chin on her arms, crimson eyes distant. I didn't understand her longing to go back to war, but then, to each their own.

The sun set slowly, coloring the stone plains and the sea in pinks and oranges as it sank beneath the horizon. Kestral insisted we set up our campsite while we still had a little light, then turn in early. It all ended tomorrow, after all.

Thick, dark storm clouds rolled in over the stone plains early the next morning. Kestral had predicted that Velyn wouldn't be able to use his fog due to the steam vents, but then sometimes when the vents were particularly active it was like the plains were covered in a warm, white fog anyway. Once again, Kila, Kestral and I awaited the approach of our brothers on a battlefield of our choosing. At least this time there wasn't a nearby village full of commoners and soldiers all telling the crown exactly where we were. Hopefully, we could fight to the finish today.

It had to end today. Every extra moment spent by Kestral's side made it harder for me to think about leaving.

Kila didn't pace today. She stood in a wide military stance, her arms crossed, hands near the weapons at her belt. Her hair and eyes were red once again, her hair wrapped about her head like a battle crown. She wore only leather armor this time—a tight leather vest, leather pants, and her high-laced leather boots. Her arms, as usual, were covered in her leather-wrapped-steel arm guards.

Kestral was similarly armored in leather with the addition of his magic-grounding gauntlets. His sword and small crossbow were clipped to his belt, but he held his spear in his hand. I hadn't seen him use it outside of practice drills, but he looked good holding it. His new boots helped the picture, too, rather than those old falling-apart sorry scraps of leather he called boots in our last battle with Velyn and Eagan.

I was dressed the same as ever—black sneak-thief clothes, low-laced boots, sheathed fae daggers. I wasn't even wearing my throwing knives as a shift would just drop them. If not for my vendetta against Velyn, I would have felt out of place next to the trained warriors, but when my brothers came into view, I knew I would fight as fiercely as either one of them.

Eagan walked a little ahead of Velyn, a self-confident smirk on his face. His sheathed sword was slung over his shoulders, arms draped over it casually. I wished I had even a tiny bit of projectile magic, just to wipe the smug expression off his face. He wasn't wearing any armor, just a flowing silk orange shirt over black leggings and embroidered boots. And people called me vain?

Velyn stalked along a pace behind, jaw set, brows drawn tightly together. He still wore the rough-spun loose clothing he always wore, pale blue vest over a cut-sleeved shirt and loose brown pants over sturdy, boring boots. His eyes flashed as he glared across the rocky field at us, cumulous hair moving in a phantom air current.

Eagan stopped well out of bow shot, Velyn stepping up beside him. We eyed each other across the rocky expanse, wondering what new tricks the others had come up with since the last time we had faced each other. I had a trick or two, but had they worked out something new as well? There was a plan, of course, but I expected it to fall apart the instant the fight began.

"Brother, Sister, it is a pleasure—" Eagan began a flowery greeting but Kestral cut him off.

"No pleasantries, Eagan. We just want this over with."

"Fine." Eagan didn't lose his smile. "Did you meet with Reina?"

"We did," I called back. "She's on her own side in all of this."

Eagan glanced over at Velyn. "I told you she wouldn't come."

"I remember. You said it half a dozen times."

"But you said—"

"I know what I Saw," Velyn snapped. "What they say doesn't mean anything."

Eagan rolled his eyes at his partner then smiled jovially at the rest of us. "Well? Are we ready to start this?"

Kila grinned, drawing her longsword and settling into an attack stance. "I'm certainly ready to end it."

Eagan lowered his sword from his shoulders, holding it low at his side. He held his free hand in front of himself, closing his eyes in concentration. At his side, Velyn faded to mist as the winds rose.

"Ready, Kila?" I asked, preparing a shift. "Just get me alone with him."

"Just distract him, Reshi," Kestral said, voice low.

"I'm going to kill him," I growled. "This is it."

"There!" Kila shouted, lifting and slamming her heel, causing a wide chunk of rock to crack and rise beneath Velyn's feet as he reformed. I raced forward, shifting as I ran. Black wings carried me to the rapidly rising stone pillar, nearly the width of a city block. Velyn dropped to one knee as he fought to keep his balance. He looked up as I landed and shifted, stalking towards him with daggers drawn. Velyn grinned, then misted.

"Coward!" I shouted, spinning to look around for him. Instead of the mist dissolving behind me, it darkened and turned to smoke. I turned back slowly as Eagan stepped forward.

"Where are you going, Reshi?" Eagan asked, friendly smile in place.

"Uh . . ." I backed a step away. "Wrong dance partner. If it's okay with you, I'll just—"

The stone platform we stood on was suddenly ringed in flame. I sighed.

"You can try flying over it," Eagan said, loosening his sword from its sheath before tossing the sheath aside. "I can make those flames jump startlingly high, though."

"I guess I'll just have to kill you, then." I crouched in a low stance, a dagger in each hand.

"Big words from such a little brother." Eagan held his sword before him, other hand back for balance, a duelist's stance.

"We're the same dusting height," I complained. "The 'little brother' thing is getting played out, don't you think?"

Eagan shrugged a shoulder. "Then become a contender. Until then, you're the adorable baby of the family."

"All of us are adorable compared to Reina," I replied. "Did you know she can—" I darted forward without completing the sentence. Unfortunately, Eagan seemed ready for that ploy. He parried my first attack and dodged the follow through. He circled his sword down and up, taking a sliding step towards me. I leaned away from the attack, using one dagger as a guard, stabbing the other down at Eagan's leg. He managed to pivot enough to earn only a scratch, then shoved his sword against my dagger, pushing me back.

Winds whipped through Eagan's flaming circle but never enough to blow the fire out. Below the stone platform, I heard the thrum of thunder and the rumble of the earth. The plan had been for Kila and Kestral to overwhelm Eagan together while I distracted Velyn;

that plan was reversed now. Hopefully, they could kill the younger brother while I kept the elder distracted.

After checking the cut on his leg, Eagan took a new stance and charged, trying to break through my daggers with his longer reach. I deflected the blade to the side, slashing out when I had the chance. We exchanged blows back and forth, neither gaining ground. Eagan never lost his grin. It was funny; I was grinning too.

"You have gotten better," Eagan admitted, breaking away and pacing back a half circle. "I would have hoped to see something new from you, though. Particularly in regard to your magic."

"I know it's hard for nobles to accept, but you can't always get what you want." I rolled my daggers in my wrists, reversing my grips. "But sometimes—" I charged again, darting low, hoping to cut through the tendons in his ankles. Those boots were too ridiculous to be any real protection to him. Eagan drove the point of his sword down and slashed up, knocking one of my daggers free of my hand. I barely got the second one up to guard, dropping to one knee as I lost my balance. With a little fancy footwork, Eagan pivoted and thrust me backwards, putting himself between me and my dropped dagger.

"Sorry you have to die like this," Eagan said, preparing another thrust. "But they were never going to allow a street rat like you take the throne anyway. Nobility always comes out on top."

"I never wanted the throne. And I wouldn't consider anyone who killed for a throne to be noble." I smirked at him. "And rats aren't the only things beneath the feet of nobles." I dropped into my snake form, coiling and lunging for my brother. He yelped and slashed, but it was hard to hit a moving, sinuous object. Lucky for Eagan, his clothes were loose enough that my fangs missed his flesh, but I did wend my way between his legs to my dropped dagger. I shifted back, picking up my dagger as I stood.

"That was well done," Eagan admitted, taking up a guard stance.

"Thanks." I grinned. "For that honest feedback, I'll tell you a secret."

"Oh? What's that?" He was too smart to lower his guard.

"I've been practicing something new." I slammed the hilts of my daggers together, holding them both in one hand. I placed my palm over the blades, sliding my hand up as the silver elongated into a narrow, double-edged sword. I whirled it once before settling into an attack stance. "And I had some truly great teachers."

I charged with a parallel thrust which Eagan nearly blocked too slowly. I turned the thrust into a slash, cutting a line through his garish orange shirt. As I prepared another attack, Eagan's surprise turned to a determined anger. He parried before moving to attack in earnest. We continued trading blows long enough for my sword arm to become weary, so I switched hands. Kestral had been impressed at how quickly I learned the sword in either hand, but then, I had always preferred fighting with both hands anyway. Eagan darted in close, thinking I had switched the sword to my weaker arm. He locked the blades at the hilts, trying to shove me back.

I punched him in the face.

Eagan cried out, shoving himself backwards off my sword. It wasn't that hard a punch, but it would leave a nasty bruise. "That's against the rules!"

I laughed so hard I nearly cried. "Nobles and their rules! This is a death match, dear brother. Only winning matters, not how you win."

Eagan snarled and charged, playful smile erased. The flames around our arena danced a little higher and burned a little hotter. I readied my sword in a guard position, preparing for another test of strength.

There was a resounding crack, one I didn't just hear, but felt beneath my boots. Eagan skidded to a halt as our stone pillar began to tip sideways. It was slow at first, as if the line where the sky met the sea had decided to rotate around us then sped up as the pillar began to tumble in earnest. Eagan cursed, puffing away in a plume of smoke. I shifted to my crow form, spiraling down to see what was happening below.

Kila and Kestral looked wind-tossed and singed, but otherwise unharmed. Several puddles of liquid steel littered the stone plains like fallen stars. Kestral still had his sword sheathed at his belt but his spear was gone, as were several of Kila's swords. Eagan materialized near Velyn, who was creating an ice bandage over his bleeding shoulder.

"All that and you couldn't kill the lightning bug?" I asked, shifting to stand between Kila and Kestral.

"We could say the same of you," Kila replied, gesturing to Eagan.

"I made him mad, though." I grinned.

Kestral rolled his eyes. "You make everyone mad. It's hardly an accomplishment worth bragging about."

Kila laughed.

"Kila, did you bring the pillar down?"

"Yeah, Kestral was worried about you." She smiled coyly. "He gets all cute and worried when he can't see his little Reshi."

Kestral glared at her but didn't argue the point.

I laughed and twisted the hilt of my sword so that it broke into daggers once again. Eagan and Velyn were working on something together and I wanted to be ready for them.

Fire spouted from the nearest steam vent, making me jump. Kila tapped her toe, making the earth groan and snap, closing old steam vents and opening new ones. This plain would never look the same again after we were done with it.

The wind picked up suddenly, tossing about debris and steam to create a veil between us and the others. I squinted, attempting to see through it.

Kestral held a hand up to block flying debris, peering through the dust veil. As I watched, the color slowly drained from his face, his jaw dropping slightly open.

"Back," Kestral said, voice hoarse. "Back!"

I shifted to my rat form, light and quick, scampering quickly ahead of Kestral and Kila as they retreated. I turned to look back, gaping in horror as fiery golems burst through the dust screen chasing after us. Each golem had to be twenty feet tall, made entirely of vortexed flames, shaping arms, legs and a head. I could guess what had shaken Kestral—these creations looked scarily similar to the slag he had described. I shifted to my crow form, letting Velyn's winds carry me closer—but not too close. There were four of the monstrosities in all. As I flew past, one tracked me with his eyeless head. He stooped, peeling a chunk of rock up with an ear-aching screech, then hurled it at me. I dove out of its path, flapping wildly to catch up with Kestral and Kila.

"What's the plan, here?" I asked, shifting human as Kila and Kestral paused to take up arms.

Kestral was panting, his eyes a little too wide, but he spoke calmly. "Kila, run the magic. Try to knock them down, crush them, whatever brings them down. Reshi, get behind them and try to engage Velyn. He's hurt, he should be weak." Kestral swallowed, eyes forward. "I'll engage."

"Kestral, that's suicide!" I protested. "There are four of those monsters!"

Kila tapped her foot against the ground. Rocks sprang up around one of the fire-golems, making it stumble. Kila held her empty hands up, then clenched them into fists. The rocks crashed together, and the beast screamed, crushed between the stones. Kila sagged to the side, sweating, but she smiled proudly as she corrected me, "Three."

Kestral nodded. "Go, Reshi." He shoved me forward before sliding his sword free of its sheath. It could only be madness, but I followed his orders. I flew past the fire-golems, distracting one for a while as Kestral engaged the other two until Kila could recover from her magic use.

As soon as I passed through the dust-and-wind veil, lightning blinded me. I tumbled free of crow form, landing lightly as a cat. I skidded across the stony ground, tucking myself beneath a stone shelf, trying to see Velyn or Eagan before they saw me.

"Oh look. They sent the baby." A dry laugh echoed against the stony plain. It was strangely quiet on this side of the dust veil.

"Told you they would," Velyn rasped, voice tight with pain. "It makes sense to protect the one with the stronger power."

That wasn't it at all, but I didn't have time to correct them. The stone above me snapped beneath an embroidered boot and Eagan sneered down at me. The point of his sword dropped towards me, but I shifted again, dodging the unwieldy weapon easily. Nothing moved quite as quickly as a rat. I ran free of the broken stone, dodging curses and thrown flames. Velyn screamed as I shifted to my snake form, fangs sinking into his shoulder.

Dust it, wrong shoulder. I got a mouthful of ice and the cold was not good for my reptilian form. I shifted to cat, leaping over Velyn's shoulder and landing as a human. An ice-pike formed in his hands as he turned to block my daggers.

Smoke plumed behind me, putting Eagan at my back. My fae blades rang as I tapped them together and slid them across each other, changing them into stilettos. One slithered between the tines of Velyn's pike, snapping the end off. The other diverted a strike from Eagan.

Kestral and Kila better hurry up, I thought, sweat pouring down my face as I struggled to fight both of my brothers at once. I couldn't keep this up for long.

I managed to trip Velyn and toss him into Eagan's path. The elder snarled, shoving Velyn aside as he charged at me, blade swinging down in an overhand blow. I crossed my stilettos, catching his blade between them but the blades simply weren't as strong as they were when they were daggers. I managed to twist away enough so that only the tip of his blade pierced me, drawing a line of agony from my shoulder to my chest. I cursed and thrust his blade away, dancing back a step.

Velyn stood up, lifting his hand to the sky to call down lightning. As I prepared to dodge, he was suddenly knocked off his feet, hitting the ground with a surprised cry. It took my mind a moment to catch up. When it did, I shifted to crow form, narrowly missing a wall of solid air. Eagan stared around puzzled until a force slammed into him, driving him back a pace.

"*Reina!*" I shouted along my bond to Kestral. "*Reina is here somewhere!*"

From above, I saw Kestral shouting to Kila, who was half-slumped over a boulder. Two fire-golems remained, one currently trapped in a stone pit, though it was slowly melting the rock around it, creating a platform to climb up. Kestral distracted the second one while Kila scraped herself up off the boulder. The heavy magic use was taking its toll on her.

Lightning split the sky and I instinctively went into a dive before realizing the strike was nowhere near me. Looking around, I saw Reina hovering in the air, her hand over her head holding up a dome of solid air. Lightning crashed against it, shattering into tiny sparks before fading.

"What did I tell you, Eagan?" Velyn snapped from far below. "I saw it during the full moon; it was prophecy!"

"Big Sis!" Eagan called cheerfully. "Come to give me a lecture, just like the old days?"

"Fool," Reina said, voice full of contempt. She flicked her fingers and Eagan was forced back another pace.

I didn't have time for them. I darted down to help Kestral and Kila. Kila had propped herself up, but she was still trying to catch her breath. Kestral's armor smoldered in several spots and sweat tracked clear paths through the ash on his face. I swooped in front of the fire-golem, hoping to distract it long enough for them to recover. As expected, the fire-golem turned from Kestral to pry up a modest-sized boulder and hurl it at me. Kestral scowled up at me, but before he could yell at me, an invisible force pushed him back.

As I watched, Kestral was swept away from the battle with the golem, putting him closer to Eagan and Velyn. When he regained his feet, he tried charging back to the fight, but met an invisible wall. He tried the sides and then behind him. It appeared that Reina had boxed him in. I dodged another golem-thrown boulder, trying to figure out what to do next.

"Reshi, go help him!" Kila shouted up to me. She placed her hand on the boulder next to her. The stone rumbled and snapped, shifting beneath her touch. When she lifted her hand, the boulder had been reshaped as a long stone lance. "I can face that monster."

Kila charged, driving the point up through the fire-golem's midsection, making it roar in fury. It brought a fist down towards her, but she pivoted expertly, tossing the golem off the end of her lance. I lost the rest of the fight as I flew to Kestral's aid.

It was a box of invisible walls, as I had thought. Kestral knelt at the bottom, scratching a rune into the base of his steel gauntlet. He looked up as I landed on top of the nearly invisible wall and shifted. The top of the wall was too high and sheer for Kestral to climb, but I was able to reach down far enough to take his hand. I grunted as his weight nearly pulled me forward. I mean, I loved his muscles, but did that have to make him so stars-cursed heavy?

Kestral braced his feet against the wall, helping with the weight until he was able to scramble on top with me.

"Why didn't she just seal the box and let me suffocate?" Kestral asked, catching his breath.

I shrugged.

"She can't," Eagan called up to us. Almost lazily, he raised his hand towards us, flames rushing forward. Kestral pulled me backwards so we tumbled back inside the invisible prison, protected from the flames but trapped once again. I scowled at Kestral; he shrugged.

"What about it, Reina?" Eagan shouted to the skies, where Reina was still hovering, sending invisible walls against Kila and blocking lightning from Velyn. "Should I tell them all your secret?"

"I have so many, I doubt you know one of any import," Reina replied in a bored tone. She flicked her fingers, sending a wall towards Eagan. He raised his hand in front of him, but instead of issuing flames, it issued smoke. The black smoke outlined the wall, allowing Eagan to dodge it neatly.

Kestral crouched, scratching again at his bracer. I started to shift but he grabbed my arm and shook his head. Over his shoulder, I watched Kila still sparring with her fire-golem. The trapped one was nearly free. We didn't have the luxury of hiding in a protective box for very much longer.

"Did Reina tell you she bartered with the fae for her magical training?" Eagan called as he vaulted another invisible wall. He pushed off it, gaining enough height for his flames to reach Reina in the air.

She sighed as she moved her fingers, creating an air-shield between herself and the flames.

"I did tell them. That's no secret."

Eagan puffed into smoke, landing safely on the ground instead of falling. He grinned wickedly. "Did you tell them the price you paid for the training?"

Reina scowled. "I forgot I told you that."

"There was a time you told me everything." Eagan said, voice mocking. "Remember how we played as children?"

"They knew each other?" I asked Kestral.

He shrugged and stood, blowing steel-dust from his gauntlet. "Noble children. Eagan's family probably visited the capital regularly."

Kestral placed his hand against the invisible wall and the new rune he had made glittered with violet light. The wall shattered, allowing us to walk free of the box.

Velyn's winds whipped at Reina, tugging at her clothes but failing to move her from her sky-high perch. "Rust it, Eagan, what is the secret?"

Eagan grinned. "She can't kill with her magic. She traded any sort of fatal magical blow for her magical education." He turned to smirk at me. "Lucky for you, Reshi. I doubt you would have walked away from her otherwise."

I had barely limped away from her even without the use of fatal magic, I thought, standing behind Kestral as he destroyed another solid air wall sweeping towards us.

There was a triumphant shout from across the battlefield. Kila, standing atop a stone spire, had speared the fire-golem through the head with her stone lance. At her cry, the lance shattered, breaking the beast's head into a thousand smoldering pieces. It slumped first to its knees before dropping heavily before her pillar. The fires swirled viciously, fighting for their lives as they slowly diminished. Kila stepped off her spire, dropping through smoke to walk over the dying flames, obviously exhausted but grinning.

"Using magic to kill is cowardly anyway," Kila declared. "I'll take any of you in mortal combat right now."

"You!" Reina shrieked, spinning on her aerial perch. "Don't you dare speak to me! How dare you even breathe the same air as me, you uneducated knuckle-dragger!"

Kila snorted. "Who put a rock in your boot?" She made a face. "I mean, slipper."

Reina's face turned ugly, blotchy and red in her fury. "You are too stupid to even begin to comprehend what you destroyed when you crushed my study. Magical history is set back decades, thanks to you. Spells that could have helped people! Spells to help the kingdom!"

Kila rolled her eyes. "You don't help people by locking yourself away in a tower and scribbling on parchment. You help the kingdom by fighting on the front lines, putting your life on the line."

"You near-sighted simpleton. How could you possibly understand?" Reina rolled her wrist and the final fire-golem rose out of its stone trap to race towards Kila.

"Reshi, distract it," Kestral ordered.

I shifted as Kestral chased after the golem. I expected Reina to try to break my crow form with solid air, as she had before, but before she could, a lightning bolt struck her invisible perch and she fell, vanishing before Eagan's flames could roast her. The battlefield quickly became chaos as lightning, fire and solid air raged against each other as well as against us. Kila, despite her earlier bravado, was barely able to keep ahead of the fire-golem. I flew at its face, flapping my wings and cawing at it, taking its attention off her and allowing her to gain a safe distance. Kestral caught up to us, slashing his sword through the flames at its ankle. It did nothing to harm the flame-beast other than make it angry. It chased Kestral while I searched for an advantage.

I wove through the air, riding Velyn's wind currents and trying to avoid walls of solid air. While Kestral held the golem's attention, I dove at Velyn, raking my claws through his hair, slicing the skin beneath. Velyn cried out, spinning to track my flight as blood dripped into his eyes. He raised his hand, intent on striking me down. I swooped low, then banked hard, narrowly missing the lightning.

The fire-golem, however, caught the full strike. It appeared stunned, head snapping back, arms flying wide.

Kestral ducked, hiding his head beneath his arm as Kila grinned wickedly, slamming her foot onto the stony ground. A rock spire erupted beneath the golem, shattering it into smoldering pieces, creating more dust to blow in Velyn's winds. Kila stood her ground, one hand on a sheath as the other moved to put her shortsword away.

It happened so fast that I couldn't even scream. One second Kila was grinning in triumph, the next a narrow blade had pierced her from behind, sprouting through her chest. She staggered forward a step, ripping the blade free of Reina's hands as she turned to face her. My eldest sister raised her chin, violet eyes flashing in satisfaction as Kila groped at the blade in her chest. I was dimly aware of Kestral running towards her as Eagan and Velyn shouted. All I could do was watch in horror as Kila dropped to one knee, then lunged forward, shortsword shining like a star of retribution.

Reina gaped as the blade entered her stomach and ripped upwards through her chest. She tumbled backwards, raising a hand as if for mercy, but Kila dove after her, burying her blade in Reina's neck. Blood sprayed as if from a steam vent. Kila fell backwards, holding one hand tight to the needle-like blade through her chest. She tried to stand, tried to scramble backwards, as the red spray turned to twining, violet mist.

Eagan and Velyn rushed forward, intent on the purple mist before turning on each other. Velyn caught an elbow in the eye from Eagan. He threw a hand out and Eagan's boots stuck to the ground encased in ice. Kestral seemed torn between running to Kila's side and defending the purple mist from my brothers. He stood halfway between them, looking from one to the other as he tried to decide.

No one noticed the tiny black spider drifting along with the wind-tossed ash and the falling smoldering remains of the fire-golem. By the time Velyn noticed and shouted, I had dropped into the center of the violet mist, reaching out with my magic to gather this new power. With a snap, the mist coalesced into a violet silk cocoon. Before my brothers could come for me, I shifted to my cat form, grabbing the cocoon in my teeth and running. Kestral, having made up his mind, caught Eagan mid-charge, blades singing as they met with a crash. Ice formed ahead of me and I slipped, sliding along towards the wounded weather mage.

Another shift carried me aloft on black wings, violet cocoon held in my beak. Lightning split the sky; I angled my wings to miss it. I was running low on magic, but then so was everyone else. I soared higher, the precious coalesced power in my beak. When the air became thin, I shifted to my human form. I looked down on the battlefield as I began to fall. Eagan and Velyn stared up with identical looks of horror. Kila was still moving, but her breath was coming in fits and starts; not a good sign. Kestral stood looking up at me, blue eyes boring through me.

I crushed the cocoon between my hands, drawing the violet light inside of me. It felt like a fire searing its way into the golden well of light in my chest. I gasped at the pain and the power. Had I nearly been out of magic? I laughed, my fall slowing as the air around me thickened. Velyn threw a hand up. I twisted—that's the only way I could describe it—and suddenly I was on the ground, standing over Kila.

"Good," Kila wheezed at me. "Glad you . . . not them."

"Hush." I knelt over her. Somewhere ahead, Kestral clashed with my brothers, keeping them back. "I don't know if this will work."

"Can't hurt," Kila replied with a shrug. She grasped the blade with both hands then shoved it backwards through her chest and out her back. Blood rushed out before I could place my hand over the wound, praying to all the stars for this to work. Kila's skin turned gray and cool, but when I pulled my hand away, the wound had healed.

"Thanks, Reshi." Kila smiled weakly. "I think I'm . . . just going to rest . . . for a while."

I smiled, relieved. "Go ahead. I think you've earned that much."

Kila's eyes fluttered shut and her breathing came even and strong. I wished I could get her somewhere safe, but that would mean leaving Kestral alone with my brothers. Instead, I left her curled up near Reina and turned around, facing Kestral and the others.

With a dramatic roll of my wrist, I placed my hand against my shoulder and healed the wound Eagan had given me earlier. I smiled as I flicked blood from my fingertips.

"What have we got here?" I shouted, drawing my brothers' attention. "Looks like baby brother just became a contender."

White-blue eyes flashed, and orange eyes flickered, staring me down. I merely grinned back, wondering which one would fall first. This new power was enormous, vast and deep like the distant sea. My brothers had to be reaching their limits; this contest was all but mine.

Velyn's hand leapt to the sky, calling down a pillar of lightning. It didn't have the presence of his earlier strikes—instead of a column of white fire, it was barely more than a blue fork, splitting the air. Velyn must have been trying to conserve whatever magic he had left. I thrust my hands out before me, envisioning the air before me becoming solid, like a shield.

The only thing that saved me was the lack of energy Velyn put into the lightning bolt. It struck at my feet, tossing me back and sending me skidding across the stony ground. I yelped as a sheer ridge sliced open my arm. I healed it quickly as I climbed back to my feet. Why hadn't the air gone solid? Reina threw around that solid air so easily.

Eagan and Velyn laughed evilly, almost in sync with each other.

"There's a learning curve, isn't there, Reshi?" Eagan called to me. "We should thank you, though. It's going to be easier taking that power from you than having to kill Reina for it."

"You mean we'll have to thank Kila." There was a hunger in Velyn's eyes as he stared at Kila's prone form.

I was close enough to see that she was still breathing but her color was still far too pale. If either one of them got too close to her, she wouldn't be able to defend herself. I couldn't let them near her.

"You could just kill her, Reshi," Eagan suggested with a shrug. "Make it a real fight."

"I'm not like you monsters," I spat, walking towards them to draw their attention away from Kila. "I never went looking for power or a throne."

"That throne should always have been mine," Eagan replied, voice cool.

"Neither of you know anything," Velyn hissed.

With a confused side-glance at Velyn, Eagan raised a hand towards me. Jets of flame raged forward and once again I tried to harden the air in front of me. Once again, the magic failed. Why could I use the healing magic and the twisting-leaping magic but not the solid air magic? I gritted my teeth and raised my arms in front of myself, bracing myself for the fire.

A powerful thrum of something like magic shuddered through ground and the air around me. The flames suddenly veered away from me, then seemed to dive into a nearby steam vent. I looked up and saw Kestral on one knee, rune-gauntleted hand pressed to the ground. The rune he had carved for Eagan's magic shimmered with a red-orange glow. He had grounded the fire magic.

Eagan cursed as his fire went out, seeming surprised and annoyed that Kestral was still in the fight. He ripped his sword free of its sheath and stalked towards the mage hunter, shouting an order at Velyn. The weather mage sneered before turning to face me.

"How long before he betrays you?" I asked, jerking my chin at Eagan. His sword met Kestral's in a spray of sparks—two swordsmen fighting at the top of their abilities. It would have been quite a show to see if I weren't facing my own battle.

Velyn shrugged callously. "Maybe I'll betray him first. If I can kill you quickly, I could beat him to Kila's power. He wouldn't stand a chance."

My hands clenched into fists that shook. "Like Cera?"

Velyn gave a resigned sigh. "Yes. Like Cera. Condemn me all you like, but you can't know the levels I would stoop to—"

I threw my hands out and something in the air moved. Velyn staggered back a pace, but he wasn't thrown as I had intended. "I don't want to hear your rationalization. I just want to hear you scream."

Velyn gritted his teeth and held his hands before him. "So be it." Freezing rain and hail dropped all around me. He didn't seem to have the strength to summon the ice storm he had before as this cyclone of ice and water swirled only around me. Rather than continue failing with new magic, I fell back on my old magic, shifting to a rat and ducking beneath a shelf of rock to hide from the hail. A rivulet of icy water diverted from its natural path, washing me out of my hiding place. Drenched as I was, I narrowly dodged the tongue of lightning that lashed down on me. Another shift and I was flying, avoiding the cone of hail and arrowing towards my brother.

I shifted again, standing behind him, daggers in both hands. He spun, forming the ice pike in his hands but I shattered it with a blow from my hilt. Velyn screamed as my second dagger found his ribs. The silver blade only scraped bone, failing to find a deeper, softer target. Velyn vanished in a puff of mist, reappearing further away, one hand clutching his bloody side.

There was a cry off to the side. Velyn and I both dared a quick look. Eagan had fallen, bleeding from various wounds, arm twisted at an unnatural angle. Kestral knelt over him, using my brother's expensive silk shirt to wipe the blood from his blade. Slowly he stood, eyes locked on Velyn, and stalked forward. Eagan moaned and shifted pitifully on the ground; he wasn't dead yet. Kestral must have left him alive on purpose.

A sound between a whimper and a cry rose from Velyn's throat. He looked from Kestral to me and back again, stepping backwards and nearly losing his balance on the uneven ground. Blood leaked freely from between his fingers. I mimicked Kila's feral grin. Predators knew when their prey was just about finished.

Velyn raised a hand to call lightning. I prepared a shift to dodge, but when Velyn brought his arm down, it wasn't towards me.

It was towards Kestral.

I twisted, and as I did, I felt the spin of the world begin to slow. The lightning was already arcing down, hot and merciless, quicker than a heartbeat. I found myself standing between Kestral and the lightning, my hands out before me.

Please let it work this time, I begged, compressing the air before me into a solid, invisible wall. Magic crashed inside me, my own personal storm. Something snapped into place and the lightning shattered as it struck my wall, dispersing into sparks and then nothingness.

I turned to look over my shoulder, smiling as cool relief flooded my body. Kestral was safe. I had figured out Reina's magic in time to protect him. My breath caught up to me. Kestral paused only a pace from me, blue eyes locking with mine.

I froze, cool relief becoming an icy chill.

In the animal world, there was no such thing as noble sacrifice. In the face of a forest fire, a parent didn't wait for the cubs to keep up—she ran and later she made new cubs. No buck stood in front of a hunter to protect a doe. No animal starved so that another could eat. Self-preservation was the all-abiding law of the animal kingdom.

So how could I stand between Kestral and death? Didn't that violate every value I ever believed in?

Kestral reached a hand out to me. "Reshi?"

I drew back, eyes wide, heart beating frantically enough to break through my chest.

I couldn't.

No, not after everything.

There was no way . . .

I couldn't be in love.

Kestral lunged forward, trying to catch my arm but using Reina's magic I twisted away. I found myself falling through the air, feeling it thicken slightly around me, slowing my descent.

Below me, Eagan had lifted himself up to his arm and knees—the other arm was piteously twisted and broken. Mist bloomed beside the wounded fire mage, revealing

Velyn by his side. He knelt beside Eagan, speaking softly. Velyn cried out suddenly as Eagan surged to his feet, lifting the weather mage by his collar. Flames swirled around Eagan's fist as Velyn's feet flailed for purchase, hands gripping Eagan's arm to keep from being strangled. A storm cloud burst into existence over their heads, pouring down rain as fire roared from Eagan's fist. Lightning lanced down from the cloud with a crack that shook the stones beneath Kila and Kestral. White steam exploded out from them both, hiding them from view. The black storm cloud dissipated first as the steam blew outwards, creating a veil.

Did they just kill each other? I wondered, shifting to my crow form to soar closer. The steam billowed outward, revealing two prone figures folded over each other on the cold stone plain. Sluggish orange mist twisted upwards, veined with white steam. Before I could bring myself any closer, a pale, shaky hand reached into the mist before clenching into a fist, turning the mist into a pale orange icicle. I banked away from the pair as Velyn pulled himself up to his knees, clothing burnt and blackened, hair standing on end, and crushed the icicle to his chest. He drew a breath, white-veined orange mist flowing into him.

Kestral whipped his sword from its sheath, stalking across the dark stone ground with grim purpose. Velyn staggered to his feet and thrust his hand out towards the mage hunter—flames drizzled from his palm, falling to die on the rocks below. With a panicked look, Velyn pulled his arm back, wrapping it around his ribs as he backed up a pace. My brother glanced up at me, fear apparent in his white-blue eyes. Before Kestral could get close, Velyn turned to mist and puffed away.

Where would he go? I circled the battlefield from above, watching for plumes of mist.

"*Reshi.*" Kestral's voice echoed in my mind. Turning one eye earthward, I saw him— solid, unyielding, shining blade in hand. His eyes tracked my flight, filling my chest with a warmth I'd been avoiding for I couldn't remember how long. "*Come back. We can finish this together.*"

No.

No. I won't be trapped again. I won't be beholden to anyone.

Not even to you, Kestral.

Soaring over the battlefield, I saw the sea off in the distance. I put my back to it, blocking the memories made there only yesterday. Instead, I faced the fae wilds, made up of trees, rivers, hills and a mist-covered lake. I sharpened my bird's eyes, watching the mist. It didn't flow like normal mist, didn't spread tendrils beyond the lake, seeking warmer air. No, it hovered, as if trapped beneath a bowl. Or by magic.

Velyn's magic veiled his boat. I performed the inner twist that allowed me to vanish mid-flight, jumping as close to the unmoving mist as I could. I told myself I wasn't running, I was chasing. This had nothing to do with . . .

I landed on the shore of the mist-covered lake, shifting back to my human form. Velyn leaned over a railing of his boat, gripping it with both hands as he panted, eyes out of focus. He had untied the boat from its mooring, but there he had paused, seeming overwhelmed with pain or fatigue or both.

I could kill him, I thought, watching as he struggled to blink consciousness back into his mind. Eagan must not have had much magic left when Velyn took it. He didn't seem to be feeling the resurgence I had felt when I took Reina's power.

Velyn finally realized I was staring up at him from the shore. He threw himself backwards, landing with a pained cry. I heard a scramble atop the deck. Velyn was still trying to run.

Why not kill him now? I wondered, taking a step into the water. I laid my hand against the wood of the boat, feeling the smooth grain of it not just beneath my fingertips, but in my mind as well. I recalled Reina turning one of Kila's stone spears to dust—that magic flowed through me now. This boat could be nothing more than dust beneath my hand.

So why hesitate?

"Reshi!" Velyn called down, his voice half-frantic. "I'm finished here, I swear it. I can't—I have nothing left!"

"But that won't stop you from coming back, will it?" I asked softly. "For me. Or for Kila."

Velyn's face twisted into an expression of anguish. "It's not that I want to. You need to understand, Reshi, it was never about a throne, not even about power. I never wanted to hurt Cera or anyone, you have to believe me!"

"Why?" My vengeance was right in front of me, but all I could feel was cold. "How could you expect me to trust you? Eagan trusted you. Cera trusted you."

Velyn licked his lips nervously, scanning the thin forest behind me. "Listen, Reshi, you have to have seen—" Velyn took a breath then let it go slowly. The sails of his ship billowed, and the boat moved backwards, hull scraping the sand as it pulled away from the shore. "You've seen the runes, haven't you?"

"The runes?" My hand dropped away from the boat, falling limply to my side. "Which runes?"

Velyn shook his head, boat bobbing as the waves caught it. "All of the runes. Think about it. How can they—" Velyn gasped, eyes going wide, before exhaling sharply. The sails billowed again, the boat gaining distance from the shore. I heard a sound behind me: boots on sand.

Kestral had caught up with me.

"Reshi."

Kestral's voice moved through me like a wave of heat and pain. I didn't turn to face him but watched as the boat disappeared into the mist.

"Reshi, come back."

I shook my head, refusing to turn around. "We said it would be over, remember? After this fight, we're done."

"It's not over," Kestral protested, his voice rough. "Velyn got away. You know he'll come after you again."

"Probably not me." I shrugged. "Kila's the weakest now. I know she'll hate me for saying this, but can you keep an eye on her? Or at least take care of her until she recovers?"

"We can both take care of her until she's on her feet again. Come back with me, Reshi."

My chin dropped, strands of loose hair falling around my face. "We said it would be over."

A near-silent scrape of leather on sand, Kestral took a step. "Neither of us want it to be over."

I swallowed past the lump in my throat and turned around, painting a smirk on my face. "Don't get ahead of yourself, Kestral. I needed to give you a reason not to kill me. None of it was ever real. It was fun, I'll give you that. But it didn't mean anything. Not to me."

Slowly, Kestral rotated his arm, turning his wrist towards me. My breath froze as hot tears seared the backs of my eyes—his liar's brand burned hot and bright against his tan skin.

I shook my head and backed up a step. "I don't want you, Kestral. I don't need you anymore. But Kila . . . she'll need you. I don't—"

The brand burned brighter. Kestral took another step, those beautiful eyes holding mine captive.

Trapped.

I won't be trapped.

Kestral lunged forward, grabbing for me as I twisted away, shifting to my crow form. Once again, I flew away from him, those blue eyes marking me from far below.

He'd come looking for me, I knew it.

But no one runs and hides better than I do.

SORCEROUS RIVALRY

APPENDIX I – MAGE-BORN BOUNTY INFORMATION

Zarapheth Bounty Information
Distributed to all military outposts
For licensed mage hunters only

Laureinaqin
Eldest daughter of Our King and his mistress Laurana
Known Aliases: None
Magic: Unknown
Combat Skills: Unknown
Location: Unknown
Appearance: Violet eyes, brown hair, average height
Additional Information: Adopted and raised by the Duke and Duchess of Hoell, educated at the Royal University, the Tower of Emlenton and Wolbridge Academy. Deemed exceptionally intelligent. Has not been seen in over ten years.

Raleagan
Eldest son of Our King and his mistress Laurana
Known Aliases: Eagan
Magic: Fire
Combat Skills: Strong Duelist
Location: Unknown
Appearance: Orange-yellow eyes, red hair, tall
Additional Information: Adopted and raised by the Baron and Baroness of Lessendri, trained and participated in several notable duels. Sightings and locations vary.

Telakishin
Son of Our King and his mistress Laurana
Known Aliases: Laki
Magic: Life to lifeless

Combat Skills: Unknown

Location: Inner Kingdom Wilds

Appearance: Green eyes, bald, short

Additional Information: Twin to Tekilashan, sworn to the Star-Strewn Sect of the Order of the Great Canvas, practices as a monk in the wilds. Fearful; approach with caution.

Tekilashan

    Daughter of Our King and his mistress Laurana

    Known Aliases: Kila, Killer

    Magic: Unknown

    Combat Skills: Extreme competence

    Location: Multiple sightings in villages along the Viaparaison border

    Appearance: Red eyes, red hair, short

    Additional Information: Twin to Telakishin, trained in the western army, served as a soldier, captain and squad leader. Deadly with any weapon; exercise extreme caution.

Navelynstra

    Son of Our King and his mistress Laurana

    Known Aliases: None

    Magic: Wind

    Combat Skills: Unknown

    Location: Unknown

    Appearance: White-blue eyes, gray hair, average height

    Additional Information: Raised as an orphan in the northern fishing village of LongNeck Port. Has not been seen in over five years.

Hacerathan

    Daughter of Our King and his mistress Laurana

    Known Aliases: None

    Magic: Psychic

Combat Skills: Unknown

Location: Unknown

Appearance: Silver eyes, blonde hair, tall

Additional Information: Raised by traveling performers of the Comet's Train troop. Has not been seen in five years.

Jereshin

Son of Our King and his mistress Laurana

Known Aliases: None

Magic: Unknown

Combat Skills: Unknown

Location: Unknown

Appearance: Unknown

Additional Information: None available

Acknowledgements

It's impossible to write without inspiration, so first, I would like to thank every fantasy writer who came before me and all those who will continue writing long after me. It takes a lot of bravery to create a world and set it down on the page for readers to enjoy. Without your worlds, I never would have had the courage to create mine. And of course, a huge thanks to all of you voracious fantasy readers! You keep us loving what we do, so you deserve a thanks all your own.

This has been my first foray into fantasy and it never would have been possible without so many wonderful people encouraging me along the way. Thank you to Janelle and Jess, who initially encouraged me to continue writing this story when it was barely more than a concept. You both gave me the encouragement I needed to make it grow! Thank you to all my beta readers, who really helped me develop this world, its magic and my characters—Lisa, David, Kevin, Sam, Marquis, Kristen, Matt and Alex, this story would not be the same without you. Special thanks to my brother Eamon, who helped critique, challenge and fine-tune this story as it grew. And of course, the greatest thanks to my husband Andy, who supports my dreams with endless enthusiasm and optimism.

I have the privilege of working with a truly fantastic editor, Monique the Editrix Fischer. You really helped me polish this piece up to a vibrant shine, I simply cannot thank you enough. And for my beautiful cover art, I thank Ivan Cakamura Cakic. Thank you for bearing with me and going through so many different versions until it was just perfect! And finally, thank you to my parents, Diana and Mark, for instilling in me a love of reading, writing and creativity.

Sorcerous Rivalry wouldn't be anything without all of you! Thank you, from the bottom of my wellspring.

About the Author

Lifelong nerd and fangirl Kayleigh Nicol earned her Bachelor's of Science in Animal Science at Cal Poly Pomona, California. After years of volunteering at zoos and aquariums in California, Kayleigh now works at a therapeutic horseback riding center in Long Island, NY. When not taking care of her own menagerie of rescued animals, she enjoys watching anime, playing video games and reading as many fantasy books as she can get her hands on.

You can follow Kayleigh Nicol on Twitter:
https://twitter.com/KayleighNicol5
Facebook:
https://www.facebook.com/Kayleigh.Nicol.1
And on her blog on Goodreads.com

Made in the USA
Middletown, DE
26 February 2019